Dear Reader:

The novels you've enjoyed ... by such authors as Kathl... Rosemary Rogers, Johanna Lindsey, Laurie McBain, and Shirlee Busbee are accountable to one thing above all others: Avon has never tried to force authors into any particular mold. Rather, Avon is a publisher that encourages individual talent and is always on the lookout for writers who will deliver *real* books, not packaged formulas.

In 1982, we started a program to help readers pick out authors of exceptional promise. Called "The Avon Romance," the books were distinguished by a ribbon motif in the upper left-hand corner of the cover. Although the titles were by new authors, they were quickly discovered and became known as "the ribbon books."

Now "The Avon Romance" is a regular feature on the Avon list. Each month, you will find historical novels with many different settings, each one by an author who is special. You will not find predictable characters, predictable plots, and predictable endings. The only predictable thing about "The Avon Romance" will be the superior quality that Avon has always delivered in the field of romance!

Sincerely,

WALTER MEADE
President & Publisher

Other Avon Books by
Elisabeth Kidd

My Lord Guardian

Avon Books are available at special quantity discounts for bulk purchases for sales promotions, premiums, fund raising or educational use. Special books, or book excerpts, can also be created to fit specific needs.

For details write or telephone the office of the Director of Special Markets, Avon Books, Dept. FP, 1790 Broadway, New York, New York 10019, 212-399-1357. *IN CANADA:* Director of Special Sales, Avon Books of Canada, Suite 210, 2061 McCowan Rd., Scarborough, Ontario M1S 3Y6, 416-293-9404.

THE DANCERS' LAND

ELISABETH KIDD

AVON
PUBLISHERS OF BARD, CAMELOT, DISCUS AND FLARE BOOKS

THE DANCER'S LAND is an original publication of Avon Books. This work has never before appeared in book form. This work is a novel. Any similarity to actual persons or events is purely coincidental.

AVON BOOKS
A division of
The Hearst Corporation
1790 Broadway
New York, New York 10019

Copyright © 1984 by Linda Triegal
Published by arrangement with the author
Library of Congress Catalog Card Number: 84-90966
ISBN: 0-380-89219-7

All rights reserved, which includes the right to reproduce this book or portions thereof in any form whatsoever except as provided by the U.S. Copyright Law. For information address Anita Diamant, Literary Agent, 310 Madison Avenue, New York, New York 10017

First Avon Printing, November, 1984

AVON TRADEMARK REG. U.S. PAT. OFF. AND IN OTHER COUNTRIES, MARCA REGISTRADA, HECHO EN U.S.A.

Printed in the U.S.A.

WFH 10 9 8 7 6 5 4 3 2 1

THEY ARE the shipped battalions sent
to bar the bold Belligerant
  Who stalks the Dancers' Land.
Within these hulls, like sheep a-pen,
Are packed in thousands fighting-men
  And colonels in command.

—Thomas Hardy, *The Dynasts*

125 kilometers
75 miles

BAQUIO

Vizcaya

• TUDELA
• ZARAGOZA
• BARCELONA

Cataluña

Mediterranean Sea

Battle of Salamanca · 22 July, 1812

SALAMANCA
Tormes River
CIUDAD RODRIGO
HUERTA
ALDEA TEJADA
LOS ARAPILES
LAS TORRES
3RD
CAVALRY
6TH
5TH
4TH
ALBA DE TORMES

British / French

CLARE CHAPMAN ©

Prologue
Paris, 1802

KATE COLLIER stepped down from the carriage and paused for a moment at the bottom of the wide marble steps. The warm August night was fragrant with the scent of roses that drifted from the gardens of the Tuileries. From behind her came the muffled clatter of carriage wheels on the graveled drive; before her the light of hundreds of candles shone out of the tall windows along the long stone front of the palace, beckoning her inside. Kate took a deep breath and glanced up at her father with her enchanting turned-up smile.

Sir Henry was a large and jovial-looking middle-aged gentleman elegantly dressed in knee breeches and a black coat with old-fashioned lace cuffs. As he watched his daughter's face, his own grew pink with pleasure. Kate looked so lovely, he thought, with her long, golden hair tied up in silk ribbons and her gray eyes shining with anticipation. He reached out to squeeze her white-gloved hand affectionately.

"Are you ready to go in, my dear?" he said, smiling.

"Oh, yes!"

Kate moved forward eagerly, holding the delicate white muslin of her skirt just off the ground. She must be especially careful of her first grown-up ball gown. It had been made for her by one of the most exclusive Paris *modistes*, who had exclaimed delightedly over Mademoiselle's exquisite figure. So tall and fine! Such a rounded figure for a sixteen-year-old. In the end, Madame had recommended against dampening the skirt to mold it more daringly to Kate's long, slim legs, and had settled on a simple green silk ribbon under the bust, for emphasis, with matching ribbons to wind through Kate's piled-up hair. No jewels—only the diamond eardrops her father had given her—for Mademoiselle's beautiful English complexion was enough to make all the other ladies at the ball *devorées d'envie.* That was, if Mademoiselle would try to stay out of the sun for a few days!

Sir Henry had smiled at that and said she was asking the impossible. If his Katie wanted to go riding hatless in the Bois de Boulogne, riding she would go. He admitted freely—almost proudly—that he indulged his only daughter. But no one could say Katie was spoiled. He had raised her to believe herself inferior to no one, and that had only made her proud, not vain or ill-mannered. Indeed, she scarcely noticed the admiring glances that followed her on the street, and she received every pretty compliment paid her with as much delight as if it were the first one.

Sir Henry had been appointed to the British diplomatic representation at King Carlos's court in Madrid, an appointment that had happily coincided with the Peace of Amiens, concluding the long hostilities between England and Bonaparte's France. But no, Sir Henry reminded himself, the First Consul called himself by the single name of Napoleon now. It would be undiplomatic in the extreme to forget that!

To be sure, this was the first time Kate had been out of England. It had been her idea to travel to Spain through France—the long sea voyage could not be nearly so exciting as Paris, she had pleaded, and Sir Henry could not resist her coaxing. So they had joined the throngs of English visitors on the roads from Boulogne—eager to see the city denied them for so long. Sir Henry carried letters of introduction to Napoleon from his old friend Addington, the prime minister, who had negotiated the present peace, but what Sir Henry most looked forward to was showing Paris to Kate—and Kate to Paris. It had been nearly twenty years since Sir Henry himself was last here. He had met Kate's mother, Leonora, in Paris.

For a moment, Sir Henry wondered if it had been a bad idea to bring Kate to Paris after all. But no, it was impossible to cut away every memory of Leonora, even though it had been years since she left them. Sooner or later Katie would have to know the truth; sooner or later she would have to learn about love and marriage. But Sir Henry was reluctant to begin her education too soon. He was—he knew it—too possessive of Katie's single-minded affection for him to risk losing any part of it. At the same time, he was proud of her and, rather selfishly, wanted to show her off.

Kate had no thought that evening for the past. She had been too young at the time Leonora left them to fully understand what had gone wrong between her father and mother. But it was clear that the affair had made Sir Henry unhappy, and that had been enough to turn Kate against the mother she knew little else about. She could not believe that her father could cause anyone unhappiness, so the fault must have been on her mother's side. It did not seem right to her, either, that Leonora had divorced Sir Henry, remarried, and gone abroad—to Italy, the rumors had it—to live quite happily after.

As she walked down the tapestry-draped entranceway on her father's arm, she was possessed with the idea that something exciting was going to happen tonight. She could feel the blood race more quickly in her veins and her pulse beat more forcefully in her temple. She was aware of the gleam of candles in the crystal chandeliers overhead, the click of heels on the hardwood floor, the soft swish of silks and whisper of velvets—and of whispers of another kind as they paused for a moment at the entrance to the ballroom behind other guests waiting to be announced.

"He has already more power than Louis ever had," one gentleman near her was saying. "He will make the consulship hereditary next, and *la pauvre* Josephine, who has given her lord no son, will have to go."

"Nonsense!" said the gentleman's companion. "Has he not said that talent is worth more than birth? You cannot deny the man's talent or his capacity for work. You live here, Armand—by his grace, I might add, so that it behooves you to tread delicately. His spies are everywhere. But anyone, even you, may see for himself the new roads, buildings, schools—he knows what will please the people. They have had enough of display and ostentation."

"Bah, all these public works are yet another form of ostentation. As for spies, there are so many of them that they will doubtless soon kill each other off so the rest of us may live in peace."

"Nevertheless, my friend, you must not parade your opinions quite so openly, nor your British sympathies. Who knows how long this precarious peace may last?"

"Doubtless until Napoleon decrees it of no further use," came the dry reply. "Until then, I will keep my busts of Pitt and Fox in my study. Like the First Consul."

Then the line of bejeweled and perfumed guests moved forward, and soon Kate heard: "Sir Henry Collier and Mademoiselle Catherine Collier!"

Kate gave her father a last private smile, and together they moved forward to be received. Tonight it was Napoleon's sister, Madame Bacciochi, who greeted the guests. She was a short, unattractive woman with an aloof manner, but aside from a slight speculative narrowing of her eyes when Kate was introduced to her, she was as coolly polite to her as to the elderly marquis who had preceded them.

They began to descend the stairs into the ballroom, which was lined with people speaking with one another, laughing behind elaborately decorated fans, pointing none too subtly at some elegant lady with more material in her gauze scarf than her bodice, or a mysterious gentleman dressed all in black, from his velvet collar to his polished boots.

One man, taller than the rest, seemed to stand alone, and Kate's eyes were drawn to him. His back was to her, displaying broad shoulders under a finely cut gray coat and burnished gold hair that gleamed in the candlelight. Kate's eyes attempted to flicker past him but were drawn back abruptly.

He had turned around and was looking directly at her out of a pair of ice-blue eyes. She felt her breath catch in her throat and she stood still—as he did, as if they were alone in that huge room—as those eyes raked over her, until she felt that she was about to catch fire. She stared back at him but did not know how long she could endure this intense heat, this unexpected assault on her senses. Was this what she unknowingly had been looking for when she

The Dancers' Land

came here tonight? She frowned in puzzlement. His mouth curled into a smile, amused and lightly mocking, but at the same time intimate, almost possessive.

"Look, Kate, there is Michel."

Her father's voice startled her. The spell was broken. Kate forced her eyes to follow her father's gaze, and she saw another man coming toward them—Michel de Vert.

Kate was to be formally presented tonight to Napoleon and his wife, Josephine, an honor secured for them by the Comte de Vert, an acquaintance of Sir Henry's, whose family had suffered greatly during the Terror. Now that Napoleon had suspended many of the laws against the *emigrés,* the comte had returned to Paris from his exile on the island of Jersey and rapidly gained a place at court.

Michel was an old friend, yet still in his forties. Since last seeing Sir Henry, he had acquired a worldliness that added to the appeal of his slim figure and dark features. He was dressed in the green velvet he favored, earning the name "the green count." Kate had always thought him attractive—up until now. Now she glanced impatiently away from the comte, back to the place where she had seen the man with the blue eyes.

He had moved to one side, following her at a distance but keeping her in his sight. He bowed slightly when she looked at him, and smiled in a familiar way. She quickly looked away again and, feeling light-headed and deliriously happy, she smiled.

"Ah, my dear Sir Henry," the comte exclaimed, shaking her father's hand. His English was excellent and only slightly accented, but he always addressed Kate in French because—he had once told her—he found her hesitant accent in that language charming.

"Enchanté de vous voir," he went on, not looking at Sir Henry at all. He narrowed his eyes at Kate, catching her involuntary smile. "And how lovely is *la petite* Ca'trine this evening! The First Consul will be pleased—Josephine not so much so, I fear, but she is at least better mannered than her husband. Did you pass Elisa's inspection? But of course you did, or you would not be standing here now! Come, let us overcome the final hurdle and get on with the dancing."

Michel led them around the edge of the room to a

smaller, but more elegant, apartment to one side. There they were again obliged to wait while a footman went to consult another, who murmured into the ear of the major domo, who nodded solemnly. Meanwhile, the comte entertained them with whispered anecdotes and sardonic observations about the people around them. Kate's lips smiled, but she scarcely heard him, and her eyes searched the room for only one man, who now stood in a corner next to a bust of the First Consul in a Roman toga. He looked at Kate, then at Michel—up and down, as if to take his measure—and shrugged lightly, as if to say she was wasting her time with such a one. Kate giggled, caught herself when her father said something to her, and then turned to find herself facing a lovely, dark-eyed lady who held out her hand to Kate and smiled.

"Welcome to Paris, Mademoiselle Collier," Josephine said in a soft voice when the comte had presented Sir Henry, and Sir Henry had brought forward his daughter. "I hope it meets with your approval?"

"Indeed, yes, Madame!" Kate curtsied quickly, a little clumsily in the strange giddiness that seemed to have overtaken her. "I have never seen such—such lovely gardens."

She could not have stumbled on anything more likely to please Josephine, who adored flowers. Her mask of polite resignation dropped for a moment, and she chatted with Kate about the English gardens she had heard so much about but had never seen, while Michel glanced approvingly at Sir Henry over Kate's head.

Napoleon, surrounded by soberly dressed lackeys who appeared to be his bodyguards, had been speaking with one of his ministers, but he moved back to his wife's side when he saw Kate and waited a little impatiently for Josephine to acknowledge him. She did at last, and Napoleon raised his wife's hand to his lips. "Who is our new guest, *ma chèrie*?"

Kate was presented and curtsied, a little more steadily this time, to the First Consul. He was handsomer than she had been led to believe, with a clear complexion, a graceful smile, and large, alert eyes. His piercing gaze assessed her boldly, but Kate stood her ground.

"Mademoiselle," he said, "you do my city great honor."

He spoke formally, but his hand, even through Kate's glove, was warm and his grip firm. Kate looked directly at him—they were nearly equal in height—and smiled her candid smile. His stare broke, but his grip tightened for an instant. Then he let her go and said to the comte, *"Charmante.* We must present your protégée to Madame de Montaillau, I think, Michel."

The comte appeared startled and began to protest in urgent, if yet tactful, terms. Napoleon cut him off. "Yes, yes, very well," he said in a distracted voice. "It was merely a fancy of mine. Think no more of it."

He gave Kate an enigmatic look and moved abruptly away to speak to another guest. The bodyguards followed and regrouped around the next object of Napoleon's scrutiny. Kate wondered who this Madame de Montaillau might be, and why she should have reminded Napoleon of her. She turned to her father, who looked perplexed, and then to Michel, who was clearly annoyed at something.

"I think it might be best to take Mademoiselle home, Sir Henry," the comte said in an uncharacteristically sharp voice.

"Oh, but I haven't—I mean, the dancing hasn't started yet!" Kate exclaimed. But then, conscience-stricken, she glanced at her father. "I'm sorry, Papa—we may go now, if you wish."

But the comte, although he continued to look grim, would not explain what was troubling him, and Sir Henry was unable to resist the pleading look in his daughter's eyes—much less her willingness to sacrifice her own pleasure to his need, however little she understood it. He soothed the comte with his most diplomatic reassurances and then bowed to Kate and begged her for the honor of the first dance. Kate's lovely smile lit up her face. She made her father a graceful curtsy and said that the honor was entirely hers.

It was when Sir Henry had led her gallantly into the first steps of the opening quadrille that Kate saw the man with the blue eyes again. The great ballroom was crowded with women in silk gowns and brilliant jewels, gentlemen in formal black knee breeches and white silk stockings, and footmen in green and gold livery discreetly mingling among them to attend to their needs and gratify their whims. The smell of perfume and candle wax hung in the air, and the heat generated by so many bodies close together was beginning to become oppressive despite the open, ceiling-high windows that gave onto the garden.

But this man did not appear uncomfortable. He stood near the musicians' circle and watched Kate take her place next to her father for the quadrille. Whenever the movements of the dance brought her around to face him, he was watching her—even more intently now, a slight frown creasing his forehead. Then, when Michel asked her for the next dance, a mazurka, the stranger seemed to lose patience and, not waiting for the dance to end, moved onto the floor to interrupt them. Michel was so surprised that he did not even protest when he found himself standing alone in the middle of the floor, amazed that Kate was being whirled away in the arms of this man she seemed to have no hesitation in following.

Her new partner said nothing for several measures. With him suddenly so close, Kate found herself staring intently at him. She was above average height, but he was taller yet, and even more devastatingly attractive than he had seemed at a distance. The hair that had gleamed like gold under the candlelight was darker than she had at first thought, the eyes lighter, like blue diamonds. His cheeks were high and broad, his mouth firm, and the smooth skin of his face lightly tanned, as if he spent a great deal of time outdoors without a hat. His large, graceful hands gripped her more tightly than even the quick movements of the dance demanded.

"You fit perfectly in my arms," he said at last. His voice was deep, the accent English.

It was true. Kate hardly felt that they were dancing; she had the dizzy sensation of having been lifted off the earth to float above it in some warm, enveloping cloud. She realized that her body had become unusually warm, with the flame that traveled down her arms from where she held his shoulders and which flared when hip lightly brushed thigh as they turned to the music. She looked up into his eyes, directly and without artifice, and she felt as if she had suddenly grown up, had gone from innocent child to knowing woman in the space of a look. She smiled at the thought.

The Dancers' Land

She could hear his sharp intake of breath as he nearly missed a step. Then he turned her around and moved her gracefully toward the windows, still keeping the rhythm of the mazurka, until they were able to slip out into the gardens. He led her by the hand down a path to a circular clearing where a fountain played merrily in the shadows.

"Who are you?" he demanded in a rough whisper. Fully aware that she had a power over him that she could increase at will, she shook her head, refusing to tell him her name.

He laughed, a low, rich laugh. "You won't tell me? Is this some new sort of game?"

She shook her head again, telling him with her look that it was no game. His eyes narrowed speculatively.

"What, are you not such an innocent as you look? Come, show me what you are."

His hands had been resting on her waist, and now they tightened as he pulled her toward him and lowered his head to her and touched her lips. She felt them burn, but she did not draw away. Her arms lifted trustingly around his neck, and she stepped closer to him. His mouth became rougher, more urgent on hers—but then it was he who pulled away.

"You're a witch, aren't you?" he said, half-laughing, gazing down at her in wonder. "And yet . . . not . . ."

He kissed her again, more gently, opening her willing mouth and entering it, exploring lingeringly inside it until she was breathless with the passion welling up in her as if from a hidden spring suddenly uncovered—and she kissed him back.

She could not have said how long they held each other like that, but the tearing apart was as sudden as their coming together, when a discreet little cough invaded their private world.

He turned abruptly, thrusting her behind him as if to shield her from something, but she could see his face in the dim light. He was frowning, and his eyes held an uncertain, wary look. The hand that held her back was tense. She glanced from him to the figure of the man who had interrupted them.

It was Napoleon.

"A thousand pardons, dear sir," he said. "I would not

have disturbed you for the world had I known, but—" He shrugged and smiled benignly but without warmth. *"Eh, bien.* What is one to do when a lady begs? Madame de Montaillau has arrived and awaits you in the gold salon."

The other man hesitated briefly, glancing into the palace, then back at Napoleon. Then, abruptly and without looking at Kate again, he whispered to her, "Wait for me," and disappeared into the ballroom. Only then did Kate realize that she had not spoken a word to him the entire time they had been together.

Napoleon looked after him thoughtfully but then turned to bow gracefully and hold out his hand to Kate. "Will Mademoiselle permit me to return her to her father?"

"Thank you."

It was barely a whisper. She was trembling so that she could scarcely stand, much less speak. He had left her, with no explanation, turning her over to Napoleon as if she were a piece of merchandise that had lost its value to him.

Suddenly she was frightened, as if she had reached out for something precious, only to have it snatched away from her and smashed to pieces before her eyes. She felt that her trust had somehow been violated, and wanted to cry out in protest. She could feel herself on the edge of tears, but she had never in her young life cried in public, and she would not let herself lose control in front of Napoleon.

As he guided her back into the ballroom, she blinked her eyes at the bright candlelight, and it was then that the room struck her as not nearly so beautiful as she had first thought. There were drops of candle wax on the furniture, she noticed now, and the velvet drapes over the windows were ragged at the hems. The guests that had so dazzled her now seemed just silly men with pomaded hair and overpainted women with crepey necks. She looked at Napoleon, seeing him differently, too, now—a small, plain, common sort of man, hardly worth the trouble it took to be polite to him. The idea gave her a kind of strength, and she put up her chin, smiled like an empress, and placed her hand on the little Corsican's arm.

Inside, her eyes flew around the room, looking for her still-unnamed cavalier, but before she could make him out in the crowd, Napoleon had found her father.

"Ah, Sir Henry," he said, making a great show of turning Kate over to her father's care by removing her gloved hand from his arm and placing it firmly on Sir Henry's. "Your lovely daughter and I have had a most interesting—ah, conversation, but I fear I must return her to you now. You will take her in to supper, *ne-c'est pas?*"

As this genial suggestion was delivered in a manner more suggestive of an order, Sir Henry could only bow politely, murmur a few conventional phrases of thanks, which were waved aside, and comply. She was glad of his diplomat's discretion. She did not fully understand herself what had just happened, and she did not think she could begin to explain it.

It was as they were passing across the ballroom to the supper rooms that Kate saw her cavalier again. He was standing in one of the large anterooms that flanked the ballroom, and she saw him only because she chanced to glance into the room just at that moment. He did not see her, being absorbed in whispered conversation with a beautiful blond woman whom Kate supposed to be the mysterious Madame de Montaillau. Kate paused to observe her critically. She was a lady no longer in the first blush of youth—in her early thirties, perhaps—but her tall figure was still slim and supple, and she was wearing a diaphanous silver-gray gown cut tantalizingly low. She listened attentively to her companion but at the same time looked glancingly around her, as if fearful of being overheard.

Suddenly, her eyes met Kate's and she smiled, and her smile was remarkably like Kate's own. As Kate stared at her in wonder, she lifted one hand and waved two fingers shyly in Kate's direction.

"Papa!" she said, pulling on her father's sleeve to get his attention. "Who is that lady?"

Sir Henry was bowing to an acquaintance on the other side of the room, but he turned at her question and said, "Which lady, my dear?"

But the words seemed to catch in his throat, and Kate barely heard the hurried answer as he took her elbow to turn her away.

"I don't know. I—come, Katie, I'm afraid we must go, after all. I'm sorry."

Kate looked up at her father's face, which had gone suddenly pale. His voice held an uncharacteristic urgency, and he did not sound as if he would be swayed by her entreaties this time.

"It's my mother, isn't it?" she said, suddenly comprehending. Her undefined fear was beginning to take shape—a cold, cruel shape.

"Yes, yes," her father admitted, "of course it is—but come along, Katie, please!"

"But who—who is that man with her?" Kate asked, dreading the answer.

"I don't know," Sir Henry answered curtly. "Her latest paramour, I imagine. Come now, Catherine—quickly!"

Kate had never seen her father angry before, but he undoubtedly was now. Stunned into silence, she followed him to the vestibule, but as he helped her hurriedly into her cloak, she looked back again. The lovely blonde was watching Kate, too, and directed her companion's attention to her. He looked at Kate with a coldness that she would not have believed him capable of half an hour ago. His mouth curved into a mocking smile, which only accented his ice-blue eyes. He said something to Leonora and threw back his head. Kate heard his laughter cutting through the noise of the ball. She watched him take the woman's arm and lead her away into the crowd.

Kate said nothing after that to her father, who gave the order to have their carriage brought around, and she held her chin up bravely as they waited for it in silence. But as she was getting into it, the strains of a polonaise drifted out from the ballroom, and the sound of gay laughter followed it, an echoing, mocking melody.

Kate clutched the strap on the side of the carriage, but in spite of her efforts to keep them back, tears began to well up in her eyes. They made no sound but flowed freely down her cheeks during the ride back to their hotel. Sir Henry gazed stonily out of the other window and pretended not to notice.

Part One
Salamanca, 1807

Chapter One

THE SPANISH sun beat down on the sere yellow hills south of Salamanca, scorched by the summer past to a dull semblance of their springtime selves. The arroyo running at their base was dry, as if the rains of the week before had never fallen. There was no breeze, no hint of moisture in the sharp, clear November air.

Three riders moved slowly along a dusty road that wound into those bleak yellow hills. Kate Collier lifted her face to the sun; her long, dark lashes closed over her gray eyes, and her lips curved in a smile. This day was her annual gift from Spain. It always came just as she had at last prepared herself for the long fierce winter and surprised her with this memory of summer.

Ramón Sariñana, who was Spanish and therefore accustomed to the vagaries of the seasons, was dressed in the same black jacket and trousers he wore throughout the year. His only concession to the sun was the wide-brimmed hat he wore pulled down over his tight black curls, so that only his long nose and wide, obstinate mouth showed beneath it. He sat erect in the saddle, holding his horse's reins in one hand; the other rested on the straw hamper that held their picnic lunch.

Kate's cousin, Christopher Benton, took the heat like any Englishman would—with a large handkerchief to wipe his uncovered forehead and a stream of halfhearted complaints about the climate. He had never understood what Kate liked about it. He cast an admiring glance at her; a few golden strands of her waist-length hair had escaped the pins that held it confined under a hat much like Ramón's. Furthermore, Kate insisted on riding around in one of Kit's white lawn shirts and a kind of skirt divided and seamed like trousers. Christopher devoutly hoped that nobody they knew would see her in it.

Other well-bred young ladies might also spend their Sundays riding in the hills and lunching on the grass, but they did so in the orthodox style—parasols open to protect their ivory complexions from the blazing sun, and skirts spread carefully over a cloth to keep them clean.

But Kate could handle a horse better than many men she knew. It was not her idea of a pleasant ride to dawdle along a perfectly good road for hours, sun or no sun. Her mouth curved suddenly into an impish smile, and before Christopher could guess what mischief she was brewing, she had snatched the hamper from Ramón's saddle and spurred her horse forward.

Christopher shouted a protest after her. He and Ramón urged their horses on to overtake her, but Kate was already around the next bend. She swerved sharply to the left and, leaving the road, started at a mad pace up a grassy knoll. The others followed, laughing and shouting good-natured insults after her.

Silhouetted against the horizon at the top of the hill stood a lone, twisted, and ancient oak. Kate pulled up abruptly when she reached it and dismounted. Ramón, close behind, jumped from his saddle and seized the precious hamper. He would have thrown it to Christopher, but Kate stopped him with a shout.

"Ramón! Remember the wine!"

"Dios!" He reached into the hamper and tenderly extracted a bottle of *vino tinto* while Kate dissolved into delighted laughter.

"Well," said Christopher, dismounting, "it's safe, no thanks to you, you crazy Basque!"

Ramón protested. "Me? It was that one—!"

He pointed an accusing finger at Kate in a fine display of outraged dignity. The laughter bubbled up in her and spilled over, but at a scowl from Ramón, she choked it back. She curtsied impertinently to Ramón, began to unpack their lunch, and served it then in humbled, if uncharacteristic, silence.

It took very little time to spread out the fresh-baked bread, mounds of cheese and spiced ham, and the cold potato *tortilla*—still less to see it disappear again. Ramón, lighting a *cigarro* by way of finishing off the meal, lay on his back and studied the sky while he smoked. Christopher poured wine into two cups, handed them to Kate and Ramón, and then sat down under the oak with his legs stretched out in front of him and drank blissfully from the bottle. When he had all but emptied it, he planted it between his knees and heaved a contented sigh.

"Fie, Christopher James!" she teased him, "What would your Mama say to your guzzling *vino* in that vulgar fashion?"

"The same, I expect, that she would say to your—ah, your costume." Christopher waved a disparaging hand in the direction of his cousin's distinctly inelegant riding habit.

Kate threw a crust of bread at him. "Shall I take to wearing skirts, then, and riding sidesaddle, and having palpitations when the sun gets too hot? Will you deny me my comfort, sir?"

"Not I! But walk into her la'ship's parlor like that and you'll give her a nervous spasm. You'll be banished from her presence for at least half an hour while she recovers. Indeed, Señorita Catarina, you show far too little respect for Mama's delicate sensibilities!" Christopher scolded, unashamed of his own dusty boots and untidy brown hair.

"Pobre Mama," Ramón grumbled, grasping at the only remark he understood. Christopher and Kate communicated in a language all their own, compounded of secret jokes and atrocious puns in a mixture of Spanish and English. Christopher was quick to see that they had inadvertently excluded him from the joke, and he turned back to him with a grin.

"It's all right for you, *hijo,* with your family hundreds of miles away in Baquio, or whatever the name of that godforsaken village is! You have your own lodgings, and *you* don't have to polish your boots and brush your coat before venturing into milady's parlor."

Ramón smiled under the shadow of his hat brim, although Kate could see that he was trying not to encourage Christopher's disrespectful comments about his mother. Ramón had a strong sense of family and, unable to see his own for years at a time, he had unobtrusively adopted the Bentons.

He had adopted Christopher first, when Kit arrived at the university where Ramón had been studying law for a year. Christopher's naturally congenial disposition had won him friends quickly but also prompted a number of pranks on the part of those who considered *el inglesito*—the English boy—fair game. Ramón had fished him out of fountains that he playfully had been dumped in, retrieved articles of clothing and books that had been pilfered from under Kit's unsuspecting nose, and generally designated himself the younger man's protector.

Mrs. Benton had been the last to accept Ramón's friendship, despite his undeniable talent for charming middle-aged ladies—not to mention their serving maids and younger daughters. Kate had watched Ramón's conquest of her aunt with some amusement, and not a little gratitude, for she had, herself, never been able to make friends with Sophie Benton. Something about Kate always rubbed Sophie the wrong way, and Kate had neither the patience, nor much interest, in finding out what it was.

Fortunately, Sophie had a daughter of her own—Kate's younger cousin, Gabriella—who listened dutifully to her mother's strictures and faithfully followed her advice, thus drawing most of Mrs. Benton's attention away from Kate. Kate was often vexed at the girl for her docility, but, of course, Gabriella was only fifteen—still a child.

Kate tried to remember if she had been that malleable at Gabriella's age. She had been innocent, certainly, and ready to be molded by whatever fate was in store for her. She had been young enough, too, to believe that her unknown fate would be a wonderful one.

But it hadn't happened quite the way she had expected.

After Paris, Kate had grown up quickly, even if she had not become fully a woman. After the initial shock of passion, suddenly ignited and just as quickly extinguished, had passed, she made up her mind never to leave herself open to pain like that again. It was not so difficult, really, for none of the men she met subsequently had the power to heat the blood in her veins and turn her heart upside down the way that one man had done.

Even the usually resourceful Michel de Vert could discover no more about the stranger than that he went by the name of "Colonel Grey." He never tried to contact Kate while she was in Paris, or later, although it must have been a simple matter for him to find out who she was. It must therefore be true, Kate had concluded, that he was Leonora's lover and had only mocked Kate by making love to her, too. She had cried herself to sleep the night of the ball and again the next night until, too exhausted to do otherwise, she fell asleep and woke determined not to let herself be destroyed by this man—or any other.

Michel had confirmed that the mysterious blond woman at the ball was Kate's mother, Leonora, divorced then from Sir Henry and remarried to Monsieur de Montaillau—and, Michel also told her, very happy in her new life. Kate could well believe it. Leonora obviously had wealth, position, lovers—a new life, indeed, for which she had no hesitation in tossing the old one aside. Michel had offered to introduce Kate to Leonora, but Kate had refused emphatically, even when Michel suggested that Sir Henry was still in love with his former wife and might even have forgiven her if Leonora had asked it. Kate found this difficult to comprehend, but when Sir Henry remained morose and ill-tempered the morning after the ball, she was alarmed enough to suggest cutting short their stay in Paris and going on to Madrid immediately. It was Kate who then began to lead her father away from the past and into a new life of their own.

Michel had found Kate's attitude over the whole affair amusing and, for some incomprehensible reason, attractive. He had even—on a whim, Kate told herself later—proposed marriage to her, shrugging indifferently at her refusal and seemingly unaffected by her instinctive recoil from his tentative lovemaking. She would break many hearts, he told her, before she learned to be a woman.

After that, Kate had been glad to leave Paris for her own sake as well as her father's. Fortunately, the years in Madrid proved happy and healing—even if Sophie Benton, to whom anything unconventional was abhorrent, declared them to have been Kate's undoing. It was Sophie's conviction that Madrid had made Kate unfeeling and selfish, but she did not know that the process had already begun in Paris.

Kate's new world was almost entirely a masculine one for those three years, for in Madrid society no woman of her age had the freedom she did because she was a foreigner. She had little feminine companionship, but because she served as her father's hostess and, on occasion, deputy, hers became a familiar face at court, in the country castles of the aristocracy, and on the fashionable avenues of Spain's bustling capital city.

If Kate did not break hearts as Michel predicted, it was only because she let no man near enough to her. She quickly discovered that, in any case, none of the men who flocked to pay court to her in Madrid cared about her as a woman. She was, rather, a challenge to them, and it became a thing worth boasting of even to have walked in the garden with *la inglesa*, or sat next to her at supper.

Other things were boasted of, too, and although Kate knew them for lies, she was helpless to combat them. In self-defense she could only adopt a mask of indifference and a manner calculated to make people see her as she presented herself and not as she was. In the beginning, the small deceits she practiced warred with her honest, open nature, but after a time, they grew to be literally second nature. It was so much easier to call her heart her own if she did not expose it to potential thieves.

It was not that she had no serious suitors. It was well known that she was her father's pet and that her father was a rich English lord, so that the man who married Catherine Philipa Collier would be able to boast of something more substantial than his amatory prowess. Kate did not even trouble to lose her temper over these fortune hunters but dismissed them contemptuously—and soon found herself with a reputation as a coldhearted coquette. If sometimes, unbidden, the image of a pair of cool blue mocking eyes rose in her mind, or a memory of fire burned in her blood, she just as ruthlessly suppressed them.

Instead, she gave her heart to her new home as if it were a new life and grew to love the country around her as she never had England, which soon receded into a vague memory of cold summers and rain. Spain was warm and wide enough to accommodate the barely discovered passions she now poured into it—for lack of any other object to lavish them on.

Sir Henry had sent Kate for Spanish lessons to an elderly cloistered nun, and Sor Inez turned out to be not only kind, but an unexpectedly astute old lady with an interest in politics. She saw immediately that her new pupil was intelligent as well as beautiful, and in return for Kate's being Sor Inez's eyes and ears in the Spanish court, she taught Kate, besides Spain's language, its history and culture. Soon Kate was as fascinated by Spain as her tutor, but unlike her, she was able to indulge her interest directly. She pursued her acquaintance with the king's First Minister, Manuel de Godoy, and with every other important person at court. She learned to be observant and to hold her tongue when necessary—and she developed strong opinions of her own.

Spain was a land in which she felt intensely alive and free. Here there were no soft pastel landscapes, no misty mornings or gray English twilights—gray was not a Spanish color. Spain was black and white, or fierce red and gold. The distant hills were not veiled in haze but stood sharply green and purple against the clear blue sky. Ramón had said once that there was no compromise in the Spanish character, nor in the country itself, but Kate simply loved Spain because it represented life to her.

Spain took life, too. In 1805, her father contracted a fever and died before Kate understood what was happening. She drifted through those days in a state of shock, and it was not until she stood by her father's grave in the Protestant cemetery on the hillside above the Manzanares River and looked down over Madrid, that she finally let the tears flow—because she was alone now, because her father's death almost certainly meant her return to England.

Kate's first instinct had been to hide herself away behind Inez's safe, impregnable convent walls, just as she had hidden her heart away from prying eyes. But her tutor had cautioned against such a move, telling Kate that she would have to learn to make her own decisions and not depend on God, or anyone else, to make them for her.

Fortunately, Sir Henry's will provided an alternative. It left her, in the event of his death before she was twenty-five, or married, to the guardianship of his brother-in-law, Philip Benton, in Salamanca, a medieval university town northeast of Madrid. Sir Henry had left his daughter financially well able to pay for her own keep, so she swallowed her pride and her reluctance to accept anything from her mother's family and went. After all, Salamanca—where Philip Benton was professor of classical languages at the university—was not Madrid, but it was still Spain.

Now, two years later, Kate was content. She sighed drowsily and stretched her slender young body on the velvet-smooth grass. She lay on her stomach with her head on her hands and loosened her long sun-gilded hair so that it fanned softly across her shoulders. She fingered a strand of it, but a sudden breeze, pungent and warm, blew it out of her hand before continuing past her and down the hillside, disarranging the yellow grass as a woman's footstep disturbs the rich pile of a carpet.

She looked up at Ramón, her lips parted to say something to him, but then she saw the black expression that had come over his face. He was staring intently down into the wide valley that spread out below them, shimmering in the brightness of the afternoon. Kate pulled herself up to where she could see out over the summit of the hill. Although the sky remained as clear as before and the low blue hills that ringed the valley still basked in the bright sun, a shadow seemed to fall over the afternoon.

Immediately beneath them, a tiny village dozed peacefully in the sun, but along the far side of the valley, over a ridge two miles or more long, a billowing cloud of dust rose behind the westward progression of what appeared at first to be a solid black column that stretched snakelike for miles back into the hills. Shading her eyes, Kate could distinguish men on horseback at the front of the column and men on foot forming its center; at its tail, teams of draught animals pulled wagons and dragged guns. Only the faintest echo of the noise reached the three on the hill, giving a sinister quality to the sight of that long column moving silently and relentlessly toward the sun.

Christopher roused himself to see what it was that so absorbed his companions, and peered down into the valley.

"What is it?" he demanded.

"Franceses."

The French. The way Ramón spat out the word made Kate turn and look sharply at him.

"Where are they going?" Christopher persisted.

"To Portugal," Kate answered for Ramón, who had

lapsed into the stony silence that customarily hid strong emotion in him. Kate's own forebodings set her heart pounding in a way that was becoming as familiar as Ramón's worried scowl.

There had been a number of such alarms since, in mid-October, the French General Junot and an army of thirty thousand had crossed the Pyrenees on their way to Lisbon to cement the alliance Portugal had been coerced into with Napoleonic France. Ramón had told Kate about it before the news had even reached the cafés of Salamanca, usually the source of all such political information. He had been in a fine fury that day, calling down curses on the Spanish king, the king's minister Godoy, the royal family in general, and the French emperor in particular. Bonaparte would be in Spain himself, Ramón said, before those fools in Madrid could be brought to see that it was not just Portugal but the whole of the peninsula that he wanted.

He had told Kate these things because she could tell him things he did not know, about the "fools" in Madrid. She had not been in the capital for two years, but she had met Godoy there; she knew his weaknesses and those of the other ministers. She had also been in Paris when Bonaparte took the first steps toward an empire, and she knew that whatever that man might be, he was neither weak nor a fool.

Ramón stood up abruptly, breaking the leaden mood as a thunderclap jolts the still air before a storm, and strode over to their horses. Kate hurriedly gathered the remains of their lunch into the hamper and put on the heavy cloak she had brought to conceal her unconventional garments and to keep her warm for the ride home. They mounted and turned their horses homeward, but their return contrasted sharply with the outward journey. Christopher soon gave up any attempt at conversation, for Kate had little to say, and Ramón, still scowling, stared straight ahead of him in silence.

They descended into the valley of the Tormes, which flowed gently among the rushes and small islands that studded its width. A donkey grazed on the long grass of one of the islands in midstream, and a barefooted boy herded his sheep up the south bank. On the far shore, the city began; its sandstone walls glowed warmly in the last lingering shafts of sunlight.

They were silent as they crossed the broad, multi-arched Roman bridge over the river. Kate looked up at the golden city rising before her. Her gray eyes took on the color of the twilight, brightened by the nearness of the night; her expression was rapt, as if she were aware of nothing but this race between darkness and day. But then she shivered. She disliked cold weather and the very thought of the coming winter, dispelled for today by the unseasonal sunshine, chilled her through. She eagerly looked forward to the fires of home.

At the end of the bridge, Ramón said a simple good night and turned toward the center of the city. Kate and Christopher took a path to the right and soon reached their home, which stood above, and some distance from, the river. The house itself was hidden among the trees, but as they brought their horses into the stables at the rear, they could hear the comfortable sounds of the servants at work, and the gleaming lights welcomed them inside.

Chapter Two

KATE STRODE into the house, swinging her riding crop as she went quickly upstairs to her bedroom under the eaves, where she sat down at her dressing table. She toyed absently with a comb as she frowned at her reflection in the glass. The fire that had been kindled for her return crackled softly, and its warm glow smoothed over the stains and signs of age in the walls. Kate's own small room suited her admirably, and its walls had absorbed her thoughts for years. The room was her refuge at those times when she felt the cold particularly keenly, when she missed her father, and when painful memories of the past crowded out more recent happiness. Now she went there to mull over in her mind the significance of what she and Ramón and Christopher had seen that afternoon. The menace represented by that column of troops had already assumed for her far greater proportions than that which actually lay in a military force that had been reduced by a long, hard march across an inhospitable land to a tattered, starving mob incapable of controlling itself, much less an entire nation. Kate feared for Spain—her Spain.

She jumped up, flinging the comb to the floor, and went to her wardrobe, rejecting useless conjecture for the mundane task of choosing a suitable dress to wear to dinner. Her Aunt Sophie liked the family to be properly dressed for meals, but Kate no longer thought very much about how she looked. Clothing was just one more reminder of the body it concealed, and that she did not want to think about, either.

Several gowns shared the comb's fate, tossed on the floor where Amelia, the housekeeper, would not be pleased to find them, and Kate was considering a light India muslin when there was a timid knock on the door.

"Who is it?" she snapped.

Gabriella poked her pretty auburn head in and regarded her cousin questioningly. "It's me. May I come in, please, Kate?"

Kate's look softened. Gabriella was a shy, yet at bottom, a valiant girl. "Of course, darling," she said. "Sit on the sofa while I dress."

Gabriella, clutching several outdated copies of *The Ladies Magazine,* clambered instead up onto the bed and spread her treasures out on the coverlet. Assuming a totally unladylike posture with her dainty feet tucked under her and her shawl covering her slim legs instead of her shoulders, she chattered brightly at Kate, now and then interrupting herself to read aloud from one of the magazines.

"I've been reading the serial story in this one," she confided, "and it's ever so thrilling!"

Kate could not help smiling but said in what she hoped was an authoritative voice, "You know your mama doesn't like you to read such nonsense. Anyway, you are too young for them."

Gabriella pursed her full lips. "I'm not! I'm fifteen. Almost. And Kate, they're not nonsense, and Mama likes to look at the fashion plates, too. Come see this one."

Kate sat down and thoughtfully examined the illustration of a pale, pink silk-and-gauze creation liberally sprinkled with jewels.

"I don't think I care for that one."

"Oh, Kate how can you say so! Of course, pink mayn't be your color, but *I* think it's beautiful! I should adore to have one like it. Do you think I might one day?"

"I think you will have many more even more beautiful, darling," said Kate, hugging her little cousin. "Now I must finish dressing so we can go down to dinner together."

However, when Amelia came upstairs a short time later to fetch the señoritas who seemed to have forgotten at what hour dinner was customarily served in the Benton household, she found the young ladies whirling around the limited dimensions of Kate's room in a frenzied dance.

They stopped when they saw her, and Gabriella attempted to explain.

"I'm teaching Kate the polka, Amelia."

Amelia, whose perpetual frown would have been quelling were it not for the twinkle in her black eyes, cast her a suspicious look and asked Kate, *"Qué es esto?"*

"It's a German dance," Kate told her, suppressing a desire to giggle. "It's very fashionable."

"Pués, a mi me parece una tontería," pronounced Amelia, and having thus passed judgment on such foolishness, informed the young ladies that Señor Benton was waiting dinner. The girls followed in her wake down the stairs, and Gabriella asked Kate about her afternoon.

"Where did you go? Wasn't it a beautiful day! I wish I might have come, too. Was Ramón with you?"

Gabriella had a schoolgirl's crush on Ramón and delighted in any news of him; but, reminded of the events of the afternoon, Kate only frowned.

She was singularly uncommunicative at the dinner table, picking at her food without really tasting it. Amelia, circling the table to serve the others, kept a watchful eye on Kate, in spite of her refusal to let Amelia coddle her as she did Gabriella. Amelia planted her short, stout figure behind Kate's chair and eyed her half-filled plate censoriously.

"You will take more *asado*, Señorita Catarina?"

"Señorita Catarina" was a mouthful Amelia never attempted unless she was upset or annoyed, so Kate smiled sweetly up at her. "No, thank you, Amelia, I have had quite enough."

Amelia was not mollified. "You do not eat enough, Señorita Catarina. You must keep up your strength."

Kate sat back, sighed, and inquired of Christopher, "If I can already outrun and outride anyone but you and Ramón, what do you suppose I must conserve my strength *for*?"

While Kit chuckled, Amelia dished out another helping of stew. Kate looked pained but dutifully picked up her fork. Amelia noted her lack of enthusiasm and said, obscurely, *"Eat and enjoy, and thee will have a good life."*

"Eat little and live happy," countered Christopher. "Take care, Kate, when she resorts to proverbs!"

Philip Benton was not the most observant man, but even he noticed that Kate was staring at her plate. He peered at her over his spectacles and inquired solicitously if there was anything the matter. She assured him that there was not, but his gentle eyes sparkled as he accused her of concealing an unrequited love. This remark caught Mrs. Benton's ear.

"That reminds me, my dear. Mr. Wilcox called this afternoon and asked particularly after you. I am afraid I was obliged to tell him you were out."

"Well, I *was* out. Really, Aunt Sophie, I wish you would not encourage that man. It is as much as I can do to prevent him from hovering over me at all hours, without you insinuating that I am flattered by the attention."

Mrs. Benton put down her fork and frowned indignantly at Kate. Her gray ringlets danced as she scolded her impertinent niece.

"You may, in your ignorance, consider Aubrey Wilcox insipid, but he certainly is no less than a perfect gentleman and one, moreover, with excellent expectations. Hasn't his father recently been given a baronetcy by his grateful government?" Mrs. Benton was not sure why, precisely, it had been given to him, but it seemed to give the family a distinction of sorts.

Philip Benton agreed with his niece's opinion of Mr. Wilcox; indeed, he rather selfishly inclined to have the same opinion of most of the young men who courted Kate. Philip had been grateful for the allowance that came with his guardianship of his niece, but he had since come to value her for herself. He admired just that attitude of self-sufficiency in her that shocked his wife and that he felt regretably lacking in himself.

The Bentons' was a marriage of opposites, and they rarely agreed on anything, although they never quarreled openly, either, maintaining rather a guarded neutrality designed to make life as comfortable as possible for everyone. Kate had recognized the absurdity of this arrangement the day she moved into Thornhill, and it served only to confirm her opinion that she wanted no part of a marriage, like the Bentons', without love—and if love, like her father's for Leonora, meant hurt and betrayal, she resolved to have no part of that, either.

"There is no need to force our Kate to receive any man she finds unattractive, my dear," Philip Benton admonished his wife gently. "She will make her own choice in good time."

"Well, she cannot afford to be so very particular," Sophie replied somewhat tartly. "The choice is not precisely unlimited—and she is already one-and-twenty!"

Gabriella shot her cousin a sympathetic glance, but Kate had retreated into her own thoughts and was not paying attention. Christopher, who sensed an imminent and eloquent repetition of his mother's dismal opinion of life in Spain, launched into a lively account of the afternoon's outing, and although he did not say how it ended, Kate was recalled to her surroundings by his vehemence and wondered if he fully realized what it meant. For surely, if war came to Spain, it would mean the end of all their lives there.

Christopher, who remembered nothing of a London he had left at the age of three, and Gaby, who had never seen it, would be more than happy to go there, Kate supposed. Mrs. Benton, not unnaturally, had long entertained visions of taking Gabriella to London to present her to society, but she had never dared to broach the subject to her husband. Sophie's memories of England had dimmed somewhat, and she remembered more vividly the joys of her youth than she had, in fact, lived them. Seen through the reminiscent haze of twenty-five years, it seemed the best time of her life, a time she wished her daughter also to enjoy.

Philip Benton loved Spain—or at least the romantic vision of Spain that had sent him off on the only adventure, however quixotic, of his quiet, scholarly life. But if his wife and family were to be placed in danger, he could scarcely ask them to remain there with him. And it would perhaps be best for him to go also. He would not be able to bear seeing Spain torn by war, seeing his golden city of Salamanca occupied by invading armies. He did not, as Kate had long since discovered, even like to think of such things. Kate would be the only one heartbroken to leave.

She had often been tempted to go to her uncle with the pieces of news Ramón occasionally brought her—as she would have gone to her own father—but she knew that he would only look up from whatever book he was reading, smile in that abstracted way of his at her anxiety, and assure her that there was no need to fret herself over such unpleasantness. She knew, too, that if he were finally convinced—if need be, by French troops billeted on his doorstep—of the seriousness of the situation, he would still fail to understand why his niece should concern herself with such matters.

To Philip Benton, history had stopped in the Middle Ages, and life between the covers of a book was more real to him than what passed on the street beneath his library window. Kate deplored this strange blindness of his but, at the same time, could envy the peace of mind and contentment that it gave her uncle.

She smiled across the table at him. He was, as usual, oblivious to whatever noise he did not wish to hear—just now his wife's reprimand of Gabriella, who had become so excited quarreling with Christopher that she had spilled caramel sauce on her pinafore—but he looked up to smile back at her. Christopher, equally unperturbed by the commotion, put a stop to it by saying that he had bet Ramón that it would snow before Christmas Day, and that he had every intention of collecting on the wager.

Kate shrugged. What was the use of trying to make them see anything beyond their own comfortable existence? Let them enjoy it while they might.

Ramón Sariñana looked down from the window of his lodgings on the Calle Libreros at the sights and sounds of the city. The evening was cold, but Salamantinos thronged the streets as if some sunny remnant of the past afternoon still lingered to warm them. Mothers called to their children from behind iron-barred balconies; hard shoes clacked on the cobblestones as two men hurried along speaking together in low voices; the clatter of dishes emanated from the open door at the rear of an inn.

Behind Ramón, a languid movement caught his ear. He turned to look at the softly curved mound in the bedclothes.

"Come back to bed, Ramón," a lazy voice said indifferently. Ramón bent over the bed to kiss the pale earlobe beneath the cloud of black hair but then stood up again and reached for his jacket.

"Where are you going?"

"I have an appointment."

A muttered curse followed him out the door, but he scarcely heard it. She knew he'd be back, but for now he did not want to be confined indoors. He wanted to walk, breathe in the air of the city. Ramón was not given to aimless wandering, but tonight, although he mentally fixed the Mesón de la Guitarra as his destination, he took his time getting there.

Wending his way through the alleyways near the university, he could see the night sky, studded with stars, above the sandstone walls of the ancient buildings that enclosed the narrow streets. Over the wider, more smoothly paved avenues near the Plaza Mayor, lights shining from upstairs windows dimmed the starlight, and passing carriages set up a clatter that drowned out the shouts of pedestrians who jumped out of the way, as if aggrieved at being robbed of their right to walk down the middle of the road.

Then Ramón emerged abruptly into the Plaza Mayor. Rather than cross the center of the square, he chose to walk around it through the cool, lofty arches. Shops and cafés opened onto this promenade, but their patrons acknowledged the evening chill by no more than the donning of a heavier cloak, and the crowd in the Plaza was as large as on any summer's day.

Most of the shaky wooden tables and chairs had been moved indoors, but café windows were still opened wide, and the voices of men loudly discussing the leading article in yesterday's *Madrid Gazette* over a bottle of *tinto* drifted out into the plaza. They mingled with the softer voices and rustling skirts of the women who promenaded in groups of two or three, ignoring the glances of the young men strolling in the opposite direction. Old women in black sat huddled together and watched the Jesuit students pass by in their red-lined black robes, and the Dominicans in their white. No one, it seemed, stayed at home.

Reaching the north side of the plaza, Ramón disappeared once again into a dark passageway and, a few steps later, was pushing aside the beaded curtain of the Mesón de la Guitarra. As Ramón walked into the smoky, overheated main room, a young man with an unlighted cigarette dangling from his lips and a three-days' growth of beard adorning his chin waved a hand in greeting. He rose, still clutching the guitar he had been studiously tuning, and with his free arm around Ramón's shoulder, guided him to another, smaller room.

There, four young men were engaged in a game of cards, and three more, less strenuously, were devouring a large portion of *gambas al ajillo,* wiping bits of bread around the sides of the plate to catch the last drops of garlic and oil that clung to it. Ramón protested that they might at least have left him a mouthful.

"*Vaya, hombre!* If you had only come a little sooner—!"

Juanito, the guitarist, clapped his hands together and called, "*Oye, muchacho!*" upon which a waiter hurried up to see what was wanted and, rubbing his hands on his grease-spattered apron, took the order and hurried off again.

"*Y otro de vino!*" Juanito shouted after him.

By the time Christopher Benton found his way to the *mesón* an hour later, the pall of smoke in the room was all but impenetrable, although the noise was by no means muffled by it, and he waved his hand in the direction of several shouts of "*Hola, inglés!*" that greeted him.

He found the four card players still intent on their game, Juanito possessively hugging his instrument, absorbed in the tune he sought to elaborate, and Ramón with his back to the wall, pensively blowing smoke rings.

Christopher sat down near him, pushed aside two empty wine bottles, and ordered another. Juanito immediately struck up a popular student song. It was not long before all of them, including the card players, were vigorously clapping their hands and shouting the verses to the guitar accompaniment Juanito kept up in good spirit.

Christopher had left home with something to tell Ramón, but it had escaped him completely by the time he entered the *mesón*. It was only when the two of them left it together sometime later that he worked himself around to his original errand. Emerging into the street, Christopher started unsteadily off in the wrong direction until Ramón pulled him around.

"Careful! You are going the wrong way, *amigo*."

"Ramón, you're the only man I know who's more sober drunk than not. How do you do it?"

"Experience," said Ramón in what Christopher would normally have recognized as a foul humor. But he was having some difficulty simply remembering that there was something he was going to say. There was silence while he searched for it.

"Kate's—um, worried over what we saw this afternoon," he remembered at last.

"I thought she might be."

"She takes some things kind of personally, you know. This—I mean, do you think she's justified? To worry?"

Ramón shrugged noncommittally. "I'll talk to her if you want me to."

"Can you reassure her?"

"No."

Ramón stopped then. They were on the edge of the Plaza Mayor, empty now and as silent as the night. Pale moonlight was reflected off the leaves of the trees in its center as they moved in the breeze. Water still played in the fountains.

"How beautiful it is."

Christopher stared at Ramón, who never said such things, and wondered if he really were drunk this time. He had guessed that lately Ramón had been more concerned about the possibility of a French invasion than he let on, but it seemed foolish to Christopher to waste mental effort on such speculation.

Ramón thrust his hands into his pockets and walked off across the plaza. Christopher followed him in silence rather than ask him what he was thinking.

Christopher, at nineteen, was just at that stage when masculine companionship meant a great deal to him. But he was, by temperament, entirely unlike Ramón, whom he considered not only his mentor but his best friend. Kit never really understood Ramón. He had never, for instance, been able precisely to define Ramón's relationship to Kate.

Ramón had more than his share of women—Christopher had had a large, heavy textbook thrown at him by the black-haired beauty in Ramón's room when he went there looking for him—but it seemed to Christopher they meant nothing to Ramón. He thought Ramón was in love with Kate, but he did not treat her the way the others who claimed to adore her did. He had more than once caught Ramón watching Kate with a curious intentness, but when, under the influence of *vino tinto,* Christopher had once asked about it directly, Ramón had reacted with one of his rare outbursts of anger. Kate was the daughter of an "English lord," Ramón reminded Kit, and far above the likes of him. Christopher was not, Ramón said further, to mention the subject again, especially to Kate. But he did not say, Christopher noticed, whether there was anything to it.

Christopher dismissed the entire matter from his mind and caught up with Ramón. Shortly, to break what seemed to him an unnatural silence, he embarked on a passionate denunciation of one of his lecturers, who had had the impertinence to suggest that he, Christopher Benton, might benefit by reading more of the texts recommended for the course. Ramón listened without comment, but Christopher was glad to see his mood had lightened. He was almost smiling, although Christopher was not entirely sure why.

Chapter Three

CHRISTOPHER, chafing good-naturedly at his lack of control over the weather, had not yet won his wager with Ramón a week before Christmas when holiday preparations at Thornhill were well under way. His mother regularly admonished him not to be so childishly inquisitive about the parcels being furtively wrapped behind closed doors, and she dispatched him with Ramón into the still dry and yellow hills to bring back pine boughs and berries for the wreaths and garlands, as well as a fine Yule log to grace the parlor. Gabriella set about designing and executing invitations to all their friends for Christmas dinner.

Mrs. Benton bustled about, needlessly upsetting whatever order there may originally have been in the proceedings, while Kate followed in her wake, overseeing somewhat more efficiently the decoration of the halls and the making of puddings and pastries. Mr. Benton savored the aromas emanating from the kitchen while reclining in his favorite chair and obligingly lifted his feet when Kate requested him to allow the maids to sweep there. But when his masculine presence became more than usually instrusive, he beat a hasty retreat to the Mesón de la Lámpera where he could generally find one of the lively—and exclusively male—discussions called *tertulias* in session.

More often than not, the *tertulia* repaired to the Benton library, and it became Kate's chore to keep the participants well supplied with brandy and coffee. She placed herself inconspicuously in a corner and listened to the gentlemen dissect a literary passage or discuss the latest publications of their colleagues in Alcalá de Henares or Seville or Madrid, as if understanding of the particular point in question were the burning issue of the day—as indeed to them it was. Nevertheless, they also found time to converse with Kate, whose company they not only tolerated but welcomed because she was their host's niece—and because they were all, secretly or openly, admirers of hers.

One of the most frequent visitors was Don Manuel Sanchez, a Castilian nobleman who had known Kate's father even before she was born and who claimed, therefore, a special relationship with her. He was a handsome but fragile-looking man with a gentle smile, which he often bestowed upon his *bella Catarina,* and he was one of the few whose smile she returned and whose conversation she enjoyed rather than merely endured.

But Kate's pet was Dr. Patrick Curtis, professor of natural history at the university. Known to Salamanca as Don Patricio Cortés, he was a large gentleman with flowing white hair who, although he had not seen Ireland for thirty years, retained a decidedly Irish twinkle in his blue eyes. He called her "Riña," a sobriquet meaning quarrelsome, which was originally invented by Christopher—as soon as he knew enough Spanish to tamper with the language—and with which Dr. Curtis frequently teased her into a temper. Then he called her a "spoilt puss" and shook his head paternally until Kate laughed herself back into a good humor.

Mrs. Benton sincerely wished that Kate would marry one of her many admirers, if only to rid herself of the troublesome girl, who appeared to take no interest in her own future, and she carefully scrutinized each new acquaintance. But there was still Aubrey Wilcox, who, for whatever Kate might say about him, continued to postpone his return to England and imposed upon his father's—the baronet's—distant kinship with Philip Benton to an impossible degree in the hope of making some more favorable impression on Kate. There was also—an acceptable second-best in Mrs. Benton's eyes—one Alan Grierson, a student of Mr. Benton's, whose silent worship of Kate he supposed to have gone unobserved.

Finally, there was a succession of young Spaniards, enchanted as much by her golden beauty as by Kate herself. When she was in an indulgent mood, she permitted their wooing, but when she was not, the echo of the front door slamming in an astonished face sounded through the house. Amelia clucked in disapproval, but Kate protested that these Don Juans were all idiots and quoted an evening's conversation in the parlor to Kit to prove it.

" 'How lovely you are, Catareen, enchantress! *Sol de mi vida!*'

" 'Thank you, Vincente (or Paulito or Antonio).' (I wish you would tell me, Christopher, why Spaniards are incapable of pronouncing *th*.)

" 'Thank you? Nothing more?'

" 'What would you have me say, sir?'

" 'That you love me!'

" 'Don't be absurd, Vincente. Of course I don't love you.'

" *'Ay, mujer!* How cold you are!'

"Really, Kit, I had only just met him, but a moment later he was sighing and clutching his chest as if—as if he had swallowed something indigestible!"

Christopher laughed, recognizing the truth behind Kate's unflattering portraits, but at the same time, he shook his head at her heartlessness.

"You sneer at them only because they sit so meekly in your pocket," he told her, "but one day, my girl, you're going to want some man who won't come running when you snap your fingers, and then what will you do?"

He was never quite sure afterward why Kate's mood had changed abruptly at his bit of teasing.

"You know nothing at all about it, Christopher James," she had said and, picking up the lace and paper pattern she had been working on at the time, had left the room without a word of explanation. Kit had stared after her, bemused. There was no figuring Kate out sometimes.

Half an hour before the first guests were to arrive for Christmas dinner, Kate stood in the front hallway, surveying herself in the tall mirror hanging behind the door. The house looked perfect—from the large vases of evergreens trimmed with red ribbons, to the scented wax candles in the wall sconces, to the sprig of mistletoe over the door—and there was nothing left to arrange. She thought she should not have been so efficient, for now she had half an hour to think about herself.

The mirror showed her that even her new gown was

perfect—red velvet that Christopher had talked her into buying when he saw it in a draper's window, with a white lace collar and cuffs. It flattered her slim figure by hinting at a good deal more of it than the demure cut and lace trim actually showed, but since the guest list included only the family and their English friends, Kate did not suppose she would cause undue alarm or unfulfillable expectations.

It ought to be a most enjoyable evening, yet it still gave her the sensation of having to perform, to play the part of a beautiful young woman with not a care in her head but the number of her admirers, and she found the prospect dispiriting. Had she really been pretending for so long that she could no longer prevent herself from doing so? She was beginning to dislike these social occasions more and more, aware that the last time she had looked forward to one— behaved freely and naturally at one—had been that fateful evening in Paris. Now, remembering that, she even shied away from the customary embraces of friends, feeling somehow that each meaningless kiss whittled away at the importance of her first kiss. She knew it was useless to feel that way, unnecessary and impolite, and that she ought to forget Paris altogether. But no matter how she forced herself, she could not.

She lectured her reflection in the glass about it, then ran her finger over her forehead to smooth away the frown, tucked an imaginary strand of golden hair back into the arrangement of curls at the back of her neck, smiled, and assumed a pose that, if not natural, was at least appropriate.

The knocker sounded then, much to her relief, and she opened the door to Ramón. Grateful that it was someone so easy to welcome as he was, she embraced him gaily and kissed him lightly on his sharply angled cheek. He stepped back and raised one black eyebrow in surprise.

"You are looking especially handsome tonight," she told him. It was true. Ramón wore an elegant black suit with a red sash at the waist; his boots were brightly polished, and his black curls perfectly brushed. "Who are you trying to impress?" Kate added in a conspiratorial whisper.

He smiled and looked around her into the hallway, as if searching for someone. *"Tu tía,* Sophie—who else?"

She laughed and told him he could impress Mrs. Benton

The Dancers' Land 41

best by helping with dinner, which might soil his splendid suit. He declared he would chance it and went off to the kitchen. Kate next heard Christopher's shout of greeting and Gabriella's dismayed shriek, as she realized that Ramón had come early and she had not yet finished dressing. She ran past Kate in her stockinged feet and up the stairs, laughing. Kate watched her with a catch in her throat at the reminder of the misty-eyed excitement she had felt at her own first grown-up party—and a sigh for the pain she hoped Gaby would never feel.

But the knocker sounded again just then. Dr. Curtis's arrival was followed quickly by that of Don Manuel, Alan Grierson, and the other guests, who came in stamping their feet against the cold, handing Amelia their wraps and Kate the gaily colored parcels they carried, and soon the house rang with footsteps and voices and laughter. And Kate remembered thankfully that there were some things she still liked about parties.

Sophie Benton liked Christmas to be English, too, at Thornhill, and so it was that year. Roast goose was served with all the trimmings that could possibly be unearthed from the Salamanca shops; mulled wine and spiced cider were poured in unlimited quantities; and the rich Christmas fruitcake that Amelia had prepared a month before under Kate and Gabriella's supervision made its appearance amid exclamations of delight.

Conversation around the table became more relaxed with every course. Despite Gabriella's determination to be grown-up and well behaved, she giggled and blushed a great deal. Kate exchanged knowing glances with Christopher whenever anyone's joking remark fell flat and felt as if she would soon be reduced to giggles herself.

Dr. Curtis saw this and deliberately provoked her. "My dear Catherine!" he exclaimed in his booming, jovial voice to catch her attention after everyone had eaten their fill and were idly talking over coffee. "You grow more beautiful every year! How is it that you are still unmarried?"

"Why, sir," Kate replied, giving him an impish smile, "because no one has asked me!"

"Well, now, how can that be possible? Have I been misled about the fires of passion that are said to burn in ardent young Spanish hearts?"

Ramón raised an eyebrow at Christopher, who grinned. The two of them had several times, at Kate's request, almost forcibly extinguished the ardor kindled by her fair beauty in the breasts of such as the unlamented Vincente.

"The truth is, sir, that now Katie's getting on a bit, she's afraid of being left on the shelf," Christopher said. "But nobody'll have her."

"Christopher!" admonished his mother in a shocked tone. Sophie had never seen the humor in her son's teasing the girls about such important matters.

But Kate only smiled at her cousin and refused to rise to his bait. The gallantry of Dr. Curtis and the others amused her as much as it did Kit, but since none of the gentlemen present had the least influence over her heart, she could also enjoy having them all flock around her, as they did when the entire company later repaired to the small parlor Mrs. Benton liked to call her "music room," and Kate sat down at the tinny pianoforte to lead the carols.

So little did she think to impress any particular one of her admirers, in fact, that she generously bestowed them on the other unattached ladies present. She charmingly persuaded young Mr. Grierson to share his carol book with Aubrey Wilcox's pale sister, Melissa (who otherwise would stand timidly in a corner and spoil the evening with her long face), and she smiled gently at Don Manuel Sanchez, who had secured a place beside her on the bench in order to turn the pages for her. Gabriella, looking charming in a light green cambric gown with a wide, dark green sash tied in a bow behind, was delighted to find Ramón assisting her with the words to the traditional Spanish *villancicos* they sang, and she continually lost track of the notes by stealing glances at him from under fluttering lashes.

Mrs. Benton and the older ladies gathered in a corner where they could observe everyone, and Philip Benton and his colleagues—with the exception of the sociably inclined Dr. Curtis—repaired to the library. Ramón elected to play the gallant to Gabriella, who might otherwise despair of attracting any masculine attention away from her cousin Kate, and complimented her on the improvement in her Spanish.

Gazing up at her idol with wide, rapt eyes, Gabriella as-

The Dancers' Land

sured him that she always spoke Spanish with Amelia and, indeed, often stole down to the kitchen to chat with the servants. "But, Ramón, I go into town only with Mama, you know, and she won't let me speak to people at all!"

"I suppose we shall have to learn a few words," said a voice behind them. "They refuse to learn English!"

Gabriella and Ramón looked up to find Dr. Curtis at their side. He sat down with them and patted Gabriella's hand.

"She said that to me once, Sophie did. As fond as I am of your mother, Gabriella, I am glad to see you have not inherited that little fault of hers. By the way, little one, you are looking especially pretty tonight."

Gabriella sighed and said with a tragic air, "That is very kind of you to say so, sir, but I know that I cannot hope to rival Kate. It is the one great disappointment of my life."

Ramón and Dr. Curtis both laughed, for despite Gabriella's youth, it was obvious that it would not be long before her delicate, dark-eyed beauty attracted its own ardent following. Both gentlemen were quick to assure her of this and to make her glow at their compliments. But seeing Kate seated on the sofa across the room, the candles softly highlighting the silver sheen in her gold hair, they could only agree that she was indeed exquisite.

Kate was smiling at Alan Grierson in what she hoped was a sisterly way, but the look in his large brown eyes—trustful eyes, she thought, like a child's—and his fair hair falling boyishly over his forehead made him look no more than sixteen and told her that she was not succeeding in dampening his infatuation with her. He had just presented her with a festively wrapped gift that she could tell by its size was some kind of jewelry, and she was searching for a way to turn it down without hurting his feelings.

But then an echo of their *villancicos* was heard from outside, and Ramón went over to Sophie Benton to whisper something in her ear, at which that lady blushed rosy red with surprise and looked up at Ramón and then at Christopher, who grinned and swept her a bow.

"It's your present, Mama—Merry Christmas!"

At that, everyone turned to the door as *la tuna*, a group of student musicians from the university, dressed in black with colored ribbons flowing from their capes and instruments, entered singing and gathered around the flustered but delighted Sophie.

After the students had gone, there was a general exchange of gifts, and Kate was able to pass over the locket Alan gave her with a lighthearted thank-you and to go on to other, less delicate offerings. She was engaged in laughingly averting a quarrel between Alan and Aubrey Wilcox over which of them might bring her a glass of wine to restore her energies after so much excitement that she did not hear a door slam until Christopher's "Dash it, Kate!" startled her out of her seat.

"I beg your pardon," he said, injecting himself into the group, "but do you know what is happening?" Kate did not. "It's snowing, by God!"

This observation was uttered loudly enough to send most of the guests to the windows to find a small blizzard in progress, but Kate merely sat back on the sofa and laughed. Christopher had waited until the very last minutes of the previous night before admitting that he had lost his wager with Ramón, and now, a mere twenty-four hours later, he was understandably dismayed to find the heavens at last obliging. Ramón, continuing to be diplomatic, settled another dispute by bringing Kate her punch. He then remarked ingenuously that he believed it to be snowing—and neatly dodged the blow aimed at him by his best friend.

Kate stopped laughing long enough to scold her cousin for being such a poor loser, a suggestion which Ramón quickly seconded. As the throng was now re-forming around Kate, Christopher complied and went off with Ramón. The snow provided a new topic of conversation, Mr. Wilcox remarking that in England a snowy evening could be enjoyed, whereas in Spain it could only be endured. Mr. Grierson took exception to this but confided that he would soon be returning to England and would not be displeased to see an English winter again. Kate, who had not been aware of his plans—nor, in truth, very much aware of Mr. Grierson—inquired politely the reason for his leaving them.

Mr. Grierson, flattered by her interest, explained shyly but with a certain pride, "Well, you see, Miss Collier, General Sir John Moore has inaugurated a training program for infantry at Shorncliffe, and I am most anxious to join it. My father is acquainted with Sir John and holds a very high opinion of his methods. He thinks I can do no better than to join one of his regiments."

The effect of this remark upon Miss Collier's countenance was scarcely what poor Mr. Grierson had intended and, thinking her to be concerned for his safety, rather absurdly assured her that it would be some time before he would see action.

Unhappily, Mr. Wilcox proceeded to make matters worse by saying to him, "On the contrary, sir, I should expect to see you back in Spain very shortly!"

Don Manuel protested in his mild way, "Surely, young sir, you do not anticipate war in Spain? Why, we are at peace with France."

The insipid Mr. Wilcox was proving unfortunately lively in his command of at least one subject, and he exclaimed earnestly, "Yes, sir, but for how long? Even now there are French troops pouring into Spain, on the pretext of passing through the country to reach Portugal. And if Spain goes to war with France, England will have to come to her aid against the common enemy."

Mrs. Benton heard the end of this speech and, puzzled, was on the verge of asking a question. Kate caught Christopher's eye and communicated a plea for help. He quickly maneuvered himself into position and asked, in a jovial tone, what the discussion was all about. Under his breath he reminded the gentlemen that this was meant to be a festive occasion, and would they for the Lord's sake not upset the ladies with talk of war.

"So you're going back to England, are you, Grierson? Shame. Miss you here. Still, if you're not taking that gray of yours, I'll make you an offer for him."

Mr. Grierson, greatly relieved to be extricated from his predicament, replied that he was, in fact, thinking of selling his horse and would inform Christopher when he had reached a decision on the matter.

The conversation continued along happier lines, but the subject that had once been introduced remained on every mind and cast a small but ominous cloud over the proceedings. Ramón left shortly thereafter, much to Gabriella's disappointment. Christopher's spirits alone seemed undampened, and his contributions to the conversation kept the smile on Kate's lips, although it had gone out of her eyes. Mr. Grierson and the others contrived to carry on with the always comforting thought of the great distance between Salamanca and the Pyrenees. None of them dared to speculate on where the next Christmas might find them.

Chapter Four

1807 BECAME 1808. Winter moved toward spring, and the Pyrenees moved closer to Salamanca. More and more French troops poured over the mountains into Spain until—to the amazement of the ministers in Madrid—the French were firmly established in the northern provinces and rapidly advancing southward. Because Spain was officially still France's ally, the northern garrisons were handed over without a shot being fired. But the tension in the occupied areas mounted as the people living there learned what it meant to be put out of their homes to make way for the interlopers.

In Salamanca, life went on much as usual—on the face of it. In February, Alan Grierson came to say good-bye to the Bentons, and Kate, remembering that he was intending to join the army, asked him if he had heard anything further about the possibility of England challenging the French invasion of the peninsula. Mr. Grierson was somewhat taken aback by this novel farewell but was rescued by Gabriella, who saw him rather as a knight departing for the Crusades who had come seeking his lady's colors to carry with him. But when Gaby later mentioned this to her cousin, Kate only laughed and told her, "You're much too sentimental for one so young."

The first days of spring came and went unheeded as Kate waited in anxious, rather than eager, anticipation of the summer ahead. Ramón's now quite frequent absences from Salamanca concerned her particularly. She never knew with certainty where he was at any given time, although he always sought her out on his return and gave her at least a partial account of his activities. Ramón's absences and Kate's unsatisfactory conversations with

Christopher, her only other confidant, added to the uncertainty of the season. And in her mind, the events in Spain and in her own life became confused, and she became possessed of the idea that any upheaval in one would be painfully reflected in the other.

Then, in the middle of the month, events occurred that caused a stir even in Salamanca. With the French rapidly approaching Madrid, the Court had retreated to Aranjuez, a village to the south of the capital. Ramón, back after a week's absence, came to call. Christopher was out, and Kate could see by Ramón's drawn face that he hadn't slept much, and tolerated Sophie Benton's fussy hospitality and proffered cups of tepid tea with diminishing patience, so she suggested they go out to find Christopher. Instead, they walked together along the river, and Ramón told her what he could of the recent confused events.

"There were crowds roaming the streets and loitering near the palace," he said. "They thought the Royal Family were trying to escape to America."

"Were they?"

Ramón shrugged. "Who knows? They stopped a carriage coming out, thinking Godoy was in it, on his way to escort them to Seville and the port. He wasn't in it. A shot was fired, and the mob rushed the house. He wasn't there, either. We found him two days later, rolled up in a carpet in his own attic, and when we let him out, he groveled like a beggar and pleaded for something to eat."

The tone of his voice told Kate precisely what Ramón thought of the king's minister. He scowled blackly but, tossing his cigarette into the water, continued calmly.

"Then Prince Ferdinand came out to speak for the king and queen. He said that his father had dismissed Godoy from office. The mob set up a cheer at that, but they wouldn't leave. When I left, the rumor was that the king would abdicate in favor of his son. Ferdinand was being hailed as the savior of Spain."

He stopped and, for a moment, leaned against the wall running along the bank of the river, silently watching the debris of winter caught up by the swollen waters and whirled downstream. Ramón's black eyes had a distant look, as if they were still watching that mob in Madrid; he hadn't shaved for several days and he looked weary. Kate would have reached out to hold his hand, tried to comfort him, but Ramón's look told her he had forgotten she was there. So she wrapped her woolen shawl closer around her, against the wind.

"*Will* the king abdicate?" she asked finally, to break the silence.

"If he believes it will pacify the mob, yes. But once Napoleon's marshal, Murat, gets to Madrid, it won't matter who rules in name. Murat will make his own law."

"But what will happen then? Surely he'll get no support."

"No more than the emperor himself. Sooner or later, the mob will rise up." Ramón smiled grimly and added with some satisfaction, "That will be the beginning of real resistance."

Not many days after this conversation, Kate came in to tea one afternoon and took her usual seat at the table. She quickly sensed that something was wrong. Christopher was silent, seated in a chair in the corner, brooding over a cup of cold tea. Gabriella sat on a cushion on the floor in front of the fire, her arms clutched around her knees—a posture that her mother ordinarily would not have tolerated for a moment. Mrs. Benton jumped nervously at Kate's entrance; her cup clattered against its saucer, and she glanced fretfully at her husband.

Kate picked up the coffeepot set out for her—for she disliked tea—but then paused to look around at Christopher, then at Gaby and her aunt. None of them met her eyes.

"What is it? Uncle Philip?"

Mr. Benton tried to smile but only managed to look wearily at his niece, his expression indicating that he did not relish having to say what was on his mind.

"Catherine . . ." he began awkwardly and paused. "My dear, I—that is, your aunt and I—feel we should tell you that we have decided, in view of the—er, present crisis, that we should, for all our sakes, return as soon as possible to England."

Kate stared at him in disbelief. She had been expecting something like this, but now that the words were spoken, she thought she had not heard them correctly. She carefully put the coffeepot down again and repeated what he had said.

"You feel you should tell me . . . ?"

Her uncle, taking her incredulity as an indication of ignorance, tried to clarify his meaning. "You see, my dear, the situation becomes every day more precarious. The French—"

"But the French are nowhere near here!"

Christopher looked up in surprise at her outburst. Kate knew that what she said was untrue, and a very short time ago she would have scorned such evasion of the truth in others.

Philip replied quietly, "Marshal Murat entered Madrid two days ago, Catherine. Madrid!"

Kate, perfectly aware of this, desperately tried another approach. "But—but, simply to leave everything and go, after all these years! Just like that? How can you?"

Her uncle looked even more uncomfortable and confessed, "It isn't *just like that*, Catherine. We have been considering this for some time, but knowing how you would feel, we thought it best not to worry you until we had more definite plans."

"What plans?"

"We have found a buyer for Thornhill. With the money we can make a new start in England. I have booked passage for all of us on an English ship leaving Vigo on the tenth of May."

May! Kate was stunned. Gabriella jumped up and threw her arms around her cousin. "Oh, Kate, don't look like that! It isn't so dreadful, really. We're going to London!"

No, it was not at all dreadful for Gaby. Kate turned questioningly to Christopher. *"Y tú?"*

He smiled wanly and shrugged his shoulders. "We can always come back, you know, Riña, when it's over."

She gazed at them all in turn, seeing them not as her family but as hostile strangers. How could they do this to her! She looked at them, trying to understand, but saw only herself being forced to leave her beloved Spain.

Stiffling a cry, Kate released herself from Gabriella's embrace and ran out of the house, her long hair flying behind her. She flew blindly up the street and soon found herself in the Plaza Mayor. As always in late afternoon, it was thronged with people. She stopped, flustered, and looked around her. Several couples passed, regarded her disheveled appearance curiously, and then continued their *paseo* in calm unconcern. Then she thought of Ramón and, stumbling on the loose paving stones as she ran, she hurried across the plaza.

Darting down a narrow lane, she quickly reached his lodgings. She swept aside the scandalized *portera*, ran up the stairs, and pounded frantically on Ramón's door. There was no answer. She jiggled the latch, but it was securely fastened. She stepped back and stood for a moment staring dully at the door, unwilling to believe that he would not be there just when she needed him most.

She turned reluctantly away and wandered out into the square that faced the main entrance to the university. There she sat down on a bench in the shadow of the statue of Luis de León, her arms folded and her foot beating a tense tattoo on the pavement. She wore no hat or cloak and gave no thought to the immodest picture she must have presented. She did not notice the carriage pull up beside her until a vaguely familiar voice made her look up.

"Catarina!"

It was Don Manuel Sanchez, with a bemused expression in his kind eyes. She smoothed her hair and stood up, attempting halfheartedly to smile at him.

"What are you doing here, Catarina?"

"I was looking for—a friend. He was not at home." Absently, she stared up the street as if Ramón would come walking along from that direction.

"But you cannot stay here like this, by yourself! Come up beside me, and I will take you home."

She moved back a step. "No! I mean—" She smiled brightly. "It's such a lovely day, is it not? I shouldn't care to go home just yet."

He frowned but did not press her. Instead, he gestured to the seat beside him. "Then come for a drive and tell me what is the matter."

Kate noticed that they were beginning to attract attention, so she reluctantly took Don Manuel's hand and climbed up into the carriage. They drove in silence for some time until Kate, feeling as if she would burst if she did not say something, told him, "We are leaving Salamanca!"

"Yes, I know," he replied quietly.

She stared at him. Her words were sharp. "You know? Then it seems that *I* am the only one who did not!"

"No, that is not precisely true. I know because it was I who offered to purchase your home. To keep until you return."

She looked at him again with new eyes. "Oh! I'm sorry. Thank you, Don Manuel."

He expressed, in the same formal terms, his willingness to be of help in any way he could, but then he was distracted from saying anything more by the difficulties of maneuvering the carriage through a crowded street. When they had reached a quieter part of town, he cleared his throat deliberately.

"I—that is, we—will be very sad to see you go, Catherine. I know you would like to stay, if you were able."

Kate felt tears burning in her eyes. Now she wanted to nurse her hurt, so she blinked back the tears and stated in a kind of stubborn litany, "I don't want to go. I want to stay. I would give anything to be able to stay."

Manuel was silent, as if giving serious consideration to her sentiment. They were driving now through a small park near the Palacio de San Boal, and he stopped the carriage at the edge of a tree-lined path. In the distance, children shouted at play, but among the trees there was no sound save the occasional jingle of a harness. The leaves above them caught the sunlight and scattered it in a thousand evanescent diamonds along the path. Manuel sat very still. She dug a handkerchief out of her pocket and looked down into it.

"Catherine, my dear, if you do so wish to stay . . . I had not intended to say this at all, and certainly not in such a way, but . . ." He paused, searching for words. Kate wondered what in the world he was trying to say. She looked deeply into his gentle dark eyes.

"I don't understand, Don Manuel. What is it?"

He fumbled with the reins that he still held and said, "Catarina, will you do me the great honor, give me the supreme joy, to stay in Salamanca to become my wife?"

She stared at him, her lips parted in amazement. She

would not that morning have believed that one afternoon could be so filled with the most astonishing revelations! Marry Manuel Sanchez? She had never imagined such a thing. She did not love Manuel—she scarcely knew him—yet she respected him, could talk to him, was comfortable with him. . . . Her mind whirled, until against her will, she was thinking, Why not? Why not take the only reprieve she was offered? But—oh, no! Impossible!

As if he understood the confusion into which he had thrown her by his unexpected offer, Manuel went on speaking so that she would not have to answer immediately. He assured her that their marriage would be in name only, that he looked upon her as a daughter, and that he would ask nothing more of her than her companionship.

"I am aware that you have many admirers, Catherine, but I believe it is true that you have no special preference for any of them?"

He paused. Kate suddenly became self-conscious, aware of how she looked and the clothing she had thoughtlessly thrown on that morning—a light gray wool gown, highly practical but with lace at the collar and cuffs that gave it a touch of soft femininity. Her hand went to her head and tucked in a stray blond strand. She wished she had worn a hat.

She became aware, too, that she was wearing that old, defensive mask and being less than honest with Don Manuel. He did not deserve that.

"No," she said. "There was—there is—no one else." She wondered if he believed that.

"I can offer you a home here in Salamanca," he went on, "and a comfortable income and the freedom to come and go as you like—not the sort of life, assuredly, that one ordinarily describes to tempt a young woman, but you are not an ordinary young woman, Catherine. I think we understand each other, my dear, in spite of the difference in our ages, which I am not foolish enough to deny."

All of it was true, Kate thought. His understanding ought to make the decision easier, and it would be so easy to fall into such a comfortable way of life with no demands made upon her and no chance of heartbreak. Had she not been trying for years to forget heartbreak? Here was her chance to put the past finally and irrevocably to rest. Why should it be so difficult to take it?

Manuel watched her anxiously as she struggled to come to a decision, but she was unaware of his scrutiny, as if the decision concerned her alone. It seemed to her that she now had to make a choice between the two forces in her life: the memory of the bitterness and unhappiness of the only kind of marriage she knew, and the present reality of Spain.

Suddenly, she thought, what if she had been mistaken, not observed carefully enough? What if there were other kinds of marriage, as there were many kinds of friendships? She was, after all, not her mother. She was not her aunt, either, who had a loveless and unequal marriage, and who, unable to enter into her husband's interests, had nothing to compensate for the lack of love. Manuel's life was much like her uncle's, but perhaps sharing it with him would be, if not a marriage, at least a relationship of mutual respect, even affection.

Finally, she took his hand and said quietly, "I am greatly honored, Don Manuel. If it is what you earnestly wish, I will be your wife."

"You must be mad!"

This was the prevailing reaction to the news of Kate's betrothal, but only Ramón expressed it quite so succinctly—and so out of keeping with his normal reticence.

"He's old enough to be your father!"

This objection had not been voiced before, but Kate knew it to be on everyone's mind. It put her out of patience.

"What does that matter? He is a good, kind man—and rich besides. No one can have any objection to Manuel himself, and—and I shall have my own house and be *Doña Catarina*." Her eyes pleaded with Ramón to believe her, as she tried to believe herself.

"But you don't love him!"

This was even less like the unemotional Ramón, and the outburst left Kate speechless for a moment. Then she looked away and said softly, staring down at her hands in her lap, "You know I don't. But he shows me every consideration, and if I cannot care for him in—as a wife should—I think I can scarcely fail to develop an affection for him in time."

This was a newly improvised part of the litany, and she was aware of how false it sounded. "Oh, Ramón, I can't, I don't *want* to marry for love," she said honestly, this time.

Ramón went to the window and leaned his head against it to cool his anger. They were alone in the music room, where he had come to give her the latest news from Madrid. He looked exhausted, and Kate thought he must be taking a greater part in the events he told her about than he revealed.

"I went looking for you that day," she said, "the day Manuel proposed. But you weren't there."

He didn't answer that but said softly, "I could have thought of some other way!"

"This is the way I have chosen," she said, her voice steadier now than his, although she did not look at him, at his stiff back and dark, bowed head. "There will be no regrets—mine or Manuel's."

When Manuel came to make his formal application to her uncle for Kate's hand, Philip was genuinely pleased at his good friend's happiness, but he later took his niece aside to ask her frankly, "Catherine, are you quite sure you wish to go through with this?" His eyes were anxious, and he looked a little weary.

"Yes, Uncle Philip."

She sounded very sure, she thought, listening to herself dispassionately. She would not let herself admit to a feeling that she was suddenly out of control of what was happening to her, that things had moved much too quickly and inexorably since that moment when she had accepted Manuel Sanchez. She might not have done it if it had not happened just that way, but now that she had committed herself, her pride would not let her back down.

"I will confess," her uncle admitted to her, "that I am grateful that you have chosen such a man as Manuel, and I do not hesitate to leave my girl in his care. I can do no more than hope you will be happy, my dear." Then he hugged Kate gently as she leaned her head on his shoulder and murmured her thanks.

Sophie Benton became very agitated at Kate's announcement, but in the face of her niece's stubborn determination, she threw up her hands in defeat. Never, she said to her husband, had she expected to see any relation of hers married in a Roman Catholic ceremony.

Gabriella said nothing, and although she continued to confide other matters to her cousin as before, Kate was never sure anymore of what she was really thinking. In truth, Gabriella was not a little disappointed in Kate's choice, although she would not for the world have said so, for she felt that her beautiful cousin could have had her pick of many more attractive suitors and, if she had only consented to come to London, would doubtless have made a brilliant match there with some highborn gentleman far more exciting than Manuel.

Christopher, as usual, was the only one who could in some way appreciate Kate's motives. Nevertheless, her news came as a shock. He liked Manuel, but he was the last man Christopher would have expected Kate to marry. And he knew without asking that she was not in love with him. What surprised him was that this seemed to matter so little to her.

He wondered, too, why Ramón made no move to stop her, but he did not care to risk igniting his friend's volatile temper by asking. He had run into Ramón a few days after Kate had let fall her bombshell, and Ramón had been in a foul mood. They had almost come to blows over some trifle, and Christopher had chosen the better part of valor and not even raised the matter of Kate's engagement. He did exert himself, however, so far as to ask Kate cautiously if she thought she would make a passable Spanish *doña*.

"Why should I not?"

"Well, you weren't bred to it, y'know. Suppose you don't—well, fit in?"

She frowned. "I'm sure I don't know what you're talking about, Christopher James. Manuel's friends treat me very kindly."

Sensing that he might well have his ears boxed by Kate, too, Christopher backed off and assuaged his conscience by telling it that he had done his best. Thereafter, he joined agreeably in with the wedding preparations and refused to be drawn into discussion of anything more momentous than the flavor of the punch for the wedding supper.

The Dancers' Land

The date was set for the end of April, and the resultant combination of preparations for the wedding and packing for the departure of the rest of the family threw the Benton household into confused disarray that mercifully prevented anyone's thinking too deeply on all that was happening. Kate took as many hours as she could spare to wander around the city and to ride into the hills, drinking in the scenes she knew so well and rejoicing that she would not now be parted from them. She rode from Santa Marta to Las Torres and deliberately pushed from her mind the price she was paying for this freedom. Then she rode back into Salamanca and looked at her future home and decided that it might be worth it after all.

Manuel lived in a house on the Plaza Mayor, an old house built in the traditional style around a central patio. It was on three levels, with the private quarters on the upper story; then the library, dining room, and parlors; and on the ground level, the kitchen and servants' quarters. Most of the windows looked out onto the plaza, but the doors led to the streets to the rear, where there were also stables. The patio was so completely cut off from the bustle and noise of the city that the gentle rhythm of water falling into the fountain could easily be heard. It was that sound that made Kate fall in love with the house at first sight.

Manuel, who was enormously pleased with everything about Kate, did not hesitate to show it. In his eagerness to display her to his friends, he took his bride-to-be to every dinner and ball given by anyone of importance in the city. Her acquaintances outside the university and the close circle of the foreign community had up to then been limited, but her father had been known in Salamanca, and some of its leading families were, not unnaturally, curious to meet her.

Kate was accepted graciously by everyone to whom Manuel presented her, and if the smiles behind the polite words were cool, Kate told herself they would warm with time. She had done this before, after all—adapted herself to a new life, new friends, and new habits. She respected the Spanish reverence for tradition, and their cautious resistance to change, but did not doubt that she belonged to their world as much as they did. They would see this, too—in time.

Ramón had taken one of his sudden departures just after her engagement and had not yet returned on the eve of her wedding. Kate fretted over the way they had parted, but she was too much occupied with her own activities, for once, to give much thought to where he might be or what he might be doing, and when Christopher asked her if Ramón would be there for the wedding, Kate only asked irritably how he expected her to know.

And then, before she knew it, the time had come.

It was a modest ceremony, for there had not been time to "make a fuss," as Christopher put it with a grateful sigh. Kate wore a simple white gown and mantilla, and Manuel beamed with pride as he watched her walk up the aisle toward him. Mrs. Benton wept through the entire ceremony and was obliged to borrow her husband's handkerchief, for in the excitement, she had forgotten her own. Christopher and Gabriella sat, dry-eyed, beside their parents. Gaby was, for all her disappointment, entranced by the beauty of the service. Christopher, to divert his mind from the growing realization that he was going to miss Kate terribly, concentrated on their coming journey—and wondered how much they had yet to do.

They did, somehow, contrive to be ready on time, and if the days before Kate's wedding had passed quickly, the week that followed it fairly raced. She spent most of it, with Manuel's understanding consent, at Thornhill to assist with the packing of the accumulated possessions of sixteen years. Most of the furniture had to be left behind, and Mr. Benton was at last able to persuade his wife that her drawing-room curtains and the rug in the hall would suffer irreparably from the sea voyage. Christopher, in his own methodical fashion, heartlessly disposed of most of his belongings to save the trouble of packing them and put aside still more to leave to Ramón, thus finishing with far fewer "necessities" to carry away than anyone else. Gabriella, between sighing over the memories conjured up by one childhood treasure and enthusiastically speculating on the usefulness of another in her future career in London, found herself three days before their departure with fully half her task still before her.

Nevertheless, on the morning of the third of May, they found themselves standing awkwardly around a loaded coach, ready but reluctant to be on their way. Manuel had quietly said his good-byes and was waiting to one side to leave Kate alone with her family. It was a bright, sunny morning, entirely unsuited to the melancholic mood although a perfect one on which to begin a journey. The coachman, eager to be off, fidgeted at his post.

The uncomfortable pause was broken only when Ramón rode unexpectedly into the scene. At the sight of him, Christopher rushed forward to embrace him firmly, not trusting himself to speak. Gabriella gazed at them, her big eyes brimming with tears that tried not to fall, but abandoned her self-control when Ramón took her small hands in his and kissed her good-bye.

Mrs. Benton then tearfully embraced her niece, kissing her wetly on both cheeks, remembering a last bottle of face lotion she had meant to give her and now fished for in her reticule. Kate was then obliged to comfort Gaby, too, for she was by then quite overcome by the emotion of the moment. But in the end, tears were dried, and the ladies were handed up into the coach. Christopher whispered an *hasta la vista* into Kate's ear and jumped up on the perch beside the driver. Mr. Benton said nothing, but squeezed Kate's hand, smiled at her, and then climbed into the coach himself and gave the order to start. As they clattered noisily away, Manuel came to Kate, put his arm around her waist, and stood with her wordlessly watching the coach out of sight.

Afterward, Ramón walked with them to the Plaza Mayor and respectfully asked Manuel if he might have a word with Kate. When he drew her aside, she noticed for the first time how tired and disheveled he looked, as if he had not slept for days.

"What is it, Ramón? What's happened?"

He looked wearily up at the arch above them, then at the trees in the plaza, and told her without looking directly at her, "There were riots all day yesterday in Madrid. French soldiers and Spanish civilians both killed by the score. Murat executes the instigators this morning."

Chapter Five

RESISTANCE had begun. The people had taken Spain's dilemma out of the bungling hands of the politicians and had begun to solve it in their own way.

With every new piece of rumor or report, Kate's mind flew back to Madrid and the still familiar scenes of her girlhood, where now such different events were taking place. The Plaza del Sol, the Royal Palace, the Toledo Gate—all now belonged not to her, but to the history that was being made there, and she felt them slipping from her. She clung to Salamanca as the only constant in her life. And Salamanca was now Manuel.

Kate had settled with unexpected ease into her new position as Doña Catarina de Sanchez. There were, certainly, a myriad of details that were different: meals were now served at the Spanish hour; Manuel's voice instead of her uncle's issued orders to the servants; she was required to adopt a different mode of dress and speech. But none of these small things seemed very important. She felt as if she had been a married woman and mistress of her own household for years instead of mere weeks.

Most important, she was more comfortable with Manuel than she had anticipated—more so than she had been with her father, who had been in his way as spoiled as she and took it for granted that the household revolved around him and his needs. Manuel, on the other hand, seemed to have no thought for himself. Over the years, he had fallen into a simple routine of rising early, taking a daily walk around the plaza, lingering over his *merienda* and newspaper in the library, and then dining lightly and reading himself to sleep. Occasionally, he would spend the day away from home, with friends or colleagues, considerately leaving a message if he expected to be late returning.

This left Kate free to do whatever she wished while Manuel was not at home, and to join him or not when he was. Increasingly, she did seek out his company, even though they sometimes said nothing to each other when they were together, each simply content to be in the other's presence.

They were less frequently invited to the homes of Manuel's Spanish friends. Kate continued to be welcomed with polite reserve—but only when she was with Manuel, who stayed protectively at her side. Kate felt her patience ebbing at their stubborn resistance to her most practiced charm, but for Manuel's sake—and partly out of her own stubbornness—she continued to batter away at it. Her smile grew fixed to her face, and flattering words tumbled from her lips as if she meant them. And at last, when one day in the plaza she encountered one of the more rigid of the elderly ladies she had met, and that lady nodded her head to Kate in greeting, Kate ran home triumphantly to tell Manuel about it.

"But certainly she would acknowledge you," he said, mildly surprised. "You are Doña Catarina de Sanchez and the inferior of no one—not even *su excelentísima* Doña Rosalia Isabel de Bustamante y Avellaneda."

That was the first time Kate had heard any hint of irony, much less censorship, in Manuel's voice, and it turned her smug victory to a bad taste in her mouth. For the first time, it occurred to her that it had cost Manuel something to marry her, and—more astonishingly still—that he had thought her worth the resistance he would have to overcome. She felt a rush of gratitude and affection for him and bent over to kiss his cheek. He looked up, but his usual, slightly bemused expression had returned, and he said nothing more than to ask her if she had brought the paper in with her.

Manuel was a continuing revelation to Kate. He had been as good as his word when he made it clear from the start that he would make no demands of her that she was not ready to fulfill. Even on their wedding night, he had only conversed politely with her over dinner and then kissed her hand and said, "Sleep well, my dear," before disappearing into his own room and closing the door firmly behind him.

Kate had lain awake wondering at his behavior, his reasons for marrying her at all. She had never said she loved him, it was true, but she hoped she had shown him that she was fond of him and wanted to be a good wife to him—but surely that was not reason enough? Was he perhaps fonder of her than she suspected? Certainly, he was admiring and quick to compliment her on a new gown or way of arranging her hair. He also had turned out to be, astonishingly, a fervent anglophile, and took great pleasure in listening to everything she could tell him about England. For the first time in her life, Kate was making a conscious effort to understand another person's feelings, but because she had never tried to puzzle out such a thing before, she was not very skilled at it.

If she could find no solution to the puzzle, however, she was determined not to make it worse by worrying over it. In time, perhaps, she would understand. Until then, she vowed to herself, she would never deliberately cause him unhappiness. When they entertained guests, she would be the perfect hostess; when they went out, she would be a genial guest herself; and when they were alone, she would be the most agreeable companion he could wish for.

And when she went riding in the hills, dressed like a gypsy, with her hair flying wildly in the wind, she would take special care that no one would see her and cause him embarrassment.

It was all so much easier than she had dreamed. And when Ramón scowled and told her she was tempting fate, she laughed; and when Amelia, who had come with her to the house on the Plaza Mayor, shook a reproving finger and reminded her, *"La mujer buena de la casa vacía la hace llena,"* Kate replied with a confident toss of her head that she *was* a good wife and that *her* house would never be empty!

A letter arrived from Vigo not long after the Bentons' departure, assuring her of their safe arrival at the port and telling her of their plan to embark as soon as possible. Each of them had written a part of the letter and, reading her uncle's brief note, her aunt's agitated tale of the overland journey, Gabriella's affectionate greeting, and Chris-

The Dancers' Land

topher's effusive and entertaining description of Vigo, brought them back to Kate more vividly than if they had magically reappeared in Salamanca. She stared at the letter for a long time and then, sighing, put it away in a drawer. That part of her life was over.

The Bentons' departure had been closely followed by that of the rest of the English residents of Salamanca, headed by Aubrey Wilcox, who was carried off by a summons from his father. Alan Grierson had written a timid little note after his arrival in Plymouth, but Kate was fast making new acquaintances and did not really miss her former neighbors.

She saw little of Ramón, although more than during those hectic days of early spring. She was still curious to know why he had not come to her wedding, but she did not ask for, and he volunteered, no explanation. Neither did he ever discuss Manuel with her, and he came only occasionally to their house.

She did know that Ramón had given up his classes at the university and had moved to a village in the northern hills, the whereabouts of which he did not disclose. But since the hostilities of the Spanish toward the French were now quite open and rapidly building into a real war, Kate could easily imagine the activities in which he was probably engaged.

In April, Napoleon had persuaded the Spanish Royal Family to meet him on the French side of the frontier. There Prince Ferdinand, who had been made king by his father's abdication was, so it was said, forced to hand the crown over to the emperor, who placed it on the unwilling head of his brother Joseph and sent him with it to Madrid.

"So now we have a French king," Manuel remarked from his newspaper one afternoon over their *merienda*.

"Ramón says they are already calling him Tío Pepe, or Pepe Botellas," Kate said, "because he likes his wine, it seems."

She placed a slice of cake on Manuel's plate as she spoke, then licked some sugar off her fingers. She was kneeling on the carpet next to the small table she served from, conscious that Manuel was smiling at her unladylike behavior over his spectacles.

"Not in public places, I trust?" he said. "However, the

sentiment is encouraging—it means *el principe* will be the beneficiary of the respect King Joseph does not get."

Ferdinand, indeed, emerged from the episode as a tragic figure, a victim of French treachery—and a rallying point for his former subjects. In the name of Ferdinand, now called *El Deseado*—the desired one—the junta of Oviedo, one of the many provincial governing boards set up after the uprisings of the second of May, had declared war on France and sent a delegation to England to seek aid for the hastily created armies of Spain. In the beginning of July, a treaty was signed with Britain, and a strange alliance was formed between the two nations that had nothing in common but their hatred of one man.

Manuel went to Palencia in July to attend a meeting of his colleagues at the university there—still the *tertulias* went on—and he was away for a fortnight. It proved a dull interval for Kate, in spite of her resolution to keep herself busy. She was forced to remain behind doors, and she had few visitors, for there were no women who would call of their own accord, and the men who used to come could not while Manuel was away. Doña Catarina, Kate was discovering, suffered disadvantages that would never have occurred to plain Miss Collier. She did not, for Manuel's sake, wish to flout convention openly, but she disliked equally the need to be furtive about her actions.

Ramón appeared one day, unannounced and unexpected, and was quick to see that her initial boredom was beginning to develop into a more dangerous mood. He had been expecting this and had already decided to offer her the only diversion he could. As if on the spur of the moment, he invited her to accompany him to a place called Santa Virgen del Arroyo, because (he said) he wanted her to meet some friends of his. Kate accepted eagerly.

It was several hours' ride to the village, and they set out early to avoid the notice of Kate's neighbors and the worst heat of the blistering July sun. When they reached the village, it proved to be no more than a few poor dwellings huddled together in the valley formed by a ring of parched, rock-strewn hills. The *arroyo* was now, in midsummer, reduced to a thin trickle almost choked by the dust that rose with the smallest breeze from its banks. The most care-

The Dancers' Land

fully tended object to be seen was a small shrine and a statue of the Virgin in the center of what passed as a square but which simply was an open space between two buildings. Ramón drew rein and dismounted in front of one of these and led Kate inside.

It was several minutes before her eyes became accustomed to the darkness. A fire, which seemed unnecessary in that heat but which gave off the only illumination, burned on the dirt floor in the center of the one large room. A gray-haired woman was seated near it, stirring a *cocido* that smelled delicious after their long ride.

"Mercedes," said Ramón to the woman, "I have brought Catarina."

The woman rose slowly and came over to inspect Kate in a familiar but, at the same time, deferential manner. Kate stared at her in frank curiosity and saw that the dress covering her big body was old but clean and that her neatly bound hair framed a kind face. Kate supposed her to be middle-aged, but her skin was still smooth and clear. The woman made a clumsy but respectful curtsy.

Kate smiled and held out her hand. "I am pleased to meet you, Mercedes."

Mercedes wiped her hand on her apron and lightly grasped Kate's. Then she grinned at Ramón, and her teeth sparkled against her smooth dark skin.

"How beautiful she is! *Tan rubia!*"

Kate laughed, and Ramón said to Mercedes, "Come, get us something to eat while we wait for the rest of the family." He beckoned to a man standing in the shadows, whom Kate had not noticed at first. He was a thickset man with short-cropped gray hair and a weathered face. Ramón introduced him as Guillermo, husband of Mercedes.

As they sat around the fire to eat, Ramón carried on an animated exchange with Guillermo about the small patch of land the older man called a farm, on which he eked out a meager living for his family. Because of its thick walls, the room was surprisingly cold away from the fire, so Kate drew nearer to it and sat quietly listening, her curious eyes darting from face to face.

Ramón seemed more comfortable here than she had ever seen him; the harsh lines around his mouth relaxed into an easy smile, and there was a warmth in his dark eyes that came from something other than the glow of the fire. Mercedes drew Kate into conversation, and she was amazed to learn how much this woman knew about herself and Salamanca—particularly since Mercedes had told her that she rarely left her village. An hour passed until Ramón, attentive to noises outside, interrupted a remark of Guillermo's.

"Someone's coming."

He got up and went outside, and the others followed. The sunlight was as startling as the sudden gloom of the house had been before, but Kate shaded her eyes and looked up to see two horsemen riding toward them. When they saw Ramón, they shouted and waved their hands. Ramón waved back.

"Rico! Ángel! *Qué tal, hombre!*"

They exchanged greetings, clasping hands and clapping each other on the back as if they had been separated for years. Ramón led them to Kate.

"Kate, this is Ricardo—we call him Rico—and his brother Ángel."

Kate held out her hand, and they took it in turn, smiling and bowing in some discomfort. They both had the same eyes and sun-browned complexions but, apart from this, bore little resemblance to each other. Rico was a tall, sturdy man of about thirty with a thatch of unruly, thick hair; Ángel was slight with delicate hands and a fragile appearance that seemed to match his name. Kate smiled at them both; their grins widened, and Rico glanced approvingly at Ramón.

"Rico and Ángel are from Valladolid," Ramón told her, "although you would not think so from their accents and those clumsy country boots you see on them!"

Rico threatened Ramón with his big fist, and the two of them launched into a spirited, if good-humored, debate on the relative merits of their two cities. They were dissuaded from coming to real blows only by the arrival of three more horsemen, who were also introduced in the same informal fashion. "This is Luis, from Alba de Tormes—and Francisco, whom we call Paco so as not to confuse this other Francisco here, who is not very clever and is called Francho."

Kate laughed and repeated their names, for the two

Franciscos did look alike, in spite of their being, as she later discovered, unrelated. Luis was somewhat older than the others, tall and sturdily built, a quiet man who seemed to study everything and everyone carefully. He would lean against the wall of the house, or whatever else might serve the purpose, and with an old, battered hat shading his eyes, scrutinize them. In time, Kate grew so accustomed to his presence that she forgot it.

Mercedes emerged from the house to greet the men and offer them the jug of wine she was carrying. Ramón poured some of it into a cup for Kate and proposed a toast.

"*A Catarina!*" suggested Francho immediately, with a gallant bow in her direction.

"To our good Mercedes!" said Rico, and drank to that stout woman's health.

"Death to the French!" cried Paco, and Francho followed with a fervent "*Arriba España!*"

Everyone drank to this. They fell silent then, but their intense expressions confirmed their agreement with the feelings that had been voiced. Kate watched their faces and felt a catch in her throat, and a surge of emotion roused by what these men, however few and ill-equipped, represented—a real chance for Spaniards to save Spain.

Ramón finished his wine and motioned to the men. They followed him and Kate to a shaded bit of ground on a hillside. Ramón squatted down and sketched a rough map of Spain in the dust with the point of his knife. He addressed himself to Kate, but the others listened attentively, uttering grunts of approval or exclamations of disgust as he spoke. While they were there, several other men materialized out of the hills and seated themselves at the edge of the circle.

"I don't know what you have guessed about us, Kate, but I think you must have an idea of what we—and others like us—are doing. The armies of Spain are worth less than nothing for fighting the French. They have almost no equipment or arms. The men are not paid and, as a result, are lazy as dogs. The fat aristocrats in command are graybeards who have been in the army so long they have forgotten what real fighting is. They win a battle now and then only by accident. As to driving the French out of Spain . . ."

He shrugged his shoulders and continued, "We think this fight is ours as much as the generals', and we are going to fight it our way. If the English get here soon—and La Romana, too, who is the only real general we have—and if Blake recovers his wits, the army may accomplish something. But they'll need the English, and until they come, there is much that we can do.

"Rico, Francho—all of us—have more men at our disposal than you see here. Perhaps a hundred in all. Not enough for a real war but enough to make life uncomfortable for the small patrols that the French are stupid enough to leave guarding vulnerable posts. We run much less risk than they do, because we all know our way around this country blindfolded. We must, because we have more chance of success by operating in the dark.

"There are still French troops in Portugal," he said, "about here." He drew a circle around Lisbon. "They and the troops in Spain get their orders from Paris, so any communication we are able to intercept spoils their plans to our advantage."

He stopped and grinned at Rico in remembrance. "Last week, some of Rico's men intercepted a communiqué intended for Marshal Bessières and, for a suitable price, sold it back to him!"

Rico chuckled. "I never thought that Jenaro, with all that education in his head, would have room there for so much wine, too. He poured *tinto* into that Frenchman until he fell over drunk and went to sleep on the floor. Then Jenaro copied the dispatch, seal and all—with different orders, of course—and sold it back to the Frenchman when he woke up!"

They all laughed loudly at this and speculated on the probable fate of the unfortunate courier when the trick was discovered. The story led to more tales of encounters with the French. Ángel cheerfully endorsed his brother's most fantastic claims, and Paco and Francho quarreled over which was to have the credit for their most recent exploit, involving the profitable picking of some French pockets.

The afternoon passed in this way, and when a cool breeze sprang up, reminding them that evening was not far away, Ramón signaled to Kate to go and get ready, for

The Dancers' Land

they must be on their way. She said good-bye to each of the men, feeling that she had come to know them and their mission well in the course of the day. After a few last words with Rico and Luis—new plans, Kate thought, wondering what they might be—Ramón joined her to say good night to Mercedes.

On the ride home, Kate found it difficult to suppress her excitement to match Ramón's maddening calm and finally burst out, "I think it's magnificent, what you're doing. How I wish I could help you!"

Ramón frowned, his brow deeply furrowed, and told her harshly, "Don't be a fool! I did not want to bring you here today, but I thought you might understand how it is. There is nothing magnificent about it. It is a dangerous business. We have had luck so far, but the war may go on for years, and sooner or later some of us are going to get killed. We'll be worn-out and discouraged and sick of fighting. We'll quarrel among ourselves, and some will just give up and go home. You think it's exciting now, but soon it will be only the French—and our hatred of them—that will keep us going."

Kate said nothing because she suspected the truth of what he said. She was silent the rest of the way but could not help thinking about the men she had met and envying them for being men and able to act for Spain—while she must sit at home and only hope.

Chapter Six

KATE WANDERED through the rooms at Thornhill, pulling dustcovers over the remaining furniture. She and Manuel had no immediate need for the house, and they had decided to close up Thornhill completely. The pressure of the Bentons' departure had created a great deal for her to do, but it was finished now. Manuel had suggested that she have a few furnishings moved into a small cottage near the stables that once had been the grooms' quarters and to make it habitable for an elderly couple to whom he paid a small wage to look after the house and grounds.

Kate looked around her old room, so empty now, and attempted to conjure up a vision of what it once had been. It was hard to believe that she had really lived there; no familiar object reached out to her, no friendly ghosts reminded her of times past. She pulled the cover from a chair and sat down, taking from her pocket a letter she had received that morning from Gabriella.

The letter contained little of substance—only Gaby's effusive descriptions of her new friends (and their handsome brothers) and of the wonderful sights she had witnessed in London. But Kate read it because it sounded so vividly like Gaby herself, and she was glad that her cousin was having her fill of pretty new dresses. For a moment, the letter conjured up the past that seemed to have escaped from Thornhill, but then its echoes faded, too, and the piece of paper in Kate's hand was no more than that.

She sat for long, silent minutes, got up then, and walked purposefully down the stairs and out of the front door, key in hand. She resisted the temptation to take one last look around before locking the door. Then she turned away and saw Manuel standing a short distance off.

The Dancers' Land

He held his hat in his hand, his head was tilted slightly backward, and his eyes were fixed on some distant point. Just for a moment he looked like an El Greco apostle, remote and unreal, but when he brought his eyes back and they found Kate, he looked like the familiar friend that he was. He smiled, and Kate went to him and took his hand. She was genuinely pleased to see him.

"Manuel! Have you just returned? How was Palencia?"

"Oh, much as usual. I arrived an hour ago, but you were not at home, so I came here. Is all the work finished now?"

"Yes, it's all over," she said with a rueful smile.

They walked up the hill hand in hand, and she asked, "Did you have a good trip? Tell me about it."

"There is very little to tell. It is not a beautiful place, and even the weather was unpleasant—it rained almost continually."

"I'm sorry. I hope you slept comfortably?"

"Oh, yes. Do you remember Diego Vargas? No, of course not—there is no reason that you should. We stayed at his home, and he and his wife were most kind. The lectures and the rest I also enjoyed, but I shall not bore you telling of them—"

He broke off and coughed fitfully for a moment. "Forgive me! I seem to have caught cold there after all."

Kate expressed wifely concern and said she would make him something hot to drink when they reached home.

Manuel laughed. "Some of your English tea, perhaps? You say you take it yourself only when you are indisposed! No, it is only a chill; as I told you, the weather was not very good."

Kate scolded him and said it would do him no harm to go to bed early and take care of himself, but in the end they both sat up late, Manuel reading one of the books he had acquired in Palencia, and Kate writing a letter to England. But then she paused to trim her pen and glanced at Manuel. He was absorbed in his book, so she laid her letter aside and pulled another from the same envelope, where she had concealed it. This one was in French.

Ramón had finally given in to Kate's entreaties to give her something useful she could do for him and had begun sending her the letters and dispatches his men intercepted from French couriers. She translated them, added any comments of her own that might be helpful, and returned them to Ramón by way of Luis. Kate suspected that Ramón had hit on this particular task not so much because the information obtained was useful but because the work would keep her safe at home.

Nevertheless, Kate was satisfied with it for now because she was learning things Ramón had not told her. There were many bands such as his, for example, all over Spain, and they were being called *guerrilleros*, because they waged their own *guerrilla*—"little war"—against the French. Indeed, the French obsession with this "little" distraction made Kate think that there would soon be more *guerrilleros* in Spain than regular army troops—and more spies in unlikely places.

The letter Kate pulled out now was more specific. It named several *afrancesados*—French sympathizers—who might be willing to go one step further to become collaborators. Kate found herself handling the letter gingerly, as if it smelled of something rotten. She knew that some of the names might be those of previously undoubted patriots who would, if the suspicion became public, be shunned by their neighbors, and even family and friends. Yet, if even one name proved to be that of a real spy, Ramón would have to know it.

Kate finished writing out the translation and put both pages back into the envelope. But she still sensed a lingering odor of unpleasant dealings and made up her mind to ride to Santa Virgen in the morning to return the letter herself.

At about ten in the morning, dressed in her split skirt, Kate rode into the plaza at Santa Virgen del Arroyo. Mercedes hurried out of her house to greet her affectionately, asking after her health and expressing satisfaction at Manuel's return to Salamanca. Ramón, who had heard the exchange from inside the house, stood in the doorway and watched. He was unshaven, and his shirt and trousers were stained, as if he had been riding on a dusty road—or kneeling in the dirt somewhere. There was a grim expression on his face.

"Are you alone?" he demanded brusquely.

Kate, walking to the door with her arm around Mercedes, looked up at him in surprise. "Yes, of course."

"You should not be riding around here unescorted. Don't do it again."

Kate smiled and teased him, "But now that our brave army has chased the French out of Valladolid, surely there is no danger anywhere near?"

His scowl blackened, and he strode angrily back into the house. Mercedes confided the reason for his mood while she buttoned Kate's blouse, which she habitually wore open at the neck when she went riding. Kate, surprised, let her do it, then handed her cloak and hat to Mercedes and brushed the dust from her boots.

Mercedes said, "There are persons—deserters from the army, *bandidos,* worse than the French!—hiding out in the hills. Last week, not far from here, a young girl was—mistreated. She was the sister of a cousin of Francho. Francho himself tracked the man down and killed him."

Kate's mood sobered quickly, and she went inside to say, "I'm sorry, Ramón. I did not mean to worry you."

With a slight shrug of the shoulders, he dismissed the subject and, leaning over the fire, picked up a glowing bit of wood to light his cigarette. Kate watched his face in the gleam of the low-burning flame that reflected orange in his eyes. She wondered if it was only her imagination that made him look suddenly older. She remembered how ready he once had always been for some new adventure with her or Christopher—careless, lighthearted, and young. But something told her that what she saw now was the real Ramón, and that her young friend had not so much grown older as emerged from behind his own kind of protective mask.

She wanted to ask him if he, too, felt alone sometimes, even with this new "family" he had adopted in this remote little village, if he, too, felt the lack of a center to his life and used Spain as a substitute for it. But she did not ask. She was afraid that for Ramón Spain really was his life, and that if she questioned that, she would have to question her own devotion to Spain's cause.

But Ramón looked so weary that she only reached out her hand silently to hold his. He drew away for a moment at the contact but then seemed to think better of it and took her hand, holding it as her warmth communicated itself to him.

She said, "I've brought those last letters you sent me, Ramón. There are names in one of them, names of possible spies."

He looked interested at that. "Who?"

She named one she knew, a French-speaking priest who had often taken part in Manuel's *tertulias*. Ramón shook his head.

"No. He is all talk. There is no backbone to him."

She named another, a contessa previously famed more for the number of her lovers and the blindness of her husband. Ramón thought about that one for a moment.

"I don't know. Perhaps."

"Ramón." Kate reached out for his other hand and turned him to face her. "Ramón, I can find out. I can go places that she does, strike up a conversation as if by accident—"

"No."

He jerked himself out of her grip, his anger flaming as suddenly as it had when she arrived.

"Why not?"

"Because you—you could not do it. They would guess what you were after in a minute. You are not devious enough."

Kate laughed. And she had thought herself such a skilled actress!

"You once said all women are devious by nature," she accused him.

"You are not like other women," he said.

Manuel had said that, too, and meant it as praise. She was not certain what either of them meant by it but, again, she was afraid to ask, afraid to discover that what they admired in her might be just those qualities she herself despised. So she did not ask.

Instead, she smiled warmly and said, "It's true. Another woman would be too delicate to ask for something to eat, but me—I'm hungry! Is there anything left of your *merienda*?"

Ramón laughed at that and got up to fetch some bread and cheese, and they sat eating it and talking nonsense. She teased the laughter out of him, as if fanning a dying flame, for it warmed her to hear Ramón laugh, however much it sounded as if he'd forgotten how. She was glad to ease the weariness in his expression somewhat by recounting some of the lighter Salamanca café gossip, so that by the time she was ready to leave, she felt that her visit had served some purpose.

She rode home with Luis at her side, a custom they were both becoming familiar with. It was late when they reached Salamanca, and Kate did not find Manuel at home. She sought out Amelia to ask after him and discovered that he had gone out with his friends. Kate frowned in annoyance at Manuel's lack of concern for his own health but said nothing and went directly to bed.

But Manuel had gone out that evening without his heavy cloak, and as a result of being caught in a sudden shower, the "slight chill" that had lingered since Palencia turned into a serious cold and confined him to his bed. Kate fussed and scolded while she kept him supplied with warm covers and stoked the fire in his room, but he would not let her send for a doctor, saying continually that it was nothing to bother a doctor with. Kate's inexperience with illness—her father's had begun and ended with appalling swiftness—made her reluctant to take sole responsibility for nursing Manuel. But he so plainly preferred her care to anyone else's that she dared not leave him for very long. She sat by his bed reading books from his library and excerpts from the Bentons' letters. Her uncle wrote in his somewhat stilted, old-fashioned style:

Since the victory at Bailén, the whole of England is fired with enthusiasm for the Spanish cause. The patriotism and bravery of the Spanish, boldly fighting to destroy the ogre Bonaparte, have caught the imagination of all. The decision of our government to throw the entire weight of England's military right into Spain has met with wholehearted support, and our young men are eagerly looking forward to "going to the peninsula."

And so, I rejoice that the campaign in Spain goes well and that British troops are being sent to reinforce the Spanish armies. I hope, and pray, too, my dear, that the calamity of war does not touch you in Salamanca. I send my best regards to Manuel and trust that he continues in good health.

But after Manuel had been in bed for a week with little sign of improvement, Kate overrode his protests and sent for a doctor—a man named Barrigo, Manuel's personal physician for many years. This elderly gentleman, who looked comfortingly professional, examined his patient and made the usual bedside noises. Then he took Kate aside, and his words were less comforting.

"Why did you not send for me before this?"

"He would not let me. He insisted it was no more than a bad cold."

"It may have been nothing more than that at the start, but he is not a strong man, as you must know. No, perhaps you don't know. Don Manuel suffered from rheumatic fever as a child and has never been strong since but regrettably refuses to take care of himself. He should have gone to bed when he first caught this chill of his, instead of staying out until all hours. These warm nights can be deceptive."

Kate listened, and apprehension began to grow in her. She opened her mouth to question the doctor further, but he sensed her anxiety and smiled at her.

"He never told you about the old fever? But do not fear, Doña Catarina. If he is well cared for, he may yet again make a recovery."

However, as the weeks went by, Manuel's illness lingered and seemed to take a stronger hold on him. Kate did what she could, but it was difficult to match her husband's ever cheerful mood, for he never regarded his illness as anything more serious than an annoyance, inconvenient in that it did not permit him to sally out of doors, but not so serious as to prevent his activities coming to him. Kate often had to interrupt a *tertulia* around his bed when the men became forgetful of the hour, and finally even to speak to them privately about it, upon which they apologized sincerely for unwittingly taxing Manuel's strength. They began to come less frequently to the house, and then only to leave some trifle, a book or newspaper, for him.

Kate left the house even less often than before, sitting, instead, for hours on end with Manuel, to talk or read to

The Dancers' Land

him and to bring him his meals on a tray. As September neared its end, she had grown accustomed to this routine and ceased to worry over Manuel's condition because, since she saw him constantly, the changes in him were lost on her; he grew thinner and older without her noticing.

The last day of September was not in any way remarkable, except perhaps for the slight trace of autumn in the air. Kate had spent the morning sewing as she sat at her husband's bedside, while he, quieter than usual, merely smiled at her and now and then reached out to pat her hand. She smiled automatically in return, but once, when he gripped her hand fiercely, she looked up in surprise. He was staring at her intently, as if searching for something.

"What is it, Manuel?"

"Eres tú?" He paused for a moment, still searching. "Are you happy, my dear?"

"Yes, of course," she said quickly, realizing only then, and with a sense of wonder, that she had been.

He looked doubtful, and Kate smiled. "How can I not be?"

"I very much wished you to be happy," Manuel said. "I loved you so much. . . ."

With that, he released his grip and fell back on the pillows wearily, staring at the ceiling as if he had already forgotten what he had just said. Kate, speechless from surprise, stared at him for a moment.

"I—I will see what is delaying your luncheon. . . ."

She got up and hurried out of the room.

A few minutes later, she was crossing the patio with the loaded meal tray when a housemaid came running noisily along the opposite balcony.

"Doña Catarina!"

Kate was about to scold the girl for creating such a disturbance, but the look on her face and the tone of her voice made Kate stop suddenly, halfway up the stairs, and demand of her, "What is it?"

"Doña Catarina—" The girl could get no more than that out, and stood on the balcony twisting her hands in her apron. A bolt of fear shot through Kate.

"Manuel!"

The tray crashed to the floor, food spilling everywhere; a cup clattered down the stairs to smash into pieces at the bottom. Kate flew up the remaining stairs and into Manuel's room. He lay precisely as she had left him, a slight smile on his lips and his hand on the coverlet as if he had just dropped off to sleep.

"Manuel!" she repeated. She moved slowly to the bed, touched the motionless hand, and then sank to her knees on the floor, burying her face in the coverlet.

Manuel was gone. Manuel, a man she had never really known, although he had been a part of her life since her girlhood. He had been her husband for five months, little enough time to try to know him, and scarcely long enough to provide her with memories.

But her grief was genuine. Snatches of conversation, glimpses of his love for her, the words he had spoken so unexpectedly at the end, all drifted across her memory, and she snatched at them greedily so that Manuel would not slip away so quickly. He had loved her, he said, but what had surprised her most at that moment was the realization that she had loved him, too. She began to understand that there were many kinds of love and to grieve that she learned of them too late.

Draped in black, she sat unmoving and seemingly unmoved through the funeral service, oblivious to the whispers and glances directed at her by those whose opinions meant nothing to her now. How could she care what strangers thought when she scarcely understood her own feelings? Even when Mercedes and Rico and her friends from Santa Virgen came to pay their respects, she withdrew into herself. She felt terribly alone. It was her own fault, she knew, for not seeing sooner how dear Manuel had become to her.

It frightened her to remain in the house by herself. For a time, she thought she must leave Spain now, but she was indecisive. Ramón, reluctant but sensing her need, crept furtively into the house each night and slept in the room next to Kate's, listening to her toss in restless slumber. Several times in the night he heard her call out indistinctly in her sleep—to Manuel, he thought, or perhaps to her father. At first he wanted to go to her, but he knew he could not—should not—try to help. She had not called him, after all. She would have to go through this alone.

The Dancers' Land

Slowly, she did. That capacity of hers to accept change saw her through. Her restlessness left her, and she began to look forward again to what life could bring. There had been so many changes so quickly—some of them must surely be for the better.

The days passed, shorter now but slower moving, one weaving into the next. The last traces of summer vanished with October, and suddenly—at last—it was November again.

Part Two
Moore's Army, 1808

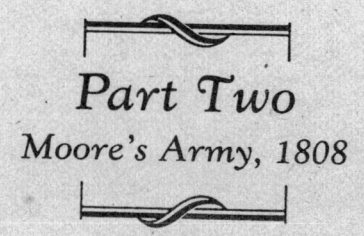

Chapter Seven

"COLONEL GREYSON!"

The tall man poised on the crest of the hill lowered his field glass and turned his ice-blue eyes to his adjutant, riding hard at him up the slope. He waited unmoving for Sinclair to reach him and smiled at the captain's prodigious energy. Greyson didn't believe in wasting any effort on show, but it was hard to convince a boy like Sinclair of that.

"General Paget presents his compliments, sir," the captain reported, "and asks, 'Where the hell are you?'"

The colonel's smile widened into a grin. "Return the compliment, captain, and—never mind, I'm coming myself."

Greyson replaced his black shako on his sleek blond hair, pulling it down a touch to shade his eyes. He checked his watch as he started toward his horse and muttered, "Devil of a hurry he's in!" He paused to take one last look at the panorama from the hill of the city that seemed so near but was still miles away.

The early-morning light filtered through the low-hanging clouds and bathed the city in a pale topaz, but Greyson thought the softness was an illusion. Beneath the welcome but superficial cordiality would lie no more real hospitality than they had encountered in other Spanish towns.

However, the president of the local junta, a marqués, had insisted at some length that Salamanca rejoiced at their arrival and that he, personally, would be at her gates to greet them. It would be sheer stupidity to refuse the invitation. And Greyson knew that Moore was prepared to swallow a good deal of his own pride in order to extract as much cooperation as possible from their reluctant allies.

Moore's orders were to rendezvous with forces under the

command of Sir David Baird, who was somewhere in northern Spain, and they would then lend their joint aid to the Spanish armies. The French were—reportedly—well away behind the distant Ebro River, and the Spanish were in force between them and the British. General Moore expected to be able to meet Baird within the fortnight—that was, if their unpredictable allies kept their promises.

Colonel Greyson's responsibilities to his regiment did not involve him in the diplomatic dilemmas of his general, however, and he had more freedom to attempt an understanding of the moody race that inhabited this wild country. He had learned Spanish and spoke with as many people—gypsies, generals, and noblemen—as he could.

He had been informed that the marqués had arranged for him to be billeted in the home of a widow who was a leading figure in Salamancan society. "Beware of widows, my lad!" he told himself as he mounted his big iron-gray horse. Then he laughed aloud and said, "She's probably eighty and deaf as a post!" He rode off to engage Edward Paget in speculation about what the day might bring them.

Kate stood in front of her mirror and gave herself a final inspection. Her gown was an old-fashioned but elegant one of black crepe she wore with no more adornment than the small ebony buttons on the sleeves and high neck, and at her throat a garnet brooch Manuel had given her. Black lace hung from her high-crowned riding hat to cover her bright hair, and she looked very much the part of the haughty aristocrat that Englishmen expected when introduced to a lady with the title of doña before her name.

This was the first public appearance she would make as a widow, and she had mixed feelings about it. On the one hand, it signified her final acceptance, by virtue of her widow's status, by Salamancan society, almost as if her bereavement automatically removed any previous disqualifications. On the other hand, she felt herself no different now from any other Salamanca matron, young or old, and while she had never particularly cared about what she wore before this, the idea that a costume donned out of respect for Manuel should deprive her of her individuality in this way chafed her in much the same way as the stiff

The Dancers' Land

black bombazine in her bodice did. But she had made up her mind to play this role, and play it she would.

She was just pulling on her gloves when Amelia entered to say that a servant of the Marqués de Cerralbo had come to inform her that Sir John Moore and his staff were now approaching the city and that the marqués would be pleased to receive Doña Catarina at his home as quickly as possible so that she might join him in welcoming the general to Salamanca.

"I am quite ready, Amelia. If we must have these creatures in the house, tracking in mud on their great clumsy boots and getting in everyone's way, then let us get on with it and hope it is over quickly."

She moved toward the door, but Amelia had folded her arms across her chest and was blocking the way with her short, square person.

"Well, what is it?" Kate said.

"I only wish to remind Doña Catarina," Amelia said in her most disapproving voice, "of how Don Manuel would have wished her to behave on such an occasion."

Kate sighed. "Oh, yes, I know. Manuel would have played the gracious host to perfection. But as you well know, Amelia, he had much more patience than I have."

But Amelia did not budge.

"Oh, very well. I promise to be on my very best behavior. But I do not promise to like it!"

Amelia seemed satisfied with this half-promise and moved aside to let her mistress pass. But she followed her downstairs, waited silently as Kate's horse was brought around, and then stood with her hands on her waist as Luis assisted Kate into the saddle. Kate settled her skirts around her, tucked her whip into her jacket pocket and, just before tossing her veil forward, flashed Amelia her most dazzling smile. Amelia grinned and waved one hand dismissively at Kate, as if to disclaim any responsibility for her, and went back into the house to complete the preparations for their guests.

The Marqués de Cerralbo, the *alcalde* and other officials of Salamanca, and representatives of its most prominent families were on hand to meet the envoy of Britannia, who had so generously come to help Spain win her war—or so the marqés phrased it. Kate sat erect in her saddle, feeling the light breeze through her veil, and glanced around her at the assembled dignitaries in all their finery. This first passing of foreign armies through Salamanca would not, Kate thought, be the last. She hoped Cerralbo had no intention of making such ceremony of every one.

They waited at the northern end of the Roman bridge as the British officers descended from the hills to the south—those same aged, yellow velvet hills from which Kate and Christopher and Ramón had watched Junot's army march to Portugal scarcely a year before. This day bore little resemblance to that other, golden November. The sky was a dull gray, and heavy clouds lay close to the earth. The storm that had been in the air all morning had not broken, but the threat of it remained. The stillness was penetrating, and only now and then did the fugitive wind send a ripple shimmering across the river or a dead leaf dancing down the road.

Kate could make out the faces of some of the approaching men now. Something about them, about the way they held themselves, stirred her strangely, as if she knew them from some place and time long ago. She frowned and quieted her horse, which had caught some of her agitation. Her companions ceased conversing among themselves, and no human voice was added to the sound of the clip-clop of hooves on the bridge and the jingle of harnesses.

Cerralbo, a young man with the classic dark Spanish handsomeness and a neatly trimmed black mustache, moved out to the center of the bridge. He smiled warmly and stretched out his immaculately gloved hand to the man who was, without a doubt, Sir John Moore. Moore sat strong and upright in the saddle and wore the uniform with the brilliant red coat proudly. He was good-looking and fair-haired like many of his men; in spite of a rather delicate mouth and lazy dark eyes, he gave the impression of great strength of character and an unshakable will. He watched the Spanish dignitaries approach with scarcely a flicker of an eyelash and then took Cerralbo's outstretched hand with a distant, polite smile. The Spaniard assured him with exquisite courtesy that Salamanca was at his service and that he held his own house and staff at the general's disposal for any and all that he might require.

The Dancers' Land

"That is quite impossible," replied Sir John stiffly. "I shall have people with me every day. I cannot think of putting you to so much expense."

Cerralbo replied with his most engaging smile and said, "But if you will not accept everything, dear sir, you shall not stay in my house!"

The general gave way, nodded his head in consent, and then rode beside the marqués into the city. The other English officers, visibly awed by this unaccustomed welcome, rode together, and the rest of the Spanish party, less willing to risk their dignity than their spokesman had been, kept themselves at a distance.

Kate rode with her head held high but watching the English with great curiosity out of the corner of her eye. Only one man among them, whom Kate later knew as Edward Paget, might have been taken for a Spaniard because of his dark good looks and black eyes. Another, older than the rest, resembled Kate's father. Several of the others reminded her astonishingly of Christopher. All of them looked strangely familiar, and it occurred to Kate almost with a shock that they were her kind—her kin and countrymen.

The officer riding beside General Paget had been watching Kate intently for some time as they passed through the narrow, cobbled streets of the city. As they turned a corner, she became aware of this scrutiny and instinctively pulled her cloak closer around her, draping what little showed of her figure with the shapeless black cloth. The gesture was not lost on the officer, who grinned impudently and removed his hat to her.

Kate caught her breath sharply at the flash of burnished gold hair when he took off his hat.

Oh, no—it couldn't be!

She stared at him, looking for something—anything—to tell her she was mistaken, that he was not the same man she had fallen so suddenly and violently in love with in Paris all those years ago. But as her eyes drank in the broad shoulders, the erect way he held himself, the high cheekbones and strong hands, memory flooded over her.

Her horse whinnied in protest at her sharp, inadvertent pull at the reins, and she put her hand to his neck to soothe him. Her hand was trembling, and she became aware of the rapid pulse beneath the black glove.

He was still looking at her, puzzlement in his frown. Kate was grateful that her black veil and hat at least hid her own hair and most of her face. He could not have recognized her; he was simply reacting to her stupidly female self-consciousness.

But she could not be certain that he would not recognize her. She swerved her horse suddenly, guiding him down a narrow side street, and rode quickly home by a shorter route.

She stormed into the house, barely seeing a startled Amelia, who was crossing the patio with a pile of freshly laundered sheets in her arms. She ran to her room, slammed the door behind her, and leaned her head back against it with a deep sigh. She felt as if she had been holding her breath all the way back from the bridge.

What was he doing here? Did he come because he knew she was in Salamanca? But if he knew, why had he never written to her? Had he, in fact, forgotten her? If so, how would she ever face him?

Kate closed her eyes, trying to shut out those tormenting questions that she had asked herself daily for years and had only recently been able to forget, thanks to Manuel. Now they all came back to her, and the ache in her heart was as fresh as before, and she had no defense against it—not Manuel, not her family, no one!

She took a deep breath and opened her eyes again. The room looked exactly the same as it had when she left it that morning, as if her world had not collapsed around her in the interim. She rang the bell, and when Amelia answered it, Kate asked her, in a voice that sounded as if it came from a long way, for a pot of tea to be sent up to her.

Amelia looked doubtful. *"Té, Señora?"*

"Yes, that's what I said." Kate gave her an uncompromising glare, and Amelia went off submissively to do as she was told. Kate sat down at her window to wait and to compose herself.

An hour later, she felt sufficiently calm to receive with equanimity an announcement of the arrival of one Colonel Greyson and his adjutant. She rose and walked quite normally along the balcony, glancing over the railing as she went. But her visitors were standing in the shadow of the entranceway and she could not see their faces. The colonel had his broad back to her as she descended the staircase, but the rustle of her skirts stopped him in the act of making some remark to the other man, and he turned toward her.

Somehow, she was not surprised that the face of her unknown guest was indeed the same one that had haunted her dreams for so long. After the initial shock on the bridge, nothing would have surprised her, she thought. She was even calm enough to look directly at him and study that face closely for the first time in six years.

He looked older—not just by the years but in experience. He was wearing the red-jacketed dress uniform of an infantry officer, but he wore it indifferently, as if unaware or uncaring of how elegant he looked in it. His mouth was set in harsh lines that looked as if he had forgotten how to laugh, and Kate thought wistfully of the way he had teased her that night in Paris. Something had happened to him since then to leave deep lines in the sun-browned skin around his eyes and the faint line of a scar across one high cheekbone. A stab of sympathy went through her for the unknown trials he had suffered, and her own uncertainties and anguish over his abandonment no longer mattered. She smiled at him.

But then she realized with a fresh shock that his mouth was set in anger and a blue fury blazed in his eyes. Her own eyes widened, and she thought she must be mistaken. She had no doubt that he recognized her now—but what could she have done to provoke that look?

He bowed then, with a stranger's formality, but with that old, cruel mockery in his voice, he said, "Good evening, madam."

Kate stiffened. "Good evening, Colonel Greyson. I am happy to welcome you to my home. This is your aide?"

"My—? Ah, yes, to be sure. Permit me, Doña Catarina de Sanchez, to present Captain Michael Sinclair."

Young Captain Sinclair, lacking his superior's powers of dissimulation, could not conceal his surprise at Kate's appearance and the unexplained lack of accent in her speech.

"Your servant, Doña Catarina," he managed to get out.

"I beg your pardon, ma'am, but I did not understand that you are English!"

"My parents were English, captain. I have lived in Spain for many years."

Colonel Greyson assumed an expression of concern. *"Were,* madam?"

Kate glanced at him but saw no reaction to her mention of her parents. The memory of the colonel's relationship to Leonora, however, strengthened her defenses. "My mother lives in England," she explained to Captain Sinclair. "My father is dead."

"Come," she said, leaving the colonel no opportunity for another provoking observation. "I will show you to your rooms. Have you any baggage? Luis will take it for you."

Captain Sinclair did his best to extend the conversation, but Colonel Greyson followed their hostess up the stairs in silence. Amelia was just putting the final touches to the two rooms looking out onto the plaza when they entered. Kate coolly explained to her guests all she thought they needed to know.

"You may ring for breakfast at any hour. The midday meal is served at two o'clock, and supper is at ten. You may come and go as you please, but if you come in late at night, you will have to clap for the *sereno*—the night watchman. I have left you keys to the main door. This is Amelia, and the porter is Luis. They are at your service at all times, and I trust they will make you comfortable."

With that, she turned and went out, resisting the temptation to slam the door behind her. Sinclair stared after her, a bemused expression on his face, then turned to his colonel.

Greyson was fingering the keys thoughtfully, and his eyes wore an expression Sinclair had not seen before, a surprisingly naked look of grief, as if he had just lost something precious. Sinclair was accustomed to his superior's normal, unsentimental, even cynical, view of the world, and while he deplored Greyson's tendency to see the worst in every situation, he admired the sense of responsibility that made him try to leave things better than he found them. But that was duty—this was a glimpse of a more private Greyson, and Sinclair was fascinated by it.

But then Greyson said, in his normal, lightly ironic tone,

"I suppose you've noticed, Michael, that our rooms are precisely at the head of the stairs and in a direct line with the passage leading to the stables? I wonder if Doña Catarina anticipates the necessity of our having to leave in a hurry some night?"

Captain Sinclair recovered his wits and laughed. "Perhaps she is better informed than we are about that."

"Nearly everyone is," Greyson said.

They parted then to make their separate rooms comfortable with their usual practical efficiency and to find amusement for themselves until ten o'clock.

Supper that evening offered little hope for the future conviviality of such meetings, however. The meal, from the *judias con chorizo* to the cheese and strong coffee that followed, was much what the gentlemen had become resigned to in their travels through the peninsula. It was well enough prepared here to make it palatable, but Sinclair was surprised at its ordinariness.

Their hostess did not make an appearance at the table. When Amelia had begged the gentlemen to be seated and proceed with their meal because Doña Catarina had been called away, Sinclair voiced his disappointment. To Greyson, he admitted in his frank way that he was intrigued by the lovely widow and would have liked to talk with her again.

"Be patient, Michael," Greyson told him calmly. "She will have to come home sometime."

Sinclair had the oddest impression then—that when she did, Greyson would be waiting for her.

Chapter Eight

KATE STRODE onto the patio, riding crop in hand, the hood of her cloak flung back to reveal her tumbled hair and a concentrated frown on her forehead. She had just come from Santa Virgen del Arroyo, where she had gone to get out of the house, but Ramón had not been there and Mercedes had been guarded in her welcome. She reminded Kate that Ramón would be none too pleased to hear that she had come there unexpectedly and after dark—even escorted by Luis. Kate told her not to mention it to him, but she knew that the honest Mercedes would not lie if asked directly, so Kate had not stayed long, returning before anyone but Mercedes and Guillermo had seen her. The ride had dissipated some of her nervous energy, but the emotional tension that had driven her out remained.

It was well after midnight, so it did not occur to her that anyone would be awake in the house. She assumed that Amelia would have offered some explanation of her absence at supper, although she knew Amelia had been offended as much by Kate's approval of a very plain menu to serve her guests as by her lack of hospitality in leaving them to eat it by themselves.

In her careless entrance, she failed to see the red glow of a *cigarro* in one corner of the patio, until its owner asked in a soft but distinct drawl, "Where have you been, Riña?"

Kate halted abruptly, one hand on the banister and her heart in her throat.

"Who's there?"

Greyson rose from the bench on which he had stretched out his long figure and bowed gravely, still holding the *cigarro* in one hand; there was a half-empty brandy glass on the bench beside the fountain. He was still in uniform, but the red jacket was unbuttoned, as if he had simply thrown it on against the night air, and his shirt collar was unfastened. Kate was acutely aware of the muscles under the linen shirt he wore and of the strong broad hands, one of which he stuffed into his pocket, where she could feel that it was as tense as his posture was casual.

"Your humble servant, Doña Catarina."

He drew once more on the *cigarro* and put it out. There was something catlike in the way he watched his hostess's efforts to compose herself, and his eyes held cool approval of her tousled hair and the effects of wind and exercise on her complexion. But that hand in his pocket told Kate he was not as cool as he seemed.

"Why, Colonel Greyson," she said with fluttering lashes and a falsely coy smile, "you did give me a start!" She was thankful that the darkness hid the blush she could feel on her face.

"I daresay," he remarked dryly. "Won't you join me?"

"Thank you, but I really must—"

"Oh, but I insist!"

He took her arm and steered her firmly to the bench. "Pray be seated."

Given little choice in the matter, Kate sat, desperately searching her mind for a suitable answer to his original query. Her flight to Santa Virgen del Arroyo, even that long ride in the cool night air, had not cleared her mind at all, she discovered now, and she had not yet formulated a defense against him that would prevent him from hurting her again. Once she had been entirely honest with him, not expecting the hurt, but now her emotions were too confused. She needed time—and some temporary disguise—to consider a response.

"Really, Colonel Greyson," she attempted with false brightness, "you must think it odd of me to be abroad at this hour, but you see, my sister-in-law is unwell and I have been with her until now."

"I am sorry to hear of it. Were you able to be of assistance?" His cool voice mocked her.

"Oh, yes." Kate felt the absurdity of this stilted drawing-room conversation, here under the stars in the middle of the night. "It was a slight fever, nothing more. But she is a delicate creature, and one cannot be too careful."

"Does she live close by?"

"Near Santa Marta, a village just outside Salamanca. Her husband is unable to be with her continually, so I rode out to spend the day with her."

She paused to see how this hastily contrived explanation had been received. Greyson scrutinized the shirt and divided skirt beneath her cloak and said accusingly, "In that?"

Kate cursed herself for falling into this trap and took her vexation out on him. "I do not see that it is any of your affair where or how I spend my time!" she snapped, so unnerved that the color left her face.

She jumped up but, laughing, he caught her arm and pulled her down again. "At last we begin to understand each other, Riña. You must not pretend with me, you know."

"Don't call me that! Where did you learn it?"

"Why not? It seems to me singularly apt, considering your present mood. The marqués told me, if you must know."

"He would."

Greyson chuckled. "Quite an agreeable fellow, that Cerralbo. I paid him a visit tonight, since my hostess was unavailable. Shortsighted, like most Spaniards, but agreeable."

Kate stiffened. "How dare you—" She stopped, aware that he was provoking her with taunts that had nothing to do with their real differences. Why did he not say what he meant! And why was he pretending with her, acting as if they never met before? For a moment, she forgot that she was being no more open with him, was indeed still casting about for a defense against honesty. Then she found one.

"I suppose you consider yourself and—and your precious General Moore far above the likes of us," she said.

"Us? Do you consider yourself Spanish, then?" he said in that maddeningly calm drawl. "Why is that, I wonder?"

Furious, she said the first thing that came into her head. "This is my home, my country."

His eyes narrowed thoughtfully. "Ah, yes. Your country. How do you say it? *La Patria.* Which is, of course, why you may even win this war, you patriots."

The Dancers' Land

"With English help, certainly," Kate responded ungraciously.

A chuckle in the darkness showed that he had succeeded in his provocation.

"You will have to meet the general, Riña. I'm afraid you've leapt to unjustified conclusions about him—and about other things."

There, he had finally acknowledged that there was something between them. But Kate was resolved not to demand any explanations from him. She'd let him offer them, as he should.

"I'm sure I don't know what you mean," she said.

"Yes, you do," he said with quiet ferocity. "What made you think I wouldn't come back for you? Didn't you care? Or did you really prefer Manuel Sanchez to me so much that you rushed into marriage with him instead?"

"I didn't rush into anything! It was only last year . . ." She hesitated, aware that he was watching her intently and that if she was going to offer a defense now, it would have to be a strong one. But then he changed his line of attack again, as if to wear her down in a dozen ways at once.

"You've changed," he said.

She temporized. "Haven't you?"

"No."

He did not explain that, as if she would understand. But she did not. Did he mean his feelings had not changed? But what were they? She could only remember the mocking look in his eyes from across that ballroom, and the cruel smile after she saw him with Leonora.

But when she looked in his eyes now, there was sorrow in them. She took a small chance and asked in a trembling voice, "Why did you not try to find me? Why didn't you write?"

He laughed mirthlessly. "It's difficult to smuggle a letter out of the *Ile des Fantômes*. It took three tries to smuggle myself out of that hellhole."

"*Ile des*—what is that?"

"The prisoners' name for a French penal colony, an island off the coast of South America."

He looked off into the night for a moment and then told her, unemotionally, "After we—after that ball in Paris, the minister of police—Fouché's—men caught me with gold and letters to be delivered to the royalist plotters. I'd been caught spying. I had no defense. I was lucky not to be shot on the spot."

Kate was silent, not knowing how to respond, ashamed of her accusations and yet aware that he had not answered them.

"A group of us finally escaped last year," he went on. "I was sick with fever all the way home and only recovered last spring—just in time to join the army and be shipped to Spain."

He did not say that he had come looking for her, that he even remembered her. She clung to the idea that he must say these things plainly, even while she knew it was unfair to ask him to say what she could not.

"I'm sorry," she whispered, aware of the inadequacy of the words. "I didn't know." Her eyes softened and she relaxed for a moment.

He was silent again. Kate sat on the edge of the bench, not looking at him, wanting to get up and leave but held there by the feeling of not yet having satisfactorily settled their differences. She still could not account for that earlier, angry look of his.

He leaned back again, and his face was hidden in the shadows. A match flared as he lighted another *cigarro*. Its fragrant aroma filled the patio.

"What was he like?" he asked finally.

"Who?" she asked, wondering whom he was referring to now.

"Your husband."

She had to think for a moment, conjure up that gentle shadow. "Manuel was a fine man. He was kind to me, and generous. I was—very fond of him." She bent to examine her hands in her lap, uncomfortable with the sadness she felt at the recollection of her husband.

"Had you been married long?"

"Only a few months. Of course, I had known him for years. He was a great friend of my father's."

There was a painful pause while he digested this.

"What color were his eyes?"

What a strange question, she thought, but immediately answered, "Why, Manuel had brown—that is, hazel—eyes. Why do you ask?"

The Dancers' Land

She hesitated, suddenly conscious of a pair of brilliant blue eyes in a sun-bronzed face, a thatch of fair hair—all unseen in the darkness—and a deep, accusing voice. "So you *did* marry him for this—this house, special position, money. Did you strike a good bargain, Riña?"

"Oh!" She did get up this time, and marched angrily to the stairs. Greyson followed her to the top and seized her hand.

"Will you leave me be!" Shaking his hand off, she took up the branch of candles that always awaited her on the landing to light her way to her room. She looked up, and his face was very close to hers, the sharply etched curve of his mouth mesmerizingly close. She thought he was going to kiss her, and she was angry at her own involuntary desire for it.

But she stood up to him and said softly, "I did care that you didn't come back—I cared a great deal, for five years. I married Manuel for many reasons—one of which was to forget you. It cost me a great deal to forget, and now you are implying that it was all wasted, that I should just forget those five years, forget Manuel."

He was halted then, as much by the sudden gleam of candlelight on her flushed face as by her words. It picked up the glint of tears in her eyes and on her cheeks. She raised her hand to wipe them away, and he stepped back, as if regretting that he had gone so far.

"Forgive me, Doña Catarina, please."

She was unprepared for this sudden change in his manner. She raised her wet, gray eyes to his; the hot words faded from her lips. There was again a long silence, and then he tore his eyes away.

"Good night, Colonel Greyson."

Her cloak had fallen off in her haste to get away from him. She picked it up and threw it over her arm, then climbed the remaining steps with an unsteadiness she could barely control.

Chapter Nine

KATE DID NOT see Colin Greyson for two days after the scene on the patio, and although Captain Sinclair murmured something evasive about "maneuvers," Kate suspected that Greyson was playing a game with her. Because her own emotions were so jumbled, it never occurred to her that it really was Greyson's duties that kept him away—and that if they had not interfered, he would by now have made his intentions clear.

In a way, then, she was glad to have a respite to prepare herself to face him again, except that if she did not know what he would say or do, she would not know how to control her reaction to him, and somehow control seemed very important. She had never responded to anyone as instinctively as she did to Colin Greyson. She was able to control, even manipulate, her earlier suitors, and she could sway Manuel with any wish or whim. But she had no control over her own instincts now, and she disliked the feeling.

At the same time, she was unwilling to let things go on in such an unsettled state. Their relationship was as yet such a fragile thing that the least misstep might shatter it, but the right word might also, ideally, restore the magic of that night in Paris. Kate knew that magic, too, was fragile; perhaps there was no way to bring it back, but there had been something between them once, some spark that needed perhaps only a gentle fanning to coax it into fire again. She was afraid to try but just as frightened not to.

Captain Sinclair, unaware of the undercurrents between Greyson and Doña Kate, as he took to calling her, intimated to his superior officer that he ought to make

The Dancers' Land

more of a push to establish himself with their hostess. In fact, after the captain's initial astonishment at meeting Kate had passed, he had taken a second look and decided that she and his colonel were a remarkably well-matched pair. It had not been lost on him that the quality of meals and service in the Plaza Mayor had improved immeasurably since that first night—surely due to their hostess. But there was Greyson all over Salamanca but where he should have been—in their ideally situated billet in the Plaza Mayor. The captain sighed.

Michael Sinclair was twenty-two years of age, a soldier by necessity but a poet by nature, and a sentimentalist. He knew that his colonel was anything but that, however, and he ordinarily avoided meddling in his personal affairs. And for that he sighed. He thought Greyson treated Doña Kate too coldly, as indeed he did other women. Michael sometimes fancied that Greyson had once been disappointed in love, and that it was this which accounted for his indifference. Lord knew women were readily attracted to him, perhaps in part because of the wall he erected between himself and them which was all the more alluring for being unscalable. He flirted with some and led others to believe they had made an impression on him. He ruthlessly set down the predators but left the innocent strictly alone. Let those who could keep their innocence, he had said once when Michael had tried to interest him in the artless daughter of a Portuguese nobleman.

Greyson seemed to look deliberately for a woman's imperfections and then to point them out to her. Whether he exposed them to the world depended on whether he thought the vices of the lady in question outweighed her virtues. He was a sharp judge of feminine foibles, as appreciative as anyone of a woman's merits, and as vulnerable as the next man to physical beauty. But his heart was harder, and since the colonel was now in his middle thirties, his very-much-junior adjutant did not think it likely that it would melt easily.

The captain would have been both pleased and astounded at the about-face the colonel performed two days later. Kate was simply incredulous when Colin returned unexpectedly to the house one morning, knocked politely on her door, and asked if she would care to go for a drive.

"I feel I must make amends," he said. "I have been an ungrateful guest, and a rude one besides, for deserting you so frequently with no explanation."

Kate did not know if this was meant as a cut at her own unexplained absences or, indeed, what it meant. There was certainly no hint of malice in Colin's presently correct and deferential manner, and yet she felt she ought to be wary.

"It is very kind of you to offer, Colonel Greyson," she said stiffly, "but under the circumstances, I am not certain that it would be a good idea."

"Circumstances?" He seemed genuinely puzzled.

"I refer to the circumstances of your residing under the roof of a single woman, however unassailable her position," she said, falling back on a dishonest defense.

"But under those circumstances, I should think it a splendid idea. You would not wish Salamanca to think you discourteous to Spain's allies, would you?"

"I think Salamanca will assume my courtesy, without my having to parade it in the streets," Kate remarked dryly. "However—"

"Excellent!" he said, sweeping aside her intended offer to compromise by making a party of it with Michael Sinclair. "I shall hire a carriage especially for the purpose."

Kate began to protest, but then, much against her better judgment, she gave in. "There is no need for that," she told him. "I have my own carriage."

Kate was not sorry for her decision, although her doubts did not immediately leave her. Apparently, Colin had decided to start over, to treat her as if there had been no Paris, no separation, and no unanswered questions. She breathed a sigh of relief and told herself it was best this way—at least for now. She knew it would not be long before the past—and what they had become since—intruded again, but if they had come to know each other better by then, perhaps it would be easier to face it.

At least for the present, Greyson was behaving with the most punctilious correctness, the weather was at its finest, and it was an unexpected treat to go out, openly, into the sunlit city again. She had not realized that, except for clandestine trips to Santa Virgen, she had been incarcerated behind her widow's weeds and protective stone walls for two months. It seemed much longer.

She had forgotten about the people living in Salamanca. At first they said a great deal, regarding the latest indiscretion of *la inglesa* as in very questionable taste. Bad enough that this *extranjero*, this foreigner, was actually living in her house—but to advertise the fact by appearing with him in public! Young women eyed her askance, disapproving in their envy of the tall, uniformed figure at her side; the older women merely disapproved while their husbands sighed and wished themselves in Greyson's place.

The British soldiers envied the colonel his good fortune and quizzed him about it later in private, attempting but failing lamentably, to get him to disclose his intentions. He admitted to nothing but continued on his best behavior, and before long, Colonel Greyson and Doña Catarina de Sanchez had become so familiar a sight as to be barely noticed by those who took their *paseo* at the fashionable hour or drank their *aperativo* in a café on the Plaza Mayor or gazing down from the balconies overlooking a busy avenue. The whispers gradually died away as the whisperers found new interests.

During the first days of the month-long British "occupation" of Salamanca, the city wore all the color and gaiety of an Andalusian city during the festival season. Behind doors, anxious conferences might be held, but except for Moore's general officers, no one else had much to do but rest and recover their energies and dissipate some of the excess in enjoyment of Salamanca.

The windows of the house of the widow of Sanchez looked out on a plaza crowded with soldiers—English, Spanish, and Portuguese. Heavily cloaked civilians strolled in the open air, and merchants bustled to take advantage of the season to press their goods, at inflated prices, upon the obliging soldiery. Pastry and sweet shops displayed traditional provincial delicacies; coffee houses, *vinaterías*, and chestnut vendors engaged in a thriving trade. Spanish women in long mantillas, children open-mouthed in admiration of the kilts of the Cameron Highlanders, students in long black gowns, and a few unkempt examples of the feminine followers of the British army could all be seen in Salamanca and most often in the Plaza

Mayor. Inns were filled to overflowing, and even the wrought-iron balconies and secretive saffron walls of private homes hinted at the increased activity behind them.

"I suppose," Greyson observed one day as they drove through one of the narrow streets leading off the plaza, "that the distinction lies in the individual blending of olive oil, garlic, *tobaco negro,* and stale humanity, but each Spanish town seems to have its own peculiar odor."

"Well, I must be inured to it," Kate replied. "I can't smell anything. On the other hand, I expect that to me, England would positively reek of salt and ratafia and wet wool. Not to mention an unmistakable odor of sanctity!"

Michael Sinclair accompanied them occasionally on these sight-seeing expeditions or, rather, cajoled them into guiding him around the city. Guidebook in hand, he would gladly tell them more about the architectural wonders of old Salamanca than Kate had ever known. She and Colin followed gamely behind as Michael explored churches and museums, convents and palaces, reverently tracing with his fingers the elegant carvings on an ancient oak-paneled door and gazing raptly up at the Byzantine dome of the Old Cathedral.

Kate had not set foot in the cathedral since the day of her wedding, and she paused for a moment in the doorway that led from the New Cathedral down stone steps into the Old. But aware of Greyson's eyes on her, she entered and dutifully followed their zealous guide through the chapels. As they passed the high altar, she stopped for a moment to kneel in front of it—hesitantly, still aware of her escort and the impression her action might make on him but sensitive also to a fading memory and a flagging duty. She felt a little ashamed, too, that this was the first time she had thought about Manuel in a week.

Once outside again, however, she recovered her equanimity and, as Michael led them on an investigation of the Convento de las Dueñas, was even moved to remark with a rueful smile, "I once had a mad notion to enter a convent."

"Why?" he asked, genuinely curious.

"Oh, because I was—unhappy, because I wanted to hide someplace where I wouldn't have to think about my unhappiness."

She realized that this was the first time she'd thought

about her father, too, in a long time, and wondered at the power of this man Greyson to erase every other man from her memory by his mere presence.

"How ignorant you are of convents, *mi vida.* They would not take you, anyway. You are hardly the ideal novitial candidate."

She had not needed Sor Inez, and certainly not Colin Greyson, to tell her that, but she wondered at the endearment he used to soften the criticism. "My life," he called her, a common enough Spanish expression that took on a different sound from his lips.

"That doesn't sound like a compliment," she said about his first remark, so as not to dwell on the second.

He smiled, "When I pay you a compliment, you'll recognize it."

Before Captain Sinclair had quite exhausted his hostess's tolerance for sight-seeing, he discovered an even greater attraction in Salamanca and was casting about for a way to introduce his colonel to it when Greyson found him browsing in Kate's library one day.

"No guidebook today, Michael? Can it be that we have seen all the churches with which this city seems so liberally supplied?"

The captain put down his book, which the colonel noted with interest was a volume of Moorish poetry—possibly the most romantic verse in Spanish literature.

"As a matter of fact, sir," Sinclair said, "I was thinking of going on—well, a picnic, sir."

The colonel was shaken but not subdued. "A picnic!"

"Yes, sir. You see, there is a young lady—"

"Ah!"

"Quite so, sir. Her name is Maria Elena."

"Tell me, Michael," the colonel inquired confidentially, "is she a young *lady,* or merely a female of tender years?"

It was the captain's turn to look nonplussed. "Oh, she is most certainly a lady, sir. The daughter of the dean of one of the colleges, a most respected man." He frowned. "That's the difficulty."

"I expect it would be."

"No, sir. I mean, Maria Elena would like to picnic with me, you see, but she won't go unchaperoned. In short—

well, I wondered if perhaps you and Doña Kate would perform that office for us if it isn't too much trouble?"

The colonel spoke to "Doña Kate" of the matter. "And her name is Maria Elena, if you please."

"What's wrong with that?"

"Haven't you noticed this bizarre Spanish penchant for compound names? Usually, some combination of Mary and Joseph—Mari José and José Maria, one assumes, are the ideals. Are they in need of two saints or two saint's days?"

"Perhaps we just don't like to be abbreviated," Kate offered, smiling in spite of herself. She wondered if Colin was going out of his way to entertain her, or was he always so amusing? How little she knew of him, really, even to such details.

They had their picnic on the banks of the Tormes on a fine clear afternoon later that week. Downstream, some women were washing their laundry in the river and spreading it out to dry in the sun. The contented murmur of their voices as they worked, the soft susurrus of the river, and the azure sky overhead made a perfect day for the occasion.

Colin ate his share of the luncheon, industriously prepared by Amelia with contributions secured from a local pastry shop by Michael, and lay down on his back on the warm, dry grass. To keep her eyes from straying to him too often, Kate studied Maria Elena. She was a small, angelically dispositioned girl with a sweet smile, which she bestowed readily on her escort. At the moment, she was finding some difficulty with his rank.

"Yo soy capitán—captain," Michael explained.

"'O he is the courageous captain of compliments,'" Greyson quoted.

"What's that from?" Kate asked.

"Shakespeare, my beautiful ignoramus. You should read more."

"I read a great deal!"

"I know, I've seen your library. I meant, in English. It is your mother tongue, after all."

"And that gentleman," Michael continued, indicating another party of young people nearby, "is a corporal."

Maria Elena hesitated. *"Cómo se dice? Cuerpo—digo,* cor-por-al, *no?"* She giggled then, and covered her mouth with her small, shapely hand. Michael pulled it toward him and kissed it lightly, smiling at her. Kate looked away.

"What's the matter, *mi vida*?"

Colin spoke softly, so that she alone could hear, but with laughter in his voice. She scowled, not understanding, herself, why she felt uncomfortable at another woman's pleasure.

He seemed to understand her better than she did. "They're falling in love," he said. "That's all. They're at that stage when there is nothing to clutter up the emotion, and they don't think about the consequences at all—why should you?"

"I'm not. I mean, it's nothing to do with me."

That wasn't what she had been thinking—or feeling. Her thoughts and emotions were becoming confused with one another. Whatever had happened to her clear head, her unemotional self-control?

"Don't frown, Riña. You are much lovelier when you smile."

She did then, and said, "Even I can recognize that as half a compliment!"

"You might be more inclined to laugh, you know, if you didn't wear black all the time—like those old crows who sit in their parlor windows all day and spy on their neighbors. Why *do* all Spanish women over the age of eighteen wear black, by the way?"

They did so only after marriage, Kate knew and, she had always thought, with cause. But she was not about to voice that opinion to Colin Greyson. Instead she said, "Most of them have lost male relations in one way or another—it is a mark of respect. Besides, it is—well, more dignified. A married woman has a certain position—"

"No! Don't remind me again of your position!" he protested, laughing and sitting up again, closer to her. "Today you have my permission to laugh as much as you please. And if you don't please, consider that an order."

She turned to him, and there was for the first time nothing to mar the pleasure of that look, which met his for a fleeting second before she turned away again, feeling herself blush with girlish confusion. It was almost as if she were sixteen again, and they were beginning all over—the way Michael and Maria Elena were doing, with no past, only a future; no broken promises, only unlimited possibilities.

She sighed, and her hand played with a strand of hair that had come loose. He sat behind her where she could hear his breathing but could not see his face. Her skin tingled with his nearness, as if he would reach out and touch her at any moment. He had not touched her, except in a polite, impersonal way, since that night on the patio. She imagined him doing so and caught her breath.

A sharp, sweet smell made her turn to Colin again. He was calmly paring an orange, and she watched his strong, brown hand, admiring the deftness of the long fingers. He used a slender knife with an elegantly engraved silver handle.

"What a beautiful knife," she said. "Where did you get it?"

"I bought it in a shop on the Praça Rossio in Lisbon. It *is* beautiful—diabolically so."

He closed the knife but, by touching a tiny hidden button, made it spring instantly open again with a deadly click, and the long blade gleamed menacingly in the sunlight. "The sort of thing one would expect to find in wide use in this country."

She frowned again. She was beginning to recognize when he made a new move in his game, always just as she thought she had begun to understand the last.

"Are you implying that we are all savages here?" she said.

"Not at all. This is a highly civilized instrument." He finished paring the orange and handed her a slice, which she picked gingerly off the point of the blade. She glanced at Michael and Maria Elena to see if they wanted anything else to eat, but they had their handsome young heads together and were unaware of any presence but their own as they thumbed through a book of verse.

She smiled. "I don't know why they bothered to invite us."

"Fie, Doña Catarina! We couldn't allow them to go about unchaperoned. What has happened to your concern for the neighbors?"

"Nonsense," said Doña Catarina. "Nothing would happen."

"Ah," he said, "there's your English upbringing for you. An English gentleman would never take advantage of a lady."

"Nor would a Spanish gentleman."

"Oh, yes, he would! It's not that his intentions are dishonorable—it's simply a matter of viewpoint. A Spaniard does not believe in respect or friendship between men and women. The difference between the sexes is too marked for such subtleties."

"Oh, that can't be true!" But she thought of her last year's admirers, who earnestly talked of her beauty but only half-listened to anything she had to say on other matters. She amended her remark. "At any rate, certainly not in all cases."

He glanced sharply at her and said lightly but carefully, "Have you such a friend? But of course, you are an exceptional woman and would be treated exceptionally. Be honest now. Does your friend treat other women as he does you?"

Kate remembered Ramón's contemptuous comments on some of the flirts who wasted their wiles in pursuit of him. "No, I suppose not. But some men, even Spaniards, must feel respect for their women, and some women must be deserving of it."

"I should be surprised to see it. A Spaniard loves a woman for her face, her body, her charm of manner; he respects a man for his brain, his opinions, or his position. A woman is not meant to have a brain or a thought in it, and a man who has beauty is not a man. They cannot therefore understand anyone who professes to love and respect at once either a man or a woman."

Kate could not help thinking that the truth could not be so clearly defined as that. She cast about for an exception to Colin's rule, but he persisted.

"What would your average Spaniard think, for example, of a British soldier who said honestly that he loved Sir John Moore?"

"He would think it a strange thing to admit, certainly."

"At the very least. And yet, it is true that this army loves and respects its commander. How many heroes of Spanish history can you name me?"

"The Cid," she said instantly.

"A mercenary. Who else?"

When Kate hesitated, he continued, "The Spanish don't revere their leaders. They tolerate them if they are worthy but would rather, if they are not, pull them from power."

"What makes you think you know so much about the Spanish?"

"Why," he said, "because I know you, and you are, or so you insist, very Spanish." He grinned. "Does it occur to you, *mi vida*, that this is a very odd sort of conversation for a Spanish lady to take part in?"

If this had not occurred to Kate, it did now. She could not help a rueful smile but frowned as she said, with some feeling, "It is, and I don't know why I let you rattle on so. But at least you do so in English, so that I need not be concerned with eavesdroppers."

They did not return home until it was nearly dark. Colin continued to be amusing, attentive, punctilious—and a stranger. Kate thought, on the one hand, that it was best this way, but on the other, that it could not go on. She would go mad soon if he did not tell her what he wanted of her—or worse, if he left before she could discover it for herself.

When he left her at her gate, with a smile and an impersonal shake of gloved hands, she was both relieved and sorry that he had to take his dinner at headquarters that night. She ate her own in solitary state—for even Michael had deserted her to take Maria Elena and her mother to a concert—and went up to her room earlier than usual. But when she opened her door, she came back to reality with a start.

Ramón was stretched out on his back on her bed, his head pillowed on his arm and his eyes closed. For a moment she did not even recognize him, so completely had her mind become absorbed by Colin Greyson in the week since he arrived. She could not even remember when she had seen Ramón last.

She thought he must be asleep, but then she saw the

lighted cigarette on the table next to the bed. He reached out for it, put it into his mouth, and opened his eyes.

"Hola."

"What are you doing here?"

He sat up wearily and looked up at her from the edge of the bed. "I'm sorry. I should not have come. I thought you wanted to hear the news."

She sat down next to him and spoke quickly. "Ramón, I'm sorry! I didn't mean it like that. You look so tired—you should have slept. The room at the end of the hall is made up. But, what is the news?"

"I've just come from British headquarters." He smiled grimly. "They were not pleased to see me. The news is that our army is routed again. At least it's moving quickly for once—in retreat, over the mountains. French cavalry are chasing ours all over the plains. The emperor himself is in personal command and has already retaken Valladolid."

"Valladolid!" Kate stared at him. The intended rendezvous of the two sections of the British army was to have been at Valladolid.

"You see why they were not diverted by my visit here. There isn't so much as a Spanish piquet between here and Valladolid."

He laughed suddenly and with an insane lilt to his laughter. "But, Kate, the most incredible thing is that the Supreme Junta still doesn't believe that the French can advance at all! They believe everything our fools of generals claim and then call them traitors when they can't win another battle, even accidentally, the way Castaños did at Bailén."

Kate was no longer interested in the opinions of the Supreme Junta. "But what about Moore? Will he retreat?"

Ramón shrugged his shoulders. "I don't have his confidence, I'm afraid. He may. Perhaps he should. He doesn't have any cavalry—they're still on their way here on the southern route, but the French don't seem to know where he is, or care, and they are concentrating their main force in the east. It's possible that Moore still has a chance to unite his army and do something with it."

Ramón's weariness was rapidly catching up with him, and Kate insisted on putting him to bed in the spare room where he fell almost immediately into a solid, dreamless sleep. Kate, however, lay awake in her own bed for some time, mentally reassessing the situation, recalling the world that had receded from her thoughts of late but seeing it in terms of her new world as well. Why had Colin not told her that the British were in such a desperate position? If it ever came to a pitched battle with the French, who now outnumbered Moore by four to one, there could be no doubt of the outcome. Even if Moore, the cavalry, and Baird's men could unite, they would still be outnumbered. It was all much too uncertain, but whatever happened, Moore—and his army—could not remain long in Salamanca.

At last she fell into a restless slumber, and when she woke, the morning was well advanced. She could hear the activity in other parts of the house. A familiar voice on the patio and the sound of two pairs of British boots crossing it made her sit up suddenly. Was Ramón still here? She opened her door a crack to see if anyone was in the corridor, then crept down it to the spare room. It was empty, and the bed had been carefully remade.

Chapter Ten

During their drives in and around Salamanca, Doña Catarina and Colonel Greyson had chanced to meet some of the men of his regiment. They greeted their commanding officer with considerably more affection, Greyson remarked caustically, when he was accompanied by his fascinating hostess than they showed under any other circumstances and, furthermore, constrained him to stop and talk for longer than he particularly cared for.

Kate had been perfunctorily introduced to one Lieutenant O'Reilly (who looked as Irish as his name), and to several privates in high spirits (proportionate to the level of spirits in the bottles they carried), who paid her lavish compliments, and to an extremely handsome young major, in company with Captain Sinclair, who stared at her in mute admiration while the captain passed the time of day with Colonel Greyson, and who had to be poked in the ribs to bring him back to reality when they had finished. Flashing a devastating smile at Kate, he bowed deeply to her and strolled on after Michael, pausing now and then to look back over his shoulder.

"I've never known Val to be speechless before," Greyson remarked as they drove on.

"Why didn't you introduce him—and why won't you let me meet the rest of your men?" Kate asked.

"I'm not such a fool as that!" he retorted with a grin. "I have an advantage over them now that I might lose if I gave you away to them."

But the day after Ramón's brief visit, and just as Kate had begun to wonder what selfish motives Colin could possibly have in keeping her to himself, he surprised her by asking her to dine with the officers of his regiment.

Moore and his personal staff had been pressed into accepting the hospitality of the Marqués de Cerralbo at the palace of San Boal, and other of the general staff had moved into the Bishop's Palace. Most of the senior officers, like Colonel Greyson, were billeted in private homes. The troops, however, and such officers as chose to remain with them, were quartered in the monasteries, inns, and taverns of the city, even in the stables of ancient and crumbling castles.

Greyson's regiment occupied a deserted college, one of many that had been closed down since the golden age of the university long before. The old stone buildings, vaulted roofs, and tiled corridors of the college rang with life now as they had not done for centuries.

Kate had dressed with more thought than she had found necessary since donning widow's black and, since no Salamancan would see her, had put aside the black for a gray silk gown she had bought in anticipation of setting aside her mourning. It was modest enough but fitted tightly in the bodice to emphasize her breasts and waist and, best of all, it moved with a luxurious shimmer that pleased her eye.

Alighting from her carriage, Kate could hear footsteps and voices before she entered the main portal and then the central patio, which was brilliantly lit and filled with men and women in a flurry of preparation. In the midst of the activity, a diminutive black-haired woman was pouring abusive Portuguese on the head of a burly private who stood with a large wooden spoon in one hand and listened to her, uncomprehending but filled with admiration of her fury.

"We do not," Greyson informed Kate unnecessarily, "stand on ceremony here."

The fiery little woman heard him and forgot the private's misdeeds in her agitation.

"*Coronel* Greyson! Oh—I am sorry, but the dinner is not yet ready! Theez-*nescio, bufão*—oh, I must fly!"

She curtsied quickly to Kate and would have hurried back to her kitchen, but Greyson laughingly caught her hand and assured her that they were ahead of time, anyway, and that she must be introduced to Doña Catarina. Mrs. O'Reilly—Maria—"the best soldier in the British

The Dancers' Land

army," according to the colonel, had been with the regiment since its first successful engagement at Vimeiro.

There were no other women present, although Kate heard feminine voices echoing down the corridors that branched off from the central patio and through rooms that had once been lecture halls and heard the echo of student voices. They were, she supposed, camp followers or the wives of some of the lower-ranking officers.

Greyson led her to a room on the first floor, which appeared to serve as both drawing room and dining hall for the officers. It was a long, narrow room with a high ceiling and a single window overlooking the rolling plains to the west of Salamanca, and through which the setting sun now beamed its soft, orange rays. A long, sturdy wooden table stood at one end, and scattered around it were chairs and desks occupied by men writing letters, perusing maps and documents, playing cards, or simply enjoying a quiet smoke or a glass of port.

Lounging in a wing chair that faced the door, with his legs stretched out in front of him, a glass in his hand, and a dreamy look on his face, was the handsome major whom Kate had seen some days previously in the company of Captain Sinclair. His eyes widened when he saw her, and with one slow, graceful movement, he rose and came toward her. He took her hand and, bowing low, kissed it lightly.

A slight twitching of his lips revealed Greyson's amusement as he introduced them. "Doña Catarina de Sanchez, may I present Major Valerian von Ehrenberg? Close your mouth, Val," he added rudely, upon which the major cast him a reproachful look.

"Dear lady! I am—indeed—truly honored and delighted!"

By this time, the other men in the room were aware of their presence and came forward to be presented. Names whirled around her, and she tried to match them to smiling faces. Lieutenant O'Reilly's orange hair and mustache were already familiar to Kate. He greeted her with some embarrassment and stepped back quickly. She smiled warmly at him, but she wondered how such an apparently reserved man had ever tamed and won the fiery little Maria. Peter Rutledge, a large, soft-spoken man, was one of the surgeons traveling with Moore's army; he took her hand gently as he bowed to her and took the black silk pelisse that had covered her gray gown. Lieutenant Vivian Harmer, a lanky individual with a habit of running his fingers through his thick, dark hair, grinned amiably at Kate and made her feel welcome.

Kate was struck by the good looks, physical vitality, and high spirits of all of them. They were like sleek young animals, in contrast to the Spaniards Kate knew, who were equally hardy but hardened, too, by their harsh lives and the country they lived in. These men were the elite of the army, Moore's "gentlemen officers." Even Ramón—young, strong, and fiercely handsome—had nothing in common with Val, glossy and finished and glowing with life like a young thoroughbred, or even with Colin, whose strength was more controlled but still lay alarmingly close to the polished surface.

Kate knew that none of this meant that the British were in any way superior to the Spanish, but she could not help admiring them and being a little surprised at how comfortable she felt with them. Someone took her arm as she crossed the room, another brought her a chair and leaned close to catch her thanks, and she felt the vitality in them affect her, too.

These were, above all, Moore's men. At Shorncliffe, Colin had told her, his officers had learned their trade by drilling alongside their men. Moore had taught them that the private soldier, too, had honor, intelligence, and the right to think for himself, and to this end he brought officer and private as closely together as possible. The men therefore followed leadership willingly, and their leaders, proud of the loyalty and eagerness of the men, did their utmost to keep morale high and themselves and their men fit and active. High morale produced high spirits and what to Kate seemed to be a lack of deference close to insolence, but no offense was taken to any remark, and good-natured insults were topped by their recipients.

There was a knock on the door, and Colin turned. "Ah, Ri—Doña Catarina, here is Captain Sinclair with, I believe, a friend of yours."

It was Alan Grierson, a lieutenant now and resplendent in a new and meticulously cared-for uniform. His brown hair was brushed another way, and he stood a little taller, but he looked otherwise very much as he had done at the Bentons' Christmas party—was it really less than a year ago? Kate thought with amazement. She smiled at seeing him, and he submitted shyly to her questions.

"Why, yes," he said, pulling up a chair beside her. "I saw your family shortly before I left England. They are all very well and send their love. Gabriella is growing into a real beauty and is enjoying London life tremendously. Christopher has become quite the dandy—fancies himself a regular Corinthian and has aspirations to a seat beside Beau Brummel himself in the bow window of White's Club. That is, when he is not badgering his father to let him join the army."

"Oh, surely not!" Kate interrupted but, realizing her error, added, "Is he not too young?"

Lieutenant Grierson, who possessed a mere six months' seniority over Christopher Benton, smiled indulgently and, to soothe her anxiety, agreed that he was. Major von Ehrenberg, impatient with this cozy chatter and at having his place at the goddess's side usurped, went to fetch a glass of sherry for her and presented it with a flourish. There ensued a lively exchange of talk, which the lieutenant, by his longer acquaintance with Kate, and the major, by selfishly pulling rank, dominated, now and then interrupted by one of the others.

Before long, however, the table had been laid, and dinner was announced. This brought Lieutenant O'Reilly back into the limelight as the recipient of comments, opinions, and speculation regarding Maria's supervision of the kitchen for the evening.

"I have no doubt whatsoever that she will produce a superlative meal," Vivian Harmer said. "For with all respect, George, Michael, Lieutenant O'Reilly, sir—she can't help but do better than what we're used to!"

O'Reilly grinned. Val threw up his hands in mock despair.

"What we're used to! We're used to never even seeing the commissariat! But stale food would be a luxury if we didn't have to fill the vacancy with Spanish fare—sausage that is three-quarters garlic, rice poisoned with saffron, salad dressed with lamp oil, beef that a bayonet couldn't sever, all washed down with wine that looks and tastes like a mixture of vinegar and ink. My dear fellow, it's insupportable!"

At that, he pulled a chair violently up to the table, swung himself into it, propped his elbows disgracefully up on the table, and sighed a long, despairing sigh while the rest of the company laughed at his antics.

"You seem to have supported it remarkably well, Val," Greyson remarked, eyeing the well-porportioned figure and energetic healthiness of Major von Ehrenberg.

"I am blessed with a remarkably strong stomach."

"What I don't understand," Dr. Rutledge interposed, "is why Val ever joined the army in the first place, accustomed as he is to mingling with the *ton* at Carleton House fêtes."

"My dear fellow," Val said, somewhat repetitively, "what was I to do? I have my poor old mother to support. Besides, Prinny—I beg his pardon, I mean our Royal Prince of Wales—is *such* a bore!"

The major seemed to thrive on provocation and received a good deal of it throughout the meal, which in quality and quantity exceeded even Lieutenant Harmer's expectations. At its conclusion, Maria was given an enthusiastic round of applause. Dr. Rutledge proposed that she be placed in permanent command of the kitchen, but her husband quickly vetoed this suggestion, causing a cheerful debate on the subject, which Maria ended by stating flatly that she had no intention of cooking every night for such a lot of slovenly sweeps as they were, particularly as she had her hands full looking after one Irishman. Major von Ehrenberg attempted an after-dinner speech, but was rapidly put down.

"These hollowed halls—"

"That's hallowed, Val."

"I'm not sure he isn't right."

". . . have seen a great deal—"

"I daresay."

"Quiet, Vivian, he's coming to the point."

". . . but never two such lovely ladies as are our welcome guests this evening."

"Hear, hear!" Thunderous clapping drowned out anything further the major said.

"That's enough now, old man, you may be seated."

The Dancers' Land

* * *

A fire had been kindled in the huge fireplace at the other end of the room, and they all gathered around it with glasses of port and brandy. Greyson requisitioned the most comfortable chair and, pulling it out of the way of the others, settled down to spend the rest of the evening in contemplation rather than active participation. Kate seated herself in the center of a long sofa with Val to one side, Vivian Harmer to the other, and Alan Grierson perched on one arm, and attempted to be equally attentive to them all, in spite of Val's generally successful endeavors to be the center of attention.

In any case, she could not help favoring Valerian von Ehrenberg. He treated her like an adored goddess, complimenting her on her gown while never even taking his eyes from her face, and she found herself flirting comfortably with him. She knew instinctively that he meant nothing by it, but he reminded her so achingly of what Colin Greyson must have looked like at Val's age that she felt as if she had been given a gift of time. For a few moments, at least, she was transported back years, memory was mercifully blurred, and she seemed able to face life directly, as she had then, rather than through a mask of pretense and self-deception.

But then, Vivian Harmer leaned over to say something to Kate. She turned her face to him and inadvertently caught Colin Greyson—the here-and-now, all-too-present Colin—looking at her. He lowered his eyes carefully, drew long and deliberately on his cigarette, and settled back into his chair in a cloud of smoke. She looked away again. The moment had passed, but Kate felt her cheeks burn and hoped no one would notice in the general gaiety that she had lost all sense of what was going on around her. She could still hear George O'Reilly's laugh, see Alan Grierson's shy smile, and feel Val's arm across the back of the sofa she sat on, but she had become detached somehow from the scene, from the men around her, from the very words she spoke. All she was aware of, as if he were illuminated by a particularly strong light, was Colin Greyson sitting across from her—looking at her with an anger in his eyes that frightened and hurt her.

What had she done? But at the same time that she asked

herself the question, she knew that it was not Catarina de Sanchez he was angry at, but Kate Collier, whom he believed had been unfaithful to him. For the moment she forgot that he had taunted her, had deceived her with her own mother, had mocked her patriotism for Spain, had misunderstood her feelings for Manuel. She could only think of how disappointed he must have been in her to lash out at her as he had that first night, and how patient he had been since, waiting for her to tell him that none of those things really mattered to her so much as he did.

But how could she? If she tried to speak to him, she would only open herself up to further hurt, for she could not be certain that she would be brave enough to try to explain herself, to find the words to make him understand that she had never stopped loving him.

Yes, that was the key. She still loved him with an ache that drove every other consideration from her mind. But how could she tell him so?

The party broke up at a very late hour. Peter Rutledge and the O'Reillys said their good-nights first. Vivian stretched, inelegantly and impolitely, begged their pardons, and followed the others. Colin rose and offered Kate his arm. She took it lightly without looking at him.

"Dear Doña Kate," Val said with the familiarity bred of low-burning embers, brandy, and good company, "you must come again—*often!*" He raised her free hand to his lips and kissed it.

It was later still when the remaining company crossed the patio to see Kate off. The night was clear and cold, the stars bright in the cloudless sky. Alan Grierson hovered near them for a moment, but when they did not invite him to accompany them, he said good night and went off alone. Val had come out without his jacket and did not wait.

Kate's wrap was insufficient and she shivered involuntarily. Colin looked at her as he handed her up into the carriage. "Are you cold?"

She smiled. "Oh, it's nothing! I'm always cold."

"Here, put this on," he said roughly, taking off the fur-trimmed greatcoat he had thrown on over his uniform, and tossed it up to her. He walked around to the other side of the carriage, climbed up, and took the reins. She put his

The Dancers' Land 119

coat on over her thin one; it still held the warmth of his body, and she wrapped it around her. But she received no warmth from him directly. She sat silently beside him on the drive home, wanting to say something but unable to think of the words.

"Thank you, Colin" was all she could find to say. "It was a wonderful evening."

"We were honored to have you."

The phrase was cordial enough, but his frown would have discouraged further conversation even if she had felt up to it. They drove the rest of the way in awkward silence and, in silence, entered her patio and climbed the stairs.

He saw her to her door and stood for a moment with her hand in his. She could feel its warmth. Like the coat, it seemed to hold something of him that flowed into her when she touched it. Then he leaned over and would have brushed her cheek with his lips had she not quickly moved to one side, afraid of adding yet another sensation.

As if a spell had been broken, the atmosphere at once was different. She heard a soft chuckle in her ear and a whispered "good night" before he stepped back, lifted the hand still enclosed in his, turned it over, and kissed it—not lightly as Val had done, but lingeringly, and with that same flow of heat from him to her. Then he turned and sauntered, hands in pockets, down the passage to his own room.

Kate closed her door behind her with one hand and found herself clutching the other, still burning with his kiss, in her skirt. She shook it out angrily, but then held it out in front of her and stared at it for a moment, as if it held some secret.

She had told Amelia not to wait up for her, and so undressed and prepared for bed by herself. She stripped the gray gown off lazily, listening to it crumple softly to her feet, and splashed over herself a little of the cold water in the basin Amelia had left, before slipping on the thin cotton shift she slept in. She crawled into bed but lay there for a long time with her eyes open and hugging her arms to her breasts against the chill of the bedding, which seemed to take longer than usual to warm up.

And then the thought came to her, frightening in its simplicity and inevitability. She had racked her brain for words to explain to Colin that she still loved him, but it was not words she needed at all—only the courage to show him what she felt, as she would have done years before if fate had not intervened.

She almost laughed aloud in the cold darkness. She had never taken any kind of action, she realized now—certainly not in the direct, simple way that it now occurred to her. Her life had simply happened to her. She had accepted her move to Spain, her father's death, the Bentons' departure, and her marriage to Manuel, as if she had no choice in any of it. Now, suddenly, there was something she wanted that was not going to come to her so easily; for the first time, she would have to take her life into her own hands.

She threw off the blankets and stood up, pausing for a moment to feel the night air send a chill through her. Making up her mind, then, she reached out to open her door and, trying not to think of what she was doing, walked through it and down the hall to Colin's room. She opened his door without knocking and went in.

He hadn't gone to bed yet. He had taken off his boots and jacket and pulled his unbuttoned shirt out of his trousers; he was sitting in the dark in a chair with his legs stretched out in front of him, looking out the window at the starlit sky. He heard the door and looked around, then stood up, startled.

It was the first time she had seen him disconcerted in any way. That was some satisfaction to her, and for an instant she considered leaving it at that. But her growing sense of inevitability drew her to him at the same time that her heretofore unvanquished pride screamed at her to get away. She closed the door behind her, and the scream fell silent, as if she had shut out the last vestiges of her pride—and, she suddenly realized, her courage, too.

"Is there something you wanted?" he said at last, impatiently, as if she were intruding. She knew that she was not, but she was no longer so brave.

"There was . . ." She hesitated. "But I—*no sé precisamente—*"

"You don't know what you wanted?" His mouth curled into a sardonic smile at her retreat into Spanish, forgetting that he spoke it as well as she. Her frightened

The Dancers' Land

eyes flew to his; gray met cool blue and held for a moment. He took a step forward.

"I think you do know," he said softly as he closed the space between them. She stepped backward but met the door she had closed herself. He took her face between his strong, brown hands. His touch sent waves of warmth flowing through her, and she knew that was truly what she had come for. She drew in her breath and closed her eyes as she felt his mouth take possession of hers and—surprisingly gently—urge her lips open.

"It's this, isn't it?" he whispered, and her "yes" came involuntarily. He kissed her again, less gently, and when she still did not resist, savagely, invading her mouth hotly with his tongue. At the same time, he pulled her more tightly to him, as if to insure that she could not break away when his hand found her breast beneath the flimsy fabric of her gown. She gasped and did try to move away then, but he held her too closely.

"Let me."

She had little choice. She had to arch her head back as his mouth moved downward, leaving hot kisses on her throat and the exposed flesh above the décolletage of her gown. She could not—did not want to—stop his slow caress as his hands, too, moved downward along her smooth waist to the swell of her hip. Finally, she could not help clutching at him desperately, as if she would fall if he let her go. Her fingers twined into his hair and then found their way under his loosened white shirt to the curls of the same gold color on his broad chest.

She heard his groan and then the tear of fabric as he tore her shift away to expose her breasts, now firm and erect with unbidden desire; she heard her own cry as he picked her up bodily and carried her to his bed. He laid her down gently but hurriedly, and when he let her go for an instant, she opened her eyes to see that he was pulling off his own clothes, tossing them anywhere on the floor. Then he leaned over her only long enough to remove the rest of her shift and replace its filmy softness with the rough, fierce, sweet touch of his hard body. Then he was on her, pressing her down against the soft bed.

"You are so beautiful, Kate—sweet Kate," he whispered between even more passionate kisses on her mouth, her throat, her mouth again, and then on those softer parts of her that no man had ever dared touch. "Why couldn't you see that this is the way it should have been from the beginning?" he murmured.

He was right; she knew he was right, but she could not just then remember why she had been wrong. She could only feel her body respond to him entirely of its own volition, and suddenly she was frightened of the force she couldn't define nor control.

"Colin—!"

He covered her mouth again, and she found herself kissing him back.

"Oh, Colin, help me—I don't know . . ."

He seemed not to hear, so that again she had no choice but to follow his lead, returning his embraces in equal measure, letting her hand caress his rough, strong body the same way that his did hers, parting her thighs when he urged them open, and, finally, when she thought she could bear no more of this exquisite torture but not knowing what more to expect, receiving him deeply inside her with a sharp, delicious pain—then deeper yet as, after an instant's surprised hesitation, he thrust himself harder and stronger as she moved rhythmically, instinctively, to keep him there inside her, until at last the agony eased and with a warm, final surge and a cry she heard from somewhere far away but which must have been her own—or both of theirs at once—he left her. He moved away, and she felt the chill of his absence until he covered her with the blanket that had fallen to the floor and held her in his arms.

"Oh, Kate, my darling Kate—I didn't know. Forgive me."

He was being absurd, she thought. What was there to forgive? She sighed contentedly and turned toward him without answering, curling her body comfortably into his. She fell asleep.

Chapter Eleven

KATE WOKE the next morning in her own bed, alone. For a moment she could not remember how she had come to be there or what was different about this morning. Still half-asleep, she was only aware of a comfortable sense of well-being. Sunlight came in her window and enveloped her in a warmth that seemed to be the remnant of some greater flame.

Then she remembered. She stretched out with a satisfied sigh. Her body felt lethargic yet oddly weightless. She pulled the covers up and tried to sleep again, to return to the sensations she had felt last night when, after Colin had waked her near dawn and carried her back to her own bed, she had lost all her fears and the last shreds of modesty and teased him into the bed with her. Their lovemaking then had been unrestrained, abandoned, but joyful, as if they had just discovered something delightfully new.

It was the first time, she realized now, that she had heard him laugh so freely, and she began to understand his earlier, cold anger, too—that it had not so much been at her but at the wasted years, the pretenses and misunderstandings—and, yes, a little at her, too, for letting those things control her. But he had no anger to spare for lovemaking, only a sure, vital passion, so that when she teased him, withholding herself, moving away when he reached for her, he finally tired of the game and laid his strong hands on her arms to keep her still and his hard mouth over hers to silence her laughter, and took her forcefully until she moaned helplessly under his unrelenting embrace and begged, not for release, but for him never to leave her.

Kate felt a hot flush of remembrance steal over her, centering in the still vivid ache between her thighs. She sat up abruptly and took a deep breath. He had to leave her when morning came, to be in his own room when Michael Sinclair came looking for him. She supposed he had then gone off to do whatever he did every morning with the regiment. She realized that she had never asked, had no notion of what his duties entailed.

She stood up, pulling her robe around her. Over the chair next to her bed where she would be sure to see it, Colin had hung the remnants of her torn nightgown. She smiled and held it to her for a moment, but practical considerations then forced themselves into her mind. She built up the embers of her fire until there was enough flame to burn the bit of cloth, and only then rang for breakfast and a hot bath. She would not go out until she was in full possession of herself again, and then she would find Colin and ask what he had done that day. She wanted to know everything about him now, to be as much a part of him mentally as they were now physically one. Suddenly, she was looking forward very much to what the day might bring.

Kate had a number of visitors that morning, including several of Colin's men. Maria and Peter O'Reilly called to repay her visit to them, quite as if following social protocol was as important under their strange circumstances as it was in normal times in Dublin or London. Alan Grierson came, but today his talk about the past held no interest for her. She could think only of the present, and her polite lack of response finally sent him away. Valerian von Ehrenberg came, bringing Vivian Harmer—"for propriety," he said—but Val did all the talking, while Lieutenant Harmer was content to admire his hostess in silence from a chair across the room.

Kate was momentarily diverted by Val's nonsense, and when he let drop that his colonel had been ordered to report to General Moore that morning, she told herself that this was an acceptable reason for his not coming back to her as soon as he could, but she was disappointed just the same. As the morning wore on and she was subjected to the de Castro sisters (who had heard, as usual, any number of wild rumors that they wanted her to confirm or deny) and to Doña Rosalia de Bustamante y Avellaneda (who, on the other hand, was barely aware of the British presence in Salamanca and wanted to complain to Kate about her dressmaker's extortionate prices), Kate began to fret. Normally, she would have handled Doña Rosalia with more tact, but this morning she had no patience with her visitors, and it was all she could do not to snap at them.

The Marqués de Cerralbo also elected to call on Doña Catarina de Sanchez that morning, and he arrived just in time to charm Doña Rosalia with a cloud of compliments that prevented Kate's growing irritation with Doña Rosalia from being noticed. And Cerralbo brought Colin Greyson with him.

Unfortunately, by then Kate had lost that perfect, early-morning happiness. She had forgotten the sheer weight of all those protective devices she had burdened herself with for all those years, and under them, her frail joy had slipped away, like water under a stone. She was not as sure as Colin was about love, and for that she wanted to weep. Instead, she borrowed his anger.

He gave her a quizzical look over Doña Rosalia's head but could say nothing to her then. They had, Cerralbo explained for him, encountered each other at British headquarters, and Cerralbo had invited himself back to the house. This, too, was explained in the most amiably civil of terms, and Colin could only indicate his wish that he could have seen Kate alone instead by caressing her lightly on the back of the neck when Cerralbo was momentarily distracted in escorting Doña Rosalia to the door. Kate's skin tingled at the touch, but determined to nurse her hurt, she forced herself not to look at him, moving away out of his reach.

"Will you take a little refreshment, marqués?" she asked when Cerralbo had resumed his seat.

"Thank you, dear lady, no. I regret I may stay only a few minutes." He cleared his throat then and assumed his most melting look. "I have come only to prevail upon you, dear Doña Catarina, to grace with your presence a most humble dinner party at San Boal tomorrow evening. It is in honor of Sir John, you understand, so I am certain you will wish to attend. It will begin at seven o'clock—an early hour, to be sure, but as I have discovered, Sir John is used to keeping early hours."

It seemed to occur to him that this might not be an inducement, and he added quickly, "But there will be dancing immediately following. All the British officers will be there, and if you will so kindly say yes, my friend Colonel Greyson will escort you, will you not, my dear sir?"

Clearly Cerralbo considered that Kate would be reluctant to attend such an affair while in mourning, but his eagerness to have her come was unmistakable. Kate wondered if he had questioned Colin about her reaction to the idea. It seemed safest to show little enthusiasm but to reply modestly that if he truly wished her there, she would gladly attend.

She lowered her eyes. "I thank you, marqués. I should naturally be honored to attend. You will, of course, forgive me if I do not dance."

She could feel Colin's smile at that. Cerralbo kept his eyes on her, but she had the idea that they had discussed this between them.

"It is such a short time," she added for emphasis, "since my husband's death. It would not be proper for me to dance."

Cerralbo patted her hand understandingly. "But of course, dear lady, it shall be as you wish." He raised her hand then and kissed it gallantly as he took his leave. He took Colin away again, insisting that he come back to San Boal for the midday meal. The Marqués would then give the colonel those maps he had promised to General Moore, so that it would look as if they had both been attending strictly to duty all along. Cerralbo made a great joke of this, and Greyson had no option but to go along with him. He shrugged at Kate and smiled as he went out, the marqués's arm companionably over his shoulder.

Kate did not smile back. Colin's calm acceptance of this absurd duty only fed her irrational anger. No, it was not even that, she knew; she was angry because the spell had been thoroughly broken. She had wanted things to continue between them as they had been last night, but reality had intruded, and now she was less sure that last night had really meant anything. Colin made light enough of it, she told herself, and that mocking smile of his had returned. She saw now, too, her folly in going to him, for letting him take over her body and mind so completely, when it was obvious that he had not really given her anything of himself. He knew how inexperienced she was, how unsure of her emotions, and he had taken advantage of that. She felt used.

But there was still one part of her life that he had nothing to do with. He had never questioned her about her prolonged absences from the house, and she had not spoken of Ramón or Santa Virgen to him. Had he asked, she could not have kept up her original fabrication about visiting a nonexistent sister-in-law, but for now at least, it remained a way of escaping the lacerations she felt her emotions had been subjected to.

She told Amelia she would see no more visitors and sent her to ask Luis to saddle their horses. In half an hour, they were on their way to Santa Virgen.

Kate had dressed against the cold, with a fur-lined cloak over her drab woolen shirt and comfortable riding skirt, for the weather had turned in the last few days. Most of her face was covered by the hood of her cloak, to protect it from the biting wind in the hills. Luis looked like a Galician shepherd in a large slouch hat, sheepskin gloves, and a bulky woolen coat.

Luis was not a garrulous man, and their journeys together to Santa Virgen were generally passed in silence, so that Kate's self-preoccupation today would have gone unnoticed. But it was evident, from his occasional glances from under the brim of his hat in her direction, that Luis had something on his mind this time. Finally, Kate asked, without much interest, *"Qué piensas, Luis?"*

A long pause indicated that Luis was forming his thoughts into words. "Forgive me, Doña Catarina, I was only wondering. . . . I mean no impertinence. Do you tell *el coronel* Greyson where you go when you come to see us?"

"Certainly not!" Kate said.

"Ah, forgive me, but you are—well—good friends, no?"

Kate scowled. "Luis, what precisely are they saying about Colonel Greyson and myself?"

He shrugged eloquently. "Precisely—*nada*. But there are certain rumors. . . ." He said no more, apparently regretting having raised the subject at all. But Kate persisted.

"Luis, have you repeated any of these rumors to Ramón?"

"No, señora."

He retreated into his layers of clothing again, and after that, neither ventured upon any further conversation until they came in sight of Mercedes, drawing water from the well in front of her house. Kate waved to her. Mercedes grinned in reply but put her finger to her lips as a sign for them not to call aloud. When they came closer, she explained, motioning in the direction of the house, "He is asleep."

"Who?"

"Ramoncito. He has just come all the way from Astorga—over one hundred miles, he marched with the soldiers there—but now he is very tired. So I let him sleep."

Kate went inside and sat down near the smoking fire and next to Ramón, who did not stir. Mercedes brought in a bucket of water, set some of it on the fire to heat, nodded in satisfaction at Ramón, and went away again. Kate wrapped her arms around her legs, rested her head on her knees, and watched Ramón, wondering what dreams he could be having in such a heavy sleep. But no, Ramón was no dreamer. He made plans, not dreams. She sighed and, with her suddenly heightened consciousness of feelings, wondered why Ramón made the plans he did, what motivated him. She would have to watch him more carefully, to learn what he was thinking. He would never tell her.

When he awoke an hour later, she was sitting with a bowl between her knees, shaving chocolate from a hard bar into it, for cocoa. The monotonous action soothed her at the same time that it dulled her mind, so that she did not think about the things she had come there to escape.

Ramón smiled drowsily and murmured, *"Hola, Riña."* She looked up and smiled.

"Where's Luis?" he asked then, looking around the room.

"I think Mercedes has put him to some work."

"Good." He sat up and stretched but showed no sign of being eager to stir himself further.

Kate asked him, "He will have reached Astorga, then?"

Ramón sighed. "Baird? Yes, much good it may do."

Kate guessed that Ramón had gone north to find out where Sir David Baird and the other half of Moore's army were. They had marched overland from La Coruña on the chance of meeting with Moore and waited now at Astorga, one hundred and twenty miles from Salamanca. Moore waited in Salamanca for his own artillery, which was being brought there via the Tajo Valley because the roads Moore himself had taken from Lisbon had been reported impassable for heavy guns. The British army was waiting, indeed, all over western Spain, waiting first for the chance to unite and make some show of strength, and then for an indication that it was feasible to advance farther into Spain—or a warning that it would be necessary to turn and make a run for safety.

But Ramón was weary of armies and volunteered nothing more, except to ask Kate to talk of something else. Mercedes came in and offered them both hot cocoa, and Kate told Ramón the Salamanca gossip and about the coming dinner party in as lighthearted a way as she could. Ramón listened willingly and smiled at her description—which did not include Greyson's part in it—of Cerralbo's invitation.

Ángel threw open the door and came in, and Mercedes immediately demanded to know what had kept him. Not waiting for an answer, she indicated the gun in the corner and told him to go out again for some game to fill the supper pot. Ramón got up and said that he would go himself. Mercedes protested but was overruled, much to the relief of Ángel, who fell wearily into a corner.

Ramón and Kate passed Luis outside and called to him to come along, but he declined. Kate commented, "I don't think Luis approves of me."

"Why not?"

"He has such a disapproving way of looking at me, and he calls me Señora or Doña Catarina, instead of Kate or Riña as the others do. I think he doesn't trust me, either, as if I might tell everyone I know about your meetings here."

"You're imagining things."

Ramón was saddling their horses and, absorbed in the task, he gave little heed to what she was saying. As they mounted and rode off into the hills, out of sight of the village, she, too, lapsed into pensive silence. The world around them was silent, too, but for the sound of their horses' passage through the underbrush. It was a dry day but cold and overcast. Gray clouds formed a solid ceiling that occasionally cracked to give passage to a stream of sunlight that illuminated one patch of country with a silver glow, making an eerie contrast to the blue-gray tint over the rest. Cypresses on a distant hill shivered in the fine breeze, but no human movement save their own could be seen.

They were alone, as if in some mysterious place where time was suspended, where they were given a respite from the world outside and from other people. Even the occasional roar and reverberating echo of Ramón's gun did not bring it back to Kate that perhaps just beyond the cypresses on the hill there was a war, a great deal of human movement, and many guns in deadly use. She had never heard guns fired in anger by men against other men and did not associate the peaceful use to which one was now being put with the more horrible purpose they could serve. Instead, she applauded when Ramón brought down a partridge, then another, until they turned homeward again, well laden with provisions for Mercedes.

Around the fire later, Kate looked again at the faces she thought she knew but now realized she could not read at all. The fire glowed dully in the center of the large, plain room—a small flame seeming to keep at bay the whole of a cold, encroaching world outside their walls.

It was reflected on Ramón's dark, solemn features. He had grown a mustache that hid the youthful, sensitive mouth, and there was a thin white scar on his temple that Kate had not noticed before. The flames illuminated Mercedes's kindly but worn face and graying hair. Guillermo's weathered skin stretched over the sharp bones of his face; his dark eyes had a hollow look, and the stubble on his chin was white. Ángel's face was still young and smooth, but his expression was an old one, and his small eyes had the unseeing, hard look typical of the Spanish peasant.

These people were never really young, Kate thought. They were born knowing too much of a harsh world. But they worked hard for their world. At night they slept the sleep of free souls, but in the morning they remembered that the country over which they rode was not free.

Kate remembered other faces then, English faces, around a fire in a college in Salamanca. They were so different, so full of hope. She had come to Santa Virgen to forget them for a few hours, but increasingly her mind went back to Salamanca, and she wondered if she had been missed—but, of course, she would have been—and what she would say to them, to Colin, when she returned. It occurred to her that despite her eagerness that morning to explore this new, strange, wonderfully stirring relationship with Colin Greyson, she had herself deliberately turned away from it.

She was no longer angry with Colin, but with herself, for these maddeningly shifting moods that she did not know how to deal with, and for her inability to be honest with him. She was at once eager to run to Colin and beg for his touch, his kisses, a renewal of the physical ecstasy he had awakened in her—and at the same time frightened of it, of exposing herself any more to him, as if to do so would lead only to the same hurt that had fallen over her first, innocent happiness with him so long ago. How unsuspecting she had been then!

But these sudden shifts in mood from hope to despair—happiness so great she wanted to weep, to sadness so deep she could not even speak—were no less agonizing. Why could she not just hold onto the happiness, not let it go, but use it to keep the despair at bay? She closed her eyes, concentrating her inner eye on the blue intensity of Colin's eyes, that arrogant mouth that could smile and turn her heart around with a laugh, the somehow touching sight of his back as he walked down the corridor, hands in pockets—and holding that vision like a talisman against future change.

She left Santa Virgen the same night, with the excuse of the marqués's dinner party the next day to prepare for. But the truth was that her volatile mood had shifted back to a passionate longing to see Colin again, to start again, to love him again. She could hardly wait to get back to Salamanca.

Ramón would have accompanied her, but Luis's presence saved the necessity of his own, and she assured him that he need not trouble himself. With a shrug of the shoulders, he let her go. He did not hear the sigh of release or see the involuntary smile on her lips when she turned her mount back toward home.

Chapter Twelve

EXCEPT for the slight flush on her cheeks, Kate succeeded in maintaining Doña Catarina's aristocratic poise as she prepared for the dinner at San Boal. She had been tempted to abandon her customary black entirely for this occasion, and only that morning had held up her red velvet gown from the Christmas before in front of her, seeing it with a slightly wistful new appreciation and wondering what Colin would say to it. But she knew that it would cause a great deal of talk, and finally she had yielded to the temptation to wear colors only to the extent of red roses in her hair. The black gown she chose had a lace overskirt and a low neckline, which she covered with a delicate lace mantilla.

As it turned out, it seemed she might have chosen her colors deliberately, for the splash of scarlet in her hair complemented that of the British uniforms in abundant display that night, and as she passed through the round arch over the entrance to the *palacio*, her black dress and bare throat, paled by the lamplight, glowed like old ivory against the cool black-and-white tiles that covered the front of the building.

Colin had given her an appreciative look when he came to escort her to San Boal, and she had displayed her gown for him, but after that he kept his distance. If he knew where she had been the night before, he did not say; and if he did not know, it seemed that he was not going to ask. This gave Kate an unworthy, but nevertheless welcome, advantage, and she used it to demonstrate her superiority to him. Her confidence added to her beauty, and that in turn made other heads than Colin Greyson's turn her way.

They ascended to the balcony on the first floor, from

which opened the principal rooms. Along the length of the balcony echoed laughter, the ring of swords, and the masculine sound of boots on stone flooring. Kate had a glimpse of women in silk and gauze gowns, in pastels overpowered by the red and white and black of uniforms. Several of the men stopped talking abruptly when she entered on Greyson's arm, leaving a confused medley of feminine sounds hanging on the air.

Valerian von Ehrenberg was the first to recover his wits on recognizing the new arrivals, and he hurried to greet his commanding officer, whom he then disregarded to devote his attention to Kate. But she was divided between amusement at his chatter and curiosity about the other officers in the room.

"Where is General Moore?" she whispered to Val.

"Doesn't seem to have arrived—but look out! Here comes the Honorable Edward with a gleam in his eye."

General the Honorable Edward Paget, a young man with a confident and formidable manner, made an impressive approach and bowed low to Kate. She remembered having seen him with Colin on the day of Moore's arrival in Salamanca and was now even more struck by his militarily erect posture and the black eyes that did indeed gleam from a tanned and weatherworn face. He stood rather stiffly before her and gazed down from his commanding height. Then, unexpectedly, he took out a snuff box, offering it to Greyson (a gesture, Val told Kate later, that was more than usually gracious of him, even knowing that Greyson would not take him up on his offer) and explaining that it had been a gift.

"What do you think of it?" he asked, and, with a little bow to Kate, added, "It's Spanish."

He was cut off at the start of what looked to be an extensive lecture on the varieties of snuff and the styles of boxes to put it in by another officer, a Major Colborne, who presented himself cordially to Kate as Sir John's military secretary. In rather too rapid succession, she also met several other officers whose names she was unable, ten minutes later, to recall.

It had been some time since this much flattering attention had been paid her, and it was an agreeably heady sensation—at least until she looked away for a moment and saw Colin Greyson standing to one side watching her handling of her admirers. It vexed her that he showed no sign of wanting to compete with them. Was he taking her for granted already? She felt her fragile confidence slip a little, and to spite him, she began flirting with Major Colborne, a tall, athletic young man, blue-eyed and fair-haired much in the manner of his commanding officer. Why should she need Colin Greyson, after all, to remind her that she was an attractive woman?

But just at that moment, Sir John himself made an unannounced appearance on the scene, bestowing greetings and smiles like benedictions, Kate thought, as he went. He entered the room in the company of the Marqués de Cerralbo, who, seeing Kate, moved to greet her and to introduce her to the General.

"I am honored, Doña Catarina," he said in a soft voice, accompanied by a slight, almost wistful, smile.

Sir John was tall, handsome, and immaculately groomed—his bâtman had outfitted him with a well-cut, neatly pressed uniform—but Kate thought he looked tired, older than he was. There were faint circles under his blue eyes, but his gaze was direct and confident. She was most struck by his look of competence and that elusive quality of leadership that inspired in others a desire to please. It affected her as well, in spite of herself, in a way that made her want to follow him, to make his wish her command.

But another part of her reacted differently, to what to her seemed an overbearing pride. He spoke to her for a few minutes, but she thought him condescending, and that the smile on his lips and his graciousness of manner were both merely assumed for the occasion.

Fortunately, given at dinner the opportunity to study the various other personalities present, Kate was able to divert her mind from uncharitable opinions of the British commander—and to disregard Colin's silent scrutiny from across the table. He seemed willing to let her find her own place in this setting, but she could not help feeling that how she did so would somehow, sometime, come back to haunt her. Fortunately, Val, who sat beside her, kept up a running commentary to divert her.

Colonel Graham, to whom Kate's attention was drawn

by his black brows and shock of white hair, leaned over to General Paget and said, "You're looking well, Edward."

"Oh, I keep pretty well," responded the younger man, "except for my rheumatism, gravel, scurvy, and gout."

"Gout? Come, come, man—at your tender age?"

"I believe it must be that," Paget insisted. "In my toe. At least, it is very red, very tender, very painful, and very glossy."

This inspired a good deal of unsympathetic laughter all around. Kate regarded General Paget critically, wondering why such a man—the son of an earl and younger brother of Lord Paget, the cavalry commander under Baird—would choose to play the buffoon. Surely in less public places, he was not so. But she soon discovered why he and the others, particularly Moore's aides, were careful to keep the conversation amusing and the atmosphere cordial.

Sir John, not a patient man, revealed a certain brusqueness of manner, and he was not always content to cast a discouraging look upon any person whom he found to be intrusive or simply stupid. One such, a Spanish lady prone to loud expressions of her patriotism, was seated on his left. She seemed unaware of the unstated ban on certain subjects and begged Sir John, in a voice that carried all too well, for news of the armies of Castile and Aragón.

There was an uncomfortable pause before he replied, "Madame, I can only guess. I am in communication with not one Spanish force, nor am I acquainted with the intentions of its generals. The goodwill and enthusiasm, such as it is, of the Spanish people is of little use while there exists no ability to bring it into action, and no capable commander to lead its lamentable armies."

Major Colborne, disregarding the likelihood of a stinging rebuke, interceded diplomatically. "Of course, we have daily reports from our agents, as well as from yours—in addition to the information intercepted by the *guerrilleros*—and a continuous flow of information on the movements of the Spanish as well as the French forces is available to us."

Sir John lapsed into silence during this speech, which Graham and Paget were quick to follow up, guiding the conversation gently but firmly into less dangerous waters.

The marqués, who had a talent for the telling of a tale, ended the meal on a note of Anglo-Spanish accord by relating a moment of history common to both countries.

"Many years ago," he began, "before Spain became a united kingdom under the Catholic sovereigns, and when England was still a very little island, Pedro the Cruel sat upon the throne of Castile. The Moor Abû Saïd, called the Red King, who had usurped the throne of Granada, came to seek Pedro's support of his cause, bringing with him many rich gifts and jewels—among them a large uncut ruby.

"Pedro set his cruel heart on this stone, and while Abû Saïd and his retinue were royally entertained in his palace, Pedro plotted to betray him. One day, he and his knights seized the Red King and murdered him.

"Later, after Edward, the Black Prince of England, together with Pedro, had won the battle of Nájara—against the French—the Castilian gave the Englishman his ruby as a token of gratitude. Our English guests will know how the stone was later worn in the helmet of Henry V at Agincourt, how in the reign of the second King Charles, Colonel Blood tried to steal it, and how from that day to this, the ruby of Abû Saïd has passed in unbroken succession to the kings and queens of England.

"And so you see," he concluded, smiling at his audience, "it is neither impossible nor unprecedented that Spain and England should meet in common cause!"

Later, in the ballroom, Kate placed herself in a matronly position on a settee with Colin standing behind her—rather, she thought, like an overly fussy chaperone. Sir John Moore stood near the door, conversing with several of the guests at once. Rather than circulating among them, he stood to let them flow past him, each receiving his share of the general's time and attention. He smiled at everyone, but that ever-present air of distraction that hung around him, the impression that in spirit he was not with them, was more than evident to Kate.

"Stop scowling, Riña. People will think you're not enjoying yourself."

Kate gave a start. She had forgotten Colin's vigilant nearness. Sir John, with a last bow, had bestowed a vague smile upon the company at large and slipped quietly out of the room, and she said, "I cannot comprehend why his men are so devoted to him. He is so far above them, so unapproachable."

Greyson considered this. "That is so, but you do not entirely see what makes him behave that way. For him, you see, there is no middle way—a thing is good or bad, right or wrong, black or white. He is at once idealist and realist. He sees all too clearly how a thing ought to be but is not, and then sets out with excessive zeal to correct it."

"Perhaps it does not only seem excessive," Kate said. "It is hardly fair of him to expect everyone to conform to his standards."

"But his men love him, you see, because he expects of them only what he would demand of himself. In the field, he shares the lot of the common soldier—his quarters, his food, all perhaps but his fear. He cannot understand fear in others because he is fearless himself. Intolerance is considered a fault, but in John Moore, I think, it must be a virtue. One either loves him or hates him, but one must grant him that."

She said nothing, not wanting to quarrel with him, not sure in any case of her arguments. He relented a little and said, with a smile in his voice, "I suppose what you particularly dislike, *mi vida*, is the general's unfortunate capacity for being almost always in the right."

"Who is always right?" demanded Valerian von Ehrenberg, coming upon the scene at that moment. "Other than your humble servant, of course."

He made himself comfortable next to Kate and proceeded to monopolize the conversation when Greyson relapsed into stony silence. Kate listened willingly to Val, preferring nonsense to being put in the wrong by Colin Greyson. And when Dr. Curtis joined the little group, she introduced him to Colonel Greyson and Major von Ehrenberg, who made the appropriate comments and surveyed with interest the imposing figure of this eminent Salamancan. The doctor showed more courtesy toward the colonel than Doña Catarina, in her present mood, thought the colonel deserved, but the doctor was never one to neglect a lady, and he soon turned his attention to her.

The Dancers' Land 139

"How is Ramón?" he asked. "I see very little of him these days."

Dr. Curtis had lately been active in formulating an intelligence service for Moore, and rumor had it that his part had been more than an advisory one. But it seemed he had not been in contact with Ramón, nor knew of Kate's trafficking in captured dispatches, so Kate avoided a direct reply by remarking that, with the present excitement, Dr. Curtis must find his lecture rooms emptier than usual.

"Yes, it's true," he said. "But since my pupils are bound to have their studies disturbed in any case, they had all much better join the British army."

Kate laughed and looked up to see how Colin had taken this blatant flattery. But he seemed not to have heard. He was looking at her with that ice-blue intensity, which told her she had committed some new folly—but what? What had she said? She searched her mind. Had she stupidly given Dr. Curtis away, or Ramón, as spies?

But just then Dr. Curtis excused himself, and she said good night to him, and Val, who had gone to fetch her a glass of punch, returned and sniffed it delicately.

"I do believe," he pronounced, "that it is almost palatable. In fact, dear lady, if you could wheedle the recipe from the marqués, I should be eternally grateful!"

The musicians struck up a new tune then, to which Kate, still puzzling out Colin's reaction to Dr. Curtis and listening with half an ear to Val's chatter, paid no immediate notice. But the sound of it caught Colin's attention.

"Do you waltz, Doña Catarina?" he asked, interrupting Val, who shot a look of indignant protest at him.

"Do I what?"

Colin indicated the couples gathering on the dance floor, and before there was time for Kate to protest, she found herself being led to join them, her arm firmly engaged in Colonel Greyson's.

"I can't dance!" she whispered. "I told Cerralbo I wouldn't—how would it look?"

But he paid no heed to her objections. "The steps are really quite simple," he was saying, "and the melody easy to follow. Come, let's try it."

She protested less strongly, but he was insistent, moving her into position as if she were a mechanical doll. But very shortly she forgot her objections, caught up in the vibrant melody that came, Colin told her, from Vienna.

"It is all the rage," he said, "and cause for a minor scandal in some quarters."

"I can see why. Is that why you were so unceremonious about getting me to dance it?"

He replied smoothly, "Naturally, it is perfectly proper for a—ah, a married lady, to dance the waltz. In your position—"

"Are you trying to take advantage of my position, Colonel Greyson?"

He leaned closer to her then and whispered in her ear, "I have every intention of doing so, Doña Catarina."

She felt an involuntary shiver go through her, and in order not to look into his eyes, she studied his hand. It was encased in immaculate white gloves, and the long tapering fingers enclosed her own in them possessively. She began to have several more reservations about this dance, which allowed her to be held by a man in public in this way—especially by a man who drew this response from her with only a touch. She shivered again.

"Beg pardon, sir," Val said, unfeelingly tripping him up in the middle of a turn, "but do give the rest of us poor fellows a chance." He grinned at Kate. "I mean, now she's got the hang of the thing."

"Really, Valerian," said his superior scathingly, "you must endeavor to acquire a little tact." But, bowing to Kate, he backed away. She was conscious of regret at being torn out of his arms, despite the uncomfortable sensations they evoked in her. But Val's arms around her were comforting and friendly, and soon she began to think she had been foolish to let a dance with Colin disturb her.

The major's initiative emboldened several other officers to ask the beautiful widow to dance. She gave preference to those she knew in Colin's regiment, although their colonel claimed the remaining waltzes. That dance continued to have a disturbing effect on her. Other rhythms made her feel light-headed, but a waltz drugged her. She moved heavily, hypnotically, over the floor, her gray eyes fastened to Colin's blue ones, as to the only fixed point in a spinning world. The music pulsed with her blood, marking time with the beat of her heart. She was abnormally con-

The Dancers' Land

scious of the melody and of the hand around her waist, and it was with a sense of escape that she was released from the spell and spun into a country dance with another partner, a quadrille with a third.

The rest of the evening passed all too quickly, but the memory of it lingered out into the night. It was all she could do to keep from dancing into her carriage, but there was no understanding smile on Colin's lips tonight; indeed, he seemed now in an even less tolerant humor than before they had danced. She did not trust him not to make some cutting, hurtful remark that would spoil her enjoyment of the aftereffects of an evening now well advanced into morning.

In the carriage on the way home, she glanced covertly at him, wondering what he was thinking. She found herself looking at him with special intensity, seeing and committing to memory the details that she could never recall about anyone else, as if she might not see them again.

He was gazing absently out of the window, but even in repose his face had great strength. The square set of his jaw gave it a solemn cast. Deeply etched lines ran from the corners of his eyes, outlining the high cheekbones, on which the skin was roughened from exposure. The light of an occasional street lamp shone in on him and undid the effect of the sun on his complexion, turning his face pale and the gold of his lashes and of the fine hairs covering his temples to silver.

She found that she was holding her breath and slowly released it, waiting for him to speak. But when he did, his voice sounded maddeningly normal.

"Look at that."

She leaned over him, and he drew back the curtain for her. What she saw made her almost forget his nearness. A bedraggled column of Spanish soldiers, recent arrivals to Salamanca, were shuffling in the cold dawn along the road leading into the city from the north. Their clothes were in tatters, many shoeless and dragging their weapons over the ground behind them. They looked up as Kate's carriage rattled by, but there was no expression in their hollow eyes. Then they were gone, and with a stifled cry, Kate looked back. But by then the carriage had rounded a corner, and the straggling rabble was lost to view.

The silence inside the carriage grew heavy with tension. Kate felt she must say something and seized upon what was the least personal.

"And the *British* army goes to a ball!"

Colin obliged her by not making the obvious retort, saying instead, "Do you think that if Blake's army had the choice, they'd not dance, too? Or that if we had the choice, we'd not sooner be in the field after this interminable waiting and indecision? At least that rabble can say they fought! Really, Riña, you must not accuse us of frivolity. Why, even Val prefers the rigors of sleeping in the open air of the patio of the college to the comfort of one of the rooms. Don't tell him I told you, however—it's meant to be a secret."

Behind the mocking tone, there was bitterness in his voice. He went on, "If the population is willing to entertain us, who are we to remind them that there is a war on? They know so well that there is, they devote the major part of their day to discussing it around a café table. We've stopped trying to describe to these 'experts' how we see the situation."

She did not try to answer him and was sorry she had said anything to provoke him. It no longer seemed important to voice her opinion—not when she thought of how, once again, the evening had been lost. What did armies and politics matter when once again they had failed to speak honestly to each other, to rekindle that passion that now seemed farther away, cooler, more irretrievable than ever? She was suddenly aware of how fast time was passing, and tears welled up behind her eyes. She stared out the window, willing them not to fall.

"Where were you last night, Riña?" he asked then, quietly but with a finality that told her he would accept no evasions this time. She understood that he was jealous of the time she spent away from him, just as he was of the harmless flirtations she carried on with other officers. She wanted to tell him there was nothing in it, to tell him anything at all he wanted to know, but what he asked now was the one thing she could not speak of to him, not without betraying Ramón. The walled-up tears spilled over, and an involuntary sob racked her body.

Startled, he moved toward her, but just then the carriage came to a halt at her front portal. Without waiting for the door to be opened and the steps let down, desperate to escape him, she forced the door and half-jumped, half-fell to the ground and ran into the house past the surprised *sereno,* who had been waiting to open the gate for her.

Still sobbing, she ran up the stairs and into her room, but she had barely slammed the door behind her before it burst open again and Colin was in her room, whirling her around to face him.

"For God's sake, Kate, what's the matter?"

He stopped, aware in the pale light of the gleam of unexplained tears on her lashes, and he was torn between wanting to comfort her and wanting an answer.

"Please leave me alone," she whispered, weary of trying and always failing to say just the right thing, make the one move that would explain everything to him. She was unaware that her refusal to speak was making its own statement.

"No, Kate," he said in a cold voice that she had not heard before. "I may have to leave you soon, and I don't want you to forget me—not this time, and certainly not in any other man's arms."

What was he talking about? He must know by now that Manuel had nothing to do with him. She looked up just quickly enough to see the blaze of angry passion that darkened his blue eyes and gasped at his harsh grip when he took hold of her and lowered his mouth to hers. Frightened, she moved her head away, but she was not quick enough. His lips burned hers, and she felt herself catch fire. Forgetting everything else, she kissed him back, drinking in the warmth of his mouth, and then moaned in disappointment when he took it away—only to bury it in the hollow behind her ear, then travel down her neck and throat, leaving hot, searing kisses down to her breasts.

She no longer cared if he loved her in anger or passion or vengeance—if he would just love her, take her! He felt for the fastenings of her gown, and she turned to help him and became aware of the open door. Every servant in the house must be aware by now of what was happening, but even that did not seem to matter. "Colin, the door."

He closed it, then slowly, deliberately began to strip off his own clothes as she watched in fascination, feeling her body respond to him even when he was across the room from her. The pale light played on his broad shoulders and narrow hips, and she saw how the muscles changed with every movement, how the skin was darker, rougher, above the waist, and below gleamed like the marble of the Greek statues she had seen in Paris.

As if aware of what she was thinking, he stood without moving for a moment as she studied him, until she, too, became aware of what she was doing and turned away, blushing. A low laugh, not amused but knowing, cruel, made her look back as he came to her and slipped the top of her gown easily down her shoulders.

"This time will be different," he whispered. "This time you will want me, but you will not have me. I will have you, and you won't forget it—ever."

She did not understand what he meant, but then, when he began to kiss her again, slowly, his warm mouth touching every part of her as he carefully removed the last of her underclothing, exposing an inch of flesh at a time until she was mad with a need for him that he would not fill, she began to understand. He held her hands away from him while he caressed her naked body with his own, light caresses that burned but did not consume.

"Oh, God, Colin—what are you trying to do to me?"

He let go of her hands then, and her arms went instinctively around his neck, her mouth seeking his. He picked her up and laid her gently down on the bed, and when he lay down beside her, she breathed a sigh of relief and expectation and reached for him. But he tortured her a little longer, touching the length of his body against hers, but only close enough so that she was aware of every inch of it, of his broad hands parting her thighs and caressing her inner softness until she began to writhe convulsively, tormented by unfulfillment.

"Colin—I love you! Please love me. Love me."

"Liar."

But the word had no strength, and she had none of her own left to protest it. He kissed her mouth, then her full breasts and the soft hollows of her body, downward to where his hand had prepared a soft home, and kissed her there and, when she moaned again, kissed her once more on the mouth so that she could taste herself and him in his deep kiss.

Then, suddenly, he entered her with a harsh thrust that was less a release than a fresh assault. She wanted him, had ached for that final ecstasy, but he was so urgent, powerful, brutal, that she could only react by moving beneath him in an instinctive rhythm that sought to ease the pain and prolong it, too.

But the same instinct that responded to his body told her that something else in him had changed. He said nothing, but she knew that now, against his will, he was making love to her and not just taking her to inflict pain on her. His caresses became gentler yet hungrier, and he was no longer angry but trembled as she did. When he left her at last, she could feel him shiver with spent passion.

But he got up quickly, scooped his clothes up from the floor, and went away without a word, leaving her to sort out by herself her jumbled emotions and the extremes of physical sensation, like fire and ice, that still coursed through her body.

And he was right. She wouldn't forget.

Chapter Thirteen

Ramón pushed his way across the Plaza Mayor. It was the kind of night, clear and full-mooned, that gave false promise of good weather on the morrow. But December had arrived, and these were the last starry skies before snow would begin to gather and the wind shift to bring the Atlantic winter in upon the plains of Castile.

He made a wide circle around a slovenly, shabbily dressed woman with dirty red hair, much the worse for drink, who hung onto the arm of a soldier no more sober than herself, and then met a group of soldiers coming in the other direction. One of them waved a bottle at him and called out, *"Bueynoz nochis, seenyor!"* in a slurred voice before being propelled on by his companions.

Ramón could not blame them for being too careless with their wine, for that morning their general had received news confirming that retreat was his only hope. A messenger, after riding five hundred miles in six days, reported to British headquarters that the Spanish had been routed at Tudela, leaving the British army the only undefeated force in northern Spain. Ramón had seen Moore that morning during a review of the troops and had thought then, seeing the anxiety and sleeplessness on his pale face, that he looked already like a man in retreat.

But in spite of his sympathy for the British and his appreciation of their effort, Ramón could not agree with the decision to retreat to Lisbon. Like any other Spaniard, he felt that having come this far, the British should at least make some push to meet the enemy. He did try to put himself in British boots, but even united, and even if the most optimistic estimates of French strength were accurate,

The Dancers' Land

they were sadly outnumbered. Napoleon himself, at the head of his army, was approaching the Spanish capital.

Ramón could understand not only the military dilemma, but also what must be Moore's thoughts at that moment. He knew that letters arrived daily from the British consul in Madrid urging him to stand firm, while letters from Spanish patriots reiterated the old pleas and promises of Spanish victories. Ramón knew that most of Moore's general staff were against his decision, the responsibility for which their commander had taken upon himself alone, and that they were deeply disappointed. Morale among the troops was even lower, and Ramón did not blame the drunken soldiers in the plaza for seeking temporary solace from the humiliation of being made to turn and run without a fight.

Kate was on the patio when Ramón made his unexpected entrance, but her smile of welcome faded swiftly at the sight of his dark, brooding expression. She called to Amelia for sherry and biscuits, with which they retired to the library.

Colin had been out of the house since early morning, but this time Kate dreaded more than she looked forward to his return.

She knew that it was now up to her to go to him and try to put things right, since it had been her actions—however unthinking and unintended—that had driven them apart again. She was beginning to understand now that what Colin wanted was for her to come to him freely, with no explanations or evasions. But the more she tried to clear her mind of all her carefully built-up defenses, the more confused it became, and the less able she was to act.

She was glad to see Ramón because she hoped that he would suggest they ride out to Santa Virgen—even while she knew that would be yet another evasion—but one look at his face told her he had no such idea and was, indeed, too exhausted to think very much at all. He sank into a chair, but Kate was too restless to sit down. She moved impatiently around the room, straightening books on the shelves and lining up the pencils on Manuel's desk into neat little rows, all the while chatting to Ramón of trivial things that she thought would distract him from what was really on his—and her—mind. But after a few minutes, he put down his sherry glass and leaned back with his eyes closed.

"For the love of God, Kate, *basta ya*—enough."

She stopped, shocked into silence, and stared at him. The old, tired look on his face struck her to the heart, and she bit her lip in shame. Silently, she knelt on the floor next to his chair and, with her arms around him, laid her head in his lap. She sighed, to keep back tears, and Ramón, regretting his own outburst, put out a hand to stroke her hair.

She did not hear a footstep on the stairs, and Colin Greyson, hearing no sound from within the library, felt at liberty to walk in the open door without knocking. As he stepped inside, his eyes met Ramón's and held them for a moment before Kate realized from a shift in Ramón's position that something had happened.

She looked up and saw Colin, but another moment passed before she fully recognized him, and the searching look that he directed at her went unnoticed until Ramón's soft, ironic chuckle brought her back to reality with a sickening lurch. Suddenly, it came to her that it had been Ramón that Colin was jealous of—Ramón! She almost laughed aloud. Oh, God, how could she have been so stupid—how could Colin, when it came to that? But his face now told her that he really believed he had cause, and she was at a loss to explain his misunderstanding to him. Instead, as if Greyson had come in upon two friends at opposite ends of a table, chatting over a cup of tea, Doña Catarina rose to greet him.

"Good evening, Colonel Greyson," she said. "May I present an old friend, Ramón Sariñana?"

Greyson bowed formally as Ramón rose from his chair; Ramón took back his outstretched hand and returned the bow with a wry smile. Kate produced another wineglass, and the three seated themselves around the fire. Greyson offered Ramón a cigarette, which was accepted with a lordly air.

For the first time since Kate met him, Colin seemed ill at ease. Ramón, on the other hand, had never been more the master of the situation. His harsh features relaxed visibly, and the lines around his eyes faded until he began to look more like the dashing *majo* of so few years before. The anxieties of recent months dissipated with the smoke of his cigarette, and a slight smile played over his long mouth. On the other hand, the frown sketched on Colin's forehead deepened, and a note of irritability crept into his voice. Kate tucked her legs up under her skirts and, ensconced in the chair nearest the fire, observed the two men in fascination.

For a few minutes, they talked of things they were all aware of but dared not probe too deeply. Ramón finished the cigarette and rose to take his leave. Colin got up, shook hands politely, and did not see him to the door. Kate did, still bemused, and watched him descend the stairs with a jauntiness foreign to him and cross the patio to the door. Then, determined to clear the additional confusion in her mind, Kate returned to the library.

Colin was leaning against the mantelpiece, gazing into the empty sherry glass he held in his hand. She was relieved, although she did not know why, when he looked at her and raised one eyebrow in mocking salute.

"Did I not say that the Spanish don't believe in friendship between men and women?" He forestalled her reply with a quick, sharp laugh. "To think it was you that never saw it! In some ways you are just as innocent as you were in Paris."

"Colin—"

"No, don't try to explain. I'm too exhausted to listen." He fell into a chair and sighed. "It's been a hellish day, Kate. Please forgive me if I don't come to dinner. Michael's here—he'll keep you entertained."

He looked up and held out a hand to her, as if in apology, but she stood where she was.

"When are you leaving?" she could not help asking.

He dropped his hand, said nothing for a moment, and then, softly, "Oh, God, not you, too! I had hoped for one word of comfort, somewhere."

She had not realized, had not intended, that her tone was the same as the Spaniards who declaimed at length on the perfidy of the British who, in a fright, were running out of Spain by the nearest exit. Or perhaps Colin, exhausted and unhappy, had read into her voice the same criticism that he had been hearing all too often of late.

In any case, her first attempt to make him understand that she did not want him to go had failed and, stung, she lashed back at him for the fear that she had not talked out with Ramón. "Comfort! When you're giving up? Do you deserve it?"

He rose wearily from his chair to face her. "Kate, don't be so damned patriotic! Stop trying to be Spanish—you don't suit the role—and look at our side of it. Do you think the army is pleased to retreat? Do you honestly believe we want to give up without a fight?

"God knows why we should want Spain's good opinion, but we do know our duty! For days now my men have been coming to blows with any Spaniard who suggested the rumors of retreat might be true and have been running to me to have them denied. Can you understand how it feels to have to confirm them now? Can you imagine the shame and the anger that prompt them to go out every night and get drunk, to forget? You are letting the passions you have invented for yourself cloud your vision, Riña. That's fatal—don't let it happen."

Kate stood her ground, however untenable. She had given her sympathy to Ramón and had none left now for this man who twisted everything she said into a personal attack.

"I am not so blinded that I can say with the rest that Spain needs no help! We do, and it's this denial of it that I cannot understand! Here you are, moving out, never having so much as caught sight of the French. How do you know they are really there? What will history say if Moore runs back to Portugal, pursued by no more than his own blind panic?"

"What would the government at home say," he countered, "if Moore lost this army? It's the only one we have, you know. You won't get another to save Spain!"

His temper was cooling as quickly as it had flared, and there was a hint of apology in his voice, but either she did not hear it or she disregarded it. She stood before him, silent, her hands clenched tightly in the folds of her skirt. He smiled ruefully.

"Don't look like that, *mi vida*—and don't take everything so personally."

Then, as if his weary mind could no longer function

The Dancers' Land

clearly, he said, half to himself, "I don't know, perhaps Ramón—incidentally, can you really be unaware of the gossip about you and Ramón?"

"What has that to do with anything?" she said, startled. It had not occurred to her that he would have heard any such gossip, but if he had, why did he believe it?

He did not seem to hear her, but picking up the empty glass again, he toyed with it abstractedly.

"Let me give you a little advice, Kate. It will be the last time I trouble you with it, but it's simple enough and it's just this: Be yourself, Kate. There's so much that's good in you that never had half a chance, so much love that you refuse to give. You've inherited too much of your father's pride, you know, too much of his stubbornness, and you're letting it govern you."

"What do you know about my father?"

"Enough. I know your mother, you see."

There—he was going to admit it at last, confirm the suspicion—nay, the certainty—she'd had from the beginning. Quickly, she threw up the defenses she needed to keep this last hurt from touching her and said contemptuously, "My mother!"

"Yes, I know what you think of her, but you couldn't be more wrong—no, wait! Hear me out."

Kate had reached for the door and flung it open, but Colin intercepted it and closed it again behind her. Kate spun around like a cornered animal.

"Do you know what she did to my father?" she said. "Any hurt to a man like that would have been unforgivable, but she treated him infamously! She was completely without principles, without a notion of common decency—"

"Did your father tell you this?"

"I could see it for myself!"

"A precocious child! How old were you then? Ten, twelve? Kate, can you never stop to look at the other side of an argument?"

"What other side?"

"Your mother's. Do you know anything at all about her? No? I'll tell you." Kate turned her head away, but he took it in his hand and turned it back, making her look at him.

"You *will* listen to me! Leonora Benton was seventeen when she married Henry Collier; he was twenty years older. It was an arranged match. Leonora scarcely knew Henry, but she was an obedient girl as well as an innocent one, and she believed her mother's assurances that she would be well-off and happy. She *was* comfortable, materially. But she scarcely saw Henry outside their bedroom. He never talked to her, never treated her like a human being, never showed the least love for that fragile, vulnerable creature who was starved for it. Was it any wonder that when other men offered her their love, she took it—and eagerly? She stuck by Henry as long as she did only because she had a sense of duty—and because she had a daughter."

He looked directly at her, his eyes searching her face for something he could not find and mirroring his disappointment. He went on quietly, almost wistfully.

"I hadn't thought before this that she was a fool to love her daughter as she did. You look so much like her, Kate! Once I thought you had her loving nature, too—it seemed so in Paris, although, of course, you were very young then. Maybe I was a fool to carry that image in my mind for five years, when there was nothing behind it, but it kept me from losing my mind on that infernal island, so I suppose it served its purpose. If only . . . There was none of your anger in Leonora, you know, in spite of Henry. She gave back kindnesses paid to her ten times over and returned love with happiness."

Kate could feel hot tears welling up inside her and wanted to be able to deny what he implied about her, but she knew it was true. Helpless, she let the question come out.

"Just how well *did* you know my mother?"

He stepped back as if she had struck him, and for a moment Kate thought he would literally hit her back.

"You should be flogged for that!"

He strode to the fire and laid his hands on the mantelpiece, letting it support him while he fought for self-control.

"You're a coward, Kate, and I hope it's only Spain that's done it to you! But you couldn't leave now, could you? Here you are something out of the ordinary and sought after because of it. But could you go home and compete with women like your mother, who are exceptional for what they are and not for what they are not? Would you have the courage to do that? Because if—oh, God, I don't know what I'm saying anymore. . . ."

His voice trailed off. For a moment there was only the sound of the fire and burning logs breaking and crumbling into it. He murmured something that might have been "Forgive me," but she could not be certain of it. He walked past her without a look, and out of the room. He left the door open and a draft came in. Kate shivered.

Chapter Fourteen

A WEEK LATER, the army was still in Salamanca. A series of events, none decisive in itself, combined to cause John Moore second thoughts and to kindle a spark of hope in the hearts of those who felt that what was at stake now was not so much England's army but her national honor.

On the first day of December, Napoleon's advance guard appeared before the gates of Madrid. Whether the French were, incredibly, still unaware of the position of the British, or were simply unconcerned over the threat they posed, was uncertain. But the disappearance of the most important part of the French forces over the mountains to the south of them left the British temporarily out of danger.

Two days later, Moore's guns and cavalry arrived at last from the south, providing Moore with a balanced force within immediate call. Then, most heartening of all, came the news of fresh revolts by the populace of Madrid, who were prepared to resist to the death Napoleon's entry into the capital.

It was imperative to the French that they hold Madrid, the center of the peninsula. And as long as Madrid held out, Moore would be free of harassment. He was forced to ignore the pleas for support from the new Junta of Defense in Madrid, because he had not the power to relieve the city. But he could, by joining forces with Baird as originally intended, strike effectively at Napoleon's communications with France. By advancing eastward instead of retreating to the west, he could strike at the French lifeline to the Pyrenees.

If Madrid held out long enough, he would have time to act and still beat a safe retreat. But if the bubble burst and

Madrid fell too soon, the safe retreat would turn into a rout.

Thus, although the odds against success had not perceptibly diminished, Moore saw the slim chance of giving Spain the aid he had been sent to give, and to keep alive in Spain the spirit of resistance. Madrid would not hold for long, but if the emperor's advance could be checked for only a few weeks, the winter would have descended. Snow-blocked mountain passes would provide a barrier against a French invasion of the south, where the patriots could work until spring to rebuild their defenses.

The tension in Salamanca mounted. No one, least of all Moore, could be certain of what change of plan the next hour might bring. Hope flickered and burned brighter, but the feeling of impending disaster combined with hope to keep the emotions of all concerned keyed to fever-pitch.

But Kate, who had once been alert, quick to catch every shift of mood, and swift to assess every change in the situation, now found that she cared less and less. She received news with a nod or a shrug, and remained unresponsive even to Ramón's noticeable excitement. It was as if she no longer cared for what had previously been an obsession with her.

For every hour that Moore remained in Salamanca, making it clear that he had no wish to abandon the Spanish to their fate, she regretted more the folly of all that she had said to Colin. If she had been wrong about Moore and the British army, after all, she must have been just as wrong about everything else. But since that night, he had neither approached nor spoken to her, as if he had abandoned any interest he might have had in her, and she was sure that it would be useless to attempt to mend things between them. In fact, he now only kept his horses and gear at the house and rarely came there himself. She saw now that she might have said something to avoid this as long ago as that night after the ball, in the carriage. She should not have gone off to Santa Virgen after that first night, either. Indeed, she continually reproached herself for saying and doing all the wrong things from the start.

Kate, like the rest of Salamanca, was more than ready and willing to be distracted, if only for a moment, and the round of balls, dinners, and other festivities continued unabated. On the evening of the eighth of December, the players at the Teatro de España presented to a crowded hall a work of Cervantes, carefully chosen for its patriotic content.

Valerian von Ehrenberg escorted Kate to the theater for the presentation of *La Numancia*, and she was grateful for his undemanding escort. He had continued to call every day since their introduction at the regimental dinner, and lately, as if aware of her estrangement with Colin, he had offered to take her on drives or shopping expeditions and had kept her amused by his uninhibited, but inaccurate, attempts at Spanish, and his apparently limitless good cheer. He reminded Kate of Christopher that way, although she suspected that Valerian von Ehrenberg's fool's facade might conceal unusual depths. But he did not burden her with his inner demons, she returned the consideration, and they found each other's company calming.

Their box at the theater was in full view of the one occupied by Colin Greyson, in company with Michael Sinclair and Maria Elena, and a Spanish woman Kate did not know—and wondered irrelevantly how it was that Colin did. He looked well and entirely untroubled by the inner turmoil that plagued her, and which she thought must show in the gray smudges under her eyes and her pale cheeks, emphasized by her black gown and shawl. But she vowed to let none of it show in her manner, and she smiled to everyone she knew and leaned over the edge of her box to wave to those below. But when the lights dimmed for the beginning of the first act, she sat back in her chair and breathed a sigh of released tension.

The performance was not an outstanding one, but the enthusiasm of the audience and the delicacy of Cervantes' poetry raised it to the heights of great drama. The story of the heroic defense of the city of Numancia against the Roman legions seemed to hold many parallels to the present, and the hall rang with cheers at each allusion to the glory of Spain and the bravery of those willing to die for her. Kate glanced across to Colin's box, wondering how much of it he understood, but his slow, sardonic smile made it clear that he missed none of the references to the Spanish as a race of individualists lacking in national unity.

The Dancers' Land 157

During the interval, Val remarked with uncharacteristic directness, "You are very quiet. Is everything all right?"

"I'm sorry. I suppose I'm not very good company."

"Of course you are. I'm only sorry that it will be for such a little time longer."

He smiled and kissed her hand in his usual, gallant way. She felt tears sting her eyes, but to avoid violating their unspoken pact against despair, she asked him, "Are you enjoying the play?"

"Can't understand the half of it," he said, dismissing it. He leaned over the edge of the box to see who of interest might be below.

Val was certainly not himself tonight, either. Could he have come on some mission from Colin? she wondered. No, that was impossible; Colin would never be reduced to such tactics. Val sat back and yawned, forgetting in his abstraction even to cover his mouth. Kate smiled. So he was merely behaving eccentrically because he was tired!

She studied the handsome profile more closely; his eyes, with the laughter lines at the corners, glittered unnaturally in the artificial light. No, not unnaturally, for Val was, by nature, brilliant. The realization that such golden beauty could be extinguished in an instant, the careless laughter stilled forever, the young, reckless spirit broken before its time, made her long for some way to keep alive the flame, to avoid exposing it to the ruthless winds.

Suddenly, she found herself wishing that the army would get out quickly, while there was yet time to do so in safety. Kate had small knowledge of death, of war and its horror, but even the thought that some of these young men might never see England and their homes again was enough to move her tremendously.

"Val, won't you—will you come to my home after the performance for—"

He read her eyes and smiled with a touch of his colonel's irony. "—For a farewell toast?"

"Yes."

Alan Grierson, Peter Rutledge, and some others from the regiment were in the theater, and she asked Val to invite them also to come. Vivian Harmer appeared in the box with a glass of lemonade for her, but she only toyed with it as they talked, waiting for the lights to dim for the next act.

In this act, the citizens of Numancia, pushed to the extreme of endurance, decided that they would all die rather than surrender or grant the victorious Romans the satisfaction of as much as one captive. Numancia was burned, her wealth destroyed, her people sacrificed to Plague, Starvation, and War.

Kate wondered if she was the only one in the cheering audience who thought the sacrifice might not be worth it.

A glimmer of light drew her attention then to General Moore's box. The curtain behind it was raised to give entrance to a messenger, who leaned over to whisper something to the general. Moore gravely heard him out, then quietly rose and left the box.

On the stage, the figure of Fame proclaimed that, triumphing over death, the memory of Numancia would live on, inspiring future generations with the same valor shown by those ancient heroes of Numancia. But the audience tonight had no thought for the generations to come. Other people had seen Moore's departure, and their only immediate interest was in the present crisis. What news?

Val took Kate home, and a dozen or more officers and wives of the regiment soon joined them, feeling that the house on the Plaza Mayor was the likeliest place of any to wait for news. Amelia, aroused to energetic activity, laid out for them an excellent cold supper, and Val was prompted to interrupt one of her frequent trips to the kitchen in order to compliment her lavishly, in his charming Spanish, on her service. Amelia, pleased that her talents should be recognized and remarked by this *señorito inglés,* dropped a flustered curtsy and ran out again to urge the harassed cook on to yet greater achievements.

"I think you've embarrassed Amelia," Kate told Val. "She isn't accustomed to such charm!"

Val replied suitably, and they fell into a harmless discussion of the play, keeping up with the rest of the party a gallant attempt at lightheartedness.

Michael Sinclair and his Maria Elena, looking as if she would burst into tears at any moment, were huddled in one corner where he clutched her hand and whispered comfort-

The Dancers' Land

ing things into her ear. The O'Reillys were at the center of a small group that stood together, glasses in hand, arguing the merits of Cervantes, and Kate silently thanked them for pretending that this evening was like any other.

The unobtrusive Peter Rutledge startled them momentarily by making an appearance with a lovely, black-eyed young woman on his arm, and Val promptly marched over to be introduced to the mysterious stranger, leaving Kate to the company of Alan Grierson. The young lieutenant attempted without much success to be cheerful, and stole wistful glances at Kate when she was looking the other way and wishing poor Alan were not so self-effacing. Of course, she supposed he could not be all that timid, or he would not have joined the army. But in social situations, he was a little trying. Colin was nowhere to be seen.

After several eternities had crept languorously by, Kate looked at the clock to discover that in fact little more than an hour had elapsed since they left the theater. Still, some news should have come by now. She considered sending Luis to San Boal, but at that moment, Vivian Harmer burst into the room, his long face shining with glee.

"Madrid has surrendered!"

No one said anything, but they all stared at him as at a madman. Madrid fallen! What possible joy was to be found in such tidings? Vivian saw that he had been misunderstood and explained, "We're moving out!" He clapped Val on the shoulder. "But eastward man, not back to Lisbon!"

His meaning came suddenly clear to their benumbed minds, and Vivian found himself the target of a volley of questions. Eastward? But with what object? Valladolid! The French had evacuated that city, apparently still unaware of Moore's presence in Salamanca. But why Valladolid? To unite there with Baird, to harass French communications, to do as much damage as they could before Napoleon turned on them. In short, to fight! When? They moved out in two days' time. No—remembering the advanced hour—tomorrow. Tomorrow!

Chapter Fifteen

THE ARMY was on the move at last. Three days saw a continuous stream of men, pack mules, loaded carts and wagons, and trains of artillery being drained out of Salamanca. Each unit moved out in high spirits, pleased with themselves and eager to meet the enemy. The Salamantinos were equally pleased with them, seeing them go forth determined to conquer.

The Spanish turned out in force to see the British off. Balconies were crowded with ladies who threw their scented handkerchiefs down on the passing soldiers and with gentlemen who waved their hands and shouted farewells. Bonfires and flares brightened the city at night.

Kate shut herself in her room and put its walls between her and the noises of packing and preparation coming from other parts of the house. She could have fled to Santa Virgen until they were gone. But she did not have the courage to do so, nor yet the resolution to go calmly about her daily routine.

On the second morning, as she sat at her desk composing a description of the scene outside for a letter to Christopher, the sounds to which she had been continually attentive stopped. She sat up and listened more carefully—but to silence. Suddenly frightened, she ran out onto the balcony and leaned over it. There was no one there.

"Colin?"

She ran down the stairs, her heart in her mouth. Surely he would not have left without a word! A jumble of confused memories flooded her mind—Colin when he laughed with her (had he ever really mocked her as she had been so quick to believe?), Colin's eyes when she caught him watching her, Colin's arms holding her as they whirled

The Dancers' Land

around the ballroom at San Boal, and the feel of his skin against hers in the lovelight of evening when all her senses came awake, as they were, wildly, now. She had been afraid to go to him, too proud to ask his forgiveness, but now, desperate, she fairly flew.

The air outside was crisp and cold, and a few flakes of snow were beginning to fall from an unfriendly leaden sky. The horses snorted and stamped, and their breath was frostily visible. Michael Sinclair was already in the saddle and struggling to control his restive horse while he buttoned his jacket up more tightly. Colin was about to mount but had paused to glance up at Kate's window, when she ran out of the doorway. She stopped, shivering in the cold. He saw her and came to take her hand. Michael saw her, too, quietly turned away down the street, and was not missed.

Colin looked into Kate's eyes, frowning with the effort to interpret the expression there. She did not speak, and he merely said, with a voice as cold as the sky, "Good-bye, Kate," and went away.

"Colin." She could scarcely force the word past her lips, and he did not hear.

"Colin!"

He looked back then, and this time there was no mistaking the meaning in her eyes and in her voice. He came quickly back to her and took her in his arms. They were comforting and strong around her, his mouth warm on hers. For a moment summer returned and the sun wrapped its warmth around her, and she returned his embrace breathlessly. While she clung to him as to a haven from the coldest of worlds outside, she felt deliciously safe and no longer alone.

But at length, he had to release her. He kissed her once more, deeply, forever, then brushed her ear with his lips as he whispered, "I'll be back, Kate, my lovely Kate. Wait for me."

Then he did turn away and did not look back again.

Kate stood in the doorway and gazed down the empty street long after Colin had disappeared, but at last the cold became too intense. She went indoors, only to spend several hours wandering aimlessly through the house. There remained not the least trace of its recent guests, but everywhere Kate turned reminded her of a moment, an hour, out of the last month. They were happy reminders again, and she was glad she had summoned up the courage to go—once again—to Colin. She was filled with an excitement and a sense of release that were overwhelming.

She sought distraction in watching the troops mustering in the plaza, from the window of the room Colin had occupied. But when she left it to have her dinner, she sat at the table doubly alone, scarcely touching her food while Amelia padded silently about, bringing in the next course or refilling Kate's wineglass. She cast concerned looks at Kate, as if uncertain whether to attempt to cheer her or to leave her alone with her thoughts.

"For heaven's sake, Amelia, must you make such a clatter?"

Amelia, who had done nothing of the sort, set her square shoulders indignantly as she went off to the kitchen again.

Possessed with a restless desire to do something—anything—Kate fetched a cloak, went outside, and stood in the plaza, watching the various units preparing to march. Then she began to walk around the city.

The high-pitched voices of bagpipes and the beat of drums that signaled a highland regiment grew louder as they approached her, and reverberated through Kate's brain as she stepped back, pressing against the people behind her to let them pass.

The kilted troops marched by with an energy amazing in men so burdened with clothing and equipment as these were. The crowd waved and called to them, holding out their hands to have them shaken in farewell, to touch once more a tartaned arm or back. One young private, carried away with the spirit of the occasion, leaned over to kiss Kate quickly on the cheek, and she could not help smiling and waving after him.

Then she was caught up in the crowd that surged in to fill the street behind the Highlanders and to follow them to the rhythmic tread of their feet and the wild excitement of the pipes. She followed along and, after a few minutes, was able to slip down a less crowded side street. But this led into another broad thoroughfare where she had to dodge soldiers and civilians alike, wagonloads of equipment, and

The Dancers' Land

the nervous prancing of horses among the tangle of paraphernalia and pedestrians.

She found her way to a large, open square where another regiment was mustering in a scene of vast confusion. The men were dressed in green jackets with black trim and had smiling, hearty faces. Their raucous, laughing voices called out jokes, ribald remarks, and orders delivered in a peculiarly informal fashion. Their high spirits made a festival of the occasion and immediately endeared them to Kate, who inquired of a young private, "Please, what men are these?"

The private, who had been attempting to make some order of his equipment, which was spread out on the ground around him, immediately sprang to attention and said, "Why, Colonel Crauford's, ma'am—the 95th!"

A voice from across the square shouted just at that moment, as if to echo his words, "The bloody 95th! Come on, you filthy sweeps, show some speed!"

A short, thickset man, who must have been their colonel, shouted to make himself heard over the din but received for his pains only a cheery "Oh, what the hell, Bob!" He ordered one soldier to button up his jacket and another to get rid of the boy he carried on his shoulders, as well as the boy's older sister, who clung to the soldier's sleeve, because he "damn well couldn't take *them* along!" A third soldier sat on the curb, the contents of his knapsack strewn over the ground near him, whistling a popular Salamancan ditty, to the delight of the lady who clung to him.

But in spite of the monumental lack of order, while Kate watched, the 95th began to form, and in a short time were ready to start. Their colonel, grinning, gave the order, which was quickly drowned in the cheers of the onlookers, and the Rifle Brigade was off.

When Kate returned home at last, she fell into an exhausted sleep, and so spent a peaceful night in spite of the continuing din of departure from outside. When she woke in the morning, the noise had not simply abated but had stopped entirely. The silence, by contrast, was deafening. She looked out into the empty plaza—empty, that was, but for the early-rising shopkeepers opening their stalls for business as they did on every other morning of the year.

The overnight change was difficult to comprehend. Kate had the sensation of having awakened from a dream and, for a few awful minutes, almost believed that was all it had been. But the house remembered the reality in a hundred little changes—a book lying on the library desk, a mark on the stairs where a boot had scraped by. And her body remembered.

She spent the morning searching for small, prosaic tasks to occupy her and to bring her back into her normal life, although she abandoned each as soon as she began it, and several times had to stop halfway across a room to remember what she had meant to do there.

Ramón appeared later in the afternoon. She watched impassively from the balcony as he crossed the patio but snapped suddenly out of her trance when he said, "Well, they're all gone."

She seemed to jerk awake then, and took violent possession of his arm, as if to pull him by it to the door.

"Ramón! Oh, please, Ramón, let's go after them! Where are they? Oh, hurry, let's go and see!"

He stared at her, astonishment and incomprehension in his scowl. "Go after them? Kate, I've just come from Fuentesauco—twenty miles from here. They must be well beyond that by now, and the rest are scattered from Toro east to Valladolid. God knows where Greyson's men are. You'll never find him—certainly not when it begins to snow in earnest!"

She winced at the mention of Colin's name but pleaded desperately with Ramón. She was not sure what arguments she used on Ramón, for she was only conscious of the questions hammering in her own brain. She had not told Colin how sorry she was—would he be sure to know? No, she must tell him herself. She could not chance Colin being away from her for so long with the wrong impression of her feelings toward him. She was blind to the impracticality of her sudden mad scheme, knowing only that she could not stay where she was while Colin rode away, farther every minute. Finally, tears streaming down her cheeks, she choked on her words and could only look entreatingly at Ramón.

In a savage voice that echoed something more than his

opinion of her foolhardy plan, he said, "I'll saddle the horses. Put something warm on."

Tearfully, Kate smiled her thanks and ran to her room to change. Within half an hour, they were well out of Salamanca, heading in the direction that Ramón guessed Colin's regiment would have taken. The ground beneath their horses' hooves was hard with the cold as they rode over the bare plain. The snow was still falling only lightly, but it had begun to turn the earth from a dull brown to a graywhite that matched the color of the sky and created the illusion of night in mid-afternoon. They rode for what seemed interminable hours, with no sign of a living thing. No birds were to be heard, the few trees in the bleak landscape were dead, and even the smoke from the fire of an occasional peasant's clay hut seemed to hang lifeless in the air.

Then, emerging from a grove of poplars bordering a narrow stream, they saw a unit of cavalry advancing up the road ahead. They spurred their horses on and caught them up as they rounded a bend. The officer in charge heard their approach and looked back, surprised to see emerging from the net of falling snow two riders who did not look to be any part of the army. He raised a hand to halt his troops and was even more surprised to hear a woman's voice call out in English.

"Captain! Please, captain, will you help us?"

He met them and saluted, vastly intrigued by the sight of this young woman, the hood of her cloak flung back, her face flushed from the ride and steadying her mount with an expert hand.

"How may I assist you, miss?"

"We are looking for Colonel Greyson's regiment. Can you tell us where they might be?"

The captain thought she said it as if she were inquiring the way from Dover Street to the Mall, but he replied as well as he was able. "I'm sorry, miss, but it's extremely difficult to say. You see, we have only just had a change of orders. An intercepted French dispatch has revealed that Marshal Soult's force is lying unprotected near Saldaña—"

Ramon's eyebrows shot up and he asked Kate a question in Spanish. She translated it for the captain.

"Doesn't Soult know how close you are?"

The captain addressed Ramón, whom he now remembered having seen at headquarters. He did not know the Spaniard's official status, but he was still doggedly determined to be cooperative with England's ally.

"No, sir," he said. "According to the dispatch, Soult is to advance west on León—since there are no troops in the way to oppose him."

He grinned. "Seems they think we're in Portugal! We are making north, then, and not east, to see if we can't catch the Frogs—sorry, sir, I mean Soult's division—unawares. But as for Greyson's men, miss—well, we passed Colonel Aspey's unit this morning. Aspey left Salamanca just behind Greyson, so I reckon they must be farther on than this by now, assuming, of course, that their orders have been changed in accordance with ours. That means they must also have veered away from Valladolid and headed north."

It occurred to the captain that he should warn these two of the danger to civilians riding about alone as they were, but before he could say so, they had thanked him and were gone.

As the true night descended, the sky turned black and the earth whiter. Reason returned to Kate, penetrating her disordered thoughts as the cold did her garments, and she knew she should turn back now. Ramón had doubtless expected her to come to her senses long before this and had only come with her so that she would not go off into this madness alone.

It had stopped snowing, but the occasional shaft of pale moonlight that filtered through the clouds only made sharper the contrast between black sky and white earth. There was no sign of any other troops, and Kate was about to ask Ramón to take her home when, suddenly, topping a ridge, they saw close ahead of them a company of British hussars. Kate started toward them, but Ramón stopped her.

"Wait! Look there."

On the opposite ridge had appeared another group of horsemen—French dragoons, looking to be half again as strong as the British force. A trumpet sounded shrilly as the British quickly formed, hampered by the stumps and low walls of a vineyard half-hidden in the snow.

The Dancers' Land

The French, little more than a quarter of a mile away, were extending in line and presented an imposing spectacle on their huge horses. The British seemed woefully weak by comparison, their soft fur caps flimsy, the hands holding their reins and swords numb with cold. When their officer gave the order to charge, the men galloped down the slope like demons, shouting and cheering.

The astonished French had loosed only a few shots before the British had covered the short distance between them and were into them with a force ferocious in its shattering impact. Men thrown from their horses were crushed by their mounts, toppled by the shock, or were ridden over by other men still mounted. Bayonets driven with maniacal force vanished into red and blue uniforms, and the men behind them tried not to look into the faces of those they had struck. Screams, the frantic whinny of a wounded horse, groans, and cries of intense excitement and of pain echoed over the plain.

Then the struggle was over, almost before it had begun. The British galloped northward in pursuit of the panic-stricken French, forgetting the cold and everything else but the thrill of slashing at the enemy as they ran.

Kate's face was ashen, and the stricken look on it made Ramón curse himself for letting her watch. He had not been able to tear his own eyes away, but now nothing was left but the huddled shapes, some attempting to move and groaning loudly in the agony of the effort, of men and horses on the frozen ground. Some moved not at all but for the ruffle of the wind on their caps; the snow beneath them was stained black. Camp followers from both sides crept down onto the scene to care for the wounded and strip the dead of their clothing and valuables.

Ramón turned Kate's mount around and forced her to take up the reins and follow him. It began to snow again, and soon it was falling so thickly that their progress was reduced to a walk in the poor visibility. He led her to Santa Virgen—it was closer than Salamanca—and delivered her, shivering with shock and cold, into Mercedes's capable hands. Mercedes looked reproachfully at Ramón as she comforted Kate, but he only shrugged his shoulders and would not explain what had happened.

Kate, her imagination fired by the skirmish she had witnessed, had passed the uncomfortable ride to Santa Virgen in conjuring up nightmarish visions of icy ghosts stalking the bleak plains, calling in vain for aid from the unhearing living. Fortunately, her inventive powers eventually wore themselves out, and she was able to fall into a dreamless sleep, guarded for most of the night by Ramón, who sat up and watched over her until he, too, fell asleep.

She woke exhausted in the morning, and Mercedes, clucking like a mother hen, brought her strong coffee and a hearty breakfast. Kate was sipping the scalding black brew when Ramón strode in the door, followed by Francho and Luis, who stooped as he came in to clear the low doorway.

"Bonaparte and the main French force have crossed the mountains from Madrid," Ramón said without preliminaries. "They are only a day's march away and are advancing in this direction. You will have to go home, Kate."

Mercedes took this in calmly and, standing by the fire with a pot in one hand, asked, *"Así—vamos ya?"*

"Sí, Mercedes, ya es tiempo."

"Where?" Kate demanded. "Where are you going?"

Ramón hesitated. "To meet Rico and the others in Medina. Then we strike north to Saldaña to try to intercept Soult. We may be able to do some damage, even if the British can't. But we can't stay here any longer."

Kate stood up and looked from Luis to Mercedes to Ramón's black eyes. Her own frightened gray eyes darted from one face to another around the room and at the door, as if she faced whatever lay beyond it.

"I won't go back to Salamanca," she said to him. "I can ride as well as any of you, and if Mercedes is going, why can't I?"

Ramón opened his mouth to order her home but stopped himself. He stared at the girl in front of him, who had the look of having burned all her bridges behind her and a determination in the set of her mouth that moved him as strongly as her tears had done.

He thought quickly. If the French still did not know— and it was more than possible—the exact position of the British army, they might well march through Salamanca in pursuit of them, making the city no more safe than these hills. Reason provided this excuse, but he knew he could not deny Kate anything she asked. He couldn't leave her alone in danger. He couldn't, in the end, leave her at all.

While Kate watched anxiously, he went into a hurried consultation with Luis, who listened, nodded, and went out the door.

"I'm sending Luis back to Salamanca for anything you might need and to leave instructions for Amelia," Ramón told her. "You won't be back soon."

Part Three
The Guerrilleros, 1809–1811

Chapter Sixteen

RAMÓN SAT on the pine-carpeted ground with his back against a massive rock, one of the many that supported the dark, rich earth and tall, straight pines making up the range of northern mountains called the Cordillera Cantábrica. It had rained heavily for most of the day, but the trees kept Ramón dry enough. He preferred the washed-earth smell, the sound of water dripping from branches, and the fresh, clean feel of the cold outside air to the warm but oppressive comforts of the nearby cave in which Kate and Mercedes were preparing the evening meal.

Ramón was waiting for Luis at this prearranged meeting place in the mountains. He would ordinarily not have lingered for so long in such a place, but the late January storms that had driven Ramón's band to shelter ten days before the appointed rendezvous would likewise discourage the nearby French troops from setting out in search of them. Still, there was no knowing anything for certain, and Ramón sat under the tree absently but expertly sharpening a knife—that fierce and violently efficient weapon with which the men of these mountains waged their *guerra a cuchillo* against the French.

Ramón did not worry that Luis might not return. Luis knew how to take care of himself; he knew not to take risks or get in the way of those who did. He would return to them safely with the report he had been sent to get about the ultimate fate of Moore's army.

Napoleon had met his marshal, Soult, at Astorga, but not before the British had been there and were gone again into the mountain passes that made pursuit next to impossible. Then, when matters demanding the emperor's personal attention in Paris became too pressing for him to continue this unprofitable game in the wilds of Spain, he handed the command over to the marshal and began the long trip home via Valladolid and Burgos. It was the first and last time the emperor would set foot in Spain.

In the course of those weeks before Astorga, Ramón had revealed a talent for choosing the seemingly unimportant target that proved in the end to be as valuable an objective as any fought for in a major engagement. Rico might protest the destruction of a small wooden bridge, high over a ravine in the middle of nowhere, as unimportant and too far from either army's course to be of any consequence, but he would discover later that its absence prevented a courier from one French unit from getting to another in time to provide the cavalry support necessary to the success of an infantry maneuver, with the result that a whole regiment of French were cut off and to pieces by the British. But much as the success of such schemes raised him in the esteem of his men, Ramón knew that any failure—any small miscalculation—could easily jeopardize his position as their leader.

Rico was—by unanimous, if untaken, vote—Ramón's second-in-command. He respected Ramón's talents, but his natural excitability and a streak of violence in him made him reckless and impatient to engage in a real fight, to strike a decisive blow instead of carrying on this everlasting chess game that Ramón made of war.

Once, Rico and part of the band became separated from Ramón's men. Hearing that Napoleon had turned back to France with minimal escort, Rico had, on a sudden heated impulse, made a wide circle around the emperor's path, coming by devious means up in front of him to lie in wait in the hills. Visions danced in his brain of the chaos France would be thrown into by the sudden death of their emperor. Strategy—bah! Maneuver—a stupid word!

But Rico badly underestimated the efficiency of the Imperial Guard, and when Ramón caught up with him, he found Rico and his men in fierce contest with a superior force. Only Ramón's intervention saved them. They lost a dozen men, but Rico never lost his resentment at being forced to express his gratitude to Ramón for saving his life. By the time the French had been beaten off, the would-be prize of the contest was long gone, blissfully unaware that for a moment, at least, his life had been in the hands of a Spanish patriot with no mercy in his heart for a foreign tyrant.

The rain came down more heavily now, and penetrated even the thickly woven branches of the pines. Ramón stood up and slapped the dead leaves from his clothing before returning to the cave.

A heavy blanket hung over the entrance; as Ramón lifted it and came in, Kate looked up and smoothed the straying strands of her hair away from her flushed face.

"It's going to rain all night, isn't it?" she said.

Ramón smiled. He had once jokingly called Kate a pampered city dweller, and ever since, she had gone out of her way to learn peasants' ways. She had already learned to predict the weather better than Guillermo, heretofore the acknowledged authority, could.

"It looks that way," Ramón said. "At least we won't get washed away here."

"We won't even get wet," Kate said as Ramón leaned over the cooking pot and sniffed appreciatively. "Unless, of course, you spill your dinner."

Ramón grinned and picked up a spoon to test the *cocido*, but Mercedes snatched it away from him and ordered him to wait with the others until the meal was ready. Ramón spread his hands in a penitent gesture. Mercedes laughed and pulled his ear in affectionate acceptance of his apology.

The cave was a large one and penetrated far enough into the mountain to accommodate a score of people. The rest of Ramón's band of about fifty were camped in other caves nearby or in makeshift shelters of pine boughs, cooking their meals or occupying themselves with some piece of mending, just as those with Ramón were doing. Ramón was glad that Luis would return today, however, because despite the bad weather, the men would already be restless to move on. This enforced idleness was bad for them. It bred quarrels and insubordination; but a quick march, a taste of danger and fighting, would cool them off fast enough. Work was the best thing for them; they were not accustomed to leisure.

Ramón had not expected Kate to adapt so easily to this life. He had forgotten the girl who had reveled in the sunshine and long rides over the rough hills of Salamanca, the girl who went hunting and fishing with him and Christopher and cooked their midday meal over an open fire. Ramón had admired her for doing that, but such activities had come to an abrupt halt when she married Manuel Sanchez and turned into an aristocrat—coolly beautiful, elegant, gracious, but far above the likes of Ramón Sariñana.

That life was natural to her, Ramón had thought, not recognizing that his own blindness made him deliberately set her above himself. On her visits to Santa Virgen, she had been like a princess masquerading as a peasant for a lark—or so Ramón had imagined. Perhaps he had been mistaken. Now she worked as hard as any of them, without complaint, untiring. She slept deeply at night and rose to the new day with no sign of missing Doña Catarina's long mornings in bed with breakfast brought to her on a tray.

Nevertheless, although she walked, rode, talked, ate, and slept in this close community where survival depended on closeness, some part of her was somewhere else, with someone else. Ramón did not attempt to bring her home. He feared that the mists she wandered in might be all too quickly dispelled by Luis's return.

A gust of cold wind blew in on them as they sat down to their meal. Luis pushed aside the covering over the door, shook off his drenched cloak, and went straight to the welcoming warmth of the fire. He squatted down to warm his hands before Mercedes pressed a plate of food into them. He consumed it in silence and spoke to no one until he had finished. Then he looked at Ramón as if to say, "All right. Now."

Luis had never been capable of more than a few words of connected narrative in front of any sort of audience, so Ramón took him aside to hear his report. He listened with his head bent, black eyes staring at the ground. Now and then he looked up to see Kate watching them as she helped Mercedes clear away the remains of their meal. She had said nothing when Luis came in and did not interrupt now, but Ramón knew that she was silently burning to know

The Dancers' Land

everything Luis was saying and that he would have to tell her. He was not sure how he was going to do it.

Most of what Luis said was only what Ramón had expected to hear. After Astorga, the British were safe enough in the mountains—safe from the French but not from the weather, the Spanish army, and themselves. The mountains were deep in snow that ran down the road in rivers of slush by day and froze to sheets of ice by night. The cold was bitter; the rain and wind penetrated tattered clothing, and the wet came in through boots that finally had to be torn from bleeding feet.

The column of marchers grew longer and longer, leaving behind it dying men and animals, and the frozen carcasses of both, lying stiff in the snow beside the supplies abandoned by those too weary to carry them farther. They had no fuel, no shelter, little to eat, and nothing but snow to drink. The Spanish bullock drivers fled with their carts, rendering the comissariat virtually useless; the march became one long struggle from one supply magazine to the next. The remains of the Spanish army, as hungry as the British, had not made for Asturias as they were meant to do, and now got in the way of the line of retreat.

These seemingly insupportable conditions set discipline to rotting like one of their abandoned corpses. Plunder, rape, drunkenness, and murder were common throughout the army, and particularly in the rear, where stragglers were continually menaced by French cavalry and were burdened with their own sick and wounded. Only floggings and hangings, administered by their desperate officers, kept the men together and, somehow, miraculously, their spirit was not broken.

The tattered remains of the army that had left Salamanca a month before with eagerness, splendid in their clean uniforms, reached La Coruña still together, still whole in spirit if not in body—and found when they arrived that the transport ships that were to take them home had not come. There was nothing to do but wait for them and hope that Soult could not bring up his reserves and heavy artillery before they could embark.

When the ships finally arrived, the hardiest survivors of the long retreat prepared to fight to cover the embarkation of the sick and wounded. Barely half of them were aboard when Soult opened fire, but he was held at bay. Moore himself was in the thick of the battle, everywhere at once, pulling the ranks together, pushing them on to fight harder. Then, while he was watching an attack on a French battery, he was struck off his horse by a cannonball. He picked himself up and resumed his duty, with his left shoulder torn away and his arm hanging by a thread of flesh. By evening, the French had abandoned the fight, and the embarkation could go on. Only then, after they told Moore of the victory, did he surrender himself to death.

There was more to the story, but Luis came to an end at last. Ramón sent him off to get some sleep, and then he joined Kate, who was doing some mending by the dying fire. She had that vacant look on her face again, as if she were somewhere else. Ramón looked at her sewing and saw that she had not set more than a few stitches. He wished he could tell her something else than what he had to say, but he repeated all of Luis's story to her, up to Moore's death.

Kate looked up at him, dry-eyed but with a stricken expression on her white face, which made him wonder how he could possibly tell her what came next. But she seemed to know, just as she knew when a change of weather was coming, that the full fury of the tale had not broken yet.

"What else? Tell me, Ramón."

He braced himself, reached into his shirt, and brought out a knife—a long, silver-handled knife. Kate took a deep breath but stared at it as if she had never seen it before. Ramón spoke more quickly now.

"Luis found this in a peasant woman's cottage. It was given to her by a British officer that she nursed for two days. She did not understand English names, and the officer spoke to her in Spanish. But his friend, who left him there, called him something that sounded like—like Greyson. He was badly . . ." Ramón hesitated. There were some things it was not necessary to tell. ". . . he had pneumonia. When he died, the woman buried him in the family plot."

It sounded so cold, so uncomforting, but Ramón knew no other way to approach death but to say the word. He searched Kate's face to see how she had taken it, but she made no sign, said nothing. She took the knife from him and turned it over in her hand before slipping it into her pocket; then she got up and silently began to prepare for bed. Ramón did not know what to do for her, so he let her go. But he could not sleep, and he watched for hours as she lay unmoving in her usual place nearest the fire, her eyes open and staring at the roof of the cave.

Sometime after midnight, when he was dropping off to sleep at last, a sudden, sharp, cold draft of air woke him. He went outside to find Kate standing alone in the darkness, the rain streaming down her face and into her light clothing. He could not tell if there were tears mingled with the rain because she stood so still, stared so blindly into the night, that there was no readable expression in her eyes. But when he came up behind her and softly spoke her name, she turned abruptly and hurled herself into his arms, sobbing out her heartbreak into his shoulder. He held her close and was able, to his own amazement, to find the right words, the means to comfort her.

Gradually, her sobs subsided, until the two of them only stood quietly together in the rain, the darkness enveloping them with its own form of oblivion. He took her in out of the wet and lay the rest of the night only a hand's length away from her, and she slept.

Chapter Seventeen

KATE NEVER later remembered the next months, which turned winter into spring and approached summer before she even felt, in the most elemental way, the change from cold to heat. She was unaware of time passing, or even of her own movements. She did everything in a kind of trance and with someone—Ramón, she supposed, or Mercedes—leading her by the hand.

But the days were less difficult than the nights, when her senses seemed to reawake even as she slept, and invented cruel, mocking nightmares to make her turn on her blanket and then toss restlessly and finally awake with a scream—except that Ramón always woke her before that, and his hands on her shoulders were her first contact with reality. His words, always the same, became a litany that steadied her racing pulse and pounding brain.

"It's all right, Kate," he would say. "It's only a dream, Kate. It can't hurt you."

"I'm sorry," she would reply. "I didn't mean to disturb you."

"It's all right, Kate. Go to sleep now."

And gradually, she did, and day and night came back into their proper order, and if her mind dwelt more on nightmares during the day, at least the pounding in her head that said, over and over, *Colin, Colin, Colin,* faded to a whisper and she could sleep again.

Nonetheless, she had lost her capacity for forgetting what was past, of casting out memories that were of no further use to her, and even after a year, the memory of one month and one man was as clear to her as it had ever been. It was as if a ghost walked with her, even though she grew to be able to disregard its presence for hours at a time and was eventually set free of the daylight nightmares, too.

Ramón, who had seen her safely through those nights, began to see a subtle change come over her. It was as if the violent flaring of love in her had made her see that she was not alone in the world, despite the loss of that love, and as a result she became more aware of other people and more open with them. She, who had once shied away from intimate contact, physical or emotional, might now be seen impulsively hugging Mercedes, to whom she had become like a daughter, or deep in conversation with Ángel or Paco or even Rico. Ramón was glad to see her finally content with life and untroubled by memories. He never knew that she appeared to be happy because she forced herself to it. He never saw in her all that Colin Greyson had, because that had been pushed into hiding in her innermost self, together with the old nightmares and the ghost.

Kate passed her time in the almost domestic tranquillity of their several and successive encampments, quietly talking with Mercedes or riding within the confines Ramón had set for her. She was willing enough to do this, for with the panorama of mountain and plain before her, and the brilliant dome of azure sky above, she had all the room she needed now.

She began to take an interest, too, in what was going on around them. She had never cared before, or asked where they would go next, but eventually a sense of the future returned to her, and she began to question Ramón about the next village beyond the valley, and the next goal of the *guerrilleros*.

Ramón carefully shielded her from the more unpleasant parts of their business, fearful that it would bring the nightmares back, and he never permitted her to accompany him on any expedition that contained the least element of danger. She noted now and then that he would return from a raid on a French outpost missing a man or two, but when she asked, she would learn only that "he was shot." Whether the missing man had actually been killed in the skirmish by the French, or wounded and finished off by his companions to keep him from falling prisoner, she never knew.

Lastly, Kate regained a consciousness of Spain, and as she listened to the men talking, events began to fall into place. It would be a little longer, she knew, before she could feel any personal interest in them, but she listened just the same.

Ramón had fallen into the habit of holding nightly meetings with his lieutenants around the fire, to go over what they had done that day and make plans for the next. He would squat down on the ground just within the light of the flickering camp fire and, with a gesture that soon became familiar to them all, drew a rough map of Spain in the dirt with the point of his knife. Then he would use the knife to point out objectives and obstacles, past mistakes and future possibilities.

Kate watched from the shadows, wrapped in a rough woolen cloak, as Rico and Francho and Paco and the others gathered around to listen and sometimes offer suggestions—although they only raised their own opinions, Kate noticed, when Ramón seemed uncertain of his. He sensed this, too, and was careful to sound confident even when he was not.

One night, in the early spring of 1810, Ramón was looking exasperated and brushed his long hair back impatiently as he talked. All the men felt it, and Ramón's quick summary of the all-too-familiar situation in southern Spain brought home to them the increased importance of their success—or lack of it—in the northern mountains.

By the spring of 1809, the French had become bored with the feeble efforts at resistance by the Spanish armies in the south. They treated them as insects to be trampled on when they became offensive, just as they had done in the north the year before, but otherwise to be ignored. But when General Sir Arthur Wellesley and a small force of crack British troops landed in Portugal in April, they looked up with interest from their pastime of flicking the wings from Spanish insects.

That summer, Wellesley drove Soult out of his Portuguese base at Oporto, uniting with the Spanish army and pushing the surprised French back toward Madrid. The French soon discovered that the smaller British forces were not so easily crushed as a Spanish insect.

Wellesley retired for the winter behind the Portuguese

frontier from where he watched with a contemptuous eye the autumn offensive of the Spanish armies, which consisted of a series of defeats culminating in disaster at Ocaña, a village south of Madrid. The road to Andalusia once again lay open to the French, and they wasted no time in taking it. Seville, Córdoba, and Málaga fell, and when Wellesley, with a sigh of exasperation, quit Portugal at the start of the campaign of 1810, only Cádiz was still in Spanish hands.

"What do we care what the English are doing?" Rico objected when Ramón, feeling some kinship with Wellesley, described the difficulties the British were having. It was not the first time Rico had objected. Despite the damning evidence of Spanish defeats, he was still convinced that they could win their own war.

"We care because the more the English can accomplish, the more trouble they will be to the French, and the more men the French will need to hold the border forts," Ramón explained patiently, pointing his knife at the sites of Badajoz and Ciudad Rodrigo.

As always, Ramón's grasp of the situation was wider than the reach of his small force, which was both an advantage and a frustration to him. He knew that the war being waged in the north against the French occupation was no less fierce in its way than that which Wellesley carried on against invasion in the south. Napoleon conducted his Spanish war from Paris, issuing orders that often had little to do with the realities his armies faced in the field. But the orders had to be obeyed, and this meant long lines of communication to be kept open and, above all, men to hold them, men that could not be released for an offensive in the south as long as roving bands of *guerrilleros* threatened the security of captured French holdings in the north.

Guerrilla bands sprang up everywhere in the path of the French. Villages that would have been content to let the war pass them by became armed camps after the French had "confiscated" their food and livestock. Every ablebodied man, from farmer and miner to hidalgo and priest, left his ravaged home and took to the hills to stalk the invaders.

Unfortunately for those who remained at home, these fighters also had to eat, and they, too, descended on the villages and farms, now being run by women and old men, to extract what they could from already much-depleted stores. Before long, the unfortunate peasants had become experts at secreting their meager belongings, at an instant's notice, from the marauders, be they French or Spanish.

The band's losses in combat were relatively light but so, too, was the influx of new members, and the band grew very little beyond its original size. Rico's visions of grandeur had received a considerable setback when he had to be rescued by Ramón from his precipitous attack on the Might of France, and Ramón had no wish to saddle himself with an army. The number of his men remained fixed at what he considered manageable.

His lieutenants were firmly fixed, too, in their relations to Ramón and to one another. Rico was the strongest, and although often at odds with Ramón, he was as loyal to him as his brother Ángel was in turn to Rico. Ángel followed devotedly in Rico's shadow, but an even fiercer attachment existed between the wild and excitable Francho and the more placid-tempered Paco; they were as inseparable as their names. Luis depended on no one but himself, and his only friendship, a tepid one at best, was with Guillermo, the nearest of them all to his own age.

As unlike to one another as they were, there existed a bond between them which extended in some part to all the men. Newcomers were regarded with suspicion and were placed on a kind of probation until they proved themselves in one way or another, worthy of a closer intimacy. One of these was El Gitano, "The Gypsy." He went by no other name, and because such nicknames were common among the *guerrilleros,* it was unanimously accepted. He was the only Andalusian among them, and the *sisisbeo* of his southern speech struck a note as incongruous as the gypsy songs he drew from his battered guitar.

Another recruit was Gilberto Higgins.

His surname was the legacy of some Irish ancestor who had long ago found his way from that small green island to the broad Iberian peninsula. The Irish in Gilberto explained his looks, too. His eyes were an unexpected green, but they looked out from under black, bristly lashes and heavy brows that almost met above them, giving his angular face a sullen look. He was tall and thin, although astonishingly strong, and could carry a load that would have staggered most of the others. When he first came, however, he carried only a blanket wrapped around a second pair of boots, a hunting knife, and a battered leather case, the contents of which remained a mystery for some time.

Kate was the first to lay eyes on Gilberto. On one of the first warm days of the spring of 1810, she had been sitting by herself on a sunny patch of turf overlooking, but invisible from, the main road between Oviedo and León. It was a convenient vantage point where she could, unobserved, study any traffic that passed and report anything of interest to Ramón.

For a long time, there had been nothing to see, and she had been lying back on a rock with her eyes closed, letting her mind drift. She was less afraid to do that now because, although the memory that drifted up was inevitably of Colin, she had discovered that the happiest ones came first—as now, when she saw him in her mind's eye lying back on the sunny grass on the afternoon of their picnic with Michael and Maria Elena. She let the image shimmer there for a moment, delicate as a cloud, still a little apprehensive of what else it might recall.

A real cloud drifted across her eyes. She opened them and sat up. She waited for the sun to return and looked down on the road again, and then she saw him—a solitary figure emerging, as she watched, from the haze to the north, walking at a steady pace that would quickly take him around the next bend and out of sight. But before he reached the bend, he turned off the road and began to climb the rocks, following no path, but with a decisiveness that made Kate sit up with interest. If he turned to the right after that stunted pine, she realized, he would find the path that led up to where she was sitting.

He turned, and she watched him come closer, until he had reached a point just below her. He put down the leather case, hoisted himself up between two rocks, and then was standing before her. He raised his black brows in surprise at finding her there, and she found herself staring into a pair of brilliant green eyes. She was startled but unafraid—and very much intrigued. He looked around.

"Ramón Sariñana?"

"Who are you?"

He seemed to remember that she was only a woman and said curtly, "I have business with Sariñana."

"Wait here," Kate told him, and got up. Five minutes later, the stranger was stating his business to Ramón.

It was not until a week later that Kate discovered the exact nature of that business, but she was more quickly gratified to see, at supper, that this newcomer had taken the first steps toward being accepted into the band. He sat on the fringe of the fireside circle, saying nothing and eating with a singular concentration, although he refused wine and drank only water. No introductions were made, and he was obliged to learn their names by hearing them mentioned in the course of the conversation. Because no one spoke to him, Kate stopped as she offered him a second helping of stew, and asked, *"Cómo te llamas?"*

He looked up and smiled. *"Gilberto. Y tú?"*

Something—that smile, perhaps—prompted her to say "Riña," and then move quickly on to someone else.

It became apparent that Gilberto had come to stay. The next morning Mercedes greeted him with a perfunctory *"Buenos!"* and a nod as he went by. Rico, Francho, and Paco in turn granted him a curt salute, although none of them spoke to him at first. Ramón, who had the final word as to whether he stayed or went, ignored him. In fact, he seemed to have taken an active aversion to Gilberto. Kate, however, liked Gilberto. There was a gentleness in his green eyes and offhand manner that appealed to her, although it was very likely part of what Rico, for example, disliked about him. He would have sensed it as weakness, but when no one else was within hearing, Kate made an attempt to talk to Gilberto. After a time he responded, and gradually the two of them came to a friendly understanding. As if to demonstrate Gilberto's increased acceptance by the others as well, he sat nearer and nearer to them around the evening fire. A week passed before he spoke up, and when he did, he caused a brief but violent explosion.

Rico had taken a dozen men on an unsuccessful foraging expedition. To cover the humiliation of his failure, he had begun, on his return, a diatribe on the ruthlessness of the French in stripping the country of food and supplies and on the incomprehensible reluctance of their own countrymen to share what they had.

"By God, there was not a sack of grain to be had, nor a strip of bacon—no, nor a bottle of wine! No cattle—one old woman had only an undersized ass, but we took it anyway—no hides, no chickens. And money! Not even paper!"

He paused for breath, and in the void created when the last echo of his words had faded, Gilberto muttered softly, "There is food in Oviedo. There is grain, flour ready-milled, wine, salt beef, biscuit. Also gold, gunpowder, cartridges, guns, mules . . ."

They stared foolishly at him—all except Ramón, who shot him a murderous look. It was Rico who recovered first. His laugh burst out like a dog's bark.

"Oviedo! Yes, there is all of that in Oviedo—and a French garrison, too! Do you expect the French to hand everything they have over to us, as a peace offering, perhaps?"

Gilberto continued quietly, disregarding Ramón's look. "The storeroom in the garrison in Oviedo is guarded by four men and two doors. The inside one is not locked because it connects with the passage to the guards' quarters. Two guards are always on watch in the storeroom. The door that connects the Plaza Menor to the garrison courtyard also has two guards. We could easily eliminate them and get out afterward by a third door, which is never used and is kept locked from the inside in the city wall. To this I have a key. From there, a narrow passage leads down between some houses and comes out well beyond the walls."

"You're mad!" Ramón sneered. "There are not four, but four hundred men in the garrison of Oviedo. How do you propose to get past them?"

"There are not four hundred men guarding the storeroom. There will not even be four hundred men near the garrison on Good Friday, next week, and if no alarm is raised to rouse those left in the main part of the garrison, we can help ourselves to the supplies."

Rico had listened to this with growing interest. "Yes!" he exclaimed. "Why not?"

Gilberto, encouraged, expounded his plan. They would go, not more than a score or so, to Oviedo in twos and threes, as if they were there for the religious observances.

They would leave their pack animals at a certain place, meet at a set time for the actual raid, then scatter again and find different ways back to camp. He had calculated every move; it sounded ridiculously simple. Kate wondered how he had come by the key he spoke of, but she was learning the difference between questions that the men accepted from her and those she should not ask, and so she did not ask—not then.

"All right," Ramón gave in gruffly. "But Higgins stays here, under guard, in case . . ." He left the sentence unfinished, but Gilberto's fate, if the men did not return, was made clear.

"Don't be a fool," Gilberto said, undisturbed by the sentence that had been implicitly passed on him. "You need me to find your way in and out again. If anything goes wrong, you can deal with me personally—if I'm still alive."

"Riña could come, too," he added as an afterthought.

That was the last straw. "Certainly not!" snorted Ramón, and stalked off with a finality that put an end to the discussion—if not to Gilberto's schemes. Kate smiled at him. She knew already that, somehow, she would be allowed to go.

Chapter Eighteen

On Good Friday morning, they set off for Oviedo. Some of the band walked, and others rode in unaccustomed luxury on the mules that would carry their spoils back to camp. They left singly or in small groups over a period of hours, so that any stranger they might encounter would not connect any one of them with any other, nor with any purpose beyond an excursion to the city to view the processions of Holy Week—La Semana Santa.

Kate sat beside Gilberto, who drove their small wooden cart. Ramón rode alongside, perched on one of the mules, his long legs dangling absurdly near the ground. His dark face, black mustache, and the thin white scar on his temple heightened the severity of his expression. Gilberto, deep in thought and unsmiling, seemed all eyebrows and angles. They roused themselves, however, when Kate laughed at their glum expressions.

"If you could only see yourselves! If I were vain, I would be very much put out that my escorts—on what is supposed to be a holiday—wore such gloomy faces and paid me not the least attention besides!"

Ramón smiled, accepted the rebuke, and spent the remainder of the journey making an effort to be cheerful. Gilberto remarked that merriment did not seem to him quite the appropriate frame of mind, considering the occasion, but he was willing to defer to the popular opinion that it was. So saying, he doffed his hat and shouted a greeting to a passing group of dusty peasants, who grinned and waved back.

It was late afternoon before they came in sight of the city. The traffic in their direction became increasingly heavy as people from the nearby villages and farms, eager to see the procession that night, hurried along in order to have time first for a glass of wine to wash away the taste of the road. As Gilberto had remarked, they were, in spite of the solemnity of this holy day, dressed in their gayest clothes, with red sashes and ribbons in profusion, for it was not often that these people had a holiday of any kind. Kate had to search for her last memory of a holiday, too, and it came to her with a stab of pain: It was the day the army left Salamanca, banners flying and a holiday air over men who knew it would not last.

She shook her head to throw off the ache in it and looked at Gilberto to clear her vision. His green eyes were narrowed, watching her. She smiled thinly.

Ramón put up his hand to shade his eyes against the setting sun; its rays, where they were unobstructed by the shadowy bulk of the city, beamed straight and strong. Oviedo was set against the hills from which it had been carved, and clung to the slopes as if its hold were in danger of loosening with the passing years. A ravine was all that finally separated them from the city gates. Trees grew in profusion along the bottom of the ravine, and among them a group of peasants—or perhaps gypsies, from the look of them—were making camp. Most of the men were, in fact, Ramón's, and there were a dozen mules, carefully guarded, tethered to the trees.

Gilberto indicated the approximate position of the hidden door in a portion of the old city walls, to their right and a few hundred yards from the trees. They could see the garrison itself rising above the walls and beyond it the tower of the cathedral. There were only a few French soldiers to be seen along their route, and those there were leaned negligently on their guns as they watched the passing parade, making occasional vulgar comments about it to one another.

It had been a long time since Kate was inside any kind of large city, and she looked around her with as much interest as the country-bred farmers displayed. There were crowds of people in the streets and cafés. Visitors and residents eyed each other suspiciously but stayed up until dawn together. Vendors sold Easter cakes carried on a long spike, plaster replicas of the saints, and confections of all kinds.

The route the procession would later take was illuminated by lanterns hung in the trees and balconies overlooking it. There were benches set up wherever there was an inch of space along the way, most of them already occupied by people who had been there for hours and had spread their belongings all around.

Kate paid little heed to the direction they were taking, for Gilberto led them unhesitatingly, sure of his destination. They found themselves inside a dimly lighted *mesón* that reeked with the odor of frying food and the spilled wine on the sawdust-covered floor.

They crossed to a vacant table, but halfway there, Kate's steps were abruptly arrested by the image of a young woman, tall and rather thin, with a brown complexion; wide, surprised eyes; and a mass of untidy blond hair—her own reflection in a wall mirror, a sight she had not seen for over a year.

How she had changed! She had scarcely noticed the old brown dress and cloak and peasant's shoes when she put them on that morning, but the sight of them now startled her. Where was the softness and elegant grace of Doña Catarina de Sanchez? Surely that woman in the glass, in whom no trace of the girl remained, could not be herself!

Gilberto came up behind her and, glancing into the mirror, guessed what she was thinking. "You are beautiful," he whispered. She laughed but was grateful to him for the gallant lie.

They lingered over their meal. The waiter was a cheerful middle-aged man who bustled about untiringly, his face red and perspiring with the effort, and always had something to say when he came their way. He lay before them a steaming dish of beans, ham, and pork flavored with peppers and saffron—a local specialty.

When at last they left the *mesón*, it had grown dark. Gilberto looked up and observed with satisfaction that there would be no moon. The men were to rendezvous outside the garrison at midnight, and although the procession had already begun, it would go on for hours, giving them a wide margin of time. They joined the crowd on the south side of the Plaza Riego. Luis would meet them there later to take Kate out of the city to where she would wait for the others, but it was early yet and he had not arrived, so they watched what they could see of the procession over the heads of the spectators, three-deep along the route.

Each of the huge litters, decked with flowers and candles, had been mounted by a different *cofradía*, or religious brotherhood. The dozens of bearers, called *costaleros*, were careful to move the litter slowly and gracefully and to negotiate corners with inches to spare. Robed and hooded penitents, some carrying crosses on their backs, accompanied each litter, followed by women in black with bowed heads and hands clutching prayer books, and young girls carrying large bunches of purple irises.

Now that it was entirely dark, save the glow of the lanterns and candles carried by the penitents, the wooden figures borne along on the straining shoulders of the *costaleros* took on a strange, bewitching aspect, almost pagan in the emotions they called up. Kate was entranced by the gradual crescendo of feeling aroused in her by the silently passing, nodding, waving, swaying human figures in black, crimson, amethyst, and white robes, and by the carved wooden ones, almost more lifelike, that illustrated the scenes of the Last Supper, Gethsemene, and Calvary.

The hollow eyes of the crucified Christ blazed in the uncertain light, and the blood of His wounds seemed really to flow forth, staining the cross, the ground, the garments of the women praying at His feet. Kate's eyes, like theirs, were drawn inexorably to the eyes of the Christ figure.

The huge crowd fell strangely silent. Many of the women knelt to pray, but the only voices Kate heard were those of the marching penitents, intoning a slow, monotonous chant, accompanied only by the thin, metallic ring of the bells carried by gold-and-white-robed priests. Their measured tread kept time with the distant, muffled tolling of the cathedral bells and the dull pounding beat of drums.

"Here is Luis. Go quickly now!"

Ramón shook her, and she broke out of her spell. She shot him a worried look but said nothing and went away with Luis.

Ramón and Gilberto left the Plaza and, as if with no purpose, meandered their way through the less crowded side

The Dancers' Land

streets of the city. Within half an hour they had come to the Plaza Menor. This was not really a plaza but a long, narrow, open space created by the destruction by the French of the buildings bordering the garrison to form a protective gap between it and the city proper.

Looking across this space, Ramón could see two sentries sitting on kegs in front of a door on the opposite side. In the surrounding darkness, he could not see but could sense the presence of his own men. He glanced at Gilberto, who nodded, and the two of them, keeping well within the shadows, walked in silence to the end of the plaza.

Then they stepped out into the open, as if they had just emerged from one of the side streets, and began the walk back on the garrison side. They sauntered along openly, gesturing and talking to themselves. Gilberto stopped once to light a cigarette and then walked on, unconcerned.

One of the sentries saw them coming and stopped Gilberto to ask, in execrable Spanish, for a light. While he obliged, Ramón moved quietly behind the second sentry. Ramón and Gilberto caught each other's eyes for an instant over the French heads. Then, simultaneously and in such a way that their victims had no time even to register surprise, each wrapped one hand over a mouth and, with the other, silently drove a knife into a fat French back.

Instantly, the other men were crossing the plaza. Ramón propped the sentries' bodies up into sitting positions on the kegs while Gilberto opened the door with one of the keys taken from the dead sentry's belt. Two minutes later they were inside, the door relocked behind them and the scene outside unchanged but for the steady drip of blood that soaked unseen into the dusty earth.

Ramón hadn't believed Gilberto's assurance that there would be few soldiers inside the garrison that night. There were, in fact, none at all to be seen. There was only one light in the guardroom, and it was likely that the men within would be more absorbed in a game of cards than in watching the storeroom. On the right was the guardroom and, against one wall, the storeroom.

Ramón quickly dispatched half a dozen men to line the courtyard, and they took up their positions in the shadows along its edge. Gilberto crossed to the wall, tried his key in the outside door, and signaled back success. Ramón and Rico led the others along the storeroom wall. Ramón looked into each of its three windows—one of which, barred, was set into the door—to ascertain, no longer to his surprise, that there really were only two sentries on duty inside. One of them even had taken his musket apart to clean it, and the pieces lay scattered uselessly on the floor. Ramón almost laughed aloud.

They paused for a moment outside the door as Ramón carefully tested it. It was unlocked. They burst in, and in a moment the two sentries had silently gone the way of their compatriots. Francho picked one of them up and, with a whoop of delight, upended him, fully clothed, into a huge cask of wine that stood inside the door.

The other men had rushed in as soon as the way was clear and were quickly and efficiently clearing the storeroom, passing their loot across the courtyard and through the door in the wall, then carrying it down the passage and a short flight of stone steps to the trees and the waiting mules.

Rico was bending over to pick up a sack when he chanced to glance out of the tiny back window of the storeroom and dropped what he was doing to give a sudden harsh exclamation.

"Caballos!"

He pulled Ramon over to the window to see for himself the horses in the corral just outside the storeroom. Ramón shook off his excited grip. "*Déjalos!* Leave them! There's no time."

But Rico had no intention of leaving such a prize. Disregarding Ramón's order, he gathered several of the men, and they unbolted the rear door, ran out to round up the horses, and threw on the bridles that hung conveniently in an adjacent shed.

"You won't be able to get them out!" Ramón called after them, half-whispering and half-shouting.

But they could. Hands over the horses' muzzles to keep them quiet, they led the frightened animals through the storeroom passage into the courtyard and out through the wall. In the end, Ramón took a horse for himself, hastily tying the sacks he was carrying onto its back and throwing himself on afterward. The horses clattered noisily down the cobbled passage outside the wall, but Ramón no longer cared if anyone heard.

The Dancers' Land

* * *

Kate, crouching unseen in one of the carts left near the ravine, thought she would go mad wondering what was happening. She could hear men moving among the trees and the sound of hooves as the mules were loaded and led away, but she could see no one and dared not emerge to look around.

Suddenly, a horse whinnied nearby, and panic sent her heart to her throat. The French! No one else, she knew, had horses. She was torn between her determination to wait where she was and the impulse to jump out and run, when the horse she had heard emerged suddenly from the darkness. Gilberto was on it, and he was leading another behind him.

She looked so surprised that Gilberto laughed aloud. He leaned over the cart, pulled her to her feet, and kissed her soundly. "We did it!" he said. "It couldn't have been easier!"

He laughed again and dismounted to unload the two horses and stow their burdens well under the straw in the cart Kate had occupied. Then he put her on the second horse. Ángel and El Gitano came up on foot, and he left them to take away the cart. In less than an hour, the last of the band was moving at a sedate pace toward the hills, like any other holiday makers returning home. By the time the alarm was raised and the French began to search all vehicles leaving the city, they were miles away. Luis, who attended to details, had even remembered to lock the door behind them.

Kate and Gilberto were halfway home when the first glimmerings of the dawn began to lighten the path and turn the surrounding darkness a little less black. Reaching a point from which they could look down almost to the sea, they paused and waited for the sun. Gilberto watched the changing colors of the valley below—black to gray to rose and blue and finally green, a silver-green near the sea but a golden green in the higher mountain meadows. Kate watched Gilberto.

"I wonder where he got that key," she mused aloud.

"Ah," Gilberto said, smiling, "he moves in mysterious ways." He volunteered nothing further until they had started up again and regained the path. Then he told her, as if he were speaking of someone else, "He was in the army once, stationed in Oviedo, before the Junta declared war on France. Not in the army precisely—he was a surgeon attached to it. When Ney took Oviedo, and the Junta and the army fled, he stayed behind and offered his services to the victors."

He glanced at Kate before continuing. "That is what is called, politely, opportunism, and less politely, treason. But he saw no reason to leave Oviedo, where he was comfortable, merely because the Spanish army found it no longer so comfortable.

"But then he had an unavoidable accident—or perhaps not so much unavoidable as inopportune. He went out one day to celebrate something—he forgets the occasion, but there was always some occasion—and the same day, the French general commanding the garrison had the impertinence to get himself shot while out hunting, and Higgins was sent for.

"The general could not, worse luck to him, defend himself against assault as efficiently as he could defend the garrison, and he died. Higgins said the general was merely sleeping after the surgery and went home to pack his bags. He spent the next months on a tour of the province, which is to say, hiding behind the nearest tree whenever a uniform came into sight. Finally, he decided to let someone else take the trouble of hiding him. Ramón Sariñana, they said, was a master of concealment."

It was a strange tale, told in a strange fashion, as if the teller were unsure whether to be ashamed of his actions or proud of them. Kate now knew why Gilberto drank no wine; she knew also what was in the mysterious leather case he carried. But the question remained.

"Gilberto, where *did* you get that key?"

He smiled again in his rueful way. "Ah, he is not such a traitor as popular opinion would have him. Not only did he study the garrison from end to end, but he knew where all the keys were kept. He borrowed that one and had a copy made. *Por si acaso.* Just in case."

They rode a little way in silence until Gilberto said, "So that is why he joined the *guerrilleros*. But now it is my turn to wonder—why did she?"

Kate smiled and felt an impulse to tell him the story, but when she tried to bring it to the front of her mind—all of it, from the beginning—she saw that it was still too heavy a weight. She would have liked to lay some of it on Gilberto's strong shoulders, but she found she could not—not yet.

"One day, perhaps, I will tell you," she said.

He seemed to understand. "I will wait."

"Will you stay with us, then?"

"Yes. I will stay with you."

They had taken a long route back to camp, and by the time they arrived, the morning was well advanced, and the others were there ahead of them. Kate saw Ramón standing on a rock, watching their approach. Suddenly, she remembered Gilberto's kiss of the night before and realized that she had been, contrary to plan, alone with him all night. What was Ramón thinking up there?

Gilberto saw him, too, and reacted, inexplicably, by running his hand over his hair to tidy it. When he dismounted, Ramón came forward, grinning, and held out his hand. Gilberto took it; they clapped each other cheerfully on the back and went off together, leaving Kate to follow after them. Ramón had not given her so much as a "good morning."

Chapter Nineteen

On a morning in mid-August, Kate sat alone in the cave, out of the direct rays of the blazing sun. The men had been gone since early morning, forced out into the heat to hunt for their supper. Mercedes had gone to the river to do the laundry, and Kate hoped it would not come back over the dusty path dirtier than it went. She had been left behind to clear away their breakfast, but that chore had been easily disposed of.

She had washed her hair in the little stream that ran past the cave to the river. It had dried quickly in the heat, and she was now leaning idly against the cool granite walls of the cave, her face up to the sun. She would get freckles again, she thought, and remembered Sophie Benton's horror of the unladylike effects of wind and sunshine. Kate's hands and arms were brown, too. She stretched them out in front of her and thought she liked the effect. She considered taking off her homespun shirt and letting the sun warm her all over, but, in the end, only unbuttoned the top of it and twisted her hair up in a loose knot to bare her neck. She took out Colin's silver knife to pare an apple and then sat fingering the knife. *I shouldn't do that,* she told herself, looking at the knife. But she did not put it away. Rather, she tested herself with memories of Colin and, relieved that the grief she lived with had lessened, she let random thoughts and memories filter through her mind.

Kate had detected, or thought she had, stirrings of jealousy in Ramón when Gilberto first came to them. But Ramón must have decided that there was nothing suspicious in their friendship, for he had ceased to keep a wary eye on them. Ramón, indeed, seemed to take her as much for granted as he did the others. She could not imagine Ramón going out of his way to find little luxuries for her, such as the soap she had used on her hair that morning, which had been a gift from Gilberto when she had threatened to cut off her long blond mane.

Since Oviedo, in fact, Gilberto had often complimented her on her looks, which made her more conscious—and more careful—of them. She thought he was doing it out of friendship, to help her to be more comfortable with her uncomfortable life, but perhaps Ramón did not see it as a gesture of a friend. What had Colin said about friendship between men and women? And why should she think of that now?

She stood up and stretched and went back into the cave to put away her soap and comb. But after she entered it, the bright whiteness at the mouth of the cave behind her was obscured as a shadow passed in front of it. Kate looked back but could see only the silhouette of a man against the opening.

"Ramón?"

There was no answer, but the man moved inside. He advanced, and she stood up, apprehensive, backing away from him. She squinted into the light, trying to make out his features.

"Who is it?"

To her relief, the intruder did not reply in French but in Spanish. "Why, good day to you, *niña*!"

He came closer, and she saw a short, heavily built man with black stubble on his chin, dressed in the uniform of the regular Spanish army. But her relief was short-lived—there was no regular force in the district, and the verminous look of the man was anything but reassuring.

"Who are you?" she asked warily.

"An honorable soldier," he replied airily, looking her up and down, "of His Majesty King Ferdinand's forces."

"There is no army near here!"

"That's right. I am—uh—on leave."

"A deserter!"

His amiability vanished with the word. "And what might you be, *niña*, eh? Are you alone here?"

"No!" she replied instantly.

He looked cautiously around him, concluded that she

was lying, and proceeded on a tour of inspection, prodding blankets and searching sacks and barrels for something worth stealing. He took little care of what he was doing and tossed bundles and bags into corners when he was done with them, treading on bedclothes and crushing utensils underfoot. Frightened, Kate moved along the wall, edging away from him but keeping a watchful eye on his movements.

"You're alone, all right," he said, "but I won't stay long. Do you have any money?"

"No."

He grunted. "Not very friendly, are you?"

Kate had drawn nearer the fire, and he looked at her more closely in the stronger light. His puffy-lidded eyes glinted appreciatively. "What a pretty *niña* it is! Where did you get that yellow hair, eh?"

He dropped the pack he was searching and came closer. She made a furtive dash for the opening of the cave, but he reached out and pinned her to the wall. She could smell his foul breath and, with a disgusted grimace, turned her head away from his face. He chuckled softly.

"What's that you've got?" he said suddenly, reaching behind her. She had forgotten the knife still clutched in one hand, until she felt his sudden, heavy grip on her wrist.

"Drop it!"

His hold hurt her, but she clenched her teeth and hung on to the knife. He swore at her and pulled her away from the wall with a painful wrench, bringing the hand with the knife in front of her while his right arm encircled her waist.

"Let me go!" she gasped out.

But he only leaned over more closely, bending her backward and attempting to shake loose the knife, which he could see only as a silver object, possibly of value, in the hand he forcibly raised higher. She beat with her free fist on his shoulder but could not loosen his hold. Desperately then, she felt for the tiny button on the knife handle and released it.

The blade slid out as smoothly as if nothing impeded it—easily and cleanly into the flesh beneath the high uniform collar.

An expression of mild bewilderment came over the soldier's face, and his staring eyes shone glassily in the firelight. He loosened his grip on her to clasp one hand around his throat. A stream of blood spurted out between the fingers. He staggered clumsily and released Kate, who backed away in horror. Then she turned and fled through the mouth of the cave.

The glaring brightness outside hit her with the force of a physical blow, and she put one arm up to ward it off as she stumbled to the nearest tree. She stood in its scant shade, propped up against the trunk for a moment, breathing deeply. The heat buzzed palpably around her, and the torrid breeze did nothing to clear her head. She crumpled slowly to the ground and was violently ill.

She could not have said how long she crouched there before Gilberto came strolling up the path with his gun cocked over one arm and carrying two plump rabbits. He stopped abruptly when he saw Kate, her knees up to her chest and her head buried in her arms.

"Kate! Are you all right?"

He pulled her to her feet and tried to look into her eyes, but she closed them against the light.

"It's the sun," he said. "Come inside where it's cool."

Her eyes flew open. "No!"

He stared for a minute into the dull gray of her eyes, abruptly turned away, and went inside to investigate. When he came out again, Ramón had returned and was trying to comfort Kate, who was sobbing on his shoulder. He looked over her at Gilberto.

"What happened?"

Gilberto held out a red hand and the blood-smeared silver knife. "You'd better see for yourself."

Ramón glanced at the knife and then back at Kate. "Kate! Kate, listen to me! Are you—are you hurt, or just frightened?"

She shook her head and murmured, "I'm not hurt."

Gilberto made a move toward her, but she turned her head away. She felt too exposed, too susceptible to bear anyone's comfort without weeping again.

Ramón moved her into the shade of the rocks nearer the cave and went inside with Gilberto to survey the wreckage—the body crumpled on the floor, the ransacked supplies—and guessed what had happened.

"But how?" he muttered. "How did she do it?"

The dead man's blood had soaked through his shirt and jacket. His hand lay in a small pool of it, and still it throbbed slowly out of the hole in his throat. Ramón grimaced at the sight.

"Let's get him out of here," he said to Gilberto.

Gilberto was calmly rifling the soldier's pockets, oblivious to the blood. "I'll do it. You get Kate out of the way."

By the time the others had returned, Gilberto had removed the body and the mess, and Kate was recovering from the fright. She helped Mercedes as usual with the evening meal and even smiled when Rico complimented her on her exploit. El Gitano was inspired to celebrate the occasion in song, comparing Kate to all the brave women of Spanish legend.

Between her adventure and the good day's hunting the men had enjoyed, they were in high spirits, lingering longer than usual around the campfire and consuming more than the usual allotment of wine. Even Rico joined in the singing.

When at last Francho fell exhausted into Paco's lap, it was after midnight, and Ramón rose to signal the breaking up of the party. He suggested in an offhand manner to Kate that, because the night was clear and warm, they might sleep outside, away from the cave, and she was quick to agree, afraid for the first time in months to go to sleep with no one near. Indeed, although the warm night lulled her easily into sleep, it was not long before her mind wandered into colder regions, into winter and darkness. She struggled up a steep mountain path to reach a cottage at the top. A woman waited there for her, a thin old woman with a cadaverous face and hands like ice, who led her to a place at the back of the cottage where Kate saw a mound of earth, on which the falling snow did not melt. She began to shiver, and the earth trembled with her. Then she was shaking violently—someone was shaking her—and struggled out of the stranger's grasp.

"Kate! Wake up, Kate!"

It was only Ramón. She opened her eyes and saw him. He always looked so stern, she thought, so forbidding; his

The Dancers' Land

black eyes were hard and cold. Why did he not smile at her? She needed his comfort.

But then he spoke her name again, more gently.

"Kate?"

She felt his hand on her cheek and looked up at him and saw the unmistakable desire that clouded his dark eyes, no longer hard or cold. But then his face blurred behind the tears that filled her eyes. She closed them and caught her tears with a sound halfway between a sigh and a sob. No. She needed comfort, but not like that. It would not be fair to Ramón to use him that way.

"I'm all right," she murmured, and turned her head away, pretending to sleep. After a moment, Ramón's hand lifted from her face, and she felt the night chill where it had been.

It was soon after this that they began to climb higher into the mountains. The air cooled as they went up and soon lost the stifling quality of the valley. They came to one of the upland meadows that were sprinkled throughout the mountains, a broad, emerald expanse dotted with wild flowers and sloping steeply down to a small lake. Rough shepherds' huts, with lichen-encrusted roofs and walls, were dispersed along the edges of the meadow, and sheep grazed on the rare, lush pasture.

On the far side of the lake, they found an abandoned stable, blown clear of dirt by the mountain winds, and Ramón decided to stop and make their camp there. Kate fell immediately in love with the site. The sweet, fresh air and greenness soothed her soul and invigorated her body. Once she even stole down to the lake to bathe but, to her disappointment, found it far too cold. Ramón watched her roaming happily through the long grass and thought that he would keep her here as long as the others did not become restless to move on.

She slept dreamlessly in the mountain air. Ramón was no longer there when she awoke—quickly and with no lingering mists to have to clear out of her mind now—and she did not know if he had watched over her during the night. During the day, he said little to her and began to go away from camp more often.

But Gilberto was there. It was almost as if he and Ramón were taking turns looking after her. She laughed at herself, remembering how once she would have resented such close supervision, but she had learned that she was not so self-sufficient after all.

She had learned to laugh again, too, and tried the sound of it on Gilberto, who responded with his crooked grin and extravagant compliments on her blooming looks, which neither of them took seriously but which they both enjoyed. They talked seriously, too, and at last she felt able to tell him about her life, her father, Manuel, and even about Colin. She had never told the story so directly before, and she was relieved to find it hurt less now to think about it.

Strengthened by the release, she asked him questions. He answered them simply, but it was the first time she had ever asked anyone for advice, and she was surprised at how comforting it was to do so.

"Did I do wrong, Gilberto, to marry Manuel?"

"No, he wanted to marry you. It made him happy."

"But I didn't love him."

"He knew that, but you treated him as if you did."

"Colin thought I should not have done it if I did not love him."

"No, he thought you should not have been false to Manuel and therefore to yourself. There are many kinds of love, Kate."

She knew that but only now understood that she had confused one with another, and even hate with love, anger with passion.

"Even between men and women?" she asked. "Can they be friends as well as lovers?"

Gilberto smiled. "Of course. Friendship is a kind of love, too."

When at last they left the mountain, Kate paused at the edge of the path, disregarding the panorama in front of her to take one last look at the place that had finally brought her a measure of peace. But the meadow seemed to travel with her. When they found a site south of Riaño, their next objective, that would suit them for a few weeks, the barren rocks and the meager stream that flowed through the pasture seemed as green and pleasant to her as the meadow had been.

The Dancers' Land

It was pleasant to linger over the evening camp fire there, where the altitude and the advent of September made its warmth all the more inviting. The men talked over the final plans for the attack on the convoy due shortly from León with winter supplies for the French garrison at Guardo. El Gitano, who only followed orders and did not formulate them, took no part in the discussion but sat back against a tree and strummed softly on his guitar.

Kate clutched a warm cloak around her and folded her chilled hands in it. She listened to El Gitano but watched Ramón: the flicker of firelight on his lean features, the quick movements of his hands as he gestured to emphasize a point, the black hair that lay in tight curls on the nape of his neck. The crisp, cool darkness of the night had an invigorating effect on her senses, tuning them to an ultrafine pitch; yet the muted crackle of the fire, the murmur of voices, and the hypnotic music of El Gitano's guitar combined to lull them once again into insensibility. Kate's skin tingled with the contrast. From the other side of the fire, Gilberto caught her eye and winked. She smiled back.

Suddenly, a sharp whistle pierced the layers of sensation. With one accord, the men sat up and listened for a repetition of the danger signal that they hoped they had not really heard. But the next sound was a gunshot, and with it, one of the men posted on sentry duty leaped out of the darkness into the light of the fire.

"Franceses!"

The next minutes moved at lightning speed. The fire was extinguished. Ramón was at Kate's side. The others picked up as much as they could find in those short minutes and then scattered, fifty of them in fifty different directions, their flight accompanied by shouts, shots, curses in French and Spanish—and then silence.

Kate found herself and Ramón on their horses a mile away from the fire where, so short a time ago, she had warmed herself. She never saw the French at all.

She was sorry now that she had not looked for her gloves when she had first needed them, for her hands quickly became numb on the reins. But she kept on, following Ramón in silence along a winding forest path. She could not tell what direction they took, because Ramón altered it constantly, but after a time they stopped and waited.

Ramón had said nothing for two hours, and when he dismounted at last, he paced back and forth in front of her, his eyes to the ground. The sky had clouded, and it began to rain softly but steadily. Water dripped from the brim of Ramón's hat. He paid it no heed, but Kate pulled up her hood and drew herself closer into her cloak.

An hour before dawn, they heard a horseman approach—Gilberto, followed by the others with Rico bringing up the rear. It was a mystery to Kate how they had found one another again. Most of them were on foot, so Ramón got back on his horse where the extra height provided a kind of defense against the grim silence of the men and the look Rico gave him. Nevertheless, Rico had come back, and so had the others, and behind them would be their men. They were still together, in spite of the loss of almost all they possessed, including the most valuable of all—pack mules and horses. Ramón made no comment and spoke only a curt order, and they prepared to move on. But Francho's voice broke the tension.

"Where's Paco?"

There was a long silence during which the rain dripped audibly from the branches of the pines, and Ramón's horse shivered and threw off the water from its flanks. The sky was brightened by a sudden flash of lightning, and Guillermo looked up and crossed himself nervously.

"He's dead," Gilberto said at last.

"You're lying!" Francho's voice rose to a frantic pitch.

"I saw him myself. He's dead. Shot. He was asleep at his post."

Gilberto had no way of knowing if this was true or not, but Paco had been known to fall asleep on sentry duty before this, and Francho could not deny it. He said no more. Kate had a glimpse in the dim light of the tears on his cheeks before he turned abruptly, motioned to his men, and whispered hoarsely, *"Vamos!"*

A dozen men followed him and disappeared into the trees. Rico looked as if he were torn between following, to prove his independence of Ramón, and, shamefully perhaps, staying behind because of loyalty to him. But then he looked at Gilberto and Luis, rocklike and unwavering at Ramón's side, and he stayed where he was.

The Dancers' Land

Ramón's face was white, and his hand clutched the reins as if all the tension in him were concentrated in his grip. Kate looked on helplessly; there was nothing she could do for him.

Chapter Twenty

As the winter closed in on them, Ramón grew more restless, his temper more precarious. No one dared to contradict his harsh judgments and the imperious orders he gave around the camp fire, stabbing his knife blade in the dirt and looking no one in the eye as he spoke. Even Rico, usually quick-tempered and combative, subsided into inaudible mumbles behind Ramón's back.

They did not desert Ramón, but Kate became concerned that his continued unapproachability would force them to it eventually. She tried to help him, as Gilberto had helped her, by persuading Ramón to talk to her—about anything, just to release some of his pent-up tensions. But Ramón was not Gilberto; he considered strong emotion unmanly. He preferred to think he had no feelings and would not acknowledge their existence by talking about them.

So Kate was silent at first, only bringing him some hot wine or an extra slice of bread and cheese late at night when everyone else was asleep, but Ramón sat awake under a tree, sharpening his knife.

And then one day he said as he accepted the cup of strong hot tea Kate offered him with an apology for not having anything else, "My mother always made tea from herbs. She said it strengthened the will."

Kate smiled. "Perhaps that's why I have always hated it. What is your mother's name? You never told me much about her."

"Concha."

There was silence as Ramón sipped the tea. Kate did not want the opening to slip away, however, and she asked, "You have brothers, too?"

208

"Yes. Augustín and Joselito—he's the youngest, always up to mischief, even as a child."

Kate grew more hopeful and carefully drew Ramón out a little further. He told her about his life, so long ago it seemed now but really less than five years, in the fishing village where he was born, in the province of Viscaya. His father was a fisherman, like every other man in the village, but he wanted something better for his sons and worked hard to send them to university—all except Joselito, who did not want to go. Papa had been sorry about that, but Mamacita was glad to have at least one son at home.

Ramón did not tell her much more than that, but Kate sensed that it had helped. He looked a little less drawn and tired when he had finished his tea, and he went away with a lighter step.

While for Kate the coming of winter brought some satisfaction and the beginning of hope that spring really would come again, over the rest of Spain the cold weather dragged weariness and hunger in its wake.

In September, Wellesley, newly created Viscount Wellington of Talavera, had withdrawn toward Torres Vedras, near Lisbon, drawing the French after him. He had planned to retire without a fight behind the fortified walls, hills, and trenches that formed the British defensive lines along the sea, and to leave the parched countryside outside to do the killing of Frenchmen for him. But a decisive victory in this campaign was essential to the morale not only of his men, but also of the people and government at home who supported Britain's last army actively fighting Napoleon in Europe.

Wellesley picked his victory from the rocky heights of Busaco in central Portugal, and then continued his careful withdrawal to Torres Vedras. Marshal André Masséna, the latest unlucky aspirant to the supreme command of the French armies in Spain, mopped his brow and doggedly followed.

During the month in which Wellington entertained Masséna at the gates of Torres Vedras—but did not invite him inside—Ramón led his band in a eastward sweep across the mountains, in a series of quick, fierce, and—

although successful—unnecessary raids on anything French that chanced into view. By November, they had established a winter base well concealed in the rocky heights near the village of Bercedo.

Kate and Mercedes set to work with a practiced efficiency to make their new home habitable. Some of the men who lived in the area begged leave to return home for the winter, but Ramón, thinking he would not get them back again, curtly refused to let them go. Kate pleaded with him on their behalf, and Gilberto remarked caustically that if they did not come back of their own accord, they weren't worth having. Rico, who knew the men best, advised Ramón to let them go or risk their desertion before spring, anyway. In the end, they went, and the band was reduced, with the exception of Gilberto and El Gitano, to the Castilians who had been the first to join it. Paco's absence was keenly felt, but no one commented on it. In fact, Kate never heard his name spoken again.

Now it was Kate who watched over Ramón during the night, waking regularly, as if by instinct, to reassure herself that his breathing remained regular and that his overburdened mind was not driving him from his bed to pace endlessly the cave or the stream or the woods.

One night, she woke and heard nothing. But when she sat up and saw that he was still there beside her and that his eyes were closed, she smiled and bent over to brush his cheek lightly with an affectionate kiss.

He awoke, although she did not at first see that he had, until he raised his hand to the back of her head to keep her from drawing away. She hesitated; his hand moved to caress her cheek, and the desire in his eyes grew brighter. This time it was Ramón who needed her comfort and not she his, so she did not draw away.

She did not know how much it would hurt him if she denied him. She did not want to find out. She leaned closer to him, trembling; his other arm came up and pulled her down to him and then, with something like a sob, he moved on top of her and kissed her on the mouth with an unexpected passion, and then on the eyes and throat.

She felt his hands move into the loose smock she wore, to her bare breast, cool to his touch at first, then warming with the moist heat of his lips on the smooth roundness of it. Then he pulled away the blanket and her smock in one swift motion. She spoke his name; he brought his mouth back to hers and urged it open, taking possession of it at the same time that he pressed her body down with every movement of his own, until she felt a welcome, long-dormant heat within her, one that she had thought dead, too, and she arched her back against the hard floor and moaned for Ramón to take her.

If Ramón was surprised by Kate's sudden surrender to him, she was not. It would have happened long before, she saw now, if it had not been for Colin Greyson. She had always believed she had given him all the love she had in her, but now she was discovering that the capacity for love he had awakened in her had many manifestations. She could not love Ramón in the same way she had Colin, but Ramón had always been there, an ever-present reality behind the dream of Colin Greyson, and the time had come to acknowledge it.

Ramón was not a comfortable lover; he was like some elusive wild animal that would come to her when she beckoned but shy away when she offered too much of herself or asked more of him than he was prepared to give. His moods were quick to come on him, and they vanished before Kate had time to adjust to them, but at least she felt no reservations about accepting this new kind of love. And life, like love, came rushing back into her. She embraced it as gratefully as she did Ramón's hard, demanding body.

Gilberto took one quick look at Ramón the following morning, said "Ah!" in his succinct way, and had the whole situation in his grasp. Mercedes took little longer to understand, and when she did, a wide smile spread over her weathered face. Rico, however, was astonished to discover that what he had assumed all along had only just come to pass, and he remarked to Luis that no good was to be expected of a leader who thought more of a woman than he did of fighting.

The winter continued, long and cold, and they were confined to the cave after fierce storms left deep snow outside. But there was much to do, and the daylight hours passed swiftly. Like the armies in the south, Ramón's small band prepared for spring. Clothing had to be mended, equipment repaired, food supplies replenished. When the snow was especially bad, it was almost easier to steal their food from the French than to hunt for it, but they could not risk an attack on the nearby garrisons for fear of having their whereabouts discovered and losing everything to another surprise raid. Ramón took extra precautions against discovery and permitted no one to venture into a town unless he returned by the most circuitous route possible. Ramón himself might be gone all day on a five-mile journey.

"He swings like a pendulum," Gilberto complained, "from one extreme to the other. In October I lived in daily fear of losing my head through his recklessness, and now, when the chances of discovery are smallest, he fusses like an overcautious old woman. God knows which way he will swing when spring comes!"

Kate was watchful, as always, for the first elusive hint of spring, after which the snows quickly subsided and patches of brown, rich earth became edged with green instead of white. The men who had left for the winter returned. There were constant discussions about their next move, and spies were sent out to discover what plans the French had that they might upset. When one of the men came back with the news that Napoleon was sending reinforcements into Spain over the Pyrenees, the issue was decided. The road from Paris to Portugal was a long one, and the more treacherous the *guerrilleros* could make it, the better.

Presented once again with opportunities to prove himself worthy of leadership, Ramón took them all. He seemed to be still haunted by that one miscalculation that had cost Paco his life, and was determined to atone for it. But instead of inspiring greater confidence in his men, his boldness gradually lessened their trust, and this made him still more desperate. Even Rico grew apprehensive.

Kate, however, began to worry less for their safety. In fact, the men had considerable success that spring, in part because of the increased guerrilla activity all over northern Spain. With success, Ramón became less tense, and the atmosphere in general clearer. For Kate, the peace of the winter returned, and although she saw less of Ramón now, their time together was the sweeter for it. The doubts of the winter were banished, and her lightened heart sang.

Because of this, the blow that fell in June was almost more than she could bear. Supposing the men to be away until dark, she had taken advantage of a quiet hour on a sun-drenched afternoon to take a walk. She climbed the hill above their camp and turned to look down over the grassy slope that ran to the foot of the river. It had rained the day before, and she thought there might be mushrooms in the copse by the water. She started down again to look.

It was then that she saw a lone horse picking its way carefully up the path, slowly because of the weight of two men on its back. Kate turned cold with fear when she realized that one of the men was holding the other upright because, otherwise, he would not be capable of staying in the saddle. She flew down the hill, stumbling over stones and roots in her path. She fell once and cut her hand cruelly but got up immediately and reached the camp, only to have her worst fears confirmed. Gilberto, still holding Ramón, whose face was ashen and expressionless, was attempting to dismount when he saw her.

"Help me!" Gilberto called out to Kate, who was too stunned to move.

Awkwardly, they carried Ramón into the shelter of the hut, which served Mercedes as a kitchen. Mercedes met them and, wasting no time in questions, quickly made up a bed for Ramón out of a collection of blankets, and helped Gilberto ease him into it. Kate watched, twisting her hands in her skirt; she realized dully that they were sticky, and she looked down to discover both hands and skirt covered with blood.

Gilberto was giving curt instructions to Mercedes while he stripped off Ramón's shirt to reveal a grim-looking wound. But as he expertly cleaned away the blood, Kate saw that there was no more to the wound than a small hole on the right side of Ramón's chest. She dropped to her knees and stared at it in fascination. Then she looked up at Gilberto. His face, in the dim light, was whiter than Ramón's.

"What happened?"

"He took a chance," he said, not looking at her.

Ramón's breathing became shallower with every passing second. Kate struggled to remain calm, surveying the damage with apparent coolness, the nausea she had felt a moment before gone now.

"Is the bullet still in there?"

"Yes."

She looked up again and stared at Gilberto until he was forced to meet her eyes. There was an uncomfortable silence before she spoke, very quietly.

"Gilberto."

"No, Kate."

"Gilberto, please take the bullet out."

"No! It's too close to the lung, and he's lost too much blood. I'd kill him!"

"He's dying now!"

Her sob broke and turned the words into a choked scream. There was no reply he could make, and her words echoed on the still air. Mercedes had been hovering nearby, listening in uncomprehending silence to this exchange, but she was galvanized into action when, at last, Gilberto gave her a series of curt orders, beginning with a demand for more light and as much boiling water as she could produce in a hurry.

"You will have to help," he said stonily to Kate. "Can you do it without fainting?"

"I'll do it."

He found his leather case and set it on the ground. He stared at it for a moment, his hands hovering over the catch. Then he opened it and spread the instruments inside it in front of him. While he swiftly prepared the area around Ramón's wound, the women wrapped the knives in clean white linen and sterilized them in the boiling water. The rest of the band arrived in the midst of these preparations, and Rico and Luis came in immediately to see what was happening. Mercedes chased them out again, telling them to keep themselves and the others out of the way.

Then they began.

It seemed to go on forever, and more than once Kate felt herself giving way to a wave of nausea. But she pulled herself back. She could even detach herself sufficiently to marvel at Gilberto's skill, unimpaired by her occasional clumsiness. When they had finished at last, he bandaged the wound and, too tired to get up, raised his head and took

The Dancers' Land

a deep breath. A curious mixture of fatigue, pride in his achievement, and relief that he had after all been capable of it showed on his face, and Kate knew without asking that Ramón would live. She sat quietly weeping and looking into Ramón's still face.

After a time, she was reminded by the throbbing pain in her hand of her own injury. She looked for Gilberto to ask him to bind it up, but he had gone. She rose and did it herself. Mercedes tried to help and suggested that she change her stained dress, but Kate only replied, "It's Ramón's blood." She broke off the ends of her bandage with her teeth and sat down again to watch over him.

It was soon evident that Ramón would make a complete recovery, but it was likewise evident that he would be an invalid for at least the remainder of the summer. Rico and Luis came to Kate after a few days and asked her frankly what she intended to do. Until then, she had not been able to decide, but when Rico brought up the question, the answer came to her.

"I shall take him home—home to Baquio."

It was the only answer. They were close enough now to the coast to make the journey feasible, and Baquio was sufficiently remote to make it the safest place for a long stay. Rico breathed a sigh of relief and, far from reluctantly, prepared to take the leadership of the band upon his shoulders. He established his new position by immediately issuing orders for a morning march.

Luis watched Rico swagger off and said to Kate, "You cannot take him there alone."

She knew it as well as he. "Will you help me, Luis?"

He had waited only for her word and left to make the preparations. Kate returned to the hut where she had left Ramón asleep and, finding him now awake, told him with no waste of words what she wanted to do. He smiled weakly up at her.

"Don't say it like that, Riña. I'm not going to fight you this time."

She smiled and bent over to kiss him. He said, "Have you told Mercedes?"

"No. I'll do it now."

Mercedes reacted with mingled pleasure and regret. She agreed that it was certainly the best thing to do.

"But, *niña,* I must go with Guillermo. I cannot leave him."

"Of course you cannot, Mercedes. Go with him. *Idos con Dios.*"

Kate put her arms around Mercedes and gave her a long hug. When Mercedes pulled away, she sniffed audibly but said only that she would go and pack.

Gilberto was not there to make the farewells more difficult. On the night after he had taken the bullet out of Ramón and made sure that Ramón could be left safely in Kate's care, she had gone to sleep at Ramón's side. When she awoke in the morning, Gilberto was gone. She never saw him again.

Chapter Twenty-one

THE MOUNTAINS crumbled into chalky, windblown hills, then into the smooth, tree-covered coastal lowlands which, although they rose now and again to new heights, ended by plunging abruptly into the sea. Craggy promontories separated and sheltered between them quiet crescent coves and strips of gray beach. There waves sped soft and foaming over the sand with none of the violent energy they expended against the cliffs on either side. From one such cove, the fishing village of Baquio faced the sea that gave it its livelihood, keeping its back resolutely to mountain, city, and plain—and to the war that raged over them.

For most of the long, slow journey down from the mountains, they had carried Ramón on a stretcher fastened by shafts to one of the horses and pulled along behind it. But when at last they came close to Baquio, late on a placid Sunday afternoon, Ramón insisted on getting up and entering the village on horseback. He ordered Luis to abandon the stretcher, and he climbed painfully onto the gentlest of the horses, where he sat stiffly erect for the last miles of their journey.

They turned off the main road onto a narrow cart track that rose to a slight crest before descending to the village. The principal street of Baquio—the only one, for the others were no more than footpaths between buildings—ran in a straight line to the seashore. At the southern end was the village church, a young cathedral with an enormous bell tower. To the north, a cluster of whitewashed houses spilled over onto the beach, leaving an empty space between them and the church. As no one had been inclined to build anything there, part of the area had been set aside for a plaza consisting of walks laid out in a rectangular pattern around a copse of trees, in the center of which stood a fountain surrounded by benches and a tiled walkway.

At the end of the street, the riders turned right along the beach, Ramón in the lead with an eager look in his eyes. They drew up to a white house in the same simple style as the rest but larger and better cared for. A dark-haired, square-set man was walking up the path to the door.

"Augustín!"

The man paused and looked up. "Ramón."

There was no surprise in his voice, and he looked as if he had last seen his brother only that morning. By the look in his eyes, Ramón's spirit would have had him jumping down from his horse, but his body would not let him. He cursed his weakness as Luis helped him down and Augustín looked on. Then Ramón embraced his brother.

"Where is Papa?" he asked in Basque. "And Mama and Joselito?"

"They are all here. Come."

He took his brother's arm, but Ramón stopped him and motioned to Kate.

"Augustín, this is Catarina."

Augustín bowed his head but did not take Kate's proffered hand.

The reception within was warmer. They stepped into a large, cheerful room with windows facing the ocean. There were two men seated there, the older, gray-haired one smoking a pipe, the younger reading a newspaper that was already well thumbed and ragged at the edges. They looked up, but before either could speak, there was a clatter of cutlery and a woman's voice from the doorway leading to the kitchen.

"Ramón! *Hijo mio!*"

Mother and son embraced with many tearful exclamations and whispered endearments before Ramón's father interrupted to embrace him as well. The younger man, aglow with excitement, took Ramón's hand between his two large, sinewy ones and shook it violently up and down. Ramón laughingly freed it but put his arm around Joselito's shoulders, as if seeking their strong support. Kate saw his face go white and took an impulsive step forward to help him, but he quickly pulled himself together and presented her to them. They all had been talking at once, but then they stopped and turned politely to her, uncertain of how to receive her. But when Ramón's mother made up her mind and embraced Kate as firmly as she had Ramón, the others followed suit.

"Concha, bring our son wine and something to eat," said the soft but authoritative voice of Ramón's father.

While she did this, the men sat down, Ramón gratefully and with a small sigh of relief. Only Augustín remained standing, leaning against the window and watching them. Ramón said nothing of his injury, and if they thought he looked unwell, no one remarked on it. Kate listened as Ramón briefly told their story—true for the most part but omitting or skimming over details. Ramón gave no explanation for his return to Baquio but let them think it was simply a desire to see them again that had brought him. His story was accepted without question, and the conversation turned to the family, their friends, and the fishing.

The garrulous Joselito interrupted the others constantly, until his father gently rebuked him and he lapsed into shamed silence. Kate decided that Joselito—all of them, in fact, even Augustín, who accepted no one easily—greatly respected the gaunt, eighty-year-old man. His wife was some twenty years younger, but over the course of the years, she had grown to resemble him until the two tall, handsome, gray-haired people looked more like brother and sister than man and wife.

The resemblance of their three sons to one another was less marked. Augustín, the eldest, was the smallest, although squarely built and still above average height. A perpetual frown marred the regularity of his features and seemed to indicate a dissatisfaction with life. Ramón told Kate later that years before, Augustín had also attended the University of Salamanca and regretted having come back to this tiny village to spend the rest of his life eking out a simple living as a fisherman.

Joselito was too young to have built up any regrets, and he faced life with unflagging enthusiasm. His square face and large, bright eyes reflected his attitude, and his big body seemed always ready to leap into action. Joselito had not wanted to go to his brothers' university. Learning was a useless possession to a man who wanted nothing more of life than the sun and the rain in their season, good fishing and the sound of the sea, and a warm bed at night. Kate could understand this; this house and this family were the best he could have had. She was acutely aware of the closeness of their family life—something she had never known and envied them for.

Luis announced his intention of departing again early in the morning, and when he had finished his supper, he went out to make his bed on the beach. Ramón's mother took her son aside and, with a worried frown, tried to explain that they had no private room "for *la señora.*" Ramón laughed and was about to tell her that none of them was accustomed to sleeping in a real bed, but then a thought occurred to him.

"*Mamacita,* the little hut on the beach where we used to keep the old boat, is it empty?"

"Yes, *mi Ramón,* but it is not clean, and the nets and such—"

"We will sleep there. Nowhere could be finer."

She protested but saw that he would not be moved. She routed Augustín and Joselito from their chairs and made them go—"quickly!"—to clean up the *casita* on the beach. "And take these blankets! And some hay from the shed, and here, also these chairs!"

A fever of activity ensued as Luis and Ramón's brothers attempted to make the hut habitable to Mama's specifications. Kate and Ramón stood on the moon-washed sand and watched them. Voices echoed over the beach, and lights shone brightly from open doors, eclipsing the moon. But in the background still beat the steady rhythm of the waves. The soft summer breeze caressed the nape of Ramón's neck and blew strands of hair over Kate's forehead. She pushed them back and looked up at Ramón, who smiled and, with his eyes, sent a kiss to her lips. She was flooded with a sense of well-being and thought how good it was to feel alive again. If she never felt the extremes of joy—and despair, too—that she once had, at least she could be content now. It was a good deal to be grateful for.

Ramón had been born within sight and sound of the sea, and its moods were familiar to him. But Kate had lived all of her life—apart from the brief voyage to Spain long ago—

The Dancers' Land

far away from it, and it was now a new and incredibly beautiful thing to her. During their first weeks in Baquio, Ramón, still recovering from his wound, was able to move very little from their hut and then only when the sun was strongest and he could lie basking in it on the beach. So Kate spent hours sitting by herself on the sand, watching the sea.

Often she would rise before dawn to watch Ramón's father and brothers set out into the still black expanse of open sea for the day's fishing. At sunset she was there to see them return, usually well laden, for it was a rich summer for fishing. Between their sailing and their return, however, the sea was hers alone. Ramón's mother, seeing how she grew to love it, would chase her from the house and send her down to the shore, like a child, to play.

"On such a day, you must not stay indoors," Concha would scold her. "I do not have so much work that I cannot do it myself."

Each wave was unlike the one preceding it—some dancing, some dreamy, some rushing onto the sand as if striving to reach something, and then failing, receding, defeated before the next gallant effort. She felt in tune with the waves, hope and melancholy ebbing and flowing within her, rising and falling with the tide, until she recognized the existence of both as natural.

The colors of the sea changed with the hours of the day—gray with the soft morning mist, bright green and blue-shadowed when wisps of white cloud played around the midday sun, hazy and violet as the sun neared the horizon, and becoming black, as if in mourning, when its last rays were extinguished.

But more than the look of it, Kate loved the sound of the sea. She lay awake on warm nights, listening to the dull roar, the sure, steady, never-ceasing fall of the waves. After love, they seemed to echo the increased tempo of her heartbeat and penetrated her senses even as she lay in Ramón's arms, drugged and drowsy with spent passion.

The sea and the care lavished on Ramón by the people who loved him best not only quickly healed his wound, but also erased the weariness from his eyes and the lines from his forehead. His mouth softened once more into young, sensual curves, replacing the thin, hard expression it had recently worn. With the loss of care, he pushed aside the thousand daily distractions that had kept them apart and drew closer to Kate. Now they were together constantly, and if his understanding of her did not increase, because it did not occur to him that there was anything to understand, there was in his attitude toward her at least a greater tenderness, and she did not fail to notice and appreciate it.

There was something deeply true about Ramón's love of her; whatever reservations Kate may have had, there was never any question in his mind. He had always loved her, and in spite of distractions along the way Kate had always been the only woman who mattered to him. Spain was his land, war his work—not by choice but by quirk of destiny, and that same destiny had given him Kate. That she had only recently begun to show a love for him he accepted as natural in the way of things. Women were weak creatures, unsure of themselves; it was not to be wondered at that they did not see things as clearly as men did. The mixture of matter-of-factness and smoldering passions that burst into flame and died as quickly again, which Kate found so incomprehensible, was not so to Ramón. Day was light and night dark, life was thus and so, and love happened another way. The powers of self-analysis that had lately been developing in Kate remained foreign to Ramón.

Still, when she did not think too much about it, it was not hard to be content with Ramón. He was strong, and his arms were sure around her, his mouth warm and caressing. It may have been that he considered that enough to be expected of him, but he took the further step of showing her a certain respect, of talking more freely with her than with other women. He told her about some of them, speaking not boastingly but not cautiously, either, as if they were merely another part of a long-gone, almost forgotten past.

"I never told any of them about the others, of course."

"Why not?"

Ramón shrugged his shoulders. "They would have had jealous tantrums and thrown things. There was no point in telling them."

"And they might have been hurt if you had."

The Dancers' Land

"No, it wouldn't have hurt them. They expect that sort of thing from a man."

"Then why do you tell me?"

"You have more sense than they. Why should you be hurt if I take some *fulana* that I will forget in the morning?"

She did not attempt to answer that. She was afraid it was true, although not for the reason he told her. Probably he meant to praise her by it, but the woman in her felt the sharp hurt that her sensible exterior pretended indifference to. She hoped she was not becoming possessive, a thing she despised in other women, and she tried to put out of her mind the nagging thought that he had never actually said he loved her.

"Te adoro, Riña!" he had said between warm, lingering kisses.

But that was not the same thing.

"Tell me that you love me," he whispered as his hands moved possessively over the curve of her breast and down the smooth hollows of her waist and hips.

"I love you, Ramón."

His hands explored her body surely and, if not with understanding, at least with gentleness, and she responded willingly to the warm flood of sensation he evoked in it. She could not make love to him with her mind, after all, so she turned it off, just as she had earlier extinguished the candle.

As the summer progressed, Kate found it easier to put aside her doubts. For long intervals she was entirely at peace with herself, and her happiness was evident to Ramón and helped to restore him to health.

Nevertheless, even in his improvement there was a menace—something that said, *And when this eternal summer is over, what then?* They never talked of the future beyond September, but it was inevitable that the clear azure sky should begin to cloud over. The clouds were tiny gray ones at first, but they seemed to be a part of the now unseen but greater, blacker storm cloud that hung over the land to the south.

One evening, as Kate approached the main house, voices reached her and she caught the words, *". . . su fulana aquí. No es desgracia suficiente que Papá y Joselito . . . ?"*

"Sshhh!" The voice of Ramón's mother stopped Augustín's, but Kate had heard enough and did not enter the house. She knew Augustín's opinion of her, but what business were Augustín's father and brother engaged in that he considered disgraceful? The riddle remained naggingly at the back of her mind.

August came in with the last wave of warmth before the gradual cooling that would lead to autumn. By day, Kate and Ramón kept to the cool of the house or, unable to resist the lure of the sea, gave in to it in body as well as spirit. The cool waves washed them, caressed them, refreshed them, so that in the evening they expended their extra energies on long walks along the beach.

On the eve of Kate's twenty-fifth birthday, they sat on a dry strip of sand, she watching the sea with never-ending fascination, he smoking—now that he could again—contentedly. He looked at her, and his eyes told her she was beautiful, and for the first time she felt that she was. The color had come back to her cheeks, the shadows had left her eyes, and in the white cotton-and-lace dresses she and Concha had sewn, she looked like a girl again.

They had finished supper, and the lights in the house were out, for the men would have to be up before dawn. There was no moon and few stars, and the only illumination was the fluorescent shimmer of the outgoing tide.

"Shall we wait for midnight and welcome your day?" Ramón asked her.

She smiled at the rare touch of sentimentality. "If you like. But it's only the twenty-fifth. Not such a special year."

"Isn't it?"

She laughed and kissed him. They got up, brushing the fine sand from their clothing and, arms around each other, walked toward the far end of the cove. There the sand rose and was augmented by stony earth into a grassy knoll. They climbed this, found a path that wound into the trees skirting the shore, and took it, wandering on oblivious to time or distance. They came to the top of a ridge overlooking another cove, where the path tumbled over tufts of grass growing in the loose, sandy soil and dropped rapidly to the beach.

"We should go back," Kate said.

The Dancers' Land

She turned, but something had caught Ramón's attention and he did not follow. He peered out at the sea, then searched the shadows of the rocks on the far side of the cove, until two of the shadows detached themselves and walked to the water's edge. Then Kate saw, still some distance out, a small boat plowing through the sea and riding low in it. Black-clad figures guided it silently but surely toward land. Ramón pulled her down onto the grass, and they lay pressed against it, watching. The muffled oars quickly closed the gap between boat and shore, but Ramón was still staring into the sea beyond the boat.

Suddenly he exclaimed, "Look! Look there! You can see it—a ship!"

Kate strained her eyes in the direction he indicated, at first unable to distinguish anything through the heavy darkness, but finally perceived between the black of sea and sky a silent, shadowy bulk, rolling phantomlike on the waves. Ramón knew now precisely what was happening, and he grinned at her.

"Would you believe it! My own father and little Joselito!"

He got up and scrambled down to the beach to join them. Kate smiled ruefully at the excited but wordless gesticulations when they met. Joselito glanced up to where she stood but then turned his attention back to the boat, which was now scraping against the sand. Two sailors jumped out and pulled it up out of the surf. Three other men, their faces blackened to match their clothing, followed and began to unload large wooden cases, carrying them well up onto the shore and standing them, hidden from view, within a cleft in the rocks.

When they had finished, they stood together talking for a time, one of the strangers carrying most of the conversation and interpreting the Spaniards' remarks to his companions. One of the sailors chanced to look up and, seeing on the hill the figure of a young woman holding a shawl tightly around her, her skirts and her long, fair hair blowing in the light breeze, turned to the interpreter.

"Captain! Look up there, sir!"

The other man turned and looked for a moment. Something about the way he stood and moved stirred a memory in her, and she held her breath, half-expecting the old ghost to rise up out of that boat. But then, reaching into the boat for something, he started with it up the hill. It was his hat, but when he put it on and threw back his black cloak to reveal the full splendor of a British naval uniform, he succeeded only in looking slightly comic, the blacking on his face contradicting the dignity of his dress and bearing. Kate was smiling when he reached her. He took the hat off again and stared at her with something near to incredulity.

"Good evening, captain," she said in English, holding out her hand.

He took it and, recovering his composure, bowed low over it. Then he smiled back at her. She liked the man; he was fair, tall, and heavily built but with the grace of one who took care to let no muscle go slack. She could not distinguish his features under the blacking, but his gray eyes reflected her own, and she felt that old, inexplicable tug of kinship with this Englishman who was, nevertheless, a total stranger.

He continued to hold her hand. Behind him, the sailors were pushing the boat into the waves, and she saw them.

"Oh, must you go immediately?"

"I fear so, ma'am," he replied softly, in a husky voice. "Mr. Ramsey has orders to sail without us if we do not return within the hour, and much as I might like to stay, I shall be glad to see my own bit of shingle at Deal once again!"

"You are a Kentish man, captain?"

"Indeed, ma'am. And where is your home?"

"It was . . ." She hesitated. "I was born in Somerset."

He turned to go but hesitated and smiled again, apologetically. "I beg your pardon, ma'am, but I scarcely expected to find, on a lonely strip of beach in Spain, such a—that is, may I know your name, ma'am?"

His gray eyes were so clear, so honest, that any other answer seemed far too complicated, and she said simply, "It is Catherine Collier."

"Captain Nicholas Calvert. Your servant, Miss Collier."

He bowed again, then turned and walked back down the hill. Kate stayed where she was as the boat moved toward the open sea. Captain Calvert wrapped his cloak around him and, his large body crouched in the stern of the boat, watched the receding shoreline. He touched his hand to his forehead, once, in salute to the woman on the hill.

When they were out of sight, Kate came down to the beach and found Ramón tearing the top from one of the crates. It came off to reveal a glittering arsenal of rifles and ammunition. Ramón stared spellbound at them, then clapped Joselito on the back.

"It's wonderful! But what happens now?"

"We leave this here," Ramón's brother said. "When the tide comes in at dawn, they will be picked up by boat."

"By whom?"

Joselito looked at his father, who said only, "By friends. Men that can be trusted."

They started homeward, Ramón in the lead with his arm around Kate's waist. The other two followed behind until they rounded the hill; then they took the inland path to the house. Kate and Ramón continued along the beach to the hut and reached it just as the bell in the church tower began to strike midnight. Ramón laughed exultantly and kissed her.

"Happy birthday, Riña!"

Chapter Twenty-two

THE GHOST that had ceased to haunt her for a few blessed months had returned. But it was a benign phantom now—a sweet memory rather than a tormenting regret—and it left no more impression on her than a faint curving of her lips in sleep. In the morning she had forgotten her dreams, but Ramón remembered the smile and, even without knowing the reason for it, strove to keep it there.

For Kate, the summer that had ended on her birthday was unwilling to die before its time and spent its final energy in a riot of halcyon days, emerald seas, and radiant skies that dissolved into star-strewn nights. The plaza was the center of all activity, and the young people of Baquio and the neighboring villages congregated there nightly to indulge in a late-summer madness of song and dance.

They were beautiful people, these young Basques, the girls lissome and charming, their gallants tall and extravagantly handsome. Kate felt old in the presence of such youth and gaiety but not yet old enough to waste the starlight indoors. She and Ramón sat on the benches around the plaza and watched the children at play. And when the world became too crowded, they still had their private part of the beach where they merely sat, her head in his lap, and watched the changing moods of the sea. Their peace was absolute—and unnatural, Kate thought, wondering if Ramón might be growing weary of it. Or of her, for being too aware of its fragility and wanting to hold on to it.

With the approach of September, the gray of the morning sea lingered longer into the day, as if in preparation for the final loss of the sun and the mourning of winter. And with September came Luis.

The Dancers' Land

Ramón was at once full of energy again, and Kate was relegated to her old role of onlooker while he and Luis held lengthy conversations on the shore. She knew what they were planning and she dreaded the thought of it. She had, rather forlornly, hoped that they might spend the winter in Baquio, but the eager look on Ramón's face told her to expect—and it soon came—a gruff announcement of their immediate departure. Ramón's eyes did not meet hers when he told her, as if he expected a voiced protest, but Kate was wiser than that now.

The farewells this time were difficult, as if Kate were losing her ability to endure such leave-takings. As she embraced Concha, she was more conscious of the finality of her good-byes than she had been with Mercedes in the spring. Even that short a time ago, she had still not quite believed in the possibility of never again seeing the people she loved. So she did not look back as they rode away to the south.

Luis had not been idle that summer. In his unassuming but competent fashion, he had organized and shaped a new band and, having built it, was now ready to hand it over to Ramón. The men were an untidy, ill-assorted collection; small, dark, and wiry, they lacked here and there an eye or a finger and, universally, razors, and their past histories were best not probed too deeply. But they were fighters, as hard as the iron buried in their mountains.

Eyeing Ramón with interest disguised as suspicion, they seemed less than ready to be handed over to a new leader. But there were enough friends among them to establish a grudging loyalty to Ramón, based on his reputation and on the expectation of successes to come. Ramón, having anticipated the need to start afresh yet again, was pleased to find old Castilians among the new men.

"Carlos! *Qué tal, hombre! Bueno, Ignacio*—welcome back! *Cómo va, Jenaro?*"

"*Bien*, Ramón! But tired of these godless mountains. We need room to move—it's the plains of Castile for us!"

Luis had taken the initiative of planting a rumor to the effect that they would move south again, toward the plains, and then assumed the further liberty of not troubling to curb the speculation that soon ran rife among the men.

The British had not yet succeeded in taking the well-fortified, French-held cities of Badajoz and Ciudad Rodrigo, which still stood between them and Spain, and had retired once again to Torres Vedras, the well-fortified lines near Lisbon. The French commander, Masséna, had been recalled to France in May, to be replaced by Auguste Marmont. Once again the lessons of peninsular warfare had to be taught to a new and not very bright pupil, and the French passed no more profitable a summer than did the British. They had it drummed into them again and again—in sharp battles at Barrosa, Sabugal, Fuentes de Oñoro, and Albuera—the oft-repeated lesson that the British, in spite of their clumsy Spanish allies, were still very much a force to be reckoned with.

Napoleon was preparing for conquest of Russia on a grand scale and to this end had begun to draw troops out of Spain. The best of them went, to be replaced by raw recruits and the emperor's indifference, for he was tired of this everlasting and inconclusive war with Spain. His most able marshals had been beaten by it, while the hated British seemed to draw strength from every adversity. Spain was a wasteland—wasteful of French lives, unproductive and unprofitable, an old vision now tarnished. Russia was a new and shining vision. He could not know that it would prove in the end more terribly destructive even than Spain.

Ramón seemed infected by the mood of his men, rather than in control of it. He still had the knack of holding their attention around the campfire at night, but the map of Spain that he drew in the dust grew more ragged and so, Kate thought, did his once carefully calculated schemes to torment the French.

Ramón discovered that one of his new band, Jorge by name and miner by profession, was something in the way of an explosives expert. Within hearing of the men, Ramón coolly discussed the possibilities of such a talent, careful not to overrate it and give Jorge—as yet an untried element—any exaggerated idea of his worth. But privately, he was bursting with enthusiasm, and he expounded to Kate on various grandiose schemes for the wholesale destruction of French installations. She smiled

The Dancers' Land

indulgently, as if at an overexcited child, but her heart sank when she thought of beginning all that all over again. She attempted, as Gilberto used to do, to curb Ramón's dangerous eagerness by pointing out every possible pitfall.

Whether it was through her influence, or because it was good strategy, Kate did not know, but Ramón postponed his more ambitious projects for the spring. They did not spend the winter in any fixed place, but rather skirted the borders of Castile, gradually acquiring explosives—never in large quantities but enough from many sources to build quite a satisfactory arsenal.

It was not an easy winter, but there was at least no snow on the plains; the fierce winds swept away any that dared to fall. There were no caves, so they slept in abandoned huts in the shells of burned-out villages or in stables that smelled vile but kept the wind out. Once or twice they were forced to move into homes that were still occupied, after a fashion, by their owners. Kate disliked intensely the necessity for this, both because of the imposition placed upon the family and because these hovels invariably smelled even more vile, and were far less comfortable than an empty barn.

But Ramón was oblivious to his surroundings, to the heavy, choking pall of smoke hanging in the windowless rooms. He passed the evening talking with the men of the house, expounding his plans for a "spring offensive" and—Kate couldn't help thinking—sounding very much like those Salamancan café idlers he had despised.

Kate's thoughts more often turned to Salamanca these days, and her eyes searched the plains as if she might see it shimmering with that illusive nearness on the horizon. As the blue mountains and dewy green meadows lost their hold on her imagination, Salamanca loomed larger and became more and more Philip Benton's glorious, golden city, even though she knew it could not have escaped the war untouched. But its heart would remain unscarred, and Kate's own heart reached out longingly to it.

In February came the news that Ciudad Rodrigo had at last fallen to the British and was being held by Spanish troops while Wellington laid hopeful plans for the siege of Badajoz. The two border fortresses were the keys to the door of Spain, and if one of them were left open to the French while Wellington ventured eastward, hard-fought-for Portugal could be retaken and his lifeline to the sea broken.

The French stepped up their southern war. Garrisons in northern Spain were cut to the bone to rush badly needed troops to Badajoz before Wellington could reduce its formidable defenses, and as a result, guerrilla activity in the north increased to an unprecedented degree.

Ramón, all fire and eagerness, rushed to complete his preparations. He turned his eye southward, to the Ebro River and the highway bridge at Miranda de Ebro. The French, Ramón's spies told him, were so sure of themselves that they had not even troubled to post a guard there. Destroying a bridge that had stood for centuries would be child's play.

Nevertheless, some hasty revision had to be made in their plans when they arrived at Miranda de Ebro to discover that there were, in fact, sentries at the crossing. Ramón saw no reason for this to stand in their way, but Jenaro was apprehensive. "Why should they suddenly put a guard there?" he asked.

Kate was even more anxious than Jenaro when Ramón announced that he and Jorge would undertake the placing of the charges under the bridge and—because they had no means of setting them off from a distance—the lighting of the fuses. It meant working by night and taking the chance of getting safely away before the bridge went up or the sentries could stop them, and although the river was not deep, it was swift, full of eddies and half-submerged obstacles and, in this season, icy cold from the melting mountain snows.

But Ramón heatedly silenced Kate's protests. The next night he and Jorge blackened their faces, covered their bodies with grease as a protection against the cold, and slipped into the river at a sheltered point just upstream of the bridge. They quickly worked their way downstream, their movements warding off numbness, but even so, their teeth were chattering by the time they reached the bridge. They worked as swiftly as possible, communicating by hand signals. The rush of water effectively drowned the slight noises they made. The sentries' tread over their heads remained solid, steady, unbroken by suspicion.

They crossed the river under the bridge and shakily fastened the first charge onto the supports nearest the sentry box. Then they moved cautiously to the center arch. This was more difficult, for the river moved swiftly here, and they had to hold fast with one hand and work with the other. But they were getting the trick of it now and soon had it done.

They were moving to the side of the river from which they had entered, when the sentries crossing directly overhead suddenly halted. Ramón and Jorge glanced at each other but kept still. Then a muffled word, the flare of a match and the fresh smell of tobacco, and the resumption of the steady pacing signaled that all was still well. They placed the last charge hurriedly but deftly, and Ramón glanced again at Jorge.

"Listo?"

His lips formed the word. Jorge nodded that he was ready and cupped his hands. Ramón removed the matches he carried in his headband and lighted one, holding it to the end of the fuse.

Two things happened at once. The fuse caught, sputtering, and a thunder of hoofbeats shattered the silence of the night. Jorge, thinking more quickly than Ramón, extinguished the fuse. Gambling that the approaching horseman had distracted the sentries' attention from the short-lived glow of the match, he edged out from under the bridge and peered over it.

On the riverbank, Jenaro was pacing back and forth in the confined space between the rocks from which Kate kept watch on the bridge through Ramón's fieldglass. Luis leaned negligently against another rock, but his eyes and the hand on his rifle were as alert as his body was motionless.

"What's taking so long?" Jenaro hissed in Kate's ear.

"Look! The fuse is lit!"

Jenaro jumped up to have a look just as the horseman clattered onto the bridge and drew up. "Where?"

"It's gone out again."

Kate could not see Ramón, but just then a shadow moved from under the bridge, paused for a moment, and slid back again. The rider above held a quick conference with the sentries, saluted, wheeled his horse, and rode back in the direction from which he had come. The river, the hills, the night became as they had been, except that the two sentries on the bridge abandoned any pretense of military correctness and lounged together talking and smoking as they watched the road.

"What are they waiting for?" Kate whispered to Jenaro.

The minutes passed. Five, ten—how long was it? She had no watch. Then came a low, drumming sound from the rocky hills on the far side of the river, increasing slowly in intensity as individual sounds distinguished themselves—horses' hooves, harnesses, accouterments. A horseman appeared around the bend, then another, then half a dozen. A column, fifty men long, with three six-pounder guns, moved toward the bridge. Kate's heart leapt with excitement.

"Jenaro!"

But he was watching, too. "Perfect! We couldn't have planned it better! What fools they are to travel at night, thinking we wouldn't be expecting them!"

"But we weren't" was Luis's dry comment from behind them.

The column approached the bridge. The first horseman, an officer, returned the salute of the now stiffly correct sentries and moved out onto the bridge. His horse, a beautiful bright chestnut mare, picked her way delicately across, as if wary of the uncertain footing.

The following riders and the guns lumbered onto the bridge unconcerned, looking neither right nor left. One of the guns was nearly across the bridge before the second reached it. The third would scarcely touch it before the first rolled off the far side, for the column was too long to fit in its entirety onto the bridge at one time.

"Now. Do it now! Don't try to get them all!"

Jenaro beat his fist on the rock with impatience. Luis moved lazily from where he stood and took up a new position, crouching near Kate, just as the first horseman stepped off the near side of the bridge.

Then came again the flare of a match. Two dark figures emerged suddenly from under the bridge and darted across the open space under the very nose of the lead rider, who started, uttered an oath, and drew out a pistol, all in the space of Kate's quick intake of breath.

But Luis was quicker, and as the officer raised his arm, a shot rang out. The pistol flew out of a shattered hand and splashed into the river.

Then the first charge under the bridge went off, sending chunks of masonry, flying bits of metal, human limbs, and screams into the air on a thunderclap of billowing smoke and yellow flame that illuminated the scene with a terrible clarity. It was eclipsed a second later by another explosion, and a third, and then the echoes of a hundred more died away among the hills, and the pieces settled again, the symmetry of the tableau reduced to a broken pile of stones and twisted metal and the stench of scorched flesh.

Nothing stirred except a few dying tongues of flame among the wreckage. One of the guns, balanced precariously on the jagged edge of the broken roadway, gave way and toppled on its carriage into the river, which worked its way quietly among the debris and soon found its course again. First a trickle, then a stream, it went on its way, carrying the remains of the convoy with it as it gained strength on its briefly interrupted journey to the sea.

Ramón and Jorge scrambled up the path and burst upon them with a shout of victory. Jorge and Jenaro embraced happily, and Ramón picked Kate up in his arms and soundly kissed her, getting water and grease and blacking all over her.

"Let's get away from here!" he said then, and would have set off wet and shivering if Kate had not stopped him.

"Wait! Put on some dry clothes first!"

"There's no time! We might be followed."

"By whom?" Kate asked, grimly indicating the chaos below them.

At the bridge, a handful of *guerrilleros* were already probing the smoking ruins and stripping the dead and dying of clothing and valuables. Ramón glanced down at them, then quickly removed his own soaking garments and, with a great show of gruffness, ordered Jorge to do the same. They were ready to move again within minutes.

Their path wound among the rocks and descended to the river before veering off to the west and away. Coming out of the shelter of the trees along the river, Kate was unprepared for the first sight that met her eyes, revealed by the eerie light of a pine torch wedged between two rocks. An involuntary scream of horror escaped her before she could avert her eyes.

Ramón, riding in front of her, had seen what was ahead and snatched at the bridle of her horse to turn it away, but not before Kate had seen the French officer, the one that had been the first over the bridge, pinned to a tree, his own saber run through him and the congealing blood on his jacket sticking it to his lifeless body. On the ground not far away lay the chestnut mare, dead, her forelegs blown off. Evidently, the officer had not been killed outright by the explosion, and the *guerrilleros* had finished him off in this fashion.

Kate covered her mouth with her hand, thinking she was going to be sick. She whispered hoarsely as she was led away, "Take him down."

Ramón left her to Jenaro and went back. She heard him demand fiercely, "Who's responsible for this?" But she did not hear the reply.

Later, no one, least of all Ramón, referred to the incident, neither to offer her sympathy nor to lament the needless cruelty. They left her to get over it as best she could by herself. She would have to, she realized; it was impossible even for Ramón to shelter her from every ugly thing. She noticed, however, that one of the men had disappeared in the night. And the same night, Ramón had gone to Luis to have a knife wound in his arm bound up, but he wore his shirt over the bandage until it healed.

Ramón seemed more elated than not as a result of the Miranda de Ebro episode. One night not long afterward, he and Jenaro made a surreptitious visit to a tavern in the town of Quintanavidas, where they chanced to overhear two French officers discussing the recent disaster. Much to Ramón's delight, one of them remarked that it looked to him like the work of "that rogue, Sariñana—and if he hadn't been reported dead last summer, I'd think he was back!"

Ramón found this premature report of his demise highly entertaining and repeated it to Kate, whose first thought was that it had more than likely been Gilberto Higgins who had instigated the rumor. Ramón felt that he should

The Dancers' Land

take full advantage of no longer being under active suspicion. He changed his appearance by shaving his mustache, brushing his hair over the scar on his temple, and adopting a dashing and more colorful style of dress. Jenaro remarked that he was beginning to look like one of Don Julian Sanchez's minions, which Ramón took to be a great compliment, for that guerrilla chief had lately been making a name for his daring exploits.

Kate had no reason to go back to Salamanca, but it had become an obsession of hers. Nothing awaited her there that she could not have where she was, with Ramón. But it had been more than three years now, and she wanted to go home. The eagerness for adventure that had burned in her brightly and for so long was dying now, and her life of constant travel was now less exhilarating, indeed more often than not just wearying.

And for the first time, she began to feel apart from the war—*their* war, as she began to think of it—that the Spanish would have to win their way. The cruelty of the episode at Miranda de Ebro had shaken her more than she would have thought a year ago.

Ramón gained new confidence, although losing some of his old scruples, with each new exploit, but Kate no longer cared to hear if they were successful or not. On the other hand, the minor annoyances—lice and no baths and the rain and the cold—that had not disturbed her before were becoming increasingly irksome. She longed to be able to remain in one place, in a home of her own again, for more than just a fleeting interval. She found herself remembering wistfully the peace of that summer in Baquio, with the soothing sound of the sea in the background. But there was no going back there.

At last even Ramón recognized that Kate was extraordinarily quiet and preoccupied. Reluctantly, he asked her what the matter was and was told it was of no importance. He pressed her and finally got an answer.

"Oh, Ramón, I want to go home!"

"Home?" He was incredulous. "To Salamanca? What for?"

"I don't know. I'm sorry—I should not have said it. Please forget that I did."

But however irritated Ramón might have been with her,

he did not forget it. He told himself that she should be perfectly content with him, that it was impractical to send her home, and inexplicable that she should want to go at all. But she became more melancholy daily, and he became so conscious of her attempts to disguise it that he finally said, "You had better go, then. If you want to."

"Oh, Ramón, thank you!" She embraced him happily.

"Luis will take you. You can start tomorrow."

Her happiness evaporated. "Luis? Won't you go?"

"My God, Kate! Do you expect me to?"

"No, of course not! I'm sorry!"

He was angry now. "I can't go! I'd have nothing left to come back to if I left now. But don't let that stop *you!* I won't make you stay if you're unhappy."

She looked to be on the verge of tears, and he dreaded the possibility. He took her in his arms, murmuring love words into her ear and stopping any further apologies with his kisses. He made love to her that night with greater tenderness than usual, but she felt that he was saying goodbye with it, even that in his eyes she had already gone and it might have been any woman lying there with Ramón, and not her. She knew that he would not ask her to stay— that would be too much like begging.

Ramón watched her preparations with a sullen eye, and when he thought she did not see him, he paced up and down along the stream, forehead furrowed and black hair rumpled from running an impatient hand through it. At last he said, "I'll see you home, then, and come back."

It was an enormous concession, and for a moment she hesitated. She had been wrong before, after all, about the depth of a man's feeling for her. But no, she could not make him do it.

"No, Ramón," she said, her voice calm and her eyes dry. "Thank you. But you were right, you can't leave and expect to find everything waiting for you when you come back. And you've worked too hard to leave it."

"Then I'll start over somewhere else. I've done it before."

She was ashamed at her willingness to leave him behind. She knew she must, if she wanted to start over herself, but he was too large a part of her life to abandon easily. It was a new sensation, this wanting to hang on to something she had valued, even if she had grown beyond it. Once she would have tossed it away without compunction. Once she had been, she realized now, much more cruel.

"Very well, *amor mío*. If that is what you want."

He held her for a moment, then broke away and said briskly, "All right. Let's go, then."

Part Four
Wellington's Army, 1812

Chapter Twenty-three

Deep golden fields of grain, mile after mile of them, rolled to the horizon, and the wind rippled over their surface like a sea breeze, raising voluptuous, sun-speckled waves. No tree marred the smooth perfection of the landscape, nor offered shade to three riders who pushed aside the yellow stalks as they would the river at a ford. It was mid-June and the sun, although still low in the sky, beat fiercely down on them. But it was only a few miles now to the Tormes and, after that, fewer still to Salamanca, and they would not be stopped now by mere heat.

It had been a long, uneasy journey. They had planned it in easy stages and by a circuitous route that would assure their meeting no obstacles, French or Spanish: But Ramón had forgotten that he did not have the freedom of movement on the plains that he had enjoyed in the mountains. Carelessness had been responsible for the loss of their horses to thieves in the predawn darkness, for an ungoverned display of temper on Ramón's part when he discovered his fault, and for a week of weary plodding on foot before Luis had commandeered—from he alone knew where—a donkey cart. But while this served to assuage Ramón's aching feet, it did not have the same effect on his wounded pride. He changed their plan of circling around Valladolid, and they passed boldly through the city for the express purpose of acquiring suitable mounts for their reentry into Salamanca. Once procured, by trading the donkey cart and all the money Kate had with her, the precious animals were carefully guarded, which meant less sleep at night for Luis and Ramón, and still shorter stages and more stops to rest themselves and their mounts.

It was at Valladolid that they heard the French were in

possession of Salamanca, but the British, having seized the fortress of Badajoz and chased Marshal Marmont out of Portugal, were now free to enter Spain for the first time in three years. Kate was stunned by this unexpected news, but Ramón only raised an eyebrow at her and asked, "Do we go on?"

Her hesitant heart had no time to make a decision, and her voice betrayed no more than a weary determination. "Yes. We go on."

She passed the remainder of the journey torn by uncertainty. If only she knew what was happening in Salamanca! Suppose the French were still in Salamanca when they arrived? Kate had yet to see a French soldier—a live one—at close range and had a certain curiosity to do so, for all she had heard about them were exaggerated tales of their cruelty and barbarous customs. "They *eat* little babies!" one peasant woman had told her, fully believing it.

Kate did not believe she would be in any physical danger if the French were in Salamanca, but Salamanca would be in for an uneasy time if both armies converged on the city. On the other hand, although the British were advancing into Spain, was Salamanca really their goal?

She longed to see her friends again—Val and the O'Reillys, Vivian Harmer, Peter Rutledge, Michael Sinclair—but how could she face them with Colin gone? Oh, God, if only she had never left Baquio!

None of Kate's inner turmoil appeared on the surface, however. She had learned from Ramón the trick of hiding her thoughts, and she meekly followed behind him and Luis as they progressed southward, their journey now measured not in weeks but in days, and then in hours. Familiar landmarks came more frequently and, instead of agitating her still more, seemed to have a soothing effect. Rolling hills and yellow fields brought memories of times farther removed than three years.

They had not left the river far behind, however, when a vivid reminder of the present intruded to impress upon her that this was not that long-ago time and that she was now no more than a returning exile.

They looked up and saw a rider appear, as if he had materialized out of the warm, heavy air on the crest of a hill. He halted, as they did, and they scrutinized one another for a moment. The lone man on the big white horse was an impressive figure. His richly embroidered jacket was unbuttoned over an immaculate white linen shirt. A wide-brimmed hat shaded his eyes but not his drooping black mustache, and a pistol was thrust into the folds of the red cummerbund at his waist. He rode slowly up to them, and, without preliminaries, demanded of Ramón, "Who are you?"

Ramón's expression betrayed no awe of the mere size of man and horse, and he replied proudly, "I am Sariñana."

A flicker of interest showed on the dark face. "We have not heard of you in Castile for some time."

Ramón smiled. "They have heard much of me in Vizcaya."

Kate had by now guessed this man to be a lieutenant of Don Julian Sanchez, one of the most notorious of the guerrilla leaders, famed for the cruelty of his methods. But Ramón had more than once expressed approval of the results he achieved, and he said, "I would speak with Don Julian."

The big man looked around pointedly. "But will Don Julian speak to you? Where are your men?"

Ramón answered, "I have no men with me, but if Don Julian would receive me, I would be honored to serve him."

The idea that any *guerrillero* leader should lower his pride so much as to be willing to serve another, even one so renowned as Sanchez, seemed to impress the man.

"Come with me," he said, and turned away.

In that time, he had paid no heed to Kate, except to run his eye up and down her in a quick, appreciative glance, and he was not now including her in his brusque invitation. Ramón turned to her with a questioning look, and she nodded a silent assent. He smiled, sketched a salute, and rode away after the big man.

And so it was not with Ramón that Kate came home, but as so often before, she rode the familiar paths accompanied by Luis. Laconic and dependable, Luis showed no inclination to return home, at least not until he had seen *la mujer de Ramón* safely to hers.

The British army had entered Salamanca two days previously. Marmont and his two French divisions had withdrawn slightly to the north, where he awaited the remainder of his army. He had left behind eight hundred men to garrison the forts of San Vicente, San Cayetano, and La Merced, which had been constructed on the southwest fringe of Salamanca on the grounds of three ruined convents. The surrounding buildings, including much of the university, had been destroyed but insufficiently leveled, and the ruins now provided cover for the siege operations of the British, who set immediately to the task of reducing the French-held forts.

The British had been unable to enter Salamanca by the Roman bridge, for that approach was guarded by the guns of La Merced. But the road was still open to civilian traffic and was crowded with every kind of vehicle, from farm carts to the carriages of the officials of the city.

And even the threat of the forts, and the French sentries that took a careful look at every vehicle and pedestrian crossing the bridge, could not check Kate's leaping heart, which had soared at her first step on the paving stones of the old bridge. Ahead of her, close enough to touch, it seemed, the spires and domes of the inner city welcomed her home. They had not forgotten her. On the other side of the bridge, she turned to the right and up the path winding around the buildings that clung to the hillside, searching the trees ahead for a glimpse of Thornhill.

She should have been able to see it before this. That orange building must have been erected since she left, but—no! She remembered it now. It had stood behind Thornhill, invisible from the road. She hastened forward and suddenly came upon the reason for her temporary confusion.

A ring of scorched poplars enclosed, as within the borders of a cemetery, an area strewn with cinders and bricks and chunks of burned wood vaguely recognizable as furniture and a staircase. A few blackened timbers still stood upright, leaning against one another for support, and one lone chimney showed naked against the trees. They were all that remained of Thornhill.

Kate gazed at the ruins for a long time, unwilling to believe what her eyes told her was true. Luis came up behind her and waited for some minutes before she remembered

The Dancers' Land

that he was there. She waved her hand in the direction of the center of the city.

"You go on, Luis. Tell Amelia I'm coming, and have something to eat."

He hesitated, but Kate had already forgotten him and dismounted. He took hold of her horse's reins and led it away.

Kate picked up a length of scorched wood and poked dully among the debris. Instinctively, she stepped over where the threshold had once been, passed down the hallway, and entered the drawing room, whose outlines were still definable. She searched for something recognizable, some link with what had once stood on this spot, but the destruction was complete.

Then, bending down, she brushed the soot from what looked like a thick sheaf of paper, once bound by twine that had been burned away, leaving an indentation along the edges. The topmost sheets were burned through and crumbled at her touch, but underneath, protected by their bulk, could still be discerned the fashion plates and flowery prose of Gabriella's back copies of *The Ladies Magazine*.

Kate had not been moved to tears at the first sight of the ruins of her old home, but now they sprang unbidden to sting her eyes. She stumbled blindly out of the rubble, staining her skirt and hands black with soot, and hurried away up the hill toward the Plaza Mayor.

That other house would surely be still there, waiting for her! What was the use of standing here amid the ruins of the past, forestalling the welcome of her own home, patio, room, by useless whimpering over what could not be brought back? But self-reproach alone would not dry her eyes. She paused, took off her hat, and wiped her eyes on a clean corner of her skirt. Then she walked on automatically, conscious only of the effort of keeping back the tears long enough to reach the Plaza Mayor.

The buildings along the Rua Mayor were decorated with flowers and banners, and the elegant ladies seated on balconies held gaily colored parasols over their elaborate coiffures. The air was heavy with the heat, the clinging scent of flowers, and an all-pervading atmosphere of carnival. The streets were thronged with noisy, celebrating crowds—the very same that had cheered Moore's army on its way to glory.

But that was in November. It was June now, summer, and the gentlemen discreetly wiped their brows while the ladies' fans fluttered languidly. Kate walked dully through the press of people, jostled from side to side, too distraught to move out of the way of a couple coming in the other direction. A carriage rattled by, and the driver shouted at her as he jerked the horses out of her path. She could feel perspiration running down her forehead, and she put up her arm to wipe her face.

A man on a horse swerved and narrowly missed her. His spur scratched her arm and she looked up, but the sun was behind the rider. She moved her hand to shade her eyes.

"Kate!"

Life, it seemed, no longer flowed by, but struck at her like a series of electric shocks. She felt she could absorb no more. She stopped, vaguely aware that the rider had dismounted. Then strong hands took hold of her shoulders and turned her to him.

"Kate! My God, what's happened to you? Where have you been?"

She looked up. That wonderful face, those amazing blue eyes—she must be dreaming again. The nightmare that had haunted her days must have returned. But she felt no throbbing pain at the bottom of her heart; there was no cold now, only heat; no darkness, only blinding sunlight. And the face that looked into hers was smiling.

"Colin?"

Then at last she succumbed gratefully to his embrace, and they clung to each other, oblivious to the crowds passing around them. Over and over he whispered her name, holding her more tightly. Realization rushed over her. Was this blinding light the reason for the blackness she had endured? Unhappiness receded further, quicker, into the past and no longer had any power over her, and she could not believe that she deserved such a reward for so little pain.

She pushed him away and looked into his smiling blue eyes and exclaimed, "You're alive!"

His first impulse was to laugh at this preposterous understatement, but he caught himself quickly.

"Alive? Of course, but—"

Someone lurched against them. He remembered where they were and postponed his questions. His arm around Kate, they continued on to the Plaza Mayor. Kate had eyes only for Colin and pressed against him as he plotted a course through the sea of arms and legs and faces. At last she was set down in the calm of her own patio, where the fountain still played and nothing seemed to have changed. Colin had taken his horse to the stables, and she stood there for a moment alone, looking around her.

Amelia, short and squat and looking not a day older, came trotting out of the kitchen, exclaiming in delighted disbelief, "Señorita Catarina, Señorita Catarina!"

Kate reached out to hug her. "Yes, Amelia, the sherry and biscuits, please! It's me. I'm home again."

Chapter Twenty-four

THE LIBRARY was a haven, soft and warm and pervaded with a peace far removed from the turmoil of the world outside. Of that world, all that dared to enter was the sun's rays, filtered through the single window to cast amber reflections on the carpet. Colin waited there while Kate, at her insistence, changed her soiled clothing. His eye was caught by a pile of letters on the writing desk. He picked them up, extracted half a dozen, and looked them over pensively, then put them in his pocket. One, franked in London and addressed in a woman's hand, he propped against a vase of flowers where it would be seen.

The door opened, and Kate came in, transformed in a long-unused, cream-colored gown of some flimsy fabric, trimmed with scarlet ribbons at the high waist and woven into the hem. Her face was free of soot and dirt and the long journey, her golden hair curled softly on her shoulders. They looked at each other for a moment, and then, with something of an effort, she moved to the window and opened it to look out. Colin came from behind her and quietly closed it again.

"No, leave everything and everybody outside."

He had never known her to look so lovely. It must have been the gown, for he had seen her only in black, and it touched him that she had put on colors just for him. It may have been, too, her thinness, that made the gay gown hang loosely on her, and that told him something of the difficulties she had been through. Or it may have been the discovery that this present reality of her far outshone his memory of her. He was afraid to touch her, afraid of shattering that exquisite beauty by saying anything.

But she had no such qualms and whispered, "I won't break, Colin."

His shaking lips met hers, and all the love and burning memories and anxious hopes of three years overwhelmed him and were communicated to her, setting her on fire and fusing her mouth and body to his. When at last the flame died to an ember and they parted, the warmth remained. They stood together in the light of the window, his arms around her waist, her head cradled on his shoulder, unaware of anything but each other and the marvelous peace of the room.

Finally, he said, "Kate, why did you think I was dead?"

She sighed, not wanting the moment to end, and he kissed her lightly behind her ear, then lifted the hair on her neck to kiss that, but then he looked at her, the question still in his eyes.

Briefly, she told him how Luis had brought her the silver knife. "The officer's friend called him a name that sounded like Greyson, and because he had your knife, I thought it was you."

He swore suddenly and broke away from her. "May God Almighty damn the Spanish and their profanation of the English language!" He stopped and muttered, as if to himself, "It wasn't pneumonia that killed him, either. . . ." He turned to face her again. "But not Greyson, Kate—not Greyson! It was Grierson."

For a moment she could not remember. "Alan?"

"Yes, Alan. I lent him the knife for some reason and then forgot about it. I didn't hear of his death until after Coruña, and the last thing I'd have thought about then was that knife!"

She was silent, thinking of the shy, gentle boy that had been Alan Grierson, and who seemed so far away now that she could scarcely remember his face. Had he been in love with her, and had she been cruel to him, too? If only she had known! But there was never any knowing. She should have learned that by now, should have realized that she would not have acted differently. All she could do now was to try somehow to make up for her past follies and not hurt anyone else, especially not Colin. And not Ramón, either. She did not know how she would do that.

Outside, a door slammed and precipitated her train of

thought. Her hand went to her mouth to keep it from voicing what came into her mind. Ramón! Colin looked at her, his ice-blue eyes narrowed, then he opened the door and glanced over the railing.

"It's Luis."

He came back, still frowning, but she had erased any trace of her agitation. She held out her hands and smiled at him.

"Tell me, how is everyone—are they all safe and well?"

He didn't answer her directly but took her hands in his. "Would you like to go and see them? Yes, you must!" he said, suddenly all eagerness. "I have a surprise for you, and it may not keep."

"A surprise?" She smiled at his impatience. "What is it?"

He shook his head and would not tell her. She laughed. "Well, at least tell me if you are billeted in that college again."

"No, camped just north of the city. The college was destroyed by the French. Half of them and a good many of the convents were, not to mention those that Marmont has converted into fortresses."

She thought of Thornhill, but she could bear no one's sympathy about that, least of all his—least of all now, when she wanted nothing to damage the moment. She laughed again, rather hollowly, and asked, "And Maria? Have you talked her into solving the regimental commissary difficulties?"

He pressed her hands and said quietly, "Maria has gone back to her family. George was killed at Badajoz."

"Oh, no!"

He looked as if he did not want to break the spell, either, but then spoke as if he wanted to get it all out at once and be done with it.

"My God, Kate, we lost five thousand men at Badajoz! A quarter of our own killed or sent home to die of their wounds, far, far too many of the Fourth and Light divisions in that mad assault . . ." He looked out of the window again, and his voice was muffled against the pane. "Crauford gone since Ciudad Rodrigo, and Michael Sinclair, too."

Kate sank down onto the sofa and shuddered. "Oh, poor Maria Elena!"

"I wrote to her immediately, but I will have to see her now, and I dread the thought of it. It isn't easy to comfort a woman who was a wife for only a week and must now be a widow for the rest of her days."

"I don't understand—they were married?"

"Didn't you know? No, I suppose not. They told no one but myself and her aunt, whom she lived with. It happened the day we saw that play—what was the name of it?"

She interrupted, suddenly struck by a new fear. "Colin, is Val—?"

He smiled again at that. "Val? Need you ask? Thriving! Except that he's thrown us up for an appointment on Le Marchant's staff. Claims he is better suited to the cavalry, anyway. I saw him prancing on Wimbledon Common when we went home after Talavera, and he may just be right. However, look, let's go! Do you still have your carriage? I'll ask Luis or have him saddle horses. Wait here."

Kate followed him to the balcony. For the first time, as he descended the stairs and crossed the patio, she noticed that he limped slightly, favoring the left leg. Was that a souvenir of Talavera or Busaco or Ciudad Rodrigo or Badajoz? She tried to piece together the scraps of information she had gleaned about the movements of the British army over the last three years. Thinking Colin dead, she had been less vitally concerned with its fate than she otherwise would have been, and now she was impressed with what they must have gone through. And what was ahead? How long would this go on? Did the long-awaited British reentry into Spain mean that the end was near? Or that the worst lay ahead?

It was some time before they were ready to leave. Three years before, Luis had dismembered the carriage to make it less attractive to marauders during Kate's absence, and he was now obliged to put it back together again. Colin returned to tell her this, a little impatiently, adding that since it would be more dignified for Doña Catarina to make her reappearance in Salamanca properly dressed and driven in a carriage than on horseback, hoyden-style, he had not told Luis to saddle the horses. But when he sat down beside her on the sofa, Kate thought he had another reason to delay.

She moved slightly, to give him room, and because the world was crowding in on her. It had been wonderful to think, for a few minutes at least, that they could start over again, but the past was not ready to let her go. She had tried to forget Colin with Ramón and had not succeeded, and now she could not deliberately put Ramón out of her heart, even for Colin.

"Please don't," she said when he reached for her.

But he was already kissing her hair and whatever else was close enough when she turned her head away. "Why not? We have time—all the time in the world now."

But they didn't. That time was long gone, and shame that she had not waited for him as he had asked—had not, again, believed strongly enough that he would be back—washed over her, and she pushed him away.

He paid no attention, pulling her to him, knowing she could not resist for long, whatever her reasons. And he was right. He took her head between his broad hands to stop her from turning it away, and she looked into his blue eyes, now filled with his need for her. They were different kinds of love, Colin's and Ramón's, different loyalties, but she did not know how to embrace the one without betraying the other. She hesitated too long; he moved forward, and his mouth touched hers.

There was a knock on the door. Colin let her go with a curse and flung himself off the sofa. She stood up shakily.

"It's Amelia. I told her to bring us something to eat. I forgot. I'm sorry. . . ."

But he said nothing, and she was not sure, away from his intoxicating touch, what it was she was apologizing for. She let Amelia in, and the luncheon was laid out for them, and they ate it in silence as the amber reflections on the library carpet lengthened. She could not speak, although he waited as patiently as ever for her to say something. But she would weep if she did. She knew from the moment she looked up again into those achingly familiar eyes that this man's love was older, deeper, stronger than any other, but she did not know how to be cruel anymore, so she did not speak.

The Dancers' Land

At last, there was another knock, and Luis stepped in to tell them that the carriage was ready for them.

When they set out into the Plaza Mayor, Kate was amazed to find that the world held so many other people. Everyone was out of doors, and all decked in their festive finest. Salamanca was the first Spanish city to be liberated by the advancing British, and its citizens felt that they had just cause for celebration. Even the houses and old buildings that never seemed to change, no matter what the season, had tied on flowers and garlands until their everyday faces had been transformed.

The excitement in the air was infectious, and Kate stared with as much curiosity as her neighbors at the passing redcoats. But she saw the change in the passing faces at once and said to Colin, "It isn't the same army."

He made no reply at first, and turned the carriage north on the Calle de Zamora. They were approaching the city gates when her attention was drawn to a man on a chestnut thoroughbred, who sat writing on a sabretache propped up on his saddle, now and again addressing a remark to one of the two orderlies accompanying him. He was a slightly built man but sat so upright as to give an impression of height to a body that was merely wiry. He had a strong face with a sturdy chin and a large nose; he was clean-shaven and immaculately, if simply, dressed in gray trousers and a plain, exquisitely tailored frockcoat.

"Colin, who is that?"

He smiled. "That, *mi vida*, is General the Earl of Wellington—and the principal reason that it isn't the same army."

Kate craned her neck to have a better look at this unimposing-looking man with the formidable reputation. Just then, a group of Salamanca matrons promenaded into view and, recognizing the general, squealed with delight and darted over to have a word with him. Wellington, startled by this sudden attack, backed away with a start. His horse shied, nearly unseating him. The two orderlies grinned and attempted to restrain the ladies, while the earl recovered his dignity and his sabretache.

The largest part of the army was encamped around the village of San Cristobal, slightly to the north of Salamanca, where they hoped that Marmont would attack to relieve the beleaguered forts. The British had few suitable siege guns, and little enough ammunition for the ones they did have, and the sound of fire from the forts to the west came only intermittently, in the intervals between cheers of celebration, to the ears of the Salamantinos. Outside the city, however, the steady barrage could be heard clearly. Kate turned in the direction of the sound but could see nothing. When she turned back, she gasped at the sight that did meet her eyes.

The British camp spread out endlessly before them: row upon row of tents in the shallow valleys; horses grazing on the grassy hillsides; piles of equipment; camp fires. There was all that Kate would have expected to see and a great deal more—a boy in uniform leading a string of greyhounds; two women arguing over a length of muslin; a smithy, stripped to the waist and perspiring freely, at work on replacing a horse's shoe while an orderly waited patiently with another animal; two nattily attired officers, oblivious to the heat, absorbed in a game of piquet, using a saddle as a card table; a private, cross-legged on the ground, mending a pair of trousers; and a girl who could not have been more than ten years old, plucking a chicken and stuffing the feathers into a sack.

Colin guided the carriage through this amazing ménage, saluting or casually waving his hand whenever they passed a man he knew. Then Kate saw someone she knew, recognizing, in spite of the ridiculous paper hat on his golden head, the elegant figure and graceful stride of Major Valerian von Ehrenberg.

"Val!"

She called out to him and jumped down from the carriage before Colin had time to get out and help her. Val turned, recognized her, tore off the hat, and swept Kate up off her feet in an enthusiastic embrace.

"Doña Kate! I was never so delighted to see anyone! *Where* have you been? *Where* have you been?"

Colin forestalled further questions by removing Kate from a rather prolonged embrace, and frowned intimidatingly at the major, who as usual paid him not the least notice. Kate looked Val up and down and decided that, although his appearance had altered in some not quite

The Dancers' Land

definable fashion, he was undoubtedly still the same sparkling, sunny young man she had known.

"Are they treating you well?" she teased him as they walked along together, Colin having surrendered the carriage to a private of his regiment.

"Oh, as well as can be expected," Val said. "I have discovered that, contrary to rumor, staff officers do not enjoy more of the comforts of life than your average subaltern. Very disillusioning it was, let me tell you! And I should very much like to know whose idea it was that I should get up at ungodly hours of the *madrugada* waiting for some fool to report to me that the French will *not* be attacking this morning, after which, and only then, mind you, allowing me my breakfast!"

"But you do get breakfast," Colin reminded him.

Val assumed an official stance and quoted, " 'The'—ahem—'the attention of commanding officers had been frequently drawn to the expediency of supplying the soldiers with'—ah—'breakfast.'

"No one," he added, "has seen fit as yet to remind the commissariat about dinner, however! Come into my parlor, dear lady—*pase usted*. There is no more natural shelter on this godforsaken field than in the middle of the Salisbury Plain in August. Although we do not, praise be, have such a sun in Wiltshire!"

He held open the flap of a tent for Kate, but Colin stopped her. "Wait. Here comes my surprise."

Kate looked up and saw a curly-haired young man advancing in their direction, unaware as yet of their eyes on him, for he had his hands in his pockets and was whistling softly to himself. Something familiar about his easy stride teased Kate's memory, but it was only when he came closer and lifted his face to them that she knew who it was.

"Christopher!"

He stopped short. The whistling ceased, the hands came out of the pockets and he stood, openmouthed, staring at her tanned face, her hair lightened from the sun to a silvery sheen.

"Good Lord—Kate!"

He ran to her, waving his arms, and caught her in a gleeful embrace before remembering Colin's presence and his dignity, and rather sheepishly letting her go. Kate laughed, but Colin reprimanded her.

"You must learn to show a little more respect in the presence of my new adjutant, Doña Catarina."

"Your what? Kit, when did this happen?"

"Last spring. Mother put me off as long as I could stand it, but then I took the first boat to Lisbon."

They adjourned to Val's tent. Kate sat Christopher down and subjected him to a barrage of questions. How was his mother? And father? Was he happy in England? And well? Were they still living in London? Colin watched in amusement, and Val sat on the floor, propped up against the cot, subdued for the moment.

"Has Gabriella had her season?"

"Yes, and her first love affair!"

"Oh, no, surely not already!"

"No, not *already*. She is nineteen now, you know, and a real beauty, if I do say so myself. That ridiculous nose of hers has all the London beaux in ecstasy. One even wrote an ode to her eyebrows."

He grew more serious. "It was terribly hard on her when Stacey was killed at Fuentes de Oñoro last year. He was a friend of mine as well, and Colin—"

He looked toward his colonel who, with an almost imperceptible shake of his head, stopped him, and Kate did not learn who Stacey was. There was a moment's awkward silence, but then a head intruded itself into the tent and demanded, "I say, is it true you fellows are hiding a perfectly drinkable bottle of port in here—oh, my word! A lady!"

Kate laughed, and Colin said resignedly, "Come in, Ferdy. Major the Honorable Frederick Harcourt, Kate, is the pride and joy of the 51st, but no one has told him that yet. He thinks he belongs to us. Ferdy, this is Doña—ah, Miss Collier."

"Honored to have you here, ma'am!" Then, almost visibly, a thought struck the major. "I say, sir, do you approve of this sort of thing?"

"It's all right," Christopher assured him. "She's got her kin here to protect her.

"Me," he added by way of amplification.

"Oh," said Ferdy, apparently satisfied that the proprieties had been observed. "But, I say, Val, about that port—"

"My dear fellow, you can't offer a lady *port*," Val said, looking pained. "However, if you look under that bedroll, you may just find a small bottle of *oleroso*."

It was very little time before a party had got under way and was augmented by several newcomers, attracted by the festive noises emanating from Major von Ehrenberg's tent. Before long, there was very little space left unoccupied. Vivian Harmer was sent for, and another happy reunion was brought about. The port was opened and finished. Val stuck a candle in the neck of the empty bottle and held it up to a new face.

"Hallo, Alastair! Didn't see you in the crush."

"Crawled in under the riggings, dear boy!"

More introductions followed. Kate was seated, or rather buffered, between Colin and Christopher and was overwhelmed by it all. Her first impression of a change in the army was reinforced by these men. They were rougher, and hardened, and now looked more like the ragtag army she had followed into the mountains. Even Ramón would have been at home here, for their very appearance indicated a lack of concern with incidentals. Their uniforms were shabby, patched with odd colors, and even the dapper Val had no scruples about sitting on the dusty floor.

No amount of polish could have hidden the tarnish in the gold braid, nor careful mending the frayed edges of oft-turned collars, but these men did not seem to mind, for their pride was now in their accomplishments as well as in their prospects. They were less careful of their language and manners than previously, and their humor was more boisterous, but their company was exhilarating, and before Kate knew it, it had grown dark. Colin leaned over to Christopher.

"I don't wish to subject your cousin just yet to our cooking," he said. "I think you had best see her home before it gets colder."

"You needn't come back immediately yourself," he added as Christopher got up, "but do be back by morning, won't you?"

The rest of the company rose, as well as they were able in the limited space, and bade Kate a cheery good night.

Colin fetched a cloak for her and put her in the carriage, and when Christopher rather pointedly went back into the tent for something he said he had forgotten, Colin quickly kissed her good night.

"I'll try to come to you tomorrow," he said, running his thumb down her cheek in a light caress that made her shiver with longing, "but it's difficult to make any arrangements. I may not be able to leave."

With a great effort, she moved his hand away from her face but held it tightly for a moment. Her mind screamed at her to hang on, but she forced her fingers open and released his hand, and in a surprisingly steady voice, she asked, "Are you expecting an attack?"

He grinned. "From Marmont? That cautious old devil has the steadiest trigger finger in Spain! But—well, one never knows."

When Christopher returned, he made some light remark to ease her concern and sent them on their way. But for all the cousins still had to say to each other, they were oddly silent as the carriage bumped along the rough road toward the lights of Salamanca. As they drove over the open ground between the camp and the city, the warm night settled over them, and a full, white moon hung on the horizon. The siege guns were silent, and if she did not look behind her, Kate could easily imagine another night long ago.

"Oh, Christopher! Thornhill—"

"I know. Don't talk about it."

She was silent for a time and then, taking a deep breath of the fresh night air, she said, "Oh, but Christopher—in spite of everything, it's good to be home!"

Chapter Twenty-five

KATE AND CHRISTOPHER talked into the small hours of the morning, and neither thought of sleep. Kate prodded out of Christopher a sketchy account of the family's activities since she had seen them last, but Christopher, who always lived in the present, was more eager to talk about the last three months than the three years before that.

From his account of his brief army career, Kate had the impression that he stood in some awe and great admiration of his colonel. He spoke of Colin in the most glowing terms and praised his generosity, his understanding, and above all his courage, although she could not persuade him to enlarge upon this. His narrative was interspersed with "Colin says . . ." and "Colin thinks . . ." and by the end of it, she had an imperfect picture of her cousin's career but a clear conception of his opinion of his commanding officer.

Inevitably, Christopher asked after Ramón. He received an unsatisfactory answer, pressed for another, and was finally told the truth. His reaction, in view of his new hero worship of his colonel, was only to be expected.

"It would kill Colin if he knew."

"Don't exaggerate, Christopher. He must know."

"You haven't told him!"

"No, I haven't." Foolishly, she had hoped there would be no need, that her dilemma would somehow solve itself. "He must have guessed."

She met with a glum silence. She thought he was going to offer some cousinly advice, but at last he only asked her, "What are you going to do, then?"

"Oh, Christopher, I don't know! Please don't ask me to talk about it now." She looked pleadingly at him, but it seemed he was as reluctant to prod a tender subject as she was. It occurred to her that he felt as badly at loving Colin over Ramón as she did; old loyalties tugged at them both.

When Christopher left at last, hastily and on a borrowed horse, there was already a thin streak of white on the horizon beyond the spires of the city. Kate went to bed, but her mind was too active and her body too weary for sleep, and when she heard Amelia moving about below, she got up and went downstairs.

Kate owed it to Amelia, who had tended her home and her belongings, even to the extent of burying her jewelry and a quantity of hard cash under the patio for safekeeping, that she could now step back into the society from which she had exiled herself as easily as if she had been only a fortnight away from it. Amelia had also given it out that Doña Catarina was spending her time quite innocently as the guest of one of her husband's relations in Santander. Neither Kate nor Amelia believed that Salamanca would accept such a story, and Salamanca didn't. But there was no one who would reveal the truth.

She took a light luncheon while she talked with Amelia of such matters, but later she felt her lack of sleep catching up with her and went upstairs again. But as she passed the library, she looked inside, for the door had been left ajar, and saw a letter propped up against the flowers on her writing desk. She had not noticed it before and went in to pick it up, curiously turning it over in her hand. It was already over a year old, and although franked in London, it could not have been from the Bentons, for it was addressed in a hand she did not know. She opened it.

"My dear daughter . . ." Kate's heart reacted strangely to the words, but she read on.

Perhaps I have not the right to call you my dear, nor my daughter, for it is no sort of mother that I have been to you. I can only pray that you will forgive me for what is long past and let us try to make a new future.

Colin Greyson has been to see me and has told me about you. Poor lad, I fear I pressed him with far too many questions, questions that he was understandably reluctant to answer. It was clear to me that I have hurt you, perhaps unforgivably, but I dearly hope not, and equally clear—please understand that this is from nothing that Colin said—that neither I nor anyone else could ever hurt you again, if only you were to grant Colin the right to shield you from all such sorrow. But I must not plead Colin's case for him; it is my own I beg.

Oh, my pretty Katie! It would please me so to see you again, and even more, to see you happy, as you were that night in Paris, which turned into such a nightmare. Will you not write to me? I should like to be able to tell you everything but, more important, to have you here and to show you everything, and take you everywhere and buy you pretty baubles, as it was once my only pleasure in life to do.

Colin tells me also how much you love Spain. But Spain, I fear, will never love you in return, and love is what we all of us need—you and I, I think, more than most. Forgive me this letter, my dear. It is long overdue.

Leonora.

Kate finished the letter and then read it again. Then she crumpled it in her hand and sank into the sofa and wept for her own stubborn pride, for the chances she had thrown away, for the goodness of a woman—and a man—who loved her in spite of it all. But how could she tell Leonora that she was unworthy of her, and Colin that she had been unfaithful to him? Finally, she wept herself into an exhausted sleep on the library sofa.

Kate awoke several hours later and raised her hands to her temples. She could feel the pulse throbbing, and a dull, driving thud beat against the sides of her skull. She closed her eyes again to shut out, if not the pain, at least the sound. But then she opened them again and listened.

She got up and opened the window. She leaned out and could hear the sound of gunfire in the distance—but not from the west and the forts. It was coming, she was certain, from the north. As she listened, however, it ceased and did not recur that evening. Neither was there any sound from the forts.

She put on a cloak and, in the warm evening air, took a walk through the city. All along the Rua Mayor she saw continual evidence of the recent French occupation of Salamanca, so she descended to the river and started across the bridge. She stopped and leaned over the wall to watch the muddy water flow past the gray, moss-clad arches of the bridge, lazily conscious of the centuries it had passed in that journey, and tranquil in the knowledge of the centuries to come. The music of the river blended with the gentle rustle of the leaves of the poplars on its banks and the chorus of night insects hidden in their branches.

A silvery moon gazed down on the river from between the drifting clouds. It illuminated La Merced, visible on the rising ground only a few hundred yards away and looking still very much more like a convent than a fortress. Lights went on, one by one, in the city, and the *farolero* came to touch a flame to the lamps on the bridge. Carriages rattled across it, and the few pedestrians hurried along, never pausing to appreciate the river or the magnificent panorama of the city.

The chimes of the cathedral recalled her to the hour. Pulling off her hood, she closed her eyes and breathed in the air and very life of the night. Then she started back, her aching head a little clearer, her sorrows, if not lifted, at least a little lighter.

The elderly gentleman coming up behind her in his carriage did not think it wise of the young lady to be abroad alone at this time of the night, and he drew up to offer her his escort.

"Why, Dr. Curtis! No, don't get down, please."

He stared in amazement at her as she climbed up onto the seat beside him. "My dear, I would not have known you!"

She smiled and took his hand. "No, I suppose not. But you are looking well."

She did not really think so, and she knew he sensed that. He looked much older, no longer the vigorous man of before the war.

"Why, yes, I am extremely well," he lied. "But we have missed you, my dear. When did you return?"

"Only yesterday."

"I see. And—er, young Sariñana?"

"He is well but not in Salamanca at present. I will bring him to see you soon."

"I wish you would do so. How like old times it will be! *Dicebamus hesterna die. . . .*" He smiled. "And not such ancient times, with the army here again. Have you met Lord Wellington?"

"Not yet. I saw him in town yesterday."

"He was kind enough to accept an invitation to dine with me last night, in spite of the pressure of his duties. A fine gentleman. I must introduce you."

"Thank you," Kate said, smiling. "I shall be happy to meet the famous earl."

He left her at the Plaza Mayor, declining her invitation to come inside for a moment, and she sadly watched him drive away. She had not asked Dr. Curtis for an account of his activities since she had last seen him, feeling instinctively that it would be best not to do so. She discovered later that he had been arrested as a spy by the French and had spent a difficult time in prison. Worse than her meeting with the doctor was her first sight of San Boal when she went there a few days later. Empty and bleak-looking now, it had been occupied last by Marshal Soult. The Marqués de Cerralbo had been imprisoned on spurious charges of treason in 1809, and in spite of efforts by the British to secure his release, he had not yet returned to Salamanca.

Again on the following morning came the sound of firing to the north, beginning with the burst that roused Kate from her bed, and continuing intermittently until early afternoon when it sputtered and died. The dull boom of the siege guns at the forts went on, although not so steadily as before, and she was becoming inured to those. But what was happening at San Cristobal? Why did Colin not come? She passed a restless day and, finally, for something with which to occupy her time, went to her room and threw open her wardrobe.

She had forgotten that she owned so much clothing and looked over the silks and muslins and brocades as if she had never seen any of it before. There were too many black things altogether, she thought, and ruthlessly pulled them out and threw them in an untidy heap on the bed. Her colored summer frocks were hidden behind them, and she drew out a pale blue gown with white trim. It had been a gift from Manuel, but she had barely had time to try it on before it had been discarded for the black. She slipped it on now; it was rather daringly cut, really, in spite of the demure color, but it fitted her now-slimmer figure well. She fastened it loosely and surveyed herself in the glass.

She had left the door of her room ajar to let in the warm air from the patio, and so that she could listen to the soft splash of water in the fountain. She had missed that sound. But then it was pushed to the background by other sounds: an opened door, a heavy tread in the patio, a male voice asking Amelia if Kate were at home. She ran out onto the balcony, her heart pounding.

"Please come up, Colin!"

She descended to the first floor and met him at the head of the stairs, where he stood smiling mischievously at her. She frowned, not realizing what it was that he found so amusing until he turned her around and did up the rest of her buttons for her.

"Now then. What has happened to upset your sense of the proprieties?"

"What has happened? Wasn't there a battle?"

"A battle! No, *mi vida*, scarcely a skirmish."

"Oh."

He was still smiling at her, and she thought that he was remarkably cheerful, even considering that the firing that had so worried her had signified so little.

But then it struck her with a flash of intuition that he was not thinking of that at all. He was simply happy to see her, no more than that. There was a light in his blue eyes that she had never seen unclouded by doubt or suspicion, and it shook her to her soul. She put one hand on the banister to steady herself and said, somewhat breathlessly, "Come into the library. We shall leave the door open—for propriety—while you tell me what news, if any, you have brought."

"Little enough, in truth," he said, seating himself on the sofa opposite her chair and speaking as if he had not noticed her trembling hands. "Marmont moved up to within artillery range of San Cristobal yesterday, but we were engaged only in a squabble over some village of little use to anyone. There was a lot of noise, which is what you heard, and by which we supposed Marmont to be signaling the forts to hold on. We should have attacked him this morn-

The Dancers' Land

ing while we had the superiority and the French had no place to run to. Even the earl was heard to remark that the situation was damned tempting, but by afternoon, two new French divisions had joined Marmont and evened the odds again."

He waved his arm in the general direction of San Cristobal. "They're still there, watching, each waiting for the other to blunder. You may be certain, however, that it won't be Wellington who does."

"I met Dr. Curtis last night," Kate told him. "He offered to present me to your precious Earl Wellington."

"You needn't trouble Dr. Curtis. I'll perform the introductions. Besides," he added with a grin, "I wouldn't care to expose you unprotected to the Beau's tender mercies. He has quite a way with a beautiful woman."

"I can take care of myself."

"I don't doubt it, *mi vida*, but permit me at least the occasional gesture."

Suddenly she remembered Leonora's letter: "If only you were to grant Colin the right . . ." She sat down on the carpet next to him and took his hand in hers. He said nothing for a moment, watching to see what she would do, perfectly still. She examined his hand carefully, turning it over several times. Then she ran her own hand up his sleeve and felt the hard, heavy muscles underneath the cloth. He was so strong, quite capable of shielding her from the world. She could hear his breathing, and it seemed to shut out every other sound, every thought in her mind. Only sensation mattered.

"Kate—"

"No," she whispered, reaching up to cover his lips with her hand. "Don't say it. Don't say anything."

He took her hand away and laughed shakily. "God knows, polite conversation is the last thing I want right now!"

He moved onto the carpet beside her, removed the pins from her hair, and ran his hands through her long blond mane, then left them there, on both sides of her head, while he stared intently at her. He was not smiling now, and she knew she should push him away but had no strength for it. She was abnormally conscious of the heat of his broad hands pressing lightly against her skull but strong enough to hold her if she tried to move away. When she did not, he leaned forward and his lips touched hers, drew away for an instant as hers parted with a gasp, and returned to claim her again. His kiss was surprisingly gentle but insistent, as if he were expecting her to resist. Instead, she felt herself melting closer into his arms, darting her tongue into his mouth, wanting to feel every part of him and nothing else.

Finally, he tore himself away and said, "You didn't order sherry or luncheon or anything, did you?"

"What?" Her mind was functioning too slowly.

"I don't want Amelia intruding this time."

She understood then, enough to whisper, "Close the door."

It took him only a second to turn the lock, and it would have taken longer than that to break the spell. She sat on the thick carpet staring straight ahead, unmoving, until he came back and she reached up to pull him down to her. His mouth covered hers again, and it felt so warm, so delicious, that she found herself silently begging for more, feeling the desire building in her until she knew she would love him this time as she never had before, pushing shame away, dismissing doubts.

He reached behind her to undo the buttons he had just done up and pulled away the pretty blue gown that was now just a hindrance. He took off his jacket, but then she stopped him, sitting up to quickly unfasten his shirt and then to strip off the rest of his clothing as he watched her in tense but delighted anticipation, barely able to wait for her to finish but stirred by her boldness.

With a groan, he kissed her mouth again and ran his hand down the smooth curve of her waist, and his mouth followed, leaving hot kisses on her cool skin. She could feel his body fit into hers, curve matching hollow, the soft mound of her breast pressed against the rough, curling, gold hair of his chest, the swelling between his legs urgent against her moist warmth.

She knew he was deliberately prolonging the ecstasy, but she could not wait. She moved her hips slightly and moaned when she felt him slip into the inviting warmth and then pull back. But he was trembling, and she knew he could not hold back much longer. She wrapped her arms

The Dancers' Land

convulsively around his strong back and pressed him down against her, until he entered her again, this time thrusting home with a force that, instead of hurting her, only deepened the exquisite pleasure, spreading heat throughout her body. She could feel herself move, rhythmically, in time to his increasingly frenzied thrusts until, unexpectedly, something exploded inside her, and she cried out.

He covered her mouth with his to silence her cry, but she could feel it echo through her very soul—even when, at length, he left her and fell onto his back beside her. She could feel him shiver, and moved closer, clinging to him as best she could in her weakness, and they lay together like that for a long time. At last she became aware of the stillness of the room, and the cool air on her skin, and moved away from him to search for her clothing.

He got up then and dressed in silence, until she had finished and picked up his jacket from the sofa to hand to him. He took it and threw it down again, putting his hands around her waist as he looked down at her. She could see the lingering light of passion in his eyes and looked away from them.

He bent his head to bury it in her loosened hair and whispered, "Marry me, Kate."

He felt her body stiffen, and then hot tears fell on the hand he raised to her cheek. Sanity came back, flooding over her, and although her heart told her, *Forget Ramón, forget everything else,* she pulled away from him and crossed the room to the window. She dried her eyes, set her shoulders with a determination she did not feel and with a consciousness of the irony of having to let go of the one thing she needed most because once she had seized upon the only thing she had. Almost inaudibly, she said, "I'm sorry, Colin. I can't."

She turned to face him, biting her lower lip in her anxiety, but he had watched her every movement and guessed what her reply would be. He put his hands on her arms, as if his touch could sway her mind as it did her body.

"That's not an answer."

His grip began to hurt her. She winced but said nothing, and after a moment, he let her go. "You look like a frightened rabbit," he said. "I'm not one of the Beau's greyhounds, you know." His voice had an edge to it.

Abruptly, he picked up his jacket and went out. Kate went with him to the front door, where he took her hand, kissed it chastely, and went out into the twilight, leaving her with a sense of incompleteness.

She hated to leave things in the air like that and wished that she could have explained to him why she could not marry him. But he would not have listened to her in any case, leaving her instead the opportunity to change her mind, and she did not think she was strong enough not to do it. Her tremulous sense of honor told her she could not accept him, but her constant awareness of her need of him might make her take him, anyway.

But she must not think about it too much now. She should see Ramón soon. He would come to her, expecting her to be waiting and, much as she might regret her newfound sense of honor, she would hang onto it until Ramón released her from it—or claimed her because of it.

Chapter Twenty-six

Two days later, on the night of June 22, Marmont withdrew from San Cristobal eastward to Huerta. Wellington let him go, in spite of the prevailing opinion that it was a mistake to do so, since Wellington's force was more than a match for him in numbers. But the earl kept to a cautious path, unwilling to risk his army except for an assured victory. And it could not hurt to let Marmont think that Wellington was unable, or unwilling, to take the initiative.

On the 23rd, an attack on one of the smaller French forts, San Cayetano, failed. The British had exhausted their small supply of ammunition before Wellington ordered a storming of the injured fort, and Salamantinos sitting down to their late suppers heard the roar of guns as San Cayetano and the untouched San Vicente both opened fire on the besiegers. Casualties were heavy, and the attack was soon given up as hopeless, but Marmont, on the other side of the Duero and not knowing that the attack on the forts had been suspended, made no further attempt either to relieve them or to engage the British.

With the lessening of tension after Marmont's withdrawal from San Cristobal, more soldiers were able to obtain a few hours' leave. They spent them in the Plaza Mayor and in the streets, cafés, and shops of Salamanca, although with their pay months in arrears, they could do little more than gaze longingly into display windows. Kate, on the other hand, had purchases to make, and when her cousin turned up alone on her doorstep one morning, she enlisted his services as escort.

Christopher soon found himself encumbered with all manner of parcels and gifts, and as Kate moved briskly on to the next shop, he demanded, "What do I get out of all this?"

"I shall mend your stockings for you," she offered, stopping to inspect a bonnet in a shop window.

"Don't buy that hideous thing. How do you know I have holes in my heels?"

"Darling, you always did, don't you remember? And I doubt very much if you would mend them yourself. Or shall I buy you a new pair instead? Come along—oh, no, I can't. I haven't any money left."

"Praise the Lord!" he said with an exaggerated sigh of relief. "Will you sit down instead, madam, and let me buy you something in the way of refreshment?"

She smiled at him. "Why, thank you kindly, sir."

They settled into a nearby café in a corner of the Plaza Mayor, at a table well away from the pavement but which commanded a view of the passing parade. Christopher ordered lemonade, which arrived with sugared biscuits and a flourish on the part of the waiter. They talked about little things for a time, but Kate had something else on her mind and asked him point-blank about it.

"Christopher, did you meet my—your aunt in London?"

"Who? Oh, you mean Leonora. Everyone calls her that, and she wouldn't let us do otherwise."

He smiled but watched Kate out of the corner of his eye as he went on. "She's not what you'd expect, considering the scandal God knows how many years ago and all the tales about her being a spy when she lived in France. She's not at all in the demi-rep style—perfectly respectable, in fact, even if she does live alone. Her French husband died a year or two ago, you know, and I suppose being a widow makes her more acceptable in any society—not to mention her fortune. She paid for Gaby's come-out, but then had half the men flocking around her as she sat demurely in the chaperones' corner."

Christopher paused to let this information sink in and added, "You'd like Leonora, Kate. You're much alike in some ways."

"So I've been told," Kate said wryly. "But direct comparison inevitably favors Leonora. You appear to have fallen under her spell, too."

Christopher grinned but did not pursue the comparison.

"You should have seen Gaby at her first ball, though. I'd never have thought the little imp would turn into such a bird of paradise with just a few new feathers. It's too bad so few girls keep that look."

"Or are allowed to," Kate said, thinking of her own first ball and feeling a pang of sympathy for Gabriella, and of envy that Leonora was obviously one of the few that survived the disappointments.

"Christopher, tell me about Stacey. Colin's being wounded has something to do with that, doesn't it?"

He hesitated and then, with some reluctance, told her about it. Gabriella, he said, had met Stacey Westover in London just before he enlisted, and they had fallen instantly in love. Stacey went off to war with the object of proving his valor to his beloved. His commanding officer took an interest in the young man during the Portuguese campaign of 1811—an interest, Christopher took pains to point out, that increased considerably when the colonel discovered that the lieutenant's betrothed had the surname of Benton.

Wellington had driven Masséna out of Portugal after that first harsh winter at Torres Vedras, and the Marshal had retired to Salamanca. But no sooner had the French recovered their breath than they were back again, and met the British at the border town of Fuentes de Oñoro. Christopher sketched for her the first stages of the battle.

"We were drawn up on a hill west of the village in reserve. The main part of town was held by the 71st and the Camerons, but then the French sent in two fresh divisions and forced them back out of the village, so we were sent down to help. We joined up with the Irish and pushed the French back to the river, east of the village. It was a bloody business, impossible to keep any kind of formation in that maze of streets, not to mention tripping over corpses and our own skirmishers, who took cover in the most unlikely places. One party of French was caught in a cul-de-sac, and the Connaughts slaughtered them to a man.

"Stacey was still new and green and a bit cut up by all the blood. I suppose he wasn't looking where he was going, because he walked right into a French bayonet. Greyson saw him go down and got the Frenchman before—before he could finish the job. He dragged Stacey out of the way but caught a bullet in the leg from a sniper on the roof. He got out all right, but Stacey was very badly hurt and he died the same night.

"Greyson wrote a masterful letter to Gabriella, all about how Stacey had died a hero's death and so forth, but I don't suppose it was much comfort to her. When I went home on leave at Christmas, she was playing the widow as if they'd been married. Mother was more upset by her behavior than by Stacey's death, even though he was a pet of hers. Papa said she'd get over it. I judge from their latest letters that she has, because a new match seems to be in the offing."

In spite of his flippant telling of the story, it had evidently affected Christopher badly at the time. He was silent for a moment and then said, "I never told this to Gaby, of course, but frankly, I think Stacey was lucky to die the way he did."

"Do you mean, because he didn't suffer?"

"Yes, but—well, if he'd lived he'd have had to be grateful to Colin for his life, for the rest of his life. I wouldn't want to be saddled with that kind of a debt."

It occurred to Kate that Christopher had always been so cheerful and lighthearted, precisely to avoid such an emotional weight. It certainly was more comfortable to avoid entanglements than to be caught up in them; she had done it herself, God knew, even when she knew she was missing something more important than discomfort by refusing to involve herself.

Christopher was staring out into the crowd passing through the Plaza Mayor, not really seeing them. Kate reached out to take his hand, and when he looked at her, his eyebrows rose quizzically in his old manner. She made some remark about the comic relief provided by an army at its leisure, and Christopher laughed.

There was indeed a motley assortment of military individuals mingling with the usual population in the plaza. A number of soldiers strolled by with pretty, dark-eyed girls on their arms; others in groups hurried past in search of greater excitement. Kate smiled at two Highlanders whose kilts had been, for lack of other material, converted to trousers. A lieutenant with leather patches on his elbows diverted attention from his tattered uniform by the well-kept but lengthy mustache he supported on his youthful upper lip. Another officer had his jacket unbuttoned to reveal a startling shade of waistcoat, but the attire of the trio of riflemen who followed him was, to say the least of it, unpretentious.

"Not very pretty, are they?"

Colin Greyson's voice jerked Christopher to his feet like a marionette. Kate looked up apprehensively, but Colin obliged her by not looking back.

"Sit down, Christopher. You're not on duty now."

"Yes, sir!" He obeyed, rather stiffly. Kate answered Colin's first remark.

"No, they're not pretty. They haven't their old splendor. But I think it is more than the surface polish that has rubbed off."

Colin signaled to the waiter, who brought him a brandy, and helped himself to a chair from the next table.

"Fighting has effectively removed that. But Wellington doesn't mind what they look like, if they go into the field with their eyes open and their muskets loaded. But you're right in that the change goes deeper than that. They are different men now. They swagger and strut and boast but not without reason. They have confidence now in their achievement as well as in themselves. Their only ambition now is to win, and hang the Glory."

"You sound as if you regret the change."

He shrugged, and smiled at a pair of green-coated riflemen gawking like country bumpkins at their surroundings.

"No, I don't regret what was inevitable. We could not have done what we have, had the men remained the same. They were young and healthy and eager then. Now they are lean, hardened cynics, but they know how to fight, and they hold no illusions about hero's deaths and last stands and forlorn hopes. Wellington doesn't believe in lost causes, and even Val admits that there is no future for gallantry in this army."

Kate heard the cynicism in his voice, yet had the notion that he missed the idealism of the earlier army, their seeking after glory, rather as Philip Benton must mourn the death of his old dream of a romantic, golden Spain—and unlike Ramón, who had known from the first what it would be like and coldly accepted the harsh reality of war.

"I say . . ." began a voice nearby and rapidly closing in.

"No, my dear fellow, don't," pleaded a second voice. "I beseech you!"

"Don't what?"

"Say anything. Just 'good morning' like a good chap and wait quietly for the lady to invite you to be seated."

The somber moment broken, Colin turned to Kate, who was having a difficult time of it to keep from laughing and said, "Do you know these ruffians?"

"I fear I do!"

"Ah!" said Major von Ehrenberg, "Recognition at last! Doña Kate, you remember Major Harcourt? Ferdy, I believe you know everyone."

"Do, indeed! Good morning to you, Miss Collier."

"Well said, old friend! Now sit down."

Kate had indicated that they should join the party, and Ferdy complied. He continued to gaze at Kate in obedient silence while Val talked for both of them. He had, he said, just abandoned a futile search for a respectable bottle of port for his commanding officer to offer to an official of Salamanca whom he was to entertain the next day. Kate suggested a likely source of supply that had thus far escaped his notice, and he thanked her profusely. She indicated a street off the eastern end of the plaza but stopped in the midst of her directions at the sight of a group of horsemen approaching from that direction. Val saw them, too.

"Here comes a cluster of dandies to put Sir Stapleton Cotton to shame," he said. "I wonder what French captain of hussars he killed for that cap?"

A Spaniard, splendidly mounted on a huge black horse and dressed in an English dragoon's pelisse with a multitude of gold braid and a French hussar's head piece with the eagle symbolically reversed, pranced into the center of the plaza. He was greeted by a tumultuous outburst of cheering from the crowd, and Kate realized with sudden terror that he must be Don Julian Sanchez. He was accompanied by a dozen of his men, all equally flamboyant in appearance, and by two aides. One of these Kate recognized as the big man on the white horse whom they had encountered coming into Salamanca six days previously. The other was Ramón.

Hoping not to be noticed herself, she glanced quickly at Christopher, but he was regarding the group with as much, but no more, interest than the others showed. Could he not have recognized Ramón? Kate looked back and realized that this must be the case, for Ramón did indeed look nothing like the man Christopher had known. Ramón turned his head in their direction, but if he saw them, he made no indication of it, and when he and his companions turned out of the plaza in the direction of San Cristobal, Kate let out her breath again.

That incident taught her that her appearance in public places invited a confrontation she was not yet prepared for. Seeing Ramón like that only confirmed her uncertainty, for she felt a kind of pride in him and his strength. She tried to detach that from her sense of obligation to him, but the two were too thickly entwined; she told herself that Ramón did not need her, but she did not believe that, either. It was he who had insisted on coming back to Salamanca with her; she had been willing to let him go then.

Colin, on the other hand, seemed not to need her. He desired her, yes, that was obvious, but he went out of his way to force her to make her own decision, not even trying anymore to make her body do it for her. That he was the only man who had ever made her feel the heat of passion from the depths of her being, had taught her a new language of giving and had shown her that great joy was worth great sorrow, made her decision no easier.

In coward's fashion, then, she sought safety in numbers. And so, when Colin called at the Plaza Mayor that evening, he found Christopher, Vivian Harmer, Peter Rutledge, and Patrick Curtis there ahead of him. He came into the library to find the two medical men engaged in quiet conversation by themselves, the rest of the party in a more lively discussion.

He greeted Kate impersonally and then each of the company in turn. He held out his hand to Dr. Curtis. "It is good to see you again, sir."

"The pleasure is mine, colonel. But now that you are here, I must insist that you bear your share of the reproaches Kate has been showering upon me. It seems, you see, that we have both promised to introduce her to the earl, and neither of us has done so. She is quite put out with us."

Kate laughed and put her arm around the doctor. "But

you must not take me in earnest, sir! I fear I should be quite tongue-tied before the great earl and make no good account of myself."

"On the contrary," said Doctor Rutledge, "I have no doubt that you and the earl would get on famously!"

Colin grinned. "Peter, that's the closest thing to flattery I've ever known you to utter. But you *shall* meet the earl, Kate—I have it on the best of authority!"

"Have you, indeed!"

"I have, indeed. Now, will you get me some sherry?"

Kate laughed at his unsubtle changing of the subject. "I shall fetch it for you myself, colonel. With your permission, gentlemen . . ."

Kate went downstairs and crossed the patio, wondering as she went what Colin had been hinting at. Then, as if in answer to the question, there came a heavy knock at the outer door.

"*Ya voy*, Amelia!" she called in the direction of the kitchen, and went to open the door.

A polite voice, in accented but presentable Spanish, said, "I understand that Colonel Greyson is here. May I be permitted to see him?"

Knowing at once who it was, Kate answered in English, "Won't you come in, my lord?"

The soft voice of an English lady stunned Lord Wellington into temporary silence. He stepped into the light of the patio and glared at Kate over that impossible nose. But he seemed to like what he saw, and his expression softened.

"You are Doña Catarina de Sanchez?"

"I am." She looked up the few inches to meet his piercing blue eyes and smiled her unconsciously captivating smile. "You are very welcome to my home, my lord. Won't you come this way, please?"

When he entered the library, the men jumped to attention—all except Dr. Curtis, who rose slowly and held out his hand. "Good evening, my lord."

Wellington took the hand, regarding the doctor somewhat curiously, but greeted him courteously. He looked around him with interest, and then back to Kate, but he remembered to say, "Sit down, gentlemen, please—sit down."

"Evening, Greyson," he added, and, under cover of

scraping chairs, said something in Colin's ear that made the colonel smile.

Kate rang for Amelia, and when she came with Colin's delayed sherry and some for the earl, the earl was already comfortably established on the sofa with Kate beside him. He beamed at her, and Colin sent a meaningful glance to Peter Rutledge, who smiled back. The earl rubbed his hands together over the fire and observed that the nights here were surprisingly chilly, even in June. Kate said that this cold snap was a trifle unusual, and he replied that he was nevertheless pleased to be in Salamanca.

Kate could not help a wry little grimace. *"We* are excessively pleased to have you here, my lord!"

The earl laughed at this, and Peter Rutledge said, "I think Lord Wellington means to say that we find Spain more agreeable than we did Portugal."

"Indeed, indeed!" the earl interrupted. "It is good to be able to walk the streets in comfort. Why, in Lisbon, during the rainy season, one had only the choice of walking at the edge of the road and being rained upon from the roofs, or in the middle, up to one's ankles in water, or between the two where—well, it was not very clean!"

"The men seem to have taken these discomforts very well, however," said Doctor Curtis. "Isn't that so, Colonel Greyson?"

"Yes, sir. They are a hardy lot."

"It's the ingredients," said Wellington. "Lords' sons, merchants' sons, shepherds, princes and paupers, vicars and roués—but we've got rid of the wastrels and those who would not take their fighting seriously. It must be taken seriously—why, if I lose five hundred men, they will have me before the bar of the House of Commons!"

The earl chuckled at his own remark, and Doctor Curtis ventured to say that the earl's many supporters would gladly take on the Commons or anyone else for his sake. The earl replied modestly and gave the credit for his successes once again to the men.

Meanwhile, Kate sat back and studied her guest. She saw by now that the inanity of some of his remarks stemmed from a simple desire to lend cheerfulness to the conversation. He seemed, in fact, to be a remarkably good-natured man, and it was difficult to credit his reputation as a commander who drove his troops hardly and unlovingly.

Colin watched her and must have read her thoughts, for when he caught her eye, he grinned broadly. She stifled a laugh, and turned back to the earl. But he must have been aware that he had overstayed the prescribed time for a first social call and rose to take his leave.

"You must forgive me, Doña Catarina. Marmont will be wondering where I've got to, don't you know! Will you accompany me, Greyson?"

"Certainly, my lord."

The party broke up rapidly after that, and only Christopher remained to take supper with Kate. She was not entirely sorry that the evening had ended like that, but once again she felt that another day had gone by, another day wasted because she could not make up her mind about her own future.

But after supper she had another caller. Amelia went to the door to let him in, and the first footfall on the stairs told Kate who it was.

"Ramón!"

But it was Christopher who was first on his feet. Kate came to the landing to find the two old friends facing one another, Ramón with a look of wonder on his face, and Christopher no less astonished by the apparition that resembled his old companion but was not, surely, the same man. Ramón laughed, his teeth flashing white in his tanned face, and tore off the elegant hat he wore over his black curls.

"*Niño!* Can you have forgotten me?"

The momentary stillness was shattered; they embraced and fired questions and laughter and good-natured insults at each other. Christopher bounded up the stairs to the library, begging Ramón to follow. He did, but paused on the landing next to Kate and smiled, and his black eyes sent a chill of mingled pleasure and apprehension through her. She had hoped desperately that at her next sight of him she might find herself changed, indifferent toward him, even resentful of the ties that still bound them. But she was still afraid to tear those bonds loose—and uncertain that there would be anything to replace them.

Chapter Twenty-seven

On the 26th, new supplies of ammunition arrived, and the siege of the forts was resumed. The heavier guns were concentrated on San Cayetano, while howitzers fired red-hot shells onto the roof of San Vicente. The fire was kept up through the night, and the noise of the guns and the excitement in the city made sleep impossible. Kate stayed by her window and watched the red glow in the sky to the west from the conflagrations that broke out in the forts, were extinguished by its defenders, and broke out anew in another place.

In the morning, the garrison still resisted but more weakly. Then a larger fire started and threatened the San Vicente powder magazine. A practicable breach had been made in San Cayetano, and a storming party was ordered forward. But before it reached the fort, white flags appeared on the battlements. The French haggled over the terms of surrender, playing for time, but Wellington lost his patience and sent the attackers in to put a quick end to the business. By noon on Thursday, Salamanca was wildly rejoicing, and by the next morning, Marmont had retreated north toward Valladolid and the defensive line of the Duero River.

After Lord Wellington had discovered Doña Catarina, he often found he could spare a little of his time to call at the house on the Plaza Mayor with no other excuse than that he "happened to be in the neighborhood." And he was grateful for the cup of tea or glass of wine and the brief moment of relaxation he found there.

Kate had little time to become fully acquainted with the earl, except to note with amusement that his appreciation of a pretty woman seemed to be even stronger than his natural shyness, which, she thought, must account for some of his reputation for brusqueness. She was impressed by the good sense of everything he said. She remembered the almost fanatical idealism of John Moore and noted the complete contrast to it of this man's inherent clear-sightedness.

Wellington was doubtless as exacting a commander as Moore, but he would not be such a popular one, if only because he did not feel he had to justify himself to his subordinates. He gave an order and expected it to be instantly obeyed, not analyzed.

He had his opinions on everything, and Kate gleaned from his visits another view of Colin. She had not seen him at all since Monday, but Wellington's brief but precise observations on his character compensated in some part for his absence.

"An excellent officer, Greyson, competent. Does as he is told and doesn't gallop off on unnecessary tangents," Wellington told her in a tone that indicated his satisfaction.

Kate thought that this seemed to indicate a lamentable lack of initiative on Colin's part. But upon further reflection, she decided that while personal initiative in a member of an irregular band of *guerrilleros* might be a good thing, in the complex organization of the regular army, it could upset the vital balance necessary to success. Small wonder that Spanish armies had no organization, as she later commented to Greyson in the hearing of the earl, who asked Greyson later what the devil she knew about it.

Lord Wellington appreciated pretty women best in what he regarded as their natural setting—at home pouring tea or, on occasion, as at a social gathering, being merely decorative. On the morning of the 28th, Kate received—through Wellington's intervention—an invitation to a private soirée to be held that evening for the victorious allies. Following a day of celebration which included a Te Deum and High Mass sung in the cathedral, all of Salamanca would make merry, for it was to be farewell on the morrow for the victorious troops.

Kate stood in the middle of the patio with the invitation in her hand as that thought struck her. Had ten days ever passed so swiftly? She had not seen Colin for the last three of them, and tonight would be the end of it. But was that not what she told herself she wanted? She had not seen Ramón, either. It seemed that no one would ease her out of her dilemma but herself. Even Christopher, who went to mass with her that morning, had little to say to her, possibly because he *had* seen Ramón and was himself torn between loyalty to his old friend and to his new idol. Kate had an impulse to tear up the invitation but knew that if she did not appear at the party, Colin would come after her and demand the reason for her absence, for her cowardice.

So she went. She had dressed unconventionally in a white, Grecian-style gown, her hair piled high on her head and the loose curls studded with white camellias. Studying herself in her mirror earlier, she had wondered at her own choice. She did not often dress deliberately to draw attention to herself and was uncertain why she did so now—to seduce Colin into making her decision for her? She hated herself for the thought but did not change her gown. The woman in her wanted him to think her beautiful for no other reason than that she was a woman.

She and Colin arrived shortly after ten o'clock, and in spite of the relatively early hour, they found a good many people there ahead of them, and the rooms were already overheated and heavy with tobacco smoke and exotic perfumes. In the candlelight her white gown glowed, and her bare, golden arms and throat attracted the quick admiration of every man in the room. Lord Wellington quickly came forward to greet her.

Kate thought that the earl was in a remarkably cheerful mood, as if he had nothing else on his mind but merrymaking. He conversed at some length with her while the ladies looked on, half-envious, half-disapproving, and his officers reflected silently that it was hardly surprising to see the Beau so at his ease with the lovely Doña Catarina.

But Colin returned quickly to her side as soon as the earl had quit his post, leading Kate to a sofa along the wall, from which they could watch people entering the room. Even Val appeared to have deserted her, and she saw him in company with an officer she did not know.

"General Le Marchant?" she asked Colin, trying to keep the conversation on an impersonal track.

He nodded. "He has only just joined the army from serving as commandant of the new Royal Military College at High Wycombe. Val is ridiculously devoted to the old schoolmaster—treats him like a father. Frankly, I would never have suspected such devotion from him."

Kate saw that he was entirely serious. General John Gaspard Le Marchant was a handsome man of about fifty, delicate of feature but possessing an excellent figure and an air of authority; he did not look as if he needed Val's support or solicitation.

Colin explained, "The general's wife died last September, Val's father at about the same time. The two families were acquainted. I don't know if Val or the general was more in need of the other, but it was then that Val suddenly decided he had had enough of the infantry and persuaded some of his connections at the Horse Guards to arrange a transfer to the cavalry for him."

"And Colin, who is that?"

Speaking with Wellington was a large, unlovely man with one eye; she was acquainted with General Beresford, one of the few who had been in Salamanca in 1808 and returned. But not far away stood a slender, dark man of about Wellington's age.

"That is General Pakenham, Wellington's brother-in-law. It has just been announced that he is to take over the command of the Third Division. The short, dark fellow with him that looks like a Corsican bandit is Alava, Wellington's aide. That trio over there is Cole, Leith, and Clinton, divisional commanders of the Fourth, Fifth, and Sixth. That's Graham, with the white hair, next to Le Marchant. I met him when I was a boy, and he came to visit my father at our home in Lyme. Even then he was an impressive figure."

Colin's mention of his home distracted her for a moment. "Do you still live there—by the sea?"

"Yes, just outside of Lyme, really, on a hill overlooking the sea." He smiled down at her. "Have I said something in my favor? Tell me, and I'll say it again."

She had to laugh. "No, it's nothing, really. I knew Sir Thomas, too, but not so long ago as that. Oh, look over there—if I am not mistaken, that must be Sir Stapleton Cotton!" She indicated a gorgeously attired cavalry officer who had just made a grand entrance.

Colin laughed. "Yes, somebody reckoned that he and his horse, fully accoutered, would be worth a neat five hundred pounds to the enemy—if they could catch him!"

Just at that moment, Don Julian Sanchez was announced, and Kate turned toward the door with a start. But the guerrilla chief was unattended, and she breathed a sigh of relief. She looked at Colin, but he was smiling at her with an indefinable look in his eyes—almost, Kate thought, of pity, as if he knew what was going through her mind. But for once it did not disturb her that he did, and it was comforting to be able to sit and just talk with him with no sense of pressure or demands on her. He asked, "Is there anything else you want to know?"

She smiled back gratefully. "Yes. When are they going to play a waltz?"

Soon afterward, they did, and Kate and Colin danced together once again. For a few minutes she had the dizzying sensation that history was repeating itself, and she tried desperately to forget the last time she had waltzed like this, the night before another army was to march away, and to hold onto the comfort she had felt only moments before.

The dancing was in a larger room at the end of a wide hall, and there the French windows were thrown open. The cool air of the gardens to the rear of the building flowed gently over the dancers. After a few turns, Colin whirled her out of the crowded room and onto the terrace. There the night air seemed to clear both of them of the drugged sensation that came from closeness, the motion of the waltz, and the heady atmosphere of the ballroom. He released his hold on her.

They walked down the stone steps into the gardens that were only faintly illuminated by colored lanterns in the trees. They were not the only couple there, but there were a great many shadowed nooks. They stopped in one of them but stood apart, in silence, for a long time.

Finally, he said, looking around him, "I am astonished at how little has changed here."

"Spain doesn't change," Kate said.

He took her hand and looked down at her. "People do, however."

She lowered her eyes. "We grow older," she said, and thought of what Leonora had written of her, as she was in Paris. Tears stung her eyes at the idea that she was no longer so beautiful for Colin after all. She had thrown that away, too.

He smiled and raised his hand to stroke her cheek. "But you, my life, grow more lovely with time. Every time I see you, just looking at you makes me forget everything ugly that has happened. I can think of nothing but how much I want you, as I have never stopped wanting you."

The tears escaped her gray eyes then, and she turned away to stifle a sob. He put his hands on her shoulders and held her still.

"Kate, I asked you once if you would marry me. If I were to ask you again, would you give me another answer?"

She struggled to control her trembling voice and whispered, "Tell me, Colin, if I will."

"No. You must decide it."

"Don't grant me that independence. I don't want it!" she cried, turning to face him again, searching his eyes anxiously. "If I say yes, will you take me with you tomorrow?"

"No. When the war is over, I shall come back for you."

"When the war is over! Colin, don't you understand that I must be with you in everything or nothing at all? I cannot let you go away again. If you are hurt, I want to be with you, and if you are really killed this time, I must know. I have too little grief left in me to waste it."

He smiled. "I shall endeavor not to be killed, my morbid darling. But if I were, you would not have been uprooted from your home—you would be free. I will not expose you to the life of a camp follower, nor to the danger of being part of a fighting army."

"Danger! Don't you think I've faced that in the last three years?"

She had never referred to that before, but he seemed to know that she had been as sheltered as it was possible to be.

"No, Kate, I don't honestly believe you knew the half of it." He continued, "Kate, I don't care twopence for the past; nothing that has happened can have any importance.

The Dancers' Land

But the future does matter. You must consider it! You must realize that if you come with me, it won't be just for the duration of the war. It will mean England and leaving Salamanca and the life you've known. And it will be forever."

"Then why should I make the sacrifice?"

"Because I love you. Because I want you near me. I want you at my breakfast table every morning for the rest of our lives, to share everything that matters most to me. I want to go home again, Kate, to look out at the sea from my own hillside, and I want you to go with me."

And so, he did make her decision for her. They remained in the garden for a long time, silent again but close again. It was strange, Kate reflected, that Colin's kisses had never required any getting used to; they were as natural as breathing. Finally, as they were going inside, she asked again, "Will you take me with you tomorrow?"

"No." The decision was not open to discussion.

Time had passed quickly in the garden, and they saw now that it was late, and the ball was drawing to a close. As they came in, Lord Wellington came up to bid them good night, for he had work to do before retiring.

Kate said, "I trust this is not good-bye, my lord?"

"No, indeed, Doña Catarina! We shall give Marmont a good hiding and be back before you know we have gone. Here is my hand on it!"

"Thank you, my lord. Good night."

The ball was held in a long, dome-ceilinged room two floors deep; at the upper level was an overhanging balcony, supported by slender white pillars encircling the room. Colin and Kate ascended to this balcony and watched the dancers below, whirling like the petals of a rose blown around and around by a capricious summer wind. The candlelight caught the glitter of a woman's ring, an officer's gold buttons, the stem of a champagne glass. Laughter as brittle as crystal or as musical as violins floated upward, leaving sad, whispering voices below unheard. The unhappy faces of friends saying good-bye and the tear-filled eyes of lovers soon to part were invisible to the two on the balcony. Then the last waltz was announced.

As the two danced, the lights in the room were extinguished by footmen who passed unnoticed among the groups quietly conversing and the equally heedless couples on the dance floor, some of whom slipped away unnoticed into the night. The room was slowly drained of all but a few dancers and the musicians, and the gay glitter faded as all but the candles on the music stands were extinguished. Then, as each player in turn laid down his instrument, he snuffed out his candle until only one violin remained to carry on the melody that faded, gently, like the last fine day of a long summer.

Kate and Colin were not dancing now but only stood silently together, silhouetted against the faint glow of the last candle, and then that, too, flickered and went out. The music stopped. A movement of leather boots and rustle of silk skirts, voices unwilling to break the mood by rising above a whisper, muffled sounds that might have been weeping took its place. Then the room was empty.

Colin took Kate to the Plaza Mayor, but when they arrived there, they found themselves unable to part before the last possible moment, to leave the magical night until it left them. They drove to San Cristobal, which at their arrival was just beginning to come to life with the first hint of dawn.

Chapter Twenty-eight

Had Kate known when she said good-bye to Colin that Lord Wellington spoke truer than he knew, and that the army would be back in Salamanca again within the month, it could not have made the leave-taking any more astonishingly easy.

She spent the early hours of the morning still in her ball gown and cape, in the midst of the lively confusion of an eager, bustling, boisterous mob forming itself into an army on the march. Between marveling at the unflagging energy of men she had seen dancing at two o'clock in the morning, and assuring Val and Christopher and Colin in turn that she was quite all right, thank you, and yes, she had just had a cup of coffee, she had no time to think. Colin kissed her and said good-bye and was gone so quickly that she was on the road back to Salamanca before she was aware that Christopher had tied his horse to her carriage, climbed up on the perch, and carried her off.

Very businesslike, he handed the carriage to Luis upon their return and declined a second breakfast.

"I must be off."

Kate kissed him on the cheek and hugging him, said, "Take care, Kit. Write."

He grinned. "Write yourself. You never were much good at it."

He mounted and was away with a clatter down the cobbled street. The morning was developing rapidly into another hot day, but Kate was too sleepy to give it any notice. She stifled a yawn and went into the house.

Three days later, the last of the French army crossed

the Duero at Tordesillas and destroyed the bridge behind them. Marmont then proceeded to spread his army along the north bank of the river as far west as Toro, guarding every bridge and ford, of which there were none too many, against a possible British crossing. Wellington planted his army firmly on the southern side, his right at Rueda and his left extending to the point where a secondary river, the Trabancos, flowed into the Duero. And there he stayed for the next fortnight, much to the wonder of the French, who thought that they must have overrated British strength.

In fact, Wellington had no intention of forcing an action that could not be successful without considerable loss, against an enemy who was at least equal to him in numbers and stronger in artillery. Furthermore, Wellington was waiting for the arrival of the Spanish Army of Galicia to make an appearance on Marmont's rear. He did not know that the Spanish were, in fact, still a hundred miles away at Astorga, to which they had decided to lay siege, tying up a ludicrously large portion of their force to do it. The only help Wellington had on his side of the Duero was a small Spanish cavalry detachment.

But while both armies waited for reinforcements—and for the other to make a move—the men enjoyed their holiday, lazing in the sun and cooling themselves in the Duero, and the pickets on both sides held cheerful conversation with their fellows across the river. They were warm, well fed, entertained, and if the men in the ranks had been asked, they might well have expressed a willingness to spend the summer where they were. What if their communications with Madrid had been cut off? said the French. *Pas de problème!* It was almost harvest time, and had they not been taught to reap the corn, grind it, and make their own bread? As for the British, their officers were hard put to keep their men sober, for the caves of Rueda had served for centuries as a huge, well-stocked wine cellar.

Greyson sent Dr. Rutledge to sort out the casualties at the Rueda taverns, not because he thought that medical assistance would be required, but because his surgeon had a steadier head than any man in the army. Lieutenant Harmer lay shirtless in the sun on the grassy

The Dancers' Land

riverbank and stirred himself only to wave languidly at a French acquaintance of his on the other side. Christopher Benton leaned back against his saddle in a field behind a tavern and obligingly wrote letters to his cousin in Salamanca.

Ramón Sariñana, with an expression bordering on the contemptuous, gazed down upon all this from the heights on Wellington's extreme right flank. Then he turned to rejoin Don Julian's band, who kept the area around Segovia, through which must pass Marmont's dispatches to King Joseph, in constant turmoil.

Ramón was in Salamanca on the 10th and called at the Plaza Mayor to inquire after Kate, who, Amelia lied apologetically, was in excellent health and spirits but not, at the moment, at home. Ramón shrugged and went off. Kate, watching from her window, despised herself for her cowardice, for she had not yet told Ramón of her betrothal to Colin. Apart from that, she would have liked to see him, for no fresh news of the deadlock on the Duero had arrived in Salamanca, and surely something must have happened by this time.

There was more excitement in Salamanca these days than in the dispatches from the north. After the three forts had surrendered, they had been stripped of their contents and destroyed. A large supply of powder found there had been moved into town. On July 7, one of the guards at the depot flicked his cigarette to the ground and, thinking it had gone out, turned his back. The resulting explosion killed him and a score of others outright, besides wrecking several houses and rattling windows as far away as the Plaza Mayor.

"*Madre de Dios!*" spluttered Amelia as a vase full of flowers danced to the edge of the table and toppled off with a crash. Kate hurried out of the house but could not penetrate the crowds and confusion at the scene of the explosion. When Ramón came into town a few days later, it was to see if she had been hurt, and he had to be content to go away not having seen her, but at least assured of her well-being.

He was back a week later, and this time Kate did not dare attempt to deceive him. She steeled her heart against his smile when he saw her, and her body against his when he took her in his arms.

"No, Ramón."

He stepped back and frowned at her. "Why not?"

She blurted out the reason and stood waiting for his reaction. There was none immediately, and then a chilled expression crept into the narrowed eyes that still stared fixedly at her.

"I would have married you," he said at last. "If you had wanted it."

"Why didn't you?" Kate cried. "I would have married you instead of Manuel, if you'd asked then. I'd have married you in Baquio, if you'd asked. Oh, God, Ramón, why didn't you?"

He looked for a moment as if she had struck him, the unexpected blow of her words leaving a red stain on his dark face. But then the chill fell over his eyes again.

"We're not alike, Kate—you must have learned that by now. Manuel and—and Baquio were out of the ordinary. We couldn't have lived an ordinary life together without one day coming to hate each other. I was . . . obsessed with you, or I would never have come back to you every time, never have taken you with me into the mountains. What came of that madness was an accident, too, or good luck, if you want to look at it that way. It wouldn't have lasted."

His voice was harsh, more self-condemnatory than angry. His eyes were cold, but as she shrank away from him, he seemed to understand that he hurt her more than himself by what he said.

"Go home, Kate," he said more gently. He picked up the hat he had laid down a moment before and added, "Go now. It may be your last chance."

Turning his back on her, he went out again, leaving her wondering at the head of the stairs. Then realization struck her—something had happened! Ramón knew something she did not, something that he had come to tell her and kept from her. She stamped her foot in vexation and then, more practically, went out on her own to discover what news she could.

Ramón did know something that she and Salamanca

did not—as yet. The army was on its way back to them. The deadlock had been broken at last on the morning of July 15, and a week of exhausting maneuvers ensued when Marmont shifted his center farther downstream toward the Guarena River, and two other French divisions briefly crossed the Duero by the Toro bridge.

On Thursday, four days later, the two armies still faced each other across the Duero, Wellington hoping to be attacked and Marmont cautiously probing the British line for a weak point. But there was none, and late in the afternoon, the French began to move again to the south. Wellington upped and followed, and they all spent the night in the same situation. Friday saw more of the same, Marmont hoping either to cut Wellington off from Salamanca or to catch him with his army too stretched out to be strong against a concentrated attack. But Wellington was not so obliging.

The Duero ran to earth and now only a narrow stretch of sand separated the armies. Wellington had his army in three columns, and Greyson was in the easternmost one as they approached the village of Cantalpino. Through the heat haze, Colonel Greyson could see the buttons on the jackets of the marching French, and he touched his hat to a French officer, who waved in return. Then the French, moving as one man, turned, and for a moment it seemed as if the two vans must collide at the next village. Colin saw French batteries halt on rolling ground only a few hundred yards away, just as a messenger galloped up to him with orders from his divisional commander.

In Salamanca, Kate dropped her fork and ran to the window as the thunder of cannon rent the still, sultry afternoon air. There was nothing to be seen, of course, but the guns were much closer now—not more than twenty miles away. Colin had told her in no uncertain terms that she was not to try to follow the army, but now that they were so close, it was all she could do to keep from saddling a horse and riding out to see what was happening for herself. But she had to be content with the reports of those who did go out to the lines every day, bringing back rather confused information, which Kate attempted to piece together in some more likely formation.

Saturday was warm and airless, and the calm of Salamanca was like that in the eye of a storm. Kate felt as restless as a wild animal, and her instinctive knowledge about a change in the weather told her the storm would come soon. The night fell quickly and from the wrong direction as huge black clouds rolled in from the west. Salamanca seemed to rush to meet them, and soon the sky above the city was blacked out.

She finally threw on her old riding clothes, and rode as far as the fringes of the city, scanning the horizon futilely for some sign of activity. She returned home just as the storm broke. A gust of wind tore the door out of her hand and slammed it behind her. The rain fell in solid sheets onto the patio. The fountain overflowed into the gutter, which ran into those in the street, where the coffee-colored water foamed over the pavement. As the storm passed overhead, the thunder was deafening and followed so closely upon wild flashes of lightning so as to seem one with them. Absurdly, Kate remembered the explanation Leonora had once given her, as a child, of a storm—that God was angry and clapped His hands to make the thunder, and that the lightning flashed from His eyes.

After one thunderclap, Kate heard a door slam, and thinking the wind must have done it, she leaned out of her own door to look. The next flash revealed the figure of a man in the middle of the patio. He bounded up the stairs, and the next clap of thunder announced Christopher's arrival. He caught Kate up in his dripping arms and shouted, "The great Kean's got nothing on me, I tell you. What an entrance!"

Kate pulled him inside and hugged him, wet clothes and all. "Oh, Kit, what an idiot you are! But I am glad to see you—come in, let me get you some dry clothes."

He shook his head. "Can't wait. Only came to tell you I'm all right. Have you a horse that isn't shy of this weather?"

"Yes, you can have Pepo. But let me at least give you some food to take with you."

His eyes lit up at that, and he followed her to the kitchen

where she pulled almost everything portable down from the shelves.

"Here," Christopher protested, "that's your Sunday dinner!"

"There's enough left for us. Please take it. Christopher, what's happening?"

He shrugged. "Nothing much. You'll have heard most everything by now. We thought we were in for it yesterday, but at the last minute Wellington ordered a turn, and we drew away from the French. They crossed the river this morning while we rested at San Cristobal. Then we followed them over Santa Marta. We're camped now on the Pelagarcia, near that ravine—you know the one—where Ramón and I used to hunt rabbits."

"But what will happen now? You can't just continue marching and countermarching until—well, until what?"

"No one seems to know. But no, we can't just go on, for it would mean abandoning Salamanca. We could have attacked when Marmont crossed the Tormes, but Wellington wasn't committing himself. I think he's still waiting for Marmont to make the first move. At any rate, we're in a good battle position now, if we aren't washed away during the night. Personally, I'd be glad to see something happen. This cat-and-mouse game can get on a man's nerves. Look, Kate, it seems to be letting up. I must go."

"Christopher, can you come back tomorrow?"

"Lord knows! I'll send you a note in any case."

He took the parcel of food, turned up his collar against the rain, and kissed her quickly.

"Regular Wellington weather, they're calling this. Oh, Colin sends his love!"

"Does he?"

"Well, he didn't say so, but I know he was thinking of it. Good-bye, darling."

He touched his cap to her and slipped out. The thunder had moved away, but rain was still pouring onto the patio and blotted her view before he had reached the door. Then there was no sound but the steady drumming of the rain on the paving stones, nothing to be seen but the candle in the kitchen that scarcely penetrated the darkness. Kate blew it out, stood for a long, lonely minute in black silence, then went upstairs to bed.

Chapter Twenty-nine

THE DAWN FOUND two sodden, sulky, aching armies tramping in parallel lines southwestward from inside the great bend of the Tormes around Huerta. The country through which they passed was rolling and lightly wooded, offering excellent opportunity for Wellington's concealment tactics. He kept his divisions out of full view of the French, on the reverse side of the low hills and in the scattered trees along the three-mile front.

At dawn, neither army had yet reached the twin hills called Los Arapiles, the faster-moving French having gained only the village of Calvarasa de Arriba. There, another hill topped by a chapel offered an excellent observation point, but a British force consisting of companies of the Seventh and Eighth Divisions beat off a French attempt to seize the chapel and held it, despite desultory fighting all around it, which kept up until the early afternoon. At about eight in the morning, by which time the sun had dispersed the early-morning mists and dried the pools of rain, the French made a rush for the higher of the twin hills, while the British occupied the smaller.

Wellington noted that Marmont seemed determined to cut him off from a safe retreat back to Portugal and was turning his eight divisions to the west around the pivotal point of the larger hill, El Grande, in order to outflank the British. Accordingly, Wellington turned his army, too, extending them behind the ridge to the rear of Los Arapiles. The marching French had their right flank thus exposed to the British, but because of the nature of the country and Wellington's skill at concealing his forces behind trees and hills, they were unaware of the full extent of the army they were attempting to encircle—or of the danger they ran at

297

thus exposing themselves. Wellington was still reluctant to risk a precipitate attack on a superior force but, as always, he kept his army in the best possible position in the event that the enemy should make a false move.

In Salamanca; the atmosphere was charged with nervous anticipation. Many of the inhabitants were hiding their valuables or packing for a hasty departure in the event of a reoccupation of the city by the French.

Kate turned a deaf ear to loud complaints of desertion echoing from the cafés—she had heard them all before—but she was nevertheless anxious for news. Too restless to stay in the city, she saddled a horse and rode over the Roman bridge, taking the first southbound road she came to. There was a fair amount of traffic on the road, but no one stopped her until she drew rein in a farmyard just behind the Allied lines. There she found Lord Wellington studying the lines of marching French across the valley through his field glass.

Wellington stepped forward when he saw Kate but said reproachfully, "My dear Doña Catarina, as delighted as I always am to see you, I am obliged to scold you for coming here at this time!"

Kate smiled appealingly at him and attempted, in a becomingly faltering voice, to explain why she had come. He interrupted her by giving a short order to one of several aides who were standing about awaiting his instructions. "You go and see if Colonel Greyson will—er—lunch with me. Quick, now!"

Kate blushed charmingly for the earl's benefit, and he engaged her in conversation, asking how she was and for all the latest Salamanca gossip, as if he had nothing else to worry about, as if he had not been worried and awake twenty hours of every day for the last two weeks. Soon, Colonel Greyson, a preoccupied frown on his forehead, came riding up to be greeted with a jovial shout from Wellington.

"Ah, there you are, Greyson! Just in time, for here is Doña Catarina come to see us, and my friend Alava wanting to give us something to eat! But first, perhaps you and the lady—that is, in the house yonder—a moment's privacy . . ."

The Dancers' Land

He stifled his embarrassment in a sandwich and picked up his telescope again. Colin escorted Kate into the nearby farmhouse, bowing his head to clear the low doorway. They stood together for a moment in the gloom behind the closed door; then he took her in his arms and kissed her, hot and roughly. The buttons of his tunic and his cartridge belt dug into her, but she cared only for the heat of his mouth on hers.

Too soon, he released her but kept his arms on hers, whispering, although he meant not a word of it, "You should not have come."

"I had to, I—Christopher said there would be a battle."

He laughed but with no humor. "And what does Christopher know about it? Would we have taken all this time and trouble avoiding one to risk it on the verge of a safe retreat? But you should have asked the earl!"

She backed up and looked at him accusingly. He faltered under her steady gaze. "God knows, Kate, for I'm sure Wellington doesn't. If Marmont gives us the opening—well, it's now or never, if you ask me."

He looked over her shoulder, toward the window, and there was an alert wariness in his eyes, like an animal when it senses danger but does not know wherein it lies.

"Are you afraid?" she asked.

He looked back at her and frowned. "Do I look it?"

"No."

"It's all right, then," he said, and she realized that he was afraid, as any sane man would be before a battle, but as an officer he could not show it. There was an undercurrent of anger, too, in his look, and she wondered if he was angry with himself or if his anger was less personal, the necessary anger of a man preparing to kill other men.

And she saw now why he had been so patient with her, so forgiving. His anger was for stupidity and betrayal and his country's enemies. He had none left for love.

She said softly, "I love you, Colin."

He seemed to understand the leap her mind had made from fear to love, but still his knuckles whitened on the hand that fiercely gripped the door handle, as if he were transmitting his emotion into it.

"No doubts now, Kate?"

"None at all."

There was a long pause before he said in another, lighter, voice, "Alava will be in a state if we don't eat his lunch. Besides, I'm hungry."

They went outside and sat down on the grass of the slope where they were served with a simple but generous cold luncheon. Kate ate automatically and was aware only of the pounding of the pulse in her throat. It echoed in her brain, beating back the thought that she might never see Colin again, never be able to make up to him for all her past mistakes and stupidities. She stared at him, drinking in every feature, as if the mere sight of him might calm her, but the blue eyes gazing intently back at her did everything but that.

She put up her hand to shield her eyes from the glaring sun and looked at Wellington instead. He was still pacing, more restlessly now, over the farmyard—first up the slope, then down, pausing now and then to study the movement across the valley. He had a chicken leg in one hand and munched on it absently between glimpses through his telescope. Alava bustled about, his fussy fluttering providing comic contrast to Wellington's preoccupied stomping, and apologized to Kate and Colin for the lack of more appetizing fare. The earl might have taken a bite of his telescope for all the attention he gave to his luncheon.

Kate's eyes were drawn to the column of troops raising dust across the valley as it twisted, snakelike and sinister, among the scattered trees at the edge of the woods. It reminded her of something, but the memory eluded her.

Then Colin sat up and watched, too. The leading French division was, for no apparent reason, putting on speed. It forged ahead, leaving a steadily increasing gap between it and the three divisions immediately following. Then, slowly, a second gap opened up between those three and the final four divisions. Wellington watched intently through his glass, standing rock-still for once, his mouth slightly open and his chin in the air. Then he grinned, snapped the telescope shut, and said, as if to himself, "That will do. By God, yes, that will do!"

He tossed the half-eaten chicken leg over his shoulder, causing Alava to give a little jump as it fell in the dust. Wellington ran for his horse and cantered up the hill behind them for a better look. Coming back, he dispensed curt instructions to his aides and to Greyson, who received them where he stood, holding his horse's reins. Then he looked approvingly at Kate, who was already in her saddle.

"I see you have the good sense, madam, to get out of the way before you have to be told. My compliments to you!"

He touched his hat and spurred his horse away. Alava, all adither, trotted after him. "But my lord. What is happening?"

Wellington gave one of his quick laughs and said jubilantly, *"Mon cher Alava, Marmont est perdu!"* Then he turned and galloped off westward, quickly outdistancing his aides, who followed doggedly after him.

Colin took hold of the bridle of Kate's skittering horse and pulled it near enough for him to swiftly kiss her and say, "Go home, Kate, quickly!" His eyes blazed unfamiliarly now.

In view of Wellington's parting words to her, and because she dared not trust her voice, Kate only nodded to him before turning her horse to the north. Mounting the ridge Wellington had just ridden over, she paused under an ancient oak tree to see Colin nearly out of sight among the troops to her right, and Wellington bearing down on Aldea Tejada, some distance off to the left. Due east of that and directly in front of her was another village, Las Torres. Reluctant to return to Salamanca just yet, she made for Las Torres instead.

She pulled up in the courtyard of a *posada* in the center of the village and found Peter Rutledge there talking to Valerian von Ehrenberg, who looked up in amazement. She told them briefly what had happened. Val asked a few questions, then replaced the jacket he had shed because of the heat, remembered to say good-bye, and made off at a gallop to where Le Marchant's cavalry was waiting a short distance away. Dr. Rutledge turned to a young Spaniard standing nearby.

"Santiago, go at once to Dr. Barnett and bring him here. Kate, may he borrow your horse? Excellent, thank you!" Then he added, "We will need help here. Can you stand the sight of blood?"

Kate remembered the last and only occasion requiring her services as a nurse and thought that she could stand anything after that. "I haven't much experience," she told him, "but I'll do what I can."

"Good girl. Come along, you can start right away getting our supplies in order. There won't be time for neatness later."

Wellington abruptly reined in his horse in front of his brother-in-law's headquarters in Aldea Tejada. General Pakenham rose to meet him and was informed of the situation in no uncertain terms.

"Ned, d'ye see those fellows on the ridge yonder? Well, throw your division at them and drive them to the devil!"

"Give me your hand, my lord," Pakenham replied with the same easy amiability he always displayed, "and the Third and I will do it!"

The earl's much-harassed staff came galloping up just as he was going off again to the east to deliver his orders personally to the other divisional commanders.

Before the Third had gotten within musket range of the French, Colonel Greyson had rejoined his regiment, which was positioned near the slope of the lower of the twin hills, waiting stoically in the scorching heat for something to happen. To Greyson's left and right, the Fifth and Sixth Divisions were also waiting, with nothing else to do but watch the yellowing grass bake, for they could not see over the slope that concealed them from the enemy's view, and they would not move until ordered to. Greyson's men, on the other hand, were in full view of Marmont himself, who was watching from the French-occupied hill across the valley and to their left. Greyson did not point this out to anyone; somebody would be bound to attempt a shot at the French commander. Anyway, Marmont ignored them, too.

The sound of insects buzzing in the sparse bushes came to them more loudly than the sporadic rattle of musketry from the west, where the guards were bickering with French *voltigeurs* over the village of Los Arapiles—or even the occasional cannonade from closer by, between the twin hills.

Then, in the unnatural stillness, they heard it. Greyson's head snapped instinctively toward the sound, a kind of dull drubbing; his eyes narrowed, looking for the dust

The Dancers' Land

that marching infantry would raise. Then he saw it. The Third was advancing.

It was all very neat, Greyson thought, watching with a detached fascination through his field glass. The Third deployed in two calm, disciplined lines, with the cavalry on their right flank, and Greyson could tell what would happen before it did. That first French division, which had hastened forward to overtake the supposedly fleeing British, was now stranded, alone on the open plain with not even the usual swarm of skirmishers to protect it. It was doomed.

The fight gradually moved east over the sun-baked plain, and now it was Leith's turn. Greyson's men cheered as the Fifth marched into sight over the ridge to their right, moving forward confidently toward the French center. Greyson grinned, watching his own men square their shoulders, knowing they were next. They had been waiting for this. Two weeks of marches and countermarches had bred frustration and near mutiny in them, but all that suddenly evaporated with the knowledge that the real fight had come at last.

Greyson looked around, mentally placing everything, everyone. He, himself, was in the center of what would be their lines, behind the colors. Over there was Vivian Harmer, an old hand now, leaning negligently on his musket and squinting up at the French battery on the hill, as if assessing its intentions. The young major who had replaced Val stood uncomfortably erect, drumming his fingers on his sword hilt. Greyson knew that his youth and his fidgets did not matter; the boy had nerve enough when he needed it.

Wickens and the other sergeants had been pacing the lines, holding back impatience and bolstering faint hearts with running jokes about the heat, the inadequacy of the morning's rations, the likelihood of plunder. But now, every man's eyes were riveted on the Fifth.

For a few minutes, the march proceeded in an eerie silence, as if the British were holding their breath. But then the British breasted the rise and shattered the silence with their muskets. The French replied, but it took only three British volleys to silence them—to teach them how infantry ought to fight. Before the smoke cleared, the British had given a tremendous cheer, charged with their bayonets, and cut the French division to pieces.

Wellington, watching from the ridge to the north, exclaimed in his excitement, "By God, I never saw anything so beautiful in my life! Well done!"

Valerian von Ehrenberg galloped wildly forward, shrieking like death itself, but then his glee was shot through with cold fear as he saw Le Marchant fall. Val wheeled about, almost without a slackening of speed, and ignored the bullets flying like angry bees all around him and the horses swerving to pass him as he jumped off his horse and knelt beside his fallen hero. Le Marchant was shot through the spine—killed instantly. It was the finest death, everyone always said, for a soldier. But Val saw only that he was dead, and the manner of his dying did not stop his tears as he pulled off the plumed helmet and smoothed the graying hair, wet with sweat.

The remaining dragoons, drunk with blood lust, sobered quickly and broke up. Three French divisions had been almost entirely annihilated in less than an hour.

Leith and Pakenham shook hands over the ground they had won, and the battle continued eastward.

Greyson raised his hand, shouted, "Prepare to advance!" and saw the regimental colors being unfurled, then those of the next units and of the rest of the division. He lowered his hand and gave the order to advance, and the men went forward as confidently and determinedly as their fellows to the right had done.

But there was less precision now. The British advance was no longer unobstructed, nor their triumph so certain. The battery on the hill no longer ignored them but poured fire directly down on them. The lines wavered when shot plowed through them, but they kept on, shifting toward the center of the line to close up the gaps as soon as they appeared. Small red-jacketed heaps lay on the trampled grass behind them, but no one looked back.

The men could see individual balls bouncing along the ground toward them at great speed, and only such hardened British troops could have marched so firmly in the face of them. So heavy, indeed, was the fire that patches of grass caught fire, and the dense smoke added to the heat and limited their vision even more than the artillery smoke had done.

Greyson tried not to think about his own vulnerability. Standing out over the men, on horseback, he was a conspicuous target. But it was more important that his men see him there than the French did. In any case, visibility farther away than a few hundred yards was getting worse with the dust and smoke—the only advantages, Greyson thought ironically, to being in the thick of things.

He had suspected they'd end up there, because the hill the French fired down from was the pivotal point in both armies' line of march. There were the reserves behind them, but they had no protection on their immediate flank. Thank God for the smoke, then.

Thank God, too, for the numbness that fell mercifully on him at such moments, blocking all feeling. He had never felt the exaltation some of his men did, going into battle, but he did not feel their fear, either. Kate had asked him if he was afraid, and he had not answered, believing this emotional chill to be a manifestation of fear. Everyone needed some crutch; this was his.

A noise of hooves to his right caught Greyson's ear, just as Christopher Benton came galloping up, wheeling in his horse with a jerk at the reins that made Greyson wince.

"Cole's sent for help," he burst out. "Pack's men are to storm the battery on the hill. You are to form in a single line."

"Done," Greyson said, but his detachment cracked for a moment, and he said, "You're sweating like a pig, Kit. And you handle that horse like a clumsy farmer." He smiled at his young aide.

Christopher grinned, and the sheen on his upper lip brightened. "Never did like this bloody climate!"

Then he was off again. Greyson gave the order to re-form and watched as the whole division fell into step in a line like a marching red wall that stretched for a mile along the sloping ridge. At the far left, Portuguese troops were hurrying up to cover the weak flank. They weren't going to be enough, Greyson realized, and as if to confirm his instinct, the French battery on the hill began firing again, aiming directly into the Portuguese.

But then the French were within range, and Greyson

had more immediate matters to worry about as the focus of battle shifted to his division, his regiment, his patch of ground. The light companies had been less effective than usual against greater numbers of *tirailleurs,* and now they fell back and melted into the red wall. The wall broke into segments to concentrate a curve of fire on the French columns.

"Prepare to fire!" Lieutenant Harmer's voice rang out. "Front rank!"

"Fire! Load!"

The first rank fired, then knelt to reload, and the rear rank fired. The front fired again, then the rear, with scarcely a breath between them. The noise was deafening. Orders could scarcely be heard, but it did not matter. The men met fire with fire with trained precision. The metal of their musket barrels was too hot to touch and the acrid smell of black powder stung their nostrils, but still they fired.

Greyson was on foot now, his horse shot from under him, his men forced back by the onslaught of the French. His face was streaked with sweat and dust, his jacket torn, and a deep streak across his boot traced the path of at least one near hit.

The line of infantry, unable to get beyond the hill, was retreating. Greyson saw his men slide backward on grass slippery with blood, tumbling over each other as they tried to stay afoot, and he felt himself sliding, too, slipping into a lethargy of surrender that took away his initiative, his will to fight back.

But then Wellington's carefully husbanded reserves made their appearance. The Sixth Division, flanked by the First and Seventh, surged over the crest of the ridge. Through the fog in his brain, Greyson heard the cheers, then caught sight of the Sixth coming up behind him.

Greyson looked around, saw the fresh lines deploy, eager to fight, and shouted a hoarse order. His men held, waiting for the reserves to reach them, and when the French drove a wedge through the red wall, they formed another wall facing them. The French turned to find the troops they had thought beaten re-forming to seal closed the opening they had just surged confidently through.

Never expecting such opposition, the French fought desperately, but they were quickly beaten and fell back, the ranks decimated as terribly as their comrades to the west had been less than two hours before. The artillery brigades abandoned their hill. The remains of Marmont's fine army, battered and bleeding, turned and fled in the failing light, down the road to the southwest and Alba de Tormes.

Chapter Thirty

GILBERTO'S IMPROMPTU surgery in that mountain cave had in no way prepared Kate for the sights to which she was now subjected. She would not have thought there were so many things that shot and shell could do to a man. Had she had the remotest idea, nothing on earth could have persuaded her to set foot in the *posada* of Las Torres.

At four o'clock, she had been occupied with rolling bandages, folding linen and blankets, and arranging menacingly sharp, shining instruments on the long wooden platform that would serve as an operating table. Then the first casualties began to come in.

One operation sufficed to suppress her nausea, two to make a nurse of her, and after the third she was able to look impassively at bone-deep saber slashes, shattered joints, bloody limbs hanging by only a thread of flesh, and even more hideous wounds without flinching. The inn stank, after an hour, of blood and festering wounds and the rum poured into the wounded men to desensitize them—and over it all, like a shroud, the pungent smell of gunpowder that drifted in through the windows and doors, which had to be kept open to let the air circulate.

At first, Kate had been afraid to look at the face of each new case that was brought in, afraid that one of them would be a familiar one. But she was soon too numb to differentiate among the pale, smoke-stained faces above the torn and bloody uniforms. Her compassion was aroused for all of them, and somehow it gave her strength to help them.

The worst cases were given the few available bedrooms, but there was little else that could be done for them. The less serious, officers and ranks alike, lay packed together

The Dancers' Land

in the corridors where Kate could sometimes stop to say a word or hold a hand. The men seemed so grateful for such little things that she began to feel of some small use. But when she glanced out of the window at all the men with minor wounds, who overflowed into the yard and lay motionless in the oppressive heat, begging a drop of water from the peasant girls tending to them, helplessness, fear, and horror washed over her again.

The short battle—forty thousand men, they said, defeated in forty minutes—was over long before the last of its victims were brought to Las Torres. In the fading light, the French reserve fought a desperate action against the British Sixth Division to cover the retreat of the broken body of Marmont's glorious army. Wellington did not press the pursuit, for he was under the impression that the village was still held by the Spanish garrison he had left there. The French were allowed to escape, but even so, the afternoon's work had cut their numbers by nearly a quarter.

Dr. Rutledge glanced out of the window at the fading light, called for a lamp, and bent his head again to his bloody task. Kate wiped her arm, in its torn and red-stained sleeve, across her forehead and helped him. The wound was bound up, and he waved the next case onto the table. The stretcher was laid gingerly down, and he lifted the blanket covering the man, took one look and motioned it away again.

"Stop!"

Kate's face went white as she tore the blanket away again. She had dreaded seeing Colin's face, Christopher's, Val's—but had never thought that it would be this one.

The black curls were matted with blood, the dark eyes closed, the wide, sensual mouth slightly open, almost smiling—as if death had caught Ramón unaware at a happy moment.

"It's no use," Peter Rutledge said brusquely. "He must have been dead when they put him on the stretcher."

His expression softened a little as he added, "I'm sorry, my dear. Do you know him? Do you want to take him home?"

She nodded dumbly. "Please, if I may—"

He looked hard at her, faintly resentful that she would

obviously be of no further assistance to him, but his kind voice betrayed no more than his weariness.

"Take him, then. Go on."

An orderly carried Ramón's body outside and laid it in one of the rickety wagons standing in the road. Numbly, Kate remembered to thank him and promised to send it back immediately, but the young corporal looked as dazed as Kate felt and did not seem to hear her. She climbed up into the wagon by herself and whipped the ancient horse into some semblance of motion. For the length of the trip back to the city, she dared not look into the rear of the wagon and concentrated instead on keeping the old horse from falling asleep in his tracks.

Her progress was minimal; traffic to and from the city was heavy, and she had to give way to larger and speedier vehicles. But at last—it was by now pitch dark—she turned into the stables in back of her house. Wearily, she got down and called out for Luis, who came out wearing a worried frown. But when he looked under the blanket in the back of the wagon, his expression changed. For the first time, Kate saw a flash of emotion on his face—a tight-lipped look of devastation that made her turn away from him.

"*Qué pasó?*" he managed finally.

"*No sé, Luis.* I didn't see it. *Lo siento.*"

He shrugged, as if to say it hardly mattered how it happened, and then gently picked up Ramón's limp body and carried it into the house. They laid him in one of the bedrooms, and Kate lit a candle for the table near Ramón's head while she struggled to think of all she had to do. Luis stood patiently by, until she asked him to drive the wagon back to Las Torres—they would need it there. He hesitated.

"Do you want me to take him away?"

"No, thank you, no. Not yet."

She forced herself to think coherently, then told Luis to wait for a moment and went to her strongbox for some gold coins. She pressed them into his hand and said, "Go now, Luis. I shall not need you anymore. *Muchísimas gracias*—For your loyalty, for everything."

"*Si, señora. De nada.* I will go, then?"

She nodded. "*Adios, amigo.*"

He touched his forehead to her and then went off to the stables without another word.

Kate went into the room where they had laid Ramón and sat down with her head in her hands, pressing them against her forehead as if to keep it from exploding. There was silence for a time, but then the door opened and Amelia came in.

"Señora—a message came for you—*ay!*"

Amelia saw Ramón for the first time and crossed herself hurriedly, dropping the paper she held in her hand. She knelt beside the bed, staring at Ramón out of wide eyes that quickly filled with tears, which streamed down her red face. Kate could not bear to watch. She picked up the paper and went out again.

In the dim light of the patio, she read Colin's note, marked half past five o'clock, near the end of the battle. He had not known she was at Las Torres and so had sent it to Salamanca. Brief and to the point, it said merely that he was unhurt and that he had seen Christopher a few minutes before and that he, too, was well; he would write again when he could. Kate wondered if he had seen Ramón fall.

Hoofbeats sounded on the cobbled street outside, but she did not distinguish them from the stream of heavy traffic in the plaza until Christopher burst onto the patio. He looked dusty and worried but unhurt. He stopped short at her bedraggled appearance, her blood-soaked clothing.

"Kate! Are you all right?" he demanded as he rushed to her.

She had forgotten what she looked like and did not understand why he should say that. She looked at him dully.

"Ramón is dead" was all she could manage.

Somehow, he did not look as surprised as she would have expected, although the light went out of his eyes as if it had been struggling against the wind for too long. He looked suddenly older. He glanced toward the candlelit room, from which Amelia emerged wiping her apron over her wet face, and then went quietly past her into it.

It was just as well Christopher had come, for Kate would not have known what to do. Her mind had stopped functioning, too heavily weighted with what she had seen that day. Christopher stayed alone with Ramón for a long time, but when at last he came looking for Kate, he had assumed an unfamiliar, cold air of authority. He made her get up from the chair where she had been sitting for an hour, unmoving and unseeing, to change her clothing, and he told Amelia to see to some supper. But Kate ate little and knew she would not sleep that night—not with Ramón lying dead under the same roof.

Christopher knew it, too, and thought quickly. It was unlikely that they could obtain permission to bury Ramón in the cathedral yard alongside Manuel, or even in the thus-far unused Benton plot in the Protestant Cemetery. But then it occurred to him that the land on which Thornhill had stood, now clear of debris, still belonged to Kate.

So they buried Ramón by the waning moonlight, under the trees that still bore the scars of fire. Christopher dug the shallow grave as the women looked on; when he had finished, the earth beneath the trees bore another scar, but that would soon vanish. Afterward, Kate sat down on the knoll that looked out over the river. She had her back to Thornhill and did not look at it again. Christopher came to sit down beside her and put his arm over her shoulder. She smiled faintly at him, grateful for his unexpected strength. But then he told her how he had come by it.

"He died for me, you know."

"Oh, Christopher—no!" Her shock showed in her eyes, and he understood that she was more concerned for him now than for Ramón.

"It was late afternoon," he said. "The battle was almost over. It was obvious that we'd beaten the devil out of the French and I—I suppose I got carried away with the excitement. I went haring off toward the woods where the only fighting was still going on—Clinton's men trying to dislodge the French rear guard. The grass was on fire, and I couldn't see much for the smoke. Before I knew it, I'd ridden right into the French lines.

"Some of the *guerrilleros* had been in the woods, picking off the French as they retreated, and Ramón must have seen what happened to me. He jumped on a horse and came galloping out of the trees—to warn me or push me out of the way, I don't know. But he'd just reached me—I

The Dancers' Land

could see him laughing and shaking his head at me—when a sniper in back of him opened fire."

Tears were running down Christopher's cheeks, but his voice was still steady. "He would have hit me; in fact, the spent ball scratched my horse and sent him galloping back to our own lines.

"It went clear through Ramón first."

He stopped then, staring ahead of him with his arms on his knees. Kate moved silently to put her arms around him, and he turned toward her, returning the embrace gratefully.

"There's no debt, after all, is there?" she said, and felt him shake his head. "He did it out of love, darling, and love doesn't know what gratitude is."

They stayed there together for a long time, the warm summer breeze caressing them understandingly, and soon Kate saw a pale pink light begin to creep into the eastern sky. She lifted her head and looked around her at the city coming back to life, its face flushed with fresh color and promising a wonderful new day.

All at once, she felt some inner force compelling her to move—but how, where? She did not know. She stood up and looked southward, barely able to make out the rim of the distant hills. No, she would not set foot in Las Torres again, or just beyond that, in the Arapiles. She thought of what that wide, rolling valley between the hills must look like now, those yellow, velvet hills so hard fought for, now bathed in revealing dawn.

Christopher stood up with her and watched her tired face, the unformed, unspoken thoughts flickering across it, and he wondered what she would do. Suddenly, she turned and walked down the hill toward the river. Christopher got up and followed a few paces behind. Silently, in step, they took the path through the poplars that shivered gently in the new day, under the now-muted guns of La Merced, and upward again, skirting the buildings of the university and into the Calle de Libreros.

Kate's stride lengthened, and she hurried purposefully on. Christopher kept up easily but could not make out where she was going or why. They bypassed the Plaza Mayor by way of the Palacio de Monterrey and turned to the right, emerging from a side street in front of San Boal, where Kate paused momentarily to study the cracked but still beautiful black-and-white facade of the palace.

Then Christopher saw what was in her mind, even if Kate did not yet suspect it. She was taking her farewell to Salamanca.

He stopped her in the middle of the pavement. "Let's go home, Kate."

Home? She thought what a strange word that was. She had always used it to refer to wherever she was going to spend the night—even those miserable hovels in the mountains, as if they were her lovely house on the Plaza Mayor, or Thornhill, or her father's rented lodgings in Madrid, or . . .

She looked around her again, as if wondering what had brought her there, and when Christopher took her arm, she followed him docilely back to the Plaza Mayor. There, she sat down in the darkness of the library, staring at the cold fireplace.

Christopher sat down opposite her, watching, and finally asked, "What are you going to do?"

The question startled her back to awareness and rekindled the light in her eyes. Christopher thought that she even looked happy, as if something wonderful had just happened.

"I'm going to Madrid!" she said. She jumped up and started up the stairs.

"Madrid!" He caught her arm and wheeled her around. "Kate, that's crazy. You can't go back there by yourself—where would you live? Besides, the army is marching to Madrid now. There may be another battle."

She laughed at that. "Of course the army is going there, darling. I'm going with it! Wait for me while I pack some things, and then you may take me, if you're so concerned about my safety. In fact, you may as well take me, because I'll go, anyway!"

"But you can't—I mean, I'm not the only one concerned. Colin isn't keen on surprises, especially when they run contrary to his orders. He'll send you straight back—he'll send you back from Madrid if he has to."

Kate tossed her head. "Not this time. He's not going to make me wait for him ever again!"

She strode up the stairs, and Christopher followed her

into her room. "It's insane, you know, all this talk of entering Madrid in a blaze of glory," he said. "They'll be back in Salamanca in a month, anyway."

Her eyes were dancing, but she said only, "In that case, I needn't pack my winter clothing."

She began opening drawers and portmanteaux, shifting things willy-nilly from the one to the other. Christopher was running out of arguments, but his mind clung stubbornly to two notions: that Kate should not be subjected to the dirty, demoralizing, dangerous life of a camp follower; and that Colin would have Christopher's head if he came riding into camp with Kate beside him.

He tried another tack and said softly, "Kate, do you really want to leave Salamanca, leave Spain—forever?"

A moment before, he had said the army would return, and the incongruity made her laugh again. "Darling, you've never approved of Doña Catarina—why won't you let me go back to plain Kate Collier?"

"All right," he said, sitting down on a pile of clothing on the bed. "I'll do anything you want. But don't do it like this. Stay here tonight and pack up tomorrow. I'll go and arrange everything with Colin. Maybe I can talk him into letting you go along if he thinks you'll be comfortable and safe and if he doesn't have to worry about you every minute. Take your carriage—take Amelia, if you like—but at least wait until tomorrow."

His tone had changed to that of a parent humoring a spoiled child, but Kate scarcely noticed. She looked down at the black veil in her hand—why was she packing that? She shuddered and dropped it.

Perhaps Christopher was right. She was exhausted, emotionally drained from lack of sleep and the cataclysmic events of yesterday. She should rest and think and put her life back to order. She was, after all, proposing to change it entirely—again.

"Very well, Christopher. I'll wait. But you need not. I'll take the carriage and be a proper lady about it, in the morning."

But he would not leave her then. Accustomed to odd hours and little sleep, he said he and Amelia would pack while Kate went to bed for a few hours. His instructions were specific and uncompromising, and Kate wearily succumbed to them. It was pleasant to have someone else make decisions for her.

When she awoke, the sky outside her window was a dark blue streaked with pink clouds. The house was perfectly still. She stretched lazily and listened to the splash of the fountain in the patio and the faint sounds of moving traffic from outside. She was still half-asleep, drugged by lingering fatigue and the warm comfort of her bed.

Then she remembered. It wasn't morning. The sun was setting, and the world had turned upside down since yesterday.

Why had no one awakened her sooner! She forced herself out of bed, but it was still several minutes before she could think clearly. She was more tired than she had realized, and it was an effort to move, even to think. She had a strong urge to lie down again and let her comfortable old house soothe her into blessed unconsciousness.

But no, she could not do that. Where was Christopher? It occurred to her that he may have wanted this to happen, for her to change her mind about leaving. She went out to the balcony to call him, but Amelia answered that he had gone out to buy something for his journey.

His journey—not hers. He did mean to leave her behind! Kate hurried back to her room, and from the still unpacked debris scattered around it, she extracted her riding habit and donned it hastily. Christopher would soon return, and she must not be there when he did. If she waited any longer, she convinced herself, she would never be able to leave.

The doubts she thought she had cast aside were still there, and Spain pulled at her as it had always done, but she had made a clean break this time. If she did not think about it too much, she might just be able to do it. Colin would be at—quickly, now, think!—Alba, perhaps, or not much beyond that. She could catch up with them somewhere on the Madrid road, and once she was there, with him, she knew Colin would not send her away again.

Half an hour later, she was on a horse riding across the Roman bridge and up into the hills. Only then did she release a sigh of relief at her escape. Over the crest and she would be out of sight of Salamanca, a few miles more—oh,

The Dancers' Land

God, no! Not that way, not over the battlefield. She would have to go by way of Huerta. She left the road to ride across the country by a quicker route. Emerging from a thicket of cork trees, she forded a shallow stream and paused again to take her bearings.

Then she made the mistake of looking back the way she had come—and saw Salamanca shimmering on the distant horizon in the last gold of the sunset. She caught her breath at its beauty. A stab of pain went through her heart, as if a part of it was being torn away.

It was only a place, she told herself, a mere collection of buildings. One of them had been her home, yes, but there was nothing left there for her now. And Spain—Spain, too, was just a place. It was where the heart lay that was really home—even when the heart misgave her.

Forgive me for what is long past, Leonora had written.

Kate's horse danced fretfully, eager to be off, but she could not summon up the will to turn him in one direction or the other. The dying sun glimmered on the water of the stream, and all other signs of life seemed to be fading, too, except for her horse's agitated movements and the thumping of her own heart.

But Spain will never love you in return. . . .

Her eyes were drawn inexorably to the golden reflections on the stream, and she recalled suddenly the memory of summer sunlight on a sparkling blue sea. Then, with a sob, she made up her mind and turned her eager horse toward home.

Epilogue
Paris, 1815

COLONEL AND Mrs. Colin Greyson arrived at the Palace of the Tuileries in Field Marshal the Duke of Wellington's own carriage. His Grace was not in it with them, declaring himself not up to the fuss a ceremonial entrance at the king's levée would entail and instead crept quietly up to the palace an hour later in a plain hired hackney coach.

But even the carriage of the Prince of Waterloo inspired little admiration among the more glittering cavalcade dispensing Paris's more fashionable residents—permanent and visiting—at the marbled entranceway. The night glittered, too, with the lighted flambeaux flanking the staircase and the lanterns suspended in the trees, their light dancing on the warm breeze.

Colonel Greyson was less interested in the other guests than in his wife, who he thought was looking particularly lovely that night. She wore an elegant pale gold gown with a low neckline, over which a flimsy lace shawl barely concealed the sparkle of diamonds at her throat. Her hair was arranged artlessly on top of her head, and diamonds shone in its golden depths, too. Her pregnancy was not yet evident except in her slightly fuller breasts, flushed cheeks, and glowing gray eyes, and thus far they had kept the new child a secret known only to them.

In their suite at the Hôtel d'Angleterre, two-year-old Master Henry Philip Arthur Greyson would be asleep by now under his nurse's watchful eye. Young Harry was much cosseted by both his doting parents, but his proud papa nevertheless wanted this second child to be a girl, who would look like her mother. He joked that he had consented to burden Harry with all those names only so that there would be none left for another boy. But Kate wanted only boys. "My own regiment," she said.

She turned her head then, and caught Colin's steady blue gaze on her. She smiled that young, captivating smile that had begun to come more easily to her, and that made his heart turn over every time.

"Are you quite sure you want to go through with this ritual?" he asked her.

"Oh, yes. I think I must, don't you?"

The carriage came to a halt, and the door was opened for Kate, who stepped down and looked around her, breathing in the soft summer evening.

"It looks the same," she said to Colin when he joined her at the bottom of the steps and took her arm. "But it feels different."

It was easy now to look back, now that the past was truly past. Their future had begun three years before at Alba de Tormes, when Kate had come riding into the British camp, her flying hair streaming behind her like a gypsy's, and had begged Colin to take her with him. He had recognized then that he had no choice, nor wanted any, and from that day on, they had never again been separated. Kate had accompanied him uncomplainingly through two more years of war in Spain, until at last the British army crossed the Pyrenees into France.

They had gone home—home to England—after Napoleon was exiled to Elba, and spent nearly a year shaking off what Colin thought was the last of the burdensome baggage of the past. But Kate's intuition told her that it was not quite over. And she had been right.

Napoleon escaped from Elba, and in a lightning-quick one hundred days had raised another army to meet the hastily reassembled Allied forces in Belgium, near a tiny crossroads village called Waterloo.

Colin had immediately rejoined the army, and Kate, in return for her consent, had demanded to go with him to Brussels. She had then refused to take Harry home in the general panic before the battle on that Sunday in June, and Colin could only get her to agree not to leave the safety of the city until he came back or sent word. She had paced the confines of their pretty little house in the Rue de la Blanchisserie all day June 18, as long as she could still hear artillery pounding to the south. Harry had sat on the floor, contentedly playing with his toys, and paid little attention to the excitement around him, except now and then to favor his anxious mother with an indulgent smile. He was already taking after his father.

Colin had escaped the fighting at Quatre Bras two days earlier and went through the worst of that terrible Sunday's battle miraculously unscratched. But then, in the final great British advance late in the afternoon, with the regiments cheering and the French retreating before them in disorder, Colonel Greyson had the ill luck to lose his horse to a rabbit hole in the field and to break his arm in the fall. It was, he remarked wryly, an ignominious end to a glorious military career.

But Kate had welcomed him as a returning hero, and his country would not let him be invalided home. Colin's acquaintance with Sir Charles Stuart, the British ambassador in Brussels, had developed into a friendship, and when Stuart was appointed to Paris, he asked Greyson to join his staff. Even Christopher Benton, who had secured an appointment to Wellington's staff before Waterloo, found diplomatic service to his taste and had become very professional at it—"starchy," Kate called it, to which Colin replied that it was only a temporary aberration, and Christopher would turn frivolous again soon enough. But Kate thought not, and smiled at the irony of Christopher's following, however unintentionally, in his Uncle Henry's footsteps. It seemed that they were indeed coming full circle. And now there remained but one ghost of the past to be exorcised.

She walked down the glittering passageway under the gleaming crystal chandeliers that had somehow survived the storms of the last twelve years and admired the silken ladies, languidly plying their ivory fans, and the bejeweled gentlemen with the white cockade of the House of Bourbon in their lapels, and the perfumes and the thousands of candles and the soft, whispering voices all around her.

There were more English voices this time and scarlet

uniforms that were not to be seen that earlier time, and Kate thought that the air had changed, too. It did not hang heavy with intrigue and suspicion but only with friendly curiosity and gay gossip—about which milord had gambled beyond his means at the Salon des Étrangers, or which opera *danseuse* had been given a vulgarly large jewel by her lover. Kate remembered her own innocent, eager anticipation the first time she came here and regretted its loss a little, now that the pain which followed it was receding mercifully into the past. She had felt then that something wonderful was about to happen; now she knew that the contentment she had finally found was more to be wondered at than the electrically charged extremes of emotion she had felt as a girl. Everything lost, she knew now, was only giving way to something better.

The Greysons were announced, and heads turned—familiar heads this time, for in the short weeks since Waterloo, Kate and Colin had become part of the small circle of English military families who had now come, with their conquering army, to Paris.

" 'All the world's in Paris,' " Colin murmured in her ear, quoting from the most popular song of the moment, and indeed it seemed so.

"Do you see Gabriella?" Kate asked her husband, looking around the huge room.

"She's dancing, of course—with poor Peter trying to keep up."

Gabriella Benton, now Lady Weston, had married Stacey Westover's older brother just that spring, after a persistent courtship on Viscount Weston's part. Peter had told Kate privately that he had been in love with Gabriella longer than Stacey had, but he had been willing to accept second place in her heart as better than none—at least as long as his more dashing brother was alive.

But Gabriella did not look as if she had settled for second best. She looked prettier than ever in a new Parisian-designed gown with the dashing short skirt a lighter blue than the bodice, and she gazed up at her adoring lord with an expression that told him he would always be first in her affections, even if, as she frequently scolded him, he was the most ungraceful dancing partner in the world.

"Kate—dearest!" Gabriella exclaimed as she came to

The Dancers' Land

greet her cousin, trailed by a somewhat more dignified, if grinning, Peter. "I'm so glad you've come. Isn't it grand? Colin, you look splendid—what a pity officers cannot wear dress uniforms all the time! We ladies would be in a continual swoon. Kate, have you seen the gardens? Do let me show you them."

Kate bent to kiss Gabriella on the cheek and gave her an amused, if belated, good evening. Colin smiled at this easy, unconscious display of affection on his wife's part—something else that he had been glad to see return to her. He turned to Gabriella, solemnly assuring her that they knew where the gardens were, thank you, and suggested that she resume dancing so that the musicians would have someone to follow when they finally took their places. Peter groaned.

"My dear Greyson, don't—I beg of you—encourage her!"

Gaby laughed, a musical laugh she reserved for Peter alone, and whispered something in his ear. "I think *we* will go and look at the gardens," she said to Kate with a meaningful look, and bore her husband off toward the long windows.

Kate and Colin resumed their rounds, speaking to acquaintances as they encountered them, until everyone's attention was drawn to the entrance where King Louis was shortly to appear. There was a hushed expectancy as they waited and then a collective swish of skirts as the ladies curtsied, the gentlemen bowed in unison, and the reenthroned Bourbon king—fat, red-faced, and vacuous-looking, but as amiable as anyone could wish, like a Gallic Sir John Falstaff—came into the room and made a grand progress across it.

Louis was followed by a lengthy cortege that included a number of émigrés, their chins in the air and deigning to speak only to one another. It also included, nearly hidden behind *le gros* Louis, Napoleon's lethally efficient Minister of Police, forced on the King by the Allies in return for Fouché's haste to call for his former master's second abdication, and because he controlled the only complete intelligence network in France.

Kate drew in her breath and glanced at Colin. He was still looking at the king, but he felt her look and said, sotto voce, "It's all right. He won't recognize me."

It was true. Fouché went by them with barely a nod, and Kate breathed easier. She supposed Colin would have enjoyed making himself known to the man who had sent him to prison in that tropical hell for four years—simply because there would be nothing Fouché could do about it now—but Kate knew the whole story of that episode now and could only be grateful that it, too, was buried in the past.

Leonora had told her about it—Leonora, who had been engaged in the same espionage game as Colin that year in Paris but had escaped unscathed. That was how Colin and Leonora had known each other, and when Kate had confessed her initial suspicions about their relationship, her mother had laughed and told her she must indeed have been a silly goose at that age.

Leonora was not in Paris this time. She said she had laid her own ghosts to rest years before and did not need to make this pilgrimage Kate found necessary. Kate had left England with mixed feelings about her lovely, warm, but unfathomable mother. She had come to be fond of her during the time she and Colin were in England, and Leonora had been delighted when Harry's arrival made her a grandmother. But despite Colin's assertion that they were two of a kind—or perhaps because of it—Kate did not feel she yet knew Leonora well. She had not said so to Colin, but she had wanted to come here tonight particularly because of Leonora. She wanted to exorcise her own lingering doubts, so that she could accept her mother as freely and lovingly as she had the rest of her life—and thus accept herself, too.

The crowd closed in behind Louis, and the voices rose again into that cheerful murmur Kate seemed to hear all over Paris now. Under cover of it, Wellington came almost unnoticed into the room with the lovely Lady Frances Webster on his arm, but those who saw him stepped back to make a passage for him, and the initial ripple of admiration around him spread slowly across the room. An irritated frown crossed the duke's forehead at the unwanted attention, but his words were as courteous as always.

"Ah, Mrs. Greyson—good evening to you," he said to Kate. "What a crush it is, eh? I don't know how the young ladies do not faint away from the heat." He patted his companion's arm, and Lady Frances gave Kate a look that was part defiance, part supplication. Kate guessed that she had not wanted to come tonight. There had been scandalous rumors about her relationship to the duke, but watching him now, Kate thought that he was only being kind, and a little protective, toward the young wife of one of his officers. Kate smiled at her, and Lady Frances, as if grateful for it, smiled back.

"Are you not pleased to be everywhere fêted and admired?" Kate said to his lordship, "not to say mobbed, as I saw you nearly were in the Faubourg Saint-Honoré yesterday!"

"Not in the least, dear lady! If I had failed, you know, they would have hanged me as readily."

He went away then, to be accosted, in spite of Lady Frances's clinging presence, by a number of other ladies who wished—they said—only a word from him that they might remember for the future.

"Poor man," Kate said to Colin. "Imagine having your every nonsensical utterance treated as a gem of wit and wisdom. But it was so even in Salamanca—do you remember?"

The musicians had finally appeared and tuned their instruments, and Colin led her to the floor, which was being cleared for dancing.

"You were not going to think of Salamanca tonight, *mi vida*—isn't that what you told me? Personally, if we must indulge in do-you-remembers, I would much rather think about the last time we danced here together."

She smiled. "It was a mazurka, was it not? Are you sure your arm is strong enough for such a challenge?"

"I am nothing if not determined," he said, holding out his hands to her.

But the first tune that was struck up was a waltz. They smiled at each other, took their positions, and let the music waft them away. With Colin's arm around her, Kate felt everything else—past and present, doubts and unhappiness, the cold of Spanish snows and the artificial brilliance of candlelight—dropping away, like layers of warm but suffocating clothing, until it seemed that they were floating above the floor in a cool green sea of sensation.

The air did suddenly become cooler, and she found herself outside in the gardens, where Colin had gently propelled her, out of the ballroom and onto the terrace. A starry sky was faintly visible above the dark trees along the paths, and they walked a little way down them to an alcove with a marble statue that shimmered palely in the night. But it was Colin she looked at, seeing the diamond-blue of his eyes soften when he bent to kiss her lightly.

"Is this as you remember?" he said.

"No. It's better."

He smiled. "I meant the gardens. The roses are gone—perhaps they died with Josephine."

He looked around, but she did not care about the roses. She put up her hand to touch his cheek, and he turned back to her.

"I never thought I could love you more than I did that first time," she said. "But I do. My love now is changed, but stronger—and better, because of everything that has happened. Do you understand?"

"Yes." He kissed her again, and the sensation of being out of the world, in his arms, flooded over her. Nothing mattered but his touch, his presence, his love. She kissed him back, more deeply, and could feel him respond, molding his body closer into hers.

His lips moved to her ear, and he whispered, "Let's go home, Kate."

She smiled. He didn't realize that she was home. It did not matter where else they went that night, or ever. She was at home in his arms.